S0-ARM-135

Praise for *Eighty-Sixed:*

"Raunchy, hilarious, and heartrending."

—The Advocate

"*Eighty-Sixed* is valuable for the look it gives at the way an embattled, plagued segment of society was and how it is now." *—New York Post*

"*Eighty-Sixed* looks at the plague nervously, but it's clear-eyed and remarkably sane, and it has a gallows humor that's almost moving in its attempt to mask the horror. The book is loose and informal and offhand, but it's also large-scale and ambitious. One doesn't have to be gay or straight to find it funny and readable, and though it is primarily about the impact AIDS has made on a community, it's also about accepting adulthood and its responsibilities." *—Bret Easton Ellis*

"Lacerations of laughter, mordancies of wit—the author takes us on a demon-journal through the circles of sexual hell with B.J. Rosenthal, who was somehow raised to believe in justice. Troubling, truthful, hilarious—a black pearl of a book. I found *Eighty-Sixed* dazzling if distressing, and quite magnificently written." *—Richard Hall, author of The Butterscotch Prince*

"Tired of all the sentimental, maudlin writing about AIDS? Well, *Eighty-Sixed* is something new: a serious, hard-nosed, yet comic chronicle of the way we gays are in the plague-ridden eighties. Comic? I wouldn't have thought there was anything funny about AIDS, but Feinberg manages to find dark humor in the ways the (as yet?) unafflicted manage to get by these days. *Eighty-Sixed* is a rollicking, risky ride, sharply depicting the resiliency gays have shown in the face of catastrophe." *—John Fox, author of The Boys on the Rock*

"David Feinberg has a perfect understanding and appreciation for the frantic life of modern New Yorkers. He uses both their dazzling wit and their frenzied neurosis to write a history of what's happened to gay men in Manhattan, first when they came out, and now when they live in the midst of crisis. Like his characters, Feinberg doesn't look away from reality—it's impossible to do so in that world—but he also never gives up his sense of humor and his belief in the healing and comforting possibilities of comedy."

—John Preston, author of In Search of a Master

· DAVID B. FEINBERG ·

EIGHTY-SIXED

GROVE PRESS
New York

Copyright © 1989 by David Feinberg

All rights reserved. No part of this book may be reproduced in any form or by any electronic or mechanical means, including information storage and retrieval systems, without permission in writing from the publisher, except by a reviewer, who may quote brief passages in a review Any members of educational institutions wishing to photocopy part or all of the work for classroom use, or publishers who would like to obtain permission to include the work in an anthology, should send their inquiries to Grove/Atlantic, Inc., 841 Broadway, New York, NY 10003.

First published in 1989 by
Viking Penguin, a division of Penguin Books USA Inc

Published simultaneously in Canada
Printed in the United States of America

In somewhat different form, Chapter 2 was first published in
Torso, "Safe Sex in the Age of Anxiety" in *Mandate,* and
"Egg Paranoia" in *The James White Review.*

FIRST GROVE PRESS EDITION

Library of Congress Cataloging-in-Publication Data

Feinberg, David B
    Eighty-sixed / David B Feinberg.
        p. cm.
    ISBN 0-8021-3902-7
    1 Gay men—Fiction. 2 Jewish gays—Fiction 3 AIDS (Disease)—Patients—
Fiction. I Title.

PS3556 E425 E34 2002
813'.54—dc 21   2002021094

Grove Press
841 Broadway
New York, NY 10003

02 03 04 05   10 9 8 7 6 5 4 3 2 1

For Glenn Person

Contents

vii

Contents

*What I claim is to live to the full the contradic-
tion of my time, which may well make sarcasm
the condition of truth.*

—*Roland Barthes,* Mythologies

PART I

1980: ANCIENT HISTORY

Prologue

*T*he priest rarely masturbated during confession. For one thing, it was too cramped, too confining. The cubicle was tiny. As soon as the priest entered the darkness of the confessional, he would unsnap the white starched collar he kept on for appearance's sake. He would sit, smoothing his pants, and wait. The tiny peephole let in some light, not enough to be distracting.

The priest could usually tell who was on the other side. He taught philosophy at a small Catholic college on Staten Island, so he was familiar with most of the students. He lived in the dorm as a resident adviser.

Usually the sins confessed were minor in nature: a broken promise, a plagiarized term paper. But on occasion, he would find himself overly engrossed in a tale of perfidy, a story of woe, a recital of uncontained eros. His interest would be aroused, his member distended. Perhaps this lay in the quality of the telling and not so much the tale. His breathing would become rapid and shallow, his cheeks flushed. The priest would be careful to control his voice, suppressing the excitement as he prompted, "And *then?*" The priest would cross and recross his legs nervously. The small dark room would seem to shrink even tinier.

Yes, it must have been the manner of the telling, perhaps even the identity of the teller. The Bible says that there is nothing new under the sun. According to Elvis Costello, there are no *original* sins. So the priest would listen, ears agog, eyes agape. When it was over, the penance would be unexpectedly light. The priest would leave the confessional and return to his room—if necessary, covering his erection with *The Confessions of Saint Augustine* or W. V. O. Quine's *Word and Object*. He would close the door and not emerge until supper.

· 1 ·

January

I met Dennis on January 5, 1980. The exact date was etched in memory because it was Day Five of my aborted Month of Celibacy. I had planned to usher in the new decade with a month of abstinence. At the time I was only expending ninety-five percent of my waking hours thinking about sex.

Let me give you an example. Say I was standing in front of a bodega in the West Forties and a Puerto Rican with bright brown eyes and two days' stubble brushed by me. What would happen? I'd be magnetized. My dick would straighten out like a divining rod, forcing me to follow more than twenty city blocks in fruitless pursuit, until a door slammed in my figurative face as I stood with hands in pockets, dejected, across the street on Twenty-first and Tenth. Or say I was going downtown on the Number 1 and the train lurched to a halt between stations, and a pair of buttocks, perfect hemispheres, bumped into my crotch. Overcome with lust, I'd peel off a card from the "Six Weeks to a Rewarding Career as a Cashier" or "*Aprenda Inglés Ahora,*" which I loosely translated into "Speak English Like a Whore," and write my name and number on it and slip it into the back pocket of my prospective boyfriend.

Or say I was in bed with some stranger, corpus delicti and all. Him, I invited over on the pretense of discussing Robert Graves's poem "The Naked and the Nude," so naturally a demonstration followed. I suppose I had a thousand and one lines, next to the jar with a thousand and one phone numbers. Anyway, we were in the middle of some act that discretion requires I don't describe in too much detail; the fact of the matter is I don't even remember it. I was lying there, thinking that the bulb needed changing, the ceiling could use another coat. He was pounding away, and I was wondering if he would ever finish. In the phonograph of my mind, Barbra Streisand

4

and Donna Summer were dueling it out with "Enough Is Enough," and the record was scratched, stuck on the refrain. And you know what I was really thinking about? The Trick That Got Away. A guy I saw on Christopher Street last Tuesday, or some other Joe that I was planning on seducing next week at the latest, or a hot number who took extra-long showers at the gym and lingered soaping his crotch and how much I wanted to be that sliver of soap.

Ten years ago I saw this sign in the library, back in junior high: "Are you reading more but enjoying it less?" Well, that was how I felt about sex. It was time to give it a rest. I had this theory about unejaculated sperm. It seeps into the bloodstream and gets reabsorbed directly into the brain, causing unprecedented spurts of creativity and genius. As for me, I'd been so busy masturbating since the age of thirteen, I didn't even have any left over for wet dreams, let alone enough to test my theory. When I thought of all of the energy I had wasted under the auspices of searching for, engaging in, and recovering from sex in the past five years, it made me sick.

I decided to go to the St. Mark's Baths on New Year's Eve to get sex out of my system.

Back when I was growing up in upstate New York, my family would usher in Passover with a massive pig-out. You know Passover; it's ten days long, and there's some biblical potboiler associated with it, something to do with killing Christian babies and smearing the blood on the doors so the Angel of Death passes over. Well, the real significant thing about it is you don't eat leavened bread-products during it. Seems during the Exodus the bakeries were closed prematurely. Imagine. No donuts for ten days! No pound cake! No Dipsy Doodles! No Sugar Frosted Flakes! The list goes on and on. It's ten days of matzo: matzo-ball soup, matzo-meal pancakes, fried matzo, matzo flakes for cereal. You get the picture. Anyway, the night before the holiday, you're supposed to clear out the house of all of your leavened products. So me and Mom and Dad and Sis would sit around the kitchen table and eat Cheetos like there was no tomorrow, Ritz crackers out of our ears, Hostess Twinkies to bulimic proportions, Sara Lee coffee cakes until you would almost explode.

Along the same lines, I went to the St. Mark's Baths on New Year's Eve for a sexual feast before my planned self-imposed famine. I had never been to the baths before. Three years ago I had tried going in Hollywood. I was so nervous I locked the keys inside my car. I asked the guy at the desk for a hanger to pull the lock up through the window. When I came back, he turned me away because I didn't have a membership card. Later I found out if I had unbuttoned my shirt to the waist, I would have been in like Flynn.

I had a pretty good time at St. Mark's. I didn't get any phone numbers, but then I guess the baths weren't the place to meet Mister Right anyhow. I managed to come at the stroke of midnight with my third companion of the night. I took the subway home at two in the morning, the car littered with beer cans and streamers.

I was living on Ninth Avenue in the Fifties. The neighborhood went by various names. Actors called it the Theater District. Accountants and secretaries called it Midtown. The Real Estate section called it Clinton. I called it Hell's Kitchenette, since it was only a few blocks north of Hell's Kitchen proper. I had just moved in late December, fleeing a nightmare roommate situation in the Village. My stoned ex-roommate had sat dazed on his bed, the eviction notice in his hands, while I packed furiously. Through some careless oversight on his part, he had neglected to pay the rent the three months I was living with him. He had not, however, forgotten to pocket my portion. I had moved to New York in the guise of a starving graduate student at N.Y.U., studying some arcane subject that turned out to be completely irrelevant. Semiology, I think. Or was it sociolinguistics?

Anyway, the new location was ideal. My apartment was sandwiched between a liquor store and Gloria's Pizza Parlor. The liquor store had a metal grating separating the customers from the wares. On the grating was a sign: "In God We Trust, All Others Pay Cash." Gloria next door must have weighed three hundred pounds. She wore jeans designed by her namesake, Ms. Vanderbilt. Several dealers sold drugs in the hallways of adjacent buildings. A block away was the third site of Madison Square Garden, now a parking lot with a lone decaying building on the corner, windows shuttered with metal plates, piss stains on the sidewalk. No one bothered scooping poop on this block.

I was almost completely isolated. The buzzer didn't work, the mailbox was locked, and the phone company couldn't install a phone until January 10. I slept on a mattress on the floor at cockroach level. The gas on the stove was turned off. The Cuban super who spoke little English had demanded five dollars for a drink before turning it back on.

I saw a lot of movies alone during Christmas vacation. My mother had invited me on a cruise, along with my sister. I didn't think the three of us could survive in such an enclosed space for ten days, so I made some excuse about a few incomplete papers I had to finish. I sat around playing the collected works of Paul Simon on my stereo and feeling sorry for myself. I made phone calls to my three friends from the pay phone on the corner and got three answering machines. All the tricks I knew were away on vacation. I read all three dailies: the *News,* the *Post,* and the *Times.* I was sitting on the bed and finishing my third crossword puzzle of the day when I heard a knock on the door.

I reached for the brick on the windowsill. Downstairs were two doors, and at least one of them should be locked at all times. Sometimes the drunk outpatients from St. Clare's Hospital across the street would jam a lock with a paper clip so they could sleep in the hallway downstairs. My doormen. Once, crazy Marvin Hirsch, who lived two floors above me, kicked in the door because he had forgotten his key. I heard about this from Betty on the fifth floor. When the police came to take him to the Bellevue psycho ward, he started shouting statutes at the top of his lungs. "You have no right to arrest me according to Penal Code Statute 245.6.b of the New York State Judicial Code." His hands were bleeding because he had smashed all of the glass in his apartment.

Another gentle rap on my door. I was ready for born-again Christians or worse. Amy, the previous tenant, was a prostitute and a drug dealer. The week I moved in, a crazed man knocked on the door and asked if Amy was here, if Amy had the stuff. "What stuff?" He pointed at some aluminum foil in his hand, containing an unidentified powdered substance. "Amy doesn't live here anymore," I said, slamming the door shut. My heart was beating a mile a minute. A few days later I found some use-them-once plastic hypodermics in the medicine cabinet. I got paranoid. I had seen too many movies. I figured that someone must have buried a brick of heroin under the floorboards and I would be meat loaf before the week was over. I didn't want the money or the drugs. I would gladly turn it over to the police, the dealers, anyone. Like Susan Hayward, I wanted to live.

The next week a pair of Jehovah's Witnesses gave me a pamphlet that told me I would burn in hell for eternity if I didn't do something quick about it. I told them I was Jewish, and they went away. I *used* to be Jewish, so it wasn't a complete lie. I was born that way. I had lost my faith when I was twelve years old and by accident in Junior Congregation I had torn a prayerbook. I expected divine retribution. Lightning or worse. And nothing happened. Perhaps my present position in Hell's Kitchenette was His punishment, but how was I expected to connect the two events? In operant conditioning, the response should directly follow the stimulus. Ring the bell, and I get an erection. But since the buzzer was out, Dennis knocked, and I merely answered.

"Who is it?"

"Hi, my name is Dennis."

"Dennis who?"

"You wrote me a letter. See? I've got it here." He produced an enveloped with a flourish. "It says that you are addicted to donuts and like the movies a lot."

I scrutinized the envelope and realized that Dennis was my dream date from the *Village Voice*. How could this be? But I wasn't ready! I was all out of cocktail peanuts and swizzle sticks, Brie and Carr's table biscuits. Should I dash out and buy candles along with my favorite flavored lubricant?

The problem with personal ads is that they never work. You answer an ad in a frenzy of lust and loneliness. By the time you get a response three weeks later, you're in an entirely different state of mind. In the interim you've tricked twice, had three minor infatuations and one major crush on a pizza delivery boy. Your mystery date is the furthest thing from mind. Although people rarely lie when they describe themselves, they never look the way you pictured them. A guy says he's blond. You envision a California beach bum. You meet him, and his hair is so dirty blond that you would mistake it for brown. Another guy says he has a gym body. You imagine him tight and lean, without a trace of fat, bulging in all the right places. You meet him and find he goes to the gym three times a week and his body is just like seventy percent of the guys at the gym, the usual mixture of muscle and paunch, tone and flab.

"Can I come in now?" asked Dennis. He was standing in the doorway.

"Uh, sure. I was hardly expecting you. I thought you would write back."

"I would have called, but you said you didn't have a phone yet. I was in the city today and thought I might catch you in."

Dennis wasn't my type physically. He was in his mid-thirties, about five ten. He wore wire-rimmed glasses. There was a touch of gray in his temples and his mustache.

He gave me his curriculum vitae in short order. Gay men always come equipped with a five-line verbal résumé. "I'm Irish. I just started to come out last year. I'm meeting people mainly through ads. I'm still pretty closeted at work. How about you?"

"Oh, I guess I've been out for four years," I replied. "I lived in California for a couple years. It's funny, I really needed the physical separation from my family. For a long time I hoped I was bisexual, able to experience everything. But now, I'm happy that I'm a Kinsey six."

"Kinsey six?"

"That's about two-hundred-percent gay."

"I really don't like fems. I prefer straight-looking guys."

I decided against the Mae West impersonation. "What do you do for a living?"

"I teach. Philosophy. At a community college on Staten Island."

"I'm in grad school now." We chatted for a while. I gave him a Fred Flintstone plastic cup of ice water. I was drinking from a Betty cup. I told Dennis how I liked to bake, especially chocolate. We discussed music. We both liked Joni Mitchell. Dennis enjoyed opera. We sat on the mattress because that was all the furniture I had. Then he kissed me.

"No. I can't," I said.

"Why not?"

"I'm trying to be celibate."

"Whatever for?"

"Sex is just too important in my life. I've lost all perspective."

"That's no reason."

I couldn't tell Dennis that I wasn't particularly attracted to him. I mean, if he had arms of steel and tits to die for, or if he was obviously going to be my lover, of course I would have said OK, eagerly. Dennis was nice. He was someone I would probably sleep with once or twice and then maybe become friends with afterward. The long-term picture didn't look so hot. But who knows? I hadn't found a lover yet. How was I to tell?

Dennis leaked. He was dripping precum when he took off his Jockey shorts. He was sweet and over-eager. He had spent a long time in the closet. Dennis's voice was soft like a whisper, like his silvery hair. I felt warm and comfortable next to him. I felt I could tell him anything and he would understand. It was easier to go ahead with it than say no.

I divided the world into two classes: those who knew I was gay and those who didn't. The latter class required mendacity, subterfuge, deceit, willful falsehoods, and outright lying. Rachel was in the former class. I had met Rachel Rosenberg through her brother Fred. Fred and I had gone to math camp at Ohio State the summer between tenth and eleventh grades, back when I was a genius. Now I was just played out, burned out at twenty-three.

I had moved to New York in the fall. Every month Rachel would invite me over for dinner, and I would respectfully decline. Eventually I gave in. Rachel lived in a doorman building in the West Seventies, above a Bagel Nosh. The mantelpiece was decorated with *tchotchkes*. A bowl containing matchbooks from every restaurant she had ever gone to sat beside a pair of wooden soldiers.

I had pretended to be straight for about three months, carefully censoring from my speech anything that might imply I was gay, hiding behind androgynous noun-phrases like "my friend." Whom was I fooling? I didn't care. But Rachel's on-again, off-again boyfriend, Chris, was of the wrong creed, and I was worried that her parents would take me for a beard. I didn't want to act as her convenience.

"Rachel, I've got something to tell you," I said one day.

"You're gay. Don't worry," she said. "I know about that. Here. Have some cheese and crackers."

"How? Who told you?"

"Oh, I read that letter you wrote Fred years ago." I searched my memory and recalled I had written Fred a coming-out letter in the early seventies. Periodically I got annoyed, testy, mad at the world, and would write bombastic letters to people I wasn't particularly close to, detailing quite explicitly my homosexual identity, not caring whether they would accept or reject me. I couldn't recall what set me off to write Fred. I might have failed a physics exam. Maybe someone called me a faggot on the street. It could have been Watergate.

"Then why didn't you tell me you knew?"

"I figured you would tell me yourself one of these days when you were ready. And you did. Discretion is the better part of valor. Are you sure you don't want a glass of white wine?"

I was irritated. "Rachel, don't you know how much energy I wasted lying?"

"It's really no big deal. How's grad school coming along?" So that was that.

Rachel was a Jewish American Princess with all of the trappings: Daddy's charge for Saks, constant complaints about her weight (even though she was thin as a rail), forty-five-dollar haircuts from Monsieur Neil that were so good you couldn't even tell she got a haircut. The time she played strip poker with Chris and his pals she came out ahead, even though she was the worst player by far, because she had so many rings and barrettes. When it came time to remove her shirt (there was no bra beneath), she said she was tired and she quit.

"I hope you like this. A new recipe." Rachel removed the casserole dish from the oven. "Oh, I hope it's not overdone." The tomato sauce had congealed. The eggplant on top was curled up. I was a starving student, in no position to complain.

"So how's your love life?" asked Rachel. "Here, let me serve you." My eyes widened as she ladled two portions on my plate and a half-portion on her own.

"I met this one guy, Dennis, who's really nice, but I don't think it's going to go anywhere."

"Why not?"

"Let's just say he's not my type. I hope he turns out to be a friend, though."

"Oh, well," she chimed. "Better luck next time."

"How's Chris doing?"

"He's down in Florida for the week, probably *shtupping* Cindy Vogel." She cut her eggplant angrily into tiny pieces. "I don't know. I know I shouldn't get jealous. We both want to be free. No ties. No commitments."

"He didn't tell you, did he?"

"A postcard from Cindy fell out of his jacket is all. Want some more wine? Are you sure you don't want something a little stronger?" Rachel took a gulp of her vodka tonic.

"No, thanks."

"Oh, and you'll have to take some of this home. I'm going to Ida and Izzie's this weekend." Rachel called her parents in New Jersey by their first names. A modern child. "It's going to spoil."

I protested. She overruled. I had my sights set on Boot Hill for a nightcap, but how can I go to a bar on the Upper West Side with a

Tupperware container of flayed eggplant? I am always laden down with the wrong thing. "Oh, and here's some salad, too." She packed efficiently, a layer of waxed paper between courses. "There. That's a complete meal." Me, so guilty, I won't throw it out. I'll eat the whole thing.

I skipped the bar and took the subway home. Across from me a woman who looked at least seventy was reading *The Happy Hooker,* a library edition.

"I've got something to t-t-t-t-t-t-t-tell you, B.J.," said Dennis. His stutter was studied—another one of his affectations he would pick up and drop at will. I think he got it from some Looney Tunes cartoon. It wasn't annoying at all; to the contrary, it was rather pleasant. "Wan-n-n-n-n-n-n-n-na see a movie?"

"Sure. How about Sunday afternoon?"

"Uh, I'm usually busy on Sundays. Could we make it Saturday?"

"Fine with me." I hung up. As I had suspected, we had sex only the first time. For some reason it's always easier for me to say no the *second* time. When I say no I feel guilty, and likewise with yes. As much as I liked Dennis, I couldn't conceive of being boyfriends with him. Boyfriends are mysterious things. I see them lined up in a row at one end of a room the size of an airplane hangar. One by one they take off and approach me at the speed of sound—prospective boyfriends, all shiny and new. After contact they zoom away, Doppler-shifting into the horizon, which is littered with failed attempts.

I wasn't asking for much. I just wanted someone who was overwhelmingly appealing physically, sexually, and mentally, who told jokes and could always keep me entertained and knew calculus and didn't go to Studio 54, which once did not admit me even though I had a pass, and read books and lifted weights and was hot enough to pose in a pornographic magazine but wouldn't for reasons of privacy and wasn't married to anyone. What I wanted was oxymoronic: a unique clone. I had always wanted to be a clone. Failing that, I wanted to own one.

Dennis and I saw something by Bergman that involved the slashing of female genitalia. "*Je me* depress," said Dennis in his fanciful fake French.

"Oh, every movie you see is depressing, Dennis. You cried during *Bambi*."

"Well," he countered, "you fell apart at *Snow White and the Seven Dwarfs*."

"That was different. I remember. I must have been five at the time; my sister, Sheila, was six. It was the first movie we ever saw alone without our parents. We were terrified when they showed the wicked witch's cottage. Afterwards, we waited outside the theater for Mom to pick us up. When she didn't show in five minutes, I started bawling. 'They're never going to come. They've left us here for good. It was just a trick. They've moved. They're in another state by now.' Sheila tried to calm me down, but I could tell she was having troubles convincing herself after another five minutes. That was an entirely different situation. I was just a kid."

"You had angst at an early age, perhaps," commented Dennis, using his Viennese accent. We went to this terrible tourist trap for coffee, a euphemism. Siegel's Delicatessen on Fifty-seventh Street. Formerly owned by Arthur Siegel, it had since gone to seed. I ordered cheesecake and tea. Dennis had his traditional Dewar's on the rocks. I went to the bathroom after ordering, and when I came back, I saw there was about an inch of scotch in Dennis's glass.

"You must have been very thirsty," I stated.

He sobbed no. He shook his head slowly.

"That's all they gave you?"

He nodded, tears in his eyes, practically. Now he paused and perked a bit. "Watch this," he commanded. "It's a magic trick." He passed his hand over the glass. He concentrated. He took out a flask from his vest pocket and poured it into the glass. His eyes were twinkling. "Voilà," he trumpeted. "It's a miracle. Water into wine. I mean, I mean, I mean, I mean scotch!"

I applauded.

"I always carry it for the commute," explained Dennis. He took the train and then the ferry to get home to Staten Island. I usually carry around a thick magazine for the subway. Once, for a month, I had one with a story by Saul Bellow. It was virtually impenetrable. It took me weeks to read. I would keep on reading the first few pages, forgetting where I had left off. The *Daily News* isn't enough. You needed something you could sink your teeth into to distract you from the fact that the train was stuck under the East River and the oxygen supply would run out in twenty-two minutes and the black man with the long flowing white robes and turban wouldn't leave the car until everyone in it made a donation to the Muslim school. Once I saw a made-for-TV disaster movie, styled on *The Poseidon Adventure,* only it took place on the BMT. The train had derailed; the tunnel was leaking; the third rail was shooting sparks; I think there were even hamster-sized rats threatening the car of survivors. I was freaked for weeks.

"I l-l-l-l-l-l-l-l-lied about my last name," Dennis was telling me. "It's really not McNiece."

"Why would you do a thing like that?"

"B-b-b-b-b-b-b-because. You never know. You never can be sure. It was just. I didn't know if I could trust you. Also, my profession. I do teach, but that's not the whole story."

"So what is it? What are we playing, twenty questions? *What's My Line?* Spit it out." Bring on the next celebrity panelist. Orson Bean would figure it out. Kitty Carlisle would play dumb bunny.

"Uh . . . it's kind of hard to tell you. It's a very respected profession among the Irish."

Is he a cop? I'm thinking, I'm really in over my head now. It's the Mafia. There must be an Irish branch. I'm going to wake up in a concrete overcoat six feet under. They'll take out a contract on me and write eighty-six: Terminate with extreme prejudice. The only way out is to be Dennis's lover forever and ever. And that, I didn't want.

"I give up. Tell me. What is it, already?"

There's a scene in *The Good Soldier* by Ford Madox Ford. A woman suddenly bolts from a room in a church and runs down several flights of stairs, breathless, to leave immediately. She rests outside. A man follows her and asks, "Why?"

"But don't you see," she says, "I am a Catholic."

"I'm a priest," said Dennis.

He couldn't be serious.

"Sure. And I am the queen of Romania."

"Do you want to see me in the full regalia? Do you want me to show you the clerical drag?"

He was. He meant it. Jesus. "Oh, for God sake's, don't call it drag. OK, you win. You're a priest. So I'm an atheist. I don't see where this is getting us. Jesus. So you're telling me that I was seduced by a priest when I was trying to be celibate. How ironic." I was dumbfounded.

"I hope this doesn't change our relationship," said Dennis.

"Sure. I mean, no, of course not. Do you take me for a fool? Give

14

me some time to think it over. A priest. I don't know any priests. I don't know any rabbis. Dennis, I can't stand religion. Remember the bit in the Old Testament about not lying with a man like a woman, for it is an abomination? Christ! When I was twelve, I had to go to Hebrew school and Junior Congregation and bar-mitzvah lessons and Sunday school. It warped me for life. It's enough to drive anyone to Satan. Do you believe in Satan? And the whole fucking Catholic church. The infallible pope screaming every sperm is sacred. Thou shalt not masturbate. Thou shalt not use a condom."

"Oh, I can't stand the pope either."

"You can't? Then why are you a priest? Organized religion. And I was thinking it was organized crime. Is there a difference? It's all laid out so neat. We are here to suffer. And later we'll get rewarded, after we're dead. After we're dead, we're dead. That's it, Dennis. No hereafter. No balloons. No burning fires or heavenly choirs. Nothing. I used to think people were dumb to believe. Now I know they're lucky. I could never believe. It would be nice, knowing that death wasn't final and forever. But I don't know, Dennis. Why are you a priest?"

"I believe. I believe in Christ."

"And you believe in sex, too."

"I don't follow the strict interpretation. Everyone knows that's folly. I don't like the organization any better than you. I feel that I'm a subversive. I can shake things up a little from where I stand. And all of the wonderful people I have known. I just can't accept that when they die, they go off into nothingness. I know that their spirit survives."

"Let's just get out of here. Give me some time to think. Don't call me for a week. Let this sink in. I don't know, Dennis; you lied to me."

"I've got to be careful. You know. When I meet someone. I have to trust them first. I mean. How was I to know you wouldn't call up the parish?"

"Well, it's a great way to get someone's trust by lying to them. Isn't lying one of the top ten?" I meant Ten Commandments, but my mouth wasn't working right.

Dennis squirmed. "Listen, I know this is a lot for you to accept all at once. Just give me a chance. Give it some time. Think it over."

"I guess." I left Dennis on the corner, confused. I just didn't know what to do.

15

Why I Always Wanted to Be a Clone

My history was sketchy, my story generic. An induced birth after thirty-six hours of false labor, the runt of a litter of twelve. At four my sister, Sheila, tossed a lamp at my head from the stairway. As I grew older, she threw progressively heavier items of furniture at me: a chaise longue, a queen-sized bed, a grand piano.

"Eat your vegetables," insisted Mother. I sat at the table silently, fork and spoon in hand, a twenty-pound can of mixed vegetables from the Civil Defense shelter before me, peas and cubed carrots in onion-salt and brine.

At nine I received a pair of glasses that each year doubled in thickness. Old pairs were donated to the Corning Glass Museum. Kids called me Four Eyes, geek, and nerd. They snatched my glasses from my face on the school bus as I protectively clutched seventeen textbooks on my lap—the glasses tossed from tormentor to tormentor, a game of catch.

Father was always busy in the basement, in his workroom, making shelves and cabinets, sawing off fingers, hammering at rats. Father worked in the cellar with the cracked concrete floor, with water seeping from groundswell, bare bulbs harshly illuminating, a cord of wood by the darkroom swarming with insects, clotheslines strewn from column to column, hanging with damp, unsoiled under things.

Hand raised in the classroom, I sat patiently in the last seat of the last row, waiting to ask permission to go to the bathroom. Miss Grimble was firm, ignoring me during the geography lecture. "Questions only after I have finished!" she snorted. A tiny stream of yellow formed at my feet. The desk floated through the door into the hallway.

The bell rang for recess. I wanted to stay and read the latest

Encyclopedia Brown detective story. Outside, boys played touch football, girls Chinese jump-rope. I leaned against the wall and observed. Ghetto kids came in a pack and used me as a punching bag. Back in class, Miss Grimble gave a lecture on racial harmony. She scolded another student for being a tattletale. I saved my breath.

At gym, last pick for kick-ball, I managed to strike out twice. "He throws the ball like a girl," they taunted afterward, bouncing me against the lockers. Then, discarding me like a broken toy, they clustered around Fred Kowalski, engrossed in baseball cards.

My life was tightly organized: school, piano lessons, Hebrew school, bar-mitzvah lessons, dance class, visits to the speech therapist at school to cure a slight lisp and stutter, swimming lessons, the orthodontist for braces, chess club, Boy Scouts, math club, Sunday school, honor society, SAT preparation classes. I set my alarm for four in the morning to give myself enough time to do homework before the paper route.

I breezed through college relatively unscathed. The first man I slept with demonstrated the difference between love and sex quite vividly. I moved to the city and went to the bars. I leaned against the wall and sipped my Lite. Men clustered and chattered lively in groups. I wished I knew how to smoke. I went home alone and lay in bed, awake, for hours.

Nothing fazes the clone. With expert detachment and practiced nonchalance, he holds the menu disdainfully, as if it were unclean. He flicks his ashes without reflection on the ground. The world is his ashtray. Behind his mirrored policeman sunglasses, the color of his eyes is anyone's guess. The glasses he removes only when showering and sleeping. They stay on for sex.

The clone wears a leather bomber-jacket. His Levi 501's are ass-clenchingly tight because he has showered in them for hours. The clone has a thick mustache hiding his upper lip. If he smiles (which he doesn't, ever), he would reveal a set of dazzling, flawless white teeth, sharp and shiny.

The clone speaks in monosyllables. He dances alone in the discotheque, pinching his own nipples. The clone is self-sufficient. The clone is hot sex. He never stays over for the night.

Invisibility is what I sought. I've always wanted to be exactly like everyone else. I wanted to blend into a crowd of clones and disappear.

· 2 ·

February

*F*rom the outside, it was a building like any other, except there were no windows. On the brown walls of corrugated metal a plaque commemorated it as the former home of James Fenimore Cooper. I opened the door, half-expecting it to be locked—a door solid enough for a safe-deposit vault, a firm barrier inscribed "The New St. Mark's Baths"—and climbed the flight of stairs to the check-in desk. My student ID allowed me a fifty percent discount on lockers during nonpeak hours. On Friday and Saturday nights, the line for rooms extended down the stairs and out the door; the wait could be as long as ninety minutes. Students must economize. I waited for a rainy Sunday afternoon. After my weekly call to Mom in Rochester, timed with a three-minute egg timer (weekend discounts apply), I hopped on the double R, got off at Eighth Street, and walked down Astor Place, past the few remaining street vendors with their soggy back issues of *Playboy* and *National Geographic* and their secondhand funky jewelry, to St. Mark's Place.

Inside, like Las Vegas, it was always night.

At the top of the stairs, above the grille, a superhero clad in loin-cloth sat astride a giant lizard, a Boris Vallejo fantasy poster. I signed the register and checked my valuables: a wallet from the Caribbean that smelled of cow dung, and a Timex. I saw a few John Smiths above my signature. The clerk gave me a key on an elastic wristband, a towel, and buzzed me in. Cute eighteen-year-old "bellhops" showed customers to their rooms for a modest tip. Those who rented lockers could find their own way.

I had eight hours to get laid.

I quickly removed my clothing in the locker room. An attractive black dressed at the adjacent locker. He was already spent. Pity. Curious queens floated like vapors through the room, eager to check

18

out the newest arrivals. In a bar one could be reasonably circumspect, casually checking the door between sips of cocktails and snippets of conversation. Here modesty and tact had little place. I was as naked as my lust.

Hard to imagine that four weeks ago I was attempting celibacy. I figured that if a priest violated my essay at chastity, it just *wasn't* meant to be. Last year I wouldn't have been caught dead at the baths. Why pay for sex? I'd take my chances at the bars. But now, especially after my New Year's Eve experience, I recognized the baths as the most direct path to sexual gratification. No deceptive advertising or flashy packaging here. Nothing to unwrap, unzip, unsnap, or unbutton: no complicated configuration of slip-lock belts and long johns to unravel, no adult equivalent of a child-proof medicine cap to struggle with. And everyone was there for one reason only: sex. I could go to Wildwood, a bar on the Upper West Side, and have a promising conversation with a cute Brazilian waiter. I'd be just about to invite Raoul to my apartment when the conversation would abruptly end as my newest acquaintance would greet his lover at the door with a hug, and I'd be left with an empty can of Bud and a hard-on. If only the semiotics of key-chains and hankies were extended to such exigencies as waiting-for-my-lover, cheating-on-my-boyfriend, recovering-from-an-infectious-disease (here a radioactive dye with the appropriate half-life would be helpful), just-here-to-collect-phone-numbers-and-bruise-egos, sorry-just-looking, third-stage alcoholic, not-interested-in-anything-under-thirty, and only-models-need-apply. I'd drain the last few drops of my beer and trudge home resentfully. My low capacity and penurious financial status required that I choose my flirtations with care, for two beers were my limit.

Apparel was democratic at the baths. We all wore towels knotted at the waist (exhibitionists carried them). Mine slipped frequently, reflecting a limited learning-disability discovered over ten years ago during the unit on knots at Boy Scouts. I held it in place, clutched at my side. The only variation in attire was how tightly the towel was rolled. Some wore them full-length; others preferred to roll them in half before knotting them. True, an occasional fetishist or off-duty porn star would be attired in leather pants or chaps, but this was rare.

Deception wasn't allowed. What you saw was what you got. Size queens quickly weeded out the unsuitable. A woman may fake orgasm with ease; faking an erection required considerable skill and talent (and the aid of Popsicle sticks and a rubber band?); it was nigh impossible to alter the length of the penis (perhaps with Play-Doh or Silly Putty?).

As I prowled through the corridors, I heard my mother's voice: "Stand straight. Remember, good posture and stately grace." I forced myself to keep the pace leisurely, fighting against the urge to walk briskly through all four floors, afraid I might miss Mister Right. I tried to construct a continuous path through the entire bathhouse such that I did not retrace my steps, similar to the equally impossible topological problem of crossing each of the seven bridges of Königsberg, Germany, once. I started with the second floor. I walked around the periphery. Each floor had about sixty rooms. The rooms contained a single bed with an inch-thick foam mattress and a small table for lubricants, poppers, and the like. Some doors were open. Men lay naked on their stomachs, passive, waiting to be fucked. Other doors were opened just a crack, just enough to see eyes glowing in the darkness. A man stood by his room in the hallway, slowly massaging his crotch through his towel. I brushed past, not wanting to touch him. Too old, too fat.

Disco music was piped through speakers on each floor, blending with the sounds of groans and dirty talk. At the stairs a short hall bisected the rectangular corridor, leading to the bathroom on the other side. This hallway was lined with pink-tinted mirrors. Two queens stood and gossiped there.

"She was a fright last night at the Paradise Garage. You should have seen what she was wearing. She looked like a walking garage-sale from Bensonhurst."

"Strictly bridge-and-tunnel."

"She was *abysmal*! Honey, you got a 'lude?"

"Just try one of these. Don't ask questions. It'll do you right."

I went to the third floor. I followed a butch number with a bear's mat of fur on his chest, but he wasn't interested. The third floor was identical to the second. I stood for ten minutes against the mirrors, watched the passing parade, and moved on to the fourth floor. The stairs on the fourth floor led to the sun deck on the roof. It was closed for the season, with a chain at the foot of the stairs. I imagined the neighbors peering over rooftops to watch the men sunbathe nude.

I descended to the ground floor, passing a man in his mid-sixties, clutching a twenty-dollar bill. I had my eyes prepared to read "not for sale," but he didn't notice me as I rushed by.

The ground floor had a snack bar and an orgy room, along with the lockers. I avoided the orgy room if possible, using it only when I met someone who also had a locker and we couldn't find an un-occupied unlocked room to borrow. There was nothing private about the orgy room. My comrade in lust and I would try to find the most remote and dark corner, but we would inevitably have to slap away hands and mouths. The maze and the orgy room were too dark for my tastes. I wanted to *see* who I was fondling. Sex for me was visual, along with tactile.

In the basement were the facilities: a steam room, a small swim-ming pool, a Jacuzzi, showers, and a sauna. I took off my glasses, left them on my towel on the tiles, and went for a quick swim. I dried off and lounged on the ledge of tiles that formed a long sitting area opposite the pool. I waited awhile. Nobody interesting. I left. Upstairs, on the second floor, I saw an attractive stud. He was blond with brown eyes, just a dusting of down on his chest and stomach. I followed him around the circuit. He went to the third floor. I didn't know if he noticed me. I started to follow, then reversed, attempting to cut him off at the pass. I just missed him as he went into his room alone and shut the door. I waited outside his door, hoping it would open a crack and he would beckon me in, but he didn't, and I left. A man with tit rings and an immense erection stared at me, licking his lips. I walked away quickly. Too heavy a scene for me.

Be patient, I reminded myself. The right guy would come along any minute now. It was just a matter of waiting. In this way the baths were no different from the bars—a lot of waiting. There seemed to be a strict hierarchy of beauty and desirability. Everyone was looking for someone more attractive than himself. Everyone thought he was more attractive than he was in fact. The syntax of desire and seduction was amazingly convoluted. If only Ann Landers had thought to write a pamphlet on gay relations. If only Miss Manners had promulgated, like the pope, an encyclical on proper gay conduct.

Finally I saw him. He had a long, thin braid down his back to the waist, and straight black hair. He was six foot two, and his eyes were burning. He saw me standing against the mirror and stopped. He looked me over carefully, appraising every visible square inch. I felt myself getting hard. He smiled, came over, and stroked my chest. I sighed. He took my hand and led me to his room without a word. The odor of poppers was noxious. I heard a cacophony of rough grunts and rhythmic thrusts over the music:

"Yeah, man. Take it."

"Oh, baby baby, that's so-o-o-o-o-o-o-o-o g-o-o-o-o-o-o-o-d."

"Uh-huh."

"Shoot it, baby."

"Shut up, bitch, and keep sucking."

"Big fat dick. Yeah."

"Eat it. Take it down your throat, the whole thing. Yeah, man."

The steady four-four beat of disco reverberated in the background, Gloria Gaynor singing "I Will Survive" in the ninety-minute version.

He shut the door behind me, and we hung our towels on the hook. He kissed me slow and deep. He removed my glasses, setting them on the table. He was huge. I stroked him slowly, then hugged him tightly. I licked his chest and then went down on him. He held my head as I pumped away. I pulled off and reached up to kiss him full. Then he licked my body and went down on me. I braced myself against the wall. It felt so good. He kneaded my ass with his fingers as he sucked me. Then he ran his fingers down the length of my back, pulled up, and kissed me.

We lay down on the bed. He opened a tiny bottle and offered me a hit of poppers. I nodded yes. He put the bottle below my right nostril, covering my left with his finger. I inhaled deeply. Then the same for the left nostril. I started to feel the rush as he inhaled. Suddenly I was all sex, he was all sex, I was overwhelmed by it, this drive, everything was sex, every touch was completely sexual, my heart was beating, all I could think of was sex, my heart was pounding, loudly, violently, I was obsessed, I wanted to touch him all over, I wanted everything inside of me at once, I wanted to envelop him, every sensation was magnified, I was a sex machine, I forced myself to take him slowly, I savored every inch of him down my throat, he was sucking me at the same time, I went deeper and then pulled away, twisting his nipples, licking his balls, tongue darting in and out, and then I felt weak, the feeling waned, I was pounding air, my head hurt a little, I slowed down and stopped.

I took another snort and offered it to him. We stopped for a moment, and he got another hit—first right nostril, then left, then right again—as I felt the rush again. He was so good, he was so hot, he was a fucking Adonis, everything about him was perfect, he was so fucking hot, I wanted him, I needed to feel him, I wanted to feel him inside me, but I wanted him in my mouth, I wanted everything at once, I went down on him again, he went down on me, I pulled him closer and clutched him by the cheeks, I could tell he was getting closer, almost ready, I felt myself starting to let go, and then he came, he shuddered, his body quivered, quickened, and died as I came a moment later.

We both rested, breathing deeply. On my back I looked at the ceiling. He had his arm around my head. The cum was cool and sticky on my stomach. I wanted to wipe it off. My head ached a bit. It was over too suddenly. I had wanted the foreplay to last hours. My dick was still hard; it took a while to soften. I felt hungry. I looked at him, and he was still beautiful. I felt the combination of a poppers' headache and *le petit mort,* post-coital depression. I felt empty. What was I doing here, naked, next to a man whose name I didn't even know? I should have been home studying, reading the latest *Journal of Contemporary Culture* or *Socio-Anthropological Research.* I should have been working on that incomplete paper from last semester, "Semiotics in the Cinema of Fassbinder." My mind had teleported to the moon, and I was being operated by remote control.

I found out his name was Brian. He was an Indian from Saskatchewan. He came to the city once a year and usually checked into the baths for the weekend. It was much cheaper than any hotel. I could hear some fairies giggling in the next room. There was no point in exchanging numbers. We went downstairs for a shower and then parted. I saw a few new hot men who must have arrived while we were having sex. I still felt a hunger inside me. I knew it was time to go, but I wasn't ready just yet. Going outside would be a shock: I needed some time to decompress before facing the real world. I figured it must be around five in the afternoon, near sunset. I rested on the tiles and then went into the steam room. Home was far away. I saw a cute Italian, and my dick got hard without my conscious involvement. I really wasn't in the mood for sex. I was and I wasn't. My dick was standing straight up. He came over and without a word sat right down on me. I pushed him off. I realized I had better go now. I took another quick shower, dressed, and left.

Three days later I was visiting a fuck-buddy on the Upper East Side, Lewis B. Pickles, an art director of dubious distinction. He took care to note my enthusiasm preceded me: I was dripping before we had even touched. On closer examination he determined the primordial ooze emanating from my member was not in fact precum but the drip of a social disease. Naturally he declined further action. I left in disbelief, for how could this happen to me? Later I experienced a curious burning sensation during micturition. Now a visit to the public health clinic was in order. I couldn't very well call home for a loan to go to a private physician. Instead, I suffered the slings and abuses of public health.

A recent high-school graduate sat at the reception desk. He greeted me cheerfully. Eyes averted, I pretended to be the unknown comic, an imaginary paper bag covering my head, with two clumsy cutouts for eye holes. Flirting was inevitable in the waiting room, for the wait was interminable, two hours easy, considerably longer than the time in which I procured this errant bacterium, *Neisseria gonorrhoeae*. I sat through lunch hour staring at a poster of a crab louse magnified to monstrous proportions. Time passed and we played musical chairs, rotating as the numbers called out got closer to the ones we were assigned. An over-friendly man greeted me effusively, having recognized me from the A&P on Fifty-fifth or perhaps Crossroads, the local hole-in-the-wall for neighborhood deviants.

The nurse in starch-white uniform gave me strict instructions to avoid intimate relations of any nature for the next fifteen days, the duration of the low-dosage penicillin they punitively dispensed, as if the U.S.D.A. had determined the minimum daily adult requirement for this antibiotic and, stingy to the core, parsimonious to a fault, kept half in reserve out of sheer perversity.

The symptoms returned after I finished the pills, and so did I. The nurse was all disbelief, citing statistics of the healed and restored, the multitudes that had passed through the portals, dripping and left cleansed, desiccated, until I displayed for her personal benefit my own particular discharge, at which point she was forced to concur. The apology I waited for I never got. Luckily the second dose, a minor variant of the first, did the trick.

On a Wednesday for lunch I met Dennis in front of the Waverly Theater at Sixth Avenue and Third Street.

"Where are we going, Dennis?"

"Oh, uh, er, I don't know, just follow me," he replied. The shortest distance between two points appeared to be a zigzag. We took a left on Houston, a left on Sullivan, then we backtracked to MacDougal. I felt like a blindfolded kidnap victim, only my eyes were open. We wound through the streets of the Village with no apparent destination and stopped abruptly on Bedford Street.

"We're here," announced Dennis.

"Which is?"

"Chumley's—another well-kept secret of the cognoscenti." Dennis delighted in showing me the out-of-the-way restaurant, the off-the-beaten-track establishment. "I uh, I uh, I uh, I wanted to make sure that we went somewhere with a w-i-i-i-i-i-i-i-i-i-ne license," explained Dennis. "After that last fiasco, huh huh, I'm not going to trust your judgment."

Envious of Dennis's talent for finding restaurants, two weeks ago I had taken him to a Thai restaurant on Eighth Avenue. We both had chicken soup with coconut and ginger that tasted like fresh vomit.

"So what's new? Are you all cleared up?" asked Dennis.

"Yep. Guess it comes with the territory," I said ruefully. "You gotta be careful at the baths."

"That reminds me," said Dennis. "I've got a question to ask you. Do they, perchance, at the baths, give a clergy discount?"

"Only for the archbishop and higher on the ecumenical scale," I replied.

"You know, I get fifteen percent off on the electric bill. It's another enticement for the laity. Perhaps you've reconsidered your faith since our last chat? Haven't you always wanted to be declared tax-free?"

"Dennis, I'm making four hundred dollars a month. There's nothing to tax. Where's our waiter? I'm starving."

"Look," said Dennis. He took his napkin and folded it in half.

"Oh, no, not the napkin trick again."

Dennis ignored me, all concentration on the napkin. This was a delicate operation, like synthesizing recombinant DNA or running a chemical solution through an ultracentrifuge. He flipped it over and folded it again. The flair was in the passion for details—all done carefully, skillfully, meticulously, methodically. Most people who do the napkin trick concentrate on speed and efficiency. Not Dennis. Every move was carefully calculated, using the principle of maximum effort. With Dennis, it was a slow and precise process. Against my better judgment, I was always drawn in, fascinated by his exacting motions.

"Finished," said Dennis. Gingerly he placed the folded napkin on his head. "It's a hat. It's bunny ears. And now"—the grand finale, the pièce de résistance, the big "schnozzola," deftly placing it on his chest—"it's a bra." I couldn't help but laugh.

"You should see me do my sermons."

"Oh, I bet they're rolling in the aisles."

The waiter arrived with a menu and two glasses of water.

"Don't worry, it's on me," said Dennis. I checked his shirt for stains. "I mean the *bill*, dummy! Anything you want so long as it's under five dollars."

"You're sure?" I protested weakly. My stipend wouldn't arrive until the end of the month.

"*Certainement. Bien sûr. D'accord.* Butt off course!!!"

"The burgers are OK here?"

"Ze entire menu eet eez *splendide*." Dennis ordered spaghetti carbonara. I got a cheeseburger platter. I picked at the fries. Dennis asked for another glass of red wine.

"So have you had any luck lately in the boyfriend department?" I asked.

(A week ago Dennis and I had made a bet. We both were desperately seeking boyfriends. If Dennis found a boyfriend before me, I'd buy him a bottle of scotch. If I found one first, he'd get me the T-shirt of my choice. We decided that we'd limit the bet to this year. "What's a boyfriend?" asked Dennis. "Dating is up to three months. I think a boyfriend is anything longer," I theorized. "OK, I'm game," he had said.)

"As a matter of fact, last week I met a guy named Anatole at the Anvil."

Shit. He's already made progress. That's not really fair, since I was out of commission. "The Anvil? Do you know what goes on there? That's one of the sleaziest leather bars on the West Side. What were you doing there?"

"Uh, er, you see, I'm doing what is called sociological research. That's it, I'm doing sociological research; I went there strictly as an observer."

"Dennis, I've been out for years, and I've never been to the Anvil." He was certainly learning the ropes fast. "Aren't you afraid?"

"What's to be afraid of? I find it fascinating." Dennis slurped some spaghetti up from his spoon. He neatly set the fork and spoon at the side of his plate. "Sure you don't want a taste?"

"Yeah. So tell me about Anatole."

"He's dark. He's about my height. He lives in Brooklyn. Brighton Beach. They have a lot of Russian immigrants there. He was a Soviet dissident. He's in his early twenties. They kicked him out of the Soviet Union two years ago. Now he works for Amnesty International and Radio Free Europe. He used to be a mathematician there."

"So get on to the big stuff. Is he good in bed? Did he bring back certain sexual secrets from behind the Iron Curtain, henceforth unknown to Western civilization? Is this the real thing or merely a facsimile?" Youth wants to know.

"I had a good time." Dennis spoke softly, his face lowered, looking at his plate of pasta. "You know, I think he was tortured in prison." Dennis paused. "He started to tell me a little about it once, but then he stopped in the middle."

People were drawn to Dennis. It wasn't just me. People wanted to confide in him, confess their deepest, darkest secrets.

"That's horrible! I hope he's OK now. I'd be a basket case."

"And he's taking me to the Mineshaft this weekend. I've got an idea that he's into S and M. I think it's related to the fact that he was tortured."

"Have you been doing any of that with him?"

"*Moi?*" In times of distress Dennis was given to using Miss Piggy's favorite word. "Of course not!"

"Maybe he should see some kind of therapist," I mused.

"He's a bit troubled, but I think he's under control." Dennis sighed.

"I've got it! You should become a psychotherapist. It's like being a priest. You get to listen to everyone's problems and then make them feel better. It's perfect!" I decided that my mission was to convince Dennis to leave the priesthood. Part of it was that I hated organized religion; part of it was that Dennis did not match my idea of a priest.

"Naaaaah. Not me. I'm too old for med school. I can't hack all of those all-nighters. And I wouldn't get to wear my Sunday finery."

"On Halloween you would."

"That's just once a year. What you don't understand is that I like my job. I like spreading the word of God. I like giving sermons."

"Wait, I've got it now. A bartender."

"A bartender?" Dennis was amused. "Now you're cooking. That's more like it."

"Think of it. You could be the kindly Irish bartender. A willing ear for everyone's troubles, along with a glass of whiskey to loosen them up. It's perfect. I'm sure we could arrange a substantial discount on wholesale liquor."

"Naaaah. Wouldn't work. I'd drink up all of the profits." He laughed.

"Oh, well, don't say I didn't try."

Miss Letitia Thing's Guide to Excruciatingly Correct Behavior Concerning Tricks, One-Night (or Afternoon) Stands, and the Like, with a Special Appendix on Relationships

1. When you see someone nice on the street, don't smile. You don't want to risk rejection this early in the game. Walk exactly three paces, then turn and stare. With any luck, he will have done the same.

2. Instead of directly approaching him, pretend to window-shop. It doesn't matter that the store you are staring at through iron gratings sells women's shoes. Be cautious if you find yourself staring at the display of the Noose, the Pink Pussycat, or a like vendor of sexual apparatuses for the more adventurous. View his reflection in the glass carefully. Determine whether to proceed.

3. Discuss the weather. Even if it's winter and the worst cold-spell of the century, describe it as "hot."

4. Find out the essentials: who lives closer, who lives alone, when his boyfriend is returning from the trip to Tahiti or work. If it is determined inconvenient for either side to meet at present, exchange phone numbers. Avoid the use of business cards. Print for legibility. Neatness counts.

5. Never call first. You don't want to appear pushy or overly interested.

6. Don't tell him he resembles your ex.

7. Do not lie about whether or not you have a lover if asked directly. However, do not feel obligated to bring it up if it would occasion discord.

8. At the entrance to the apartment building, it is the responsibility of the host to (a) apologize for the state of disarray; (b) give an accurate count of the number of flights to climb if it is a walk-up.

9. Hugs and kisses are allowed once inside the apartment. It is the responsibility of the host to first offer a beverage of some sort before going down on the guest. Groping should not be too excessive initially (that is, in the first thirty seconds).

10. The guest should make agreeable comments on the apartment's decor, location, view, size, or bargain status, as appropriate, before undressing the host.

11. Courtesy dictates introducing the guest to the roommate should he not be your lover. After a decent interval the roommate should disappear on an errand or into his room for an extended period.

12. Once in the bedroom, it is proper to remove all clothing. If you are a size queen and he is less than you had hoped, try to conceal your disappointment.

13. Never defile a lover's bed. Be imaginative. Use the couch, the fireplace, the bearskin rug, the linoleum kitchen floor, the closet, the bathtub, the fire escape.

14. Disco tapes are appropriate background music. If he requests classical, offer earplugs and a Walkman.

15. Share all recreational drugs. If he says no to poppers, try to refrain from using them yourself.

16. Ask before you tie him up.

17. Do as much as he does in bed unless (a) you are at least five years younger; (b) you are at least twenty pounds more muscular; or (c) you are at least fifty percent cuter.

18. Try to keep individual quirks to a minimum. By concealing your personality defects, you can appear to be his ideal. For example, don't converse if it would cause disappointment.

19. In the event that both of you turn out strictly active or passive, the host should supply a suitable board game, e.g., Monopoly or Clue.

20. After you come, stay awake until he does. Bring a cassette of moans if you are incapable of feigning enthusiasm. After he comes, stop pulling his nipple and tying it into complicated knots you learned in macramé class.

21. It is the responsibility of the host to supply the cum towel after ejaculation. Do not accept paper towels. Insist on the union label.

22. Stay at least fifteen minutes after you come. If he swallows, you are obligated to give him a back rub.

23. If it's after midnight, let him stay the night. Otherwise, you may discreetly kick him out.

Remember, the one-night stand will not be repeated. You want to leave the best impression, since you will probably never see this person again. Courtesy counts.

RELATIONSHIPS: To keep a relationship fresh, think of it as a series of one-night stands.

· 3 ·

March

I had met Carlo Montagna, a pumped-up film major, at N.Y.U.'s makeshift gym on the fourth floor of the Education Building. A new gymnasium had been under construction for several years. Each semester I received a mailing from the school informing me that the opening had been delayed another six months. I doubted that the Coles Athletic Center would open before I graduated.

The gym was a joke. The locker room—filled with broken lockers, fluorescent tube-lights sputtering from the ceiling, gum embedded in the concrete floor—belonged in a high school for juvenile delinquents at the turn of the century. A metal cage encased the weight-lifting area, which consisted of two tiny rooms. Unfortunately, a row of lockers lined the wall separating the gym from the locker room, obstructing the view. Cruising was suboptimal. The only way to keep abreast of current activity in the locker room from the weight room was to do pull-ups on the grips of the Universal weight-machine station, and the view would necessarily be intermittent. Similarly, from the locker room the only way to check out the weight-lifting room was by standing on a stool, a much too obvious cruise tactic.

I had seen Carlo a few times over the past few months and spoken to him once or twice. He wore a thick weight-lifter's belt and leather gloves. While the other queens sat and debated whether Elizabeth Taylor was the greatest film star who ever lived or dished about last night at the Flamingo or 12 West, Carlo would assiduously go through his workout—one day arms and legs, the next chest and back. Every day he would do two hundred sit-ups on the slant board.

I was lucky. I could get away with only forty twist sit-ups. One day when I set the board at the highest angle and was doing my sit-ups, Carlo was watching.

"That's pretty good," he commented.

32

"Thanks," I replied, flustered. In the presence of great beauty I am often left speechless. I went on to another exercise. He moved the board down two notches and began his first set of fifty.

Carlo was gorgeous, and he knew it. His eyes were ice-blue, his hair soft and tousled brown, his mustache immaculately trimmed. Carlo reeked of sex and masculinity. He had huge thighs and delicate nipples atop boulderous pecs. I'd get hard whenever I was near him. He had that rare combination of size and definition. Most men as big as Carlo were thick-waisted. Carlo was large as a steroid junkie yet not puffy—firmly outlined, with a chest like an armor breastplate. His body tapered down in a V to a small, tight stomach and waist.

A few weeks later I saw Carlo as I walked through Washington Square Park. The park was swarming with students and drug dealers, tourists and derelicts. Taking advantage of a brief break in the weather, people covered the fountain. Its seven or eight jets had been killed for the winter, yet it remained a silenced centerpiece of the park. Three teens with ivory legs in shorts played Frisbee across the fountain. Bottles littered the walkways. A man in dreadlocks accosted all with cries of "Loose joints, loose joints." I shook my head no and continued down the path. A few steps later a pockmarked man in a leather jacket mumbled, "Good smoke."

Graffiti covered the arch at the base of Fifth Avenue. Ghetto blasters spewed Jamaican rhythms. A pair of sullen punks from the East Village were talking quietly beneath a bare tree. A man stood in the sod, juggling three sticks.

"Carlo!" I shouted. I crossed the park and rushed to approach him.

"Oh, hi."

"Which way are you going? I'll walk you." Anywhere.

"I'm going home now. I'm supposed to meet some friends for dinner in a few hours."

"I was a prisoner in a university library," I said.

"I hear you."

"After three hours in the basement my mind turns to oatmeal."

We walked to East Seventh and Second Avenue. I felt the conversation was but a subtext for a more visceral, nonverbal communication.

"Here we are. You want to come up for some tea or something?" I hoped tea was a euphemism for you-know-what.

"Sure."

Carlo lived on the fifth floor, facing the street, in a railroad apartment he shared with a girlfriend from high school. She was out. Carlo brewed some tea. I examined the posters on the wall. *Three Women* by Robert Altman. *Casablanca* with Humphrey Bogart and Ingrid Bergman. His bookshelves were plywood and cinder blocks. He had *James Agee on Film, The Definitive Citizen Kane, Beowulf,* and *The Canterbury Tales,* along with Truffaut's book on Hitchcock. Next to the books were two years of Joe Weider's weight-lifting magazines arranged in chronological order and a copy of *Pumping Iron.* On a small table were arrayed the latest issues of *Interview, Film Comment, American Film Quarterly,* and *Honcho.*

We chatted noncommittally in the kitchen, neutral territory. His plaid shirt was half-unbuttoned. I forced myself to stop staring at his chest and looked instead around the room. A Colt calendar was on the wall. A bathtub sat prominently in the center of the kitchen, covered with a door to make a table. Cheery yellow curtains were placed on the window, facing an air shaft. Above the stove and refrigerator ran a row of shelves painted white, neatly stacked with dishes and silverware, pots and pans, buckling slightly in the middle.

"It's very homey here," I commented.

"Thanks. I'm glad you like it."

"I just don't seem to have the touch myself."

"And you call yourself a self-respecting faggot?"

"I know. It's embarrassing. Maybe I should wallpaper my apartment with pages from *Architectural Digest* and *Better Homes and Gardens.* I'd be too embarrassed to take a course on design at the New School. Maybe I can try a correspondence course through the cooperative extension at Rochester."

"Why upstate?"

"That's where I'm from."

"I grew up on Long Island," said Carlo.

"Do you see your folks much?"

"About once a year."

"And you're this close?"

"I have my life, and they have theirs. I'm working on an independent film project now. You have no idea how much time it takes."

"And you still have time for the gym."

"I make the time."

"You look pretty good." Again my eyes went to his open shirt.

"You've got a pretty good stomach yourself."

"It used to be one of the ten best stomachs in Manhattan."

"What happened?"

"I ate lunch. Now it's one of the twenty best."

"How do you do it? I spend three times the amount of time you do on sit-ups, and I still can't get results like you."

"I guess it's just luck. Heredity." Thank God. We were finally talking about bodies. I was wondering whether he would ever make a move. Maybe he was shy. I didn't want to be the aggressor and risk rejection. He didn't invite me up here for sex. This was his apartment. He had dinner to go to. There probably wasn't enough time anyway.

"And you've got a nice dick." Bingo. I blushed.

"How do you know?"

"Oh, I've changed next to you in the locker room. I notice these things." Did Carlo notice that I got hard every time I was near him? At least he was unobtrusive. If only I could cruise without having my eyes bug out. Maybe I should wear dark glasses. Sure, and why not a cane to poke at baskets? Many's been the time when I would skip an exercise in the hopes of catching some hot man naked in the showers. I hadn't seen Carlo because he typically didn't shower at the gym. Maybe he didn't sweat much. Maybe Carlo *was* shy. Then again, maybe he knew from experience that he would set off a stampede toward the showers. I had gotten it down so I could strip in ten seconds. The only thing holding me up would be fumbling at the combination lock or renting a towel. While precious seconds would be ticking away, I'd curse the attendant for his sluggish pace as he reluctantly tore himself away from the *New York Post* and waddled over to fetch me a towel.

"What about *your* dick, Carlo?"

"You want to find out?" His voice had grown husky. Yet at the same time I felt he was indulging me, a squalling child begging to be fed in the middle of the night. We went to the bedroom. He told me to remove my clothes one by one. He stripped while watching me. His dick was as big as I had imagined it would be. He stood, imposing, facing me. He knew that I wanted him more than anything. This was why he kept his distance. He would let me look. No more. I wanted to cover him with my tongue. He wouldn't let me. He laughed softly.

"I love to torture Jewish boys," he said, slowly stroking his massive dick. He stood, facing me on the bed. I lay there naked watching him jerk off. Carlo was just talking trash. Where were the whips, the chains? Which way to the gas chamber? I moved to sit up and approach him. "Stay on the bed," he ordered. "Don't get any closer." He breathed, hard and hot. "Touch me and you'll pay the consequences." I stayed on the bed. I erupted ten minutes later, and Carlo soon followed. We cleaned up with Kleenexes, exchanged phone numbers. I had to rush home. He was late for dinner.

Maybe next time he'd let me touch him. Maybe it was a plan to heighten desire by withholding pleasure. Maybe Carlo was more sophisticated than me and he knew what I wanted. Or maybe he was just a cock tease.

Over the next few weeks I called Carlo at various times. He was never home. Occasionally I got his roommate, Leslie. "Uh, just tell him I called," I said. Or, "No, don't bother leaving a message. I'll try him later." Embarrassed that he should realize the depths of my desperation, I grew disconsolate. I fully realized the futility of this enterprise, an unrequited obsession, a one-sided infatuation. We had nothing in common except that I was head over heels in lust with him and he wouldn't give me the time of day if my life depended on it.

I lingered at the gym, hoping to catch him there. I rearranged my schedule, split my workout, went to the gym two, three times a day. No luck. Once I ran into Carlo as he was leaving. He smiled and dashed out without even saying hello. Crushed, I changed into shorts and a T-shirt and sat at the slant board without moving for five minutes, dazed and confused. My head was spinning.

"Anything wrong?" asked Zack, a cute sophomore with a single gold hoop through his left ear.

"Oh, uh, nothing," I replied. I woke myself up. I finished my sit-ups and left. There was no point in hanging around any longer. At home as I emptied my backpack, a slip of paper fluttered to the floor. Zack had slipped me his number while I was in the showers.

I called Carlo one more time, ten o'clock that night. Then I called Zack. "Why don't you hop on the subway and come down for a bit? We can fool around." His voice was breathless. Zack was about five six. He had a sprig of green in his curly brown hair. He lived in Weinstein Dorm on Fifth Avenue and Ninth. I took the double A down to see him. For that added romantic touch, the subway lights had been dimmed on the first two cars. I closed my eyes. All we needed was a little Sinatra crooning "Strangers in the Night." In the subway one faced the eternal mystery of lust and desire. At rush hour, was that hand smoothing your buttocks filled with carnal desire for you, a stranger in hot and horny pursuit, or merely a pickpocket? I kept my wallet in front. The square crotch kept them guessing. Cruising was practically de rigueur in the subway, if only to stay awake, to keep alert for the endless horrors one encountered. I've seen so many disabled beggars that I suspected the hospitals sent out amputees for occupational therapy. I always checked wheelchairs for false bottoms to hide missing limbs.

The train lurched to a halt at West Fourth. I scrambled out the exit, past a nodding ten-year-old boy with a cardboard sign hanging from his neck, "Homeless and Hungry," and a hat with small change at his feet, and walked down Tenth Street to Fifth. At Weinstein Dorm I took the elevator to the ninth floor. Zack let me in and chained the door behind us. He was drinking grape Tang and vodka, a demented dormitory drink when mixers were scarce. I refused a grape-jelly glass. Instead I started nibbling on his neck. A David Bowie tape played in the background. Zack mouthed the words as I undressed him. Zack knew the words to everything that David Bowie and Lou Reed have ever written. He bragged that he had made it with all five of the New York Dolls when he was sixteen. For me it was all slurred nasality, guitars whining, and cacophonous drums. I picked up one word in three. I found out he had also dyed a small patch of his pubic hair green to match his hair.

I stripped, and we rolled around the bed. I was aggressive, flipping him over, eager to get a taste of all of him at once. Part of it was frustration. I knew I would never have another chance at Carlo. Later Zack told me he was afraid of me a little. But as soon as he came, he rushed to the bathroom to shower. I was left pumping air. The quiet moment of intimacy after sex never arrived. He was as efficient as a prostitute. What about me? I called him my Lady Macbeth, running to the bathroom and compulsively washing his hands, over and over again, gasping, "Out, damned spot! Out, I say!" But he was merely washing his genitals and gargling with Listerine. He told me he had had so many venereal diseases at this point that he knew to wash up immediately afterward. I heard pounding on the door.

"Oh, that's just my roommate."

"You locked him out?" I asked incredulously.

"Yeah. He does the same when he has a girlfriend over. Well, now that we're done, I might as well let him in."

"Hey, wait." I was embarrassed. "Can I get dressed?" I said, trying to scramble into my pants. Two legs did not fit into one hole.

"All right," he said. "Benno, just a minute, OK? Here, could you get me a Planters peanut bar from the vending machine down the hall? Thanks." He turned his attention to me. "It's no big deal. He's seen other boys here before."

I left, feeling a little uncomfortable. I could sense that Zack had just checked me off his list of potential tricks and was ready to start in on another page of the Manhattan white pages. But then again, I saw him only because I couldn't get to Carlo. So much for sloppy seconds. I guessed I could write both of them off as potential boyfriends. I wondered how Dennis was doing with romance. I hoped better than me.

"Is Dennis still a priest?" Rachel whispered in my ear. She had invited us over for dinner. I was in the kitchen with Rachel, helping with the drinks. Dennis had brought a bottle of Beaujolais.

"It's not exactly sacramental," apologized Dennis, "but I think you'll like it."

"Dennis!" I scolded.

He chuckled and sat down on the couch. The coffee table was littered with Italian *Vogue*s and *New Yorker*s.

"I'm having vodka and grapefruit juice. Does anybody else want one?"

"I could go for that," said Dennis.

"Just juice for me," I answered. Rachel mixed the drinks, and I delivered two brimming glasses from the kitchen to the living room.

"The coasters should be on the side," informed Rachel. I opened a red lacquer box and took out three cork coasters.

"Dinner should be ready in a few minutes. Here, have some cheese and crackers." Rachel fumbled with her pot holders and removed a meat-loaf pan covered with aluminum foil. No smoke yet. A good sign.

"I hope I didn't put too much garlic in." Dinner was pesto meat-loaf. "I was on the phone to Ida and Izzie in New Jersey while I was pulverizing the pesto in the Cuisinart, and I lost track of how many cloves of garlic I had put in."

"I'm sure everything will be fine," I lied. Dennis looked at me questioningly. I mouthed, "P-i-z-z-a l-a-t-e-r."

"Could you help me with the vegetables?" asked Rachel.

"No problem." I carried the green-bean casserole to the dinner table, placing it on a bamboo trivet. Crushed bread-crumbs and Parmesan cheese formed an impenetrable topping. We sat down to dinner.

"Hey, I got a dinner joke," said Dennis, giggling. "What happened to the cannibal who came late for dinner?"

"I don't know."

"He got the cold shoulder!" Dennis laughed.

Rachel smiled. "So tell me, Dennis, exactly what is it that you do?" she asked.

"Oh, the usual. Perform ecclesiastical duties. A sermon here, a confession there. Disseminate the knowledge of Kant, Spinoza, and Schopenhauer. A little epistemology and some existentialism. Oh, I almost forgot," said Dennis, spearing some string beans with his fork. "I'll be also teaching ethics."

I choked on my wine. A gay priest teaching ethics?

"Now, now, B.J., we don't drink wine like that. Try sipping. See?" He demonstrated. "Voilà! Not a single drop wasted."

The vegetables tasted surprisingly good. The meat loaf, however, was an unqualified disaster.

"B.J. tells me you studied anthropology at Radcliffe?" prompted Dennis.

"Yes. My thesis was on the role of women on a Sioux reservation in North Dakota. After I graduated, I got a job at the Museum of the American Indian. But there was a budget cut after a year, and I was laid off. Now I'm on unemployment."

"Tell Dennis what you're doing now," I urged.

"You have to promise not to tell. It's under the table."

"You have my word," said the professor of ethics.

"I'm cataloging the estate of Estelle Wentworth. You remember her from the papers, don't you? She was the most famous debutante of 1925. She died a few months ago. She left a considerable collection of modern couture at her home in Brooklyn."

"Gee. Sounds nice. Who turned you on to it?" asked Dennis.

"It was the 'old girl' network. Someone I went to Radcliffe with— her parents knew Miss Wentworth's lawyers. Oh, but you must have seconds."

Dennis demurred. "I had a late lunch," he confessed.

"The food stamps should come through any day now," I announced.

"Food stamps! How could you?" Rachel was horrified.

"I don't see a whit of difference between food stamps and unemployment," I contended.

"Oh, don't be ridiculous! They couldn't be further apart! Unemployment is money that *I* paid into a fund, just like insurance," reasoned Rachel. "It's *my money*. They've just socked it away for me for an emergency. Which I am currently in."

"I want to be on the public dole. Come on, Rachel. Face it. Nobody can live on what I'm getting from grad school. My assistantship is just peanuts. Every time I have to ask my mom for money I feel six inches tall."

"Oh, no, he's going to go on about his height again," groaned Rachel. "You're just too sensitive, B.J. When I said I thought you were short, I merely meant in comparison with me."

"That's not fair. You were wearing heels." I pouted.

"So, I know a place where you could have picked up some wedgies dirt cheap," she suggested.

"I bet they wouldn't have been designer," I bemoaned.

Rachel was about an inch taller than me. She had told me her rule of thumb was that if a guy was shorter than she was, he was short.

My contribution to dinner was dessert. I brought a carton of Häagen-Dazs rum-raisin ice cream. "Uh, er, uh, I usually don't mix," claimed Dennis, "but in this case I suppose I can make an exception."

"So how's it going with Anatole?" I asked Dennis.

"Baaaaad. He tells me he loves me, but he's not ready for a relationship. He's back to going to the bars on West Street." For Rachel's sake he didn't elaborate. Dennis sighed. "How about you?"

"I had a crush on a guy I met at the gym, but he hasn't reciprocated." I left out names and descriptions. Why complicate matters?

"Why don't you introduce Dennis to Gustave?" suggested Rachel. Gustave taught Romance languages at Hunter. "I'm sure they have a lot in common."

"A blind date? Naaaaah. I'm too old for that sort of thing."

"C'mon, Dennis, I'll lend you my cane and Seeing Eye dog."

"Why bother? I'm down on love. I'm never going to get a boyfriend."

"Dennis, you just started looking a year ago. Look at me. I've been looking for a boyfriend for five years."

"I don't know how seriously," said Rachel, sipping her postprandial brandy.

"Rachel, these things take time. It's not as if the city is swarming with unattached gay men. You know the percentages. There are a lot more straight men out there."

"Funny, my impression is there are a lot less unattached straight men in New York than gay," said Rachel.

"Yeah, and how many of them are really interested in being in a relationship?" I asked.

"Are you?" she replied.

"Sure," asserted Dennis.

"Of course. I'm tired of spending Saturday nights alone with the Sunday *New York Times,*" I said.

"So you want someone to fight over 'Arts and Leisure' with?" asked Rachel.

"We'll compromise. I'll read over his shoulder," I replied.

"OK. Just asking. I just wanted to be sure. Sometimes it seems to me that you're more interested in playing the field than settling down is all."

"That's the only way to find a boyfriend in Manhattan. You know, comparison-shop. Look for bargains. Sample the merchandise." I'll find a boyfriend if it kills me. I'll find a boyfriend if I have to sleep with every gay male from Houston Street to Ninety-sixth Street between the ages of eighteen and forty.

Rachel was the local problem lady. From her I could get advice on anything: how much to send for a bar-mitzvah present (a Cross pen or an equivalent check), what to tip the super for Christmas (twenty-five dollars), where to buy suits at a discount (Moe Ginsburg's), and how many times to call a prospective boyfriend after meeting him (exactly once). Rachel organized lives and romances as easily as her shoe-closet. She always knew what to do and what to say in any social situation. I had a feeling that she could give Barbara Walters a few pointers. Her only blind spot was with Chris, her live-in boyfriend.

"How's Chris?" I asked.

"Oh, he's between jobs again. He's spending the week with some friends in Jersey." Chris had worked driving a cab, selling tickets at the Regency Theater, waiting on tables at an Ethiopian restaurant in SoHo, and doing free-lance ad-copy work, all in the past two years. He'd save up some money and then go traveling for several months. Rachel waited patiently for him to settle down.

"Hey, I'd better be going soon," said Dennis. The ferry didn't leave that often late at night. "Thanks for dinner, Rachel. Sorry I wasn't hungrier."

"That's perfectly fine. It was a pleasure meeting you, Dennis," said Rachel.

"Aw, shucks. Nice meeting you, too, Rachel." We left together and walked over to the Seventy-second Street subway stop. On the way Dennis gave a beggar some change. "I'd lose it eventually anyways." He never refused anyone.

"I like Rachel. She's nice," said Dennis. "Next time—"

"Let's go *out* to dinner," I chorused in.

We laughed. "Bye, guy."

"You know, maybe you would like Gustave." A plan started forming in my head. "Sure, Rachel's a yenta. But I think he just might be what you're looking for."

"I guess I'd be willing to give it a try," said Dennis cautiously.

In hindsight, an unalloyed catastrophe of monstrous proportions was inevitable. Both Dennis and Gustave had at various times in the recent past been passionately enamored with me, or so I suspected. Setting them up with one another proved a big mistake. Later, Gustave expressed resentment that I had in effect told him that although he wasn't quite good enough for me, he would do for Dennis. Dennis, in turn, felt I was fobbing him off as a second, slightly damaged goods, reduced for spring clearance. In trying to play matchmaker and kill two birds with one stone, I nearly annihilated three.

A native of Italy, Gustave was full of European charm and obliqueness. His verbal tenses were all askew; everything he spoke of happened in the present progressive. His black hair was thinning slightly in the back. He cut a dashing figure in his black-leather jacket and blue jeans. Around his neck he wore a gold ingot engraved with his birthday, a present from his sister. When I had met Gustave the previous fall, he was lamenting his lately departed boyfriend, Michael. On our dinners and dates he talked of nothing but Michael. In a fit of jealousy I contrived to be his lover for approximately twenty-three hours and fifteen minutes, thus attaining the status of ex-lover in short order. As his most recently departed boyfriend I thought he would at last give me the attention I deserved. This turned out to be not the case.

Dennis and I met Gustave at the Art on Eighth Street, a tiny theater buried in the highest per-capita concentration of shoe stores in North

America. Gustave had brought along Paul, an old bar crony who lived on the Upper East Side, to make the meeting appear less contrived. Everyone was walking on eggs, eager to make a good impression for my benefit only. They suppressed the automatic reactive cringe they must have felt on being introduced. I was the Duco cement that held everyone together. Had I not been present, they would have doubtlessly ditched one another immediately, claiming toothache or allergy, only to run into one another a few hours later at the Spike.

We saw a movie by Herzog that concluded with a chicken in a Midwest sideshow that played tic-tac-toe. Gustave, who also taught German, corrected the mistranslated subtitles.

"What is being said here is really 'For such things I am having no patience,' and not 'I'm bored.' "

"Shhhhhh," said Dennis.

I was oblivious to all tension and discomfort, too busy playing Dolley Madison, the hostess with the mostes', refilling imaginary drinks and keeping the conversation flowing. Afterward, I suggested cocktails, but the hour was late. Dennis excused himself, saying he had to make an early start the following morning.

Dennis fidgeted on the walk to the train.

"Well, that went much better than I expected," I said.

"Sure, B.J., it was fine. Sorry I got tired."

"That's OK. But you didn't get a chance to exchange phone numbers. If you like, I can always give Gustave your number."

"Hey, guy, wait a minute. Stop right there. Unh, unh! I was perfectly ready to let this pass as a folly of youth, but you're going too far. Forget it. No way, José. It was a fiasco."

"It was?" The truth slowly dawned upon me.

"Couldn't you tell? Wake up and smell the coffee!"

I felt like an idiot. "But I thought—"

"You weren't thinking. You vere merely projectink," said Dennis in his Viennese accent.

"Gee, I'm sorry."

"It's OK. That's the way the cookie crumbles. Chalk it up to experience."

The next day Gustave called me up. "Dennis isn't my type, but my friend Paul liked him a lot. Perhaps I should give Paul Dennis's number?"

"I think not." Dennis had liked Paul even less. I decided to stick to my own boyfriend problem and leave others well enough alone.

Boyfriends: Pros and Cons

Pro: *He shares grocery expenses.*
Con: *He eats all the cashews, leaving only Spanish peanuts from the Planters mixed-nut assortment.*

Pro: *You don't have to worry about V.D. anymore if you're strictly monogamous.*
Con: *You have to blame the gym sauna for poor hygiene when you give him crabs.*

Pro: *He's someone you can confide all of your problems to.*
Con: *If you hear the story of his twisted boss one more time, you may poison his hamster.*

Pro: *He makes a wonderful Indonesian dinner every Friday night.*
Con: *The sink always overflows with dirty dishes. He operates under the assumption that the mysterious "dish fairy" will clean them up.*

Pro: *You don't have to worry about going home at three o'clock in the morning: you're already there.*
Con: *He snores.*

Pro: *You have a chance to deeply explore one another's sexuality; you aren't limited to the basic trick repertoire, and you can try new things.*
Con: *One day he brings home handcuffs.*

Pro: *No more lonely Saturday nights.*
Con: *When you want privacy, you may be forced to lock yourself in the bathroom.*

Pro: *Now you finally have someone to cheat on.*
Con: *Guilt.*

· 4 ·

April

*T*he invitation to Carlo's birthday party said, "Dress festive." For the occasion, I bought a Hawaiian shirt at Unique Clothing Warehouse on lower Broadway. I was looking for the tacky shirt that Robert De Niro wore in *New York, New York*—it was all colors and skyscrapers—but the closest I could get was one along the lines of Tom Selleck in *Magnum, P.I.* I wasn't sure why Carlo had invited me, but there was no question as to whether or not I would go.

I arrived at the apartment at nine. Carlo, fresh from the shower, was drying his hair. I realized that it was still early, even though the invitation had said nine. I went to the kitchen to help his girlfriends set up while he finished dressing.

Carlo knew a lot of people. I discovered later that so many people had been invited that he staggered the invitations so people would arrive in two shifts, half at nine and the rest at ten. I was in the less glamorous nine o'clock shift.

Rachel had told me that once you go to a party you have to stay at least an hour or else the host will be insulted. I stationed myself next to the curried-yogurt veggie dip and prepared myself for a bracing evening. At ten-fifteen people began arriving in droves. Five men came in a group, each wearing metal bands on their biceps. I tried to match up couples with complementary hankies and key-chains. Left goes with right. Make sure they're color-coordinated. I didn't know a single person there. I felt tense and gawky. I couldn't talk to Carlo; it was his party, and he was busy mixing with the crowd. I didn't feel comfortable introducing myself to a host of strangers. I melted into the wall and listened to snatches of conversation. In the kitchen a large woman in paisley slacks sliced a roll of Pillsbury chocolate-chip dough and transferred the putty disks onto a cookie sheet.

*   *   *   *

"And he had shaved his body *completely!* It was like having sex with an emery board."

"Studio is dead dead dead. I can't believe Rubell was dumb enough to get caught. What was it, laundering money?"

"It's called skimming. Everybody does it."

"But they got sloppy."

"So he turns around and says that Hamilton Jordan was doing coke in the men's room."

"Big deal. How can they prove it ten months later? Give him a blood test?"

"And it's not like they're being sent to prison. I hear it's a fucking country club."

"The rich are different."

"They buy it by the kilo. We have to settle for a gram."

"You heard of any new clubs?"

"Bond's is opening in a few months."

"That old shell of a department store? It's the largest empty men's clothing store in all of Times Square. It's been closed for years. They might as well make a disco out of Klein's on the Square."

"A disco on Fourteenth Street? Get serious, girl. Can you imagine taking a cab to that sleaze street? Nobody would go out of their way to Union Square. It would never work."

"Unless there was a sale on at Wig City."

"And it was Halloween."

"I like Paradise."

"The Garage?"

"You ever go to the Ice Palace?"

"That cha-cha palace? No espeaka espanish."

"The Anvil's always good for a laugh."

"Have you been to the Mineshaft?"

"I'm still a virgin."

"A man wanted me to pee on him in the basement."

"What about the Club Baths?"

"It's so elegant. I could scream!"

"I could die laughing. You know the room with the faggy palm trees and the fountain that looks like it came from some cheap Italian restaurant? They've got those rattan chairs there. I swear, Katharine Hepburn sat on one of them in *Suddenly, Last Summer*."

"You mean *Sodomy, Last Summer.*"

"Whatever."

"I know Andy Warhol," said James Bellefleur just before he passed out on the couch. I overheard his name in conversation. I couldn't approach him; I was too intimidated. James was so beautiful that it was painful to look at him. He had the face of an angel, surrounded by a halo of tight blond curls. His Navajo cheekbones dazzled; his classic Romanesque nose left one breathless. He was never in any but the best of lighting. Even his flaws, few as they were, succeeded in adding additional allure. The tiny bags beneath his eyes gave him the drawn look of a suffering artist, the mystique of a morphine addict. His body was agonizingly slender and lithe. I stood there, watching him rhythmically breathing on the couch, sleeping off his fifteenth cocktail.

"Last month George got eighty-sixed from the West Side Y for fooling around in the sauna."

"You should have been there."

"He was kicking and screaming."

"You wouldn't believe the commotion he made."

"I was eighty-sixed from the Anvil for not removing my jacket. This brute of a bouncer—"

"Was his name Fernando? Did he have a tattoo that looked like a black chain-link fence?"

"I wasn't paying attention, dear. Anyway, this bouncer grabs me by the scruff of the neck and tells me that if I was good-looking, I would have taken my coat off, and ejects me."

"He probably thought you were a pickpocket."

"Could be."

"I've got one that tops them all. A week ago Thursday, Rob got eighty-sixed from the Athens Diner on Tenth Street."

"How in hell can you get thrown out of a horrible Greek coffee-shop like that?"

"Is nothing sacred?"

"Rob was with a couple of drag queens, and I guess they really caused a ruckus. The manager went over and told them never to darken his doorstep again!"

"But Athens is just a pit."

"That's what makes it all the more impressive. Imagine, being tossed from the Ninth Circle of Hell."

"Not to be confused with the Ninth Circle Steakhouse on Tenth Street."

"Oh, it's all the same."

"If Rob could get thrown out of Athens, he could get eighty-sixed out of anything."

"He could give lessons."

"He could write the book."

I decided that since Carlo was lost to me, maybe I could pick up someone else at the party. I looked around for someone who wasn't engaged in conversation. The room was filled with groups of threes and fours. On the other side, by the kitchen entrance, stood a cute redhead. I felt ashamed for judging people solely on physical appearance, but what else did I have to go on? No one was wearing name tags that said "Nuclear physicist who reads Thomas Pynchon" or "Broadway playwright into Thai cuisine." The best I could do was to steer away from those who had the ten-pound key-chains ripping a hole in their back pockets, the red hankies (fisting was not my style), and the large tattoos (somehow they made me think of pain).

"Having a good time?" I asked. "Hi, I'm B.J."

"My name is Frank." He danced with the Feld Ballet. It turned out he had a crush on Carlo, too. Oh, well. Another lost cause. Having done my duty by approaching and initiating one conversation with a stranger, I felt free to leave.

"Carlo's such great sex!" said Frank. "We just met two weeks ago. We got together three or four times. I can't get him out of my mind. I wish he'd come up to me and give me a hug."

"It's a big party. Don't let it bother you." We nursed our beers. I wondered how many broken hearts Carlo was responsible for and how many of us were in the room at that moment. Frank had a perfect bubble-butt and massive thigh muscles clearly outlined in his khaki pants. Perhaps if I tried to offer him physical consolation for his imminent loss of Carlo? At that moment Carlo was entertaining a group of leather-men with some story about a lost weekend at the baths in Denver.

"Do you know Carlo well?"

"Naaah, we just work out at the N.Y.U. gym." No reason to tell him about our abortive sex.

"Oh, he's coming over. Listen, nice talking to you." Frank turned to greet Carlo. He gave him a kiss on the lips. Carlo hugged Frank, gave him a friendly pat on the ass, smiled, and departed. As he passed me, he caught my questioning glance and shrugged as if to say, "I can't help it. I'm just gorgeous. He'll get over me soon enough."

Half an hour later I slipped out the door without saying good-bye, even though Rachel told me I should. I can't stand being stuck at a party, waiting twenty minutes to interrupt a conversation so I can thank the host for a wonderful party, when I've in reality had a quite shitty time, and then being forced to come up with a lie or two when the host insists I stay for another hour or so because the party's just getting going. I walked to the subway station on West Fourth and took the train home at quarter to one. Farewell, Carlo.

I was getting tired of the starving-student routine. I spent half my free time at the library. I did grunt work for the secretary at the department twenty hours a week. I wrote papers and read dissertations. The only fun I had was going to the gym. I missed being able to afford to go to a movie once in a while. Dennis told me that Juilliard gave free student concerts every week. I decided to give it a shot, even though I wasn't wild for classical music.

I met Bob Broome at the concert that Thursday. I had gone alone, and he happened to sit next to me. Bob was over six feet tall, with light-blond hair and big, goofy ears. He had a light complexion that looked like it burned easily. Bob was very pale. His eyes were pale blue.

He placed his Harris tweed on his lap, over folded hands. During the first movement of the Bartók concerto his left hand snaked out from under the overcoat and surreptitiously began to gently massage my crotch. All the time his eyes were kept straight ahead, as if he were unaware of these activities, as if his hand bore no relation to the rest of him. He sat, impassive, removing his hand from my swollen groin only to applaud at the end of the piece.

I was in love with James Bellefleur and in lust with Carlo Montagna. Both were lost causes. I left with Bob during intermission.

Bob lived on Columbus Avenue in the Seventies. At every block a new sidewalk café was opening. His apartment was an appalling mess. Piles of unread *Scientific American*s and *National Geographic*s filled the loft space. The floor was littered with boxes, junk mail, the last six months of the Sunday *New York Times,* and a partially assembled Radio Shack home-computer kit. Bob unearthed a pair of cognac glasses from the overflowing sink and rinsed them. "Care for some Courvoisier?" he asked. He turned the stereo to WBLS, a black disco-station.

What happened next I don't recall. I'm not exactly sure what transpired. A few cocktails later, enough to addle my memory, I found myself in bed with Bob. The next thing I knew it was the following morning. We exchanged addresses. I made my excuses and left.

This was the first time I had ever blacked out. I was frightened. Was I an alcoholic? Was I responsible for my own actions? Why couldn't I learn from experience? Why was lust such a powerful feeling? I should know not to go home with the first man that came along just because I felt lonely or horny. Whenever I did this and substituted whoever was handy for the person I was attracted to, disaster struck. I wasn't even particularly attracted to Bob in the first place. In the morning light this was apparent.

I vowed to be more cautious in the future. I promised to myself to watch what I drank. I pledged to never again go home with someone on the spur of the moment. That was no way to find a boyfriend.

The first thing Dennis did when he came over to my apartment was make a beeline to my porn.

"Hey, Dennis, what are you doing? You could at least say hi."

"Uh, er, just doing some more sociological research," he said.

I shook my head. "You make me feel like the kid who only got to play baseball with the gang when he supplied the bat," I said.

"Hey, guy, you know I can't bring this sort of stuff into the college. Wow! I didn't think this position was possible!" Dennis lifted the magazine by the side and craned his neck back and forth. He squinted and frowned.

"It's all done with mirrors."

"Hey, B.J., how come these pages don't come apart? How'd they get stuck together?" Dennis pretended to struggle with two pages he held together with his two forefingers. I started to blush. "Just fooling, see?"

I toddled off to the kitchen. I'd bought a bottle of scotch for Dennis. I had crossed out "Dewar's" and wrote "Dennis's" in its place. I poured a few fingers into a tumbler over ice. I gave myself a glass of ice water.

"Off the sauce?" asked Dennis as he gratefully received his drink.

"You know I hardly ever drink," I said. Then I told Dennis about meeting Bob Broome and getting plastered last week.

"Oh, well. Bottoms up!" saluted Dennis. "Hey, look! Mister May was listening!" Dennis displayed a nude's ass for my benefit from the May issue of *Blueboy* and laughed.

"Any news on The Prisoner?" Dennis had told me a few weeks ago he was corresponding with a prisoner. His name was Frank, but I called him The Prisoner because of the TV series.

Dennis looked down. "It's over."

"What do you mean? He was supposed to come last week after he got out, wasn't he?"

"Yeah, he was supposed to stay with me for a few weeks. He never showed."

"Did he call?"

"No."

"That's lousy."

"I was going to let him stay with me at the college for a few weeks. He just disappeared. You know what's funny?"

"No."

"I met him the same way I met you. Frank answered my ad in the *Voice*. You know, I've got a private post-office box in the city at Roosevelt Station. I can't afford getting that kind of mail at the college. Every Wednesday I come into the city and go to the Metropolitan Museum. I really like the Egyptian collection. Did you ever see the Frank Lloyd Wright room? It's so soothing. So one day on my way to the museum, I picked up my mail, and there was a letter from Frank. He's in a minimum-security prison located in South Carolina. He's in for possession of stolen property. How was he to know that his friend sold him a hot stereo receiver? He thought it was just used. So Frank gets six months. He's lonely. He answered my ad. B.J., I fell in love with him from the first letter."

"Not again."

"He's really sweet. He has bad handwriting; he prints the letters. His grammar isn't the best. He's only twenty. His letters are long and sincere. He writes me about his sadness and loneliness, his hopes and fears, his dreams and plans. I'm touched. Once in a while he'll ask me to send him something. Small stuff. How could I refuse? I sent him writing utensils, paper clips, envelopes, and other office supplies purloined from the school. I sent him CARE packages with Gillette Trac Two razors and Rachel's brownies. I sent him three-packs of Hanes underwear, size thirty-two. Frank was scheduled to be released on probation at the end of this month. He asked me if he could come up and stay with me for a while. He was going to hitch up north to meet me, but I sent him some money so he could take a bus. I don't want him arrested for vagrancy. I counted the days until April twentieth."

"And then?"

"And then nothing. He never showed. I don't know, maybe he was ashamed to meet me. Maybe he knew it would never work out. Maybe he felt we came from such disparate backgrounds that any deeper relationship would be doomed to failure."

"Maybe he was a convicted ax-murderer doing a life sentence, and he just wrote letters to pass time. Maybe it was just another prisoner scam."

"Naaaaah, that couldn't be."

"Well, then, maybe he was an Orthodox Jew and didn't want an interfaith marriage."

"I'm depressed. *Je me depresse.*"

"Dennis, we're never going to get ourselves boyfriends at this rate."

"I know."

"I think your problem is that you fall in love too easily."

"And yours?"

"That I fall out of love too easily?" I asked.

"Maybe. I don't know. I'm tired of men. I'm tired of trying."

"I think you should just give it a rest for a few weeks. You need a break."

"I guess you're right." Dennis stood up and cracked his neck. He went to the bathroom. "Tiny tanks," he said by way of explanation.

"So are we seeing a movie today or what?" I asked.

"What?" shouted Dennis from the bathroom. He flushed, jiggled the door. "Help! I'm trapped!"

"Turn it the other way."

"Oh," said Dennis. He carefully extricated himself from the loo. "The old lock-'em-in-the-bathroom routine. B.J., you should be ashamed of yourself! You got me all riled up. I think I'll take just a teeny nip to calm down," he said, pouring himself one more Dennis-on-the-rocks.

*　　*　　*　　*

It was Saturday night. The Stud had a three-dollar cover charge. The bouncer checked me out for weapons at the door. I was in no mood to stay at home and read the Sunday *New York Times* or another appalling article badly translated from the French for my course work. Graduate school seemed less and less relevant. Gustave had told me about the Stud. Feigning innocence, I had refused to go there with him. But this weekend he was up in Maine with his latest conquest. My curiosity had gotten the better of me. I felt I could safely explore the Stud without Gustave's tutelage and inconstant attention.

The Stud was in the deepest recesses of the West Village. Dennis had an early service the following Sunday, so I was relatively assured of not interrupting one of his "sociological investigations." I wandered to the back room. A projector was going with a fuck film. The only light in the room was from the projector. I could barely make out the men there. Most seemed to be in caustic middle age, faces blank or scowling. Some had their pants down by their knees. Others had cocks sticking out of flies. The men having sex were in groups of four or five. It was impossible to have sex simply in pairs without someone finding another erogenous zone to stimulate, another orifice or appendage to genuflect before or caress or suck or twist or fuck or yank or lick or bite or pull.

To my horror I saw James Bellefleur, shirtless, hairless, wandering around with a blithe look of idiocy, cocktail at hand. He was the closest thing to underage. A slender youth for the carnivores. I shied away. Delicately poised, he took a deep breath and inhaled a cocktail, then strode into the masses of men like a virgin sacrifice. They parted and then closed on him. I watched as he was enveloped by flesh and groans. I made a cry and turned to leave. A man, arms folded at his chest like the Mr. Clean genie, tit rings prominent, dim in the dusk, stood by the door. His eyes bore right through me. I looked down. His pants were closed, tight. The fabric was straining. He licked his upper teeth. I brushed against his arms. He held me firm. I felt the ravenous spell of the place. My heart beat loudly. He kissed me hard on the mouth. I would do anything for him. He pulled me to the back. I felt many hands as I walked past. He unbuttoned his Levi's one button at a time. Suddenly I didn't care about the rest. It was only me and him. Their touches meant nothing. I would do anything.

How to Get Eighty-Sixed from the Restaurant or Cocktail Lounge of Your Choice

Eschew reservations. Force your way past the maître d' or the bouncer, insisting that you are "on the list." Dress inappropriately. Go to Lutèce in inexpert drag; neglect to shave. Leave your fly unzipped. Forget to wear underwear. Ask for complicated cocktails and dispute their execution. Do some target practice by tossing drinks at your companions; avoid clear and colorless beverages, as they seldom leave stains—stick to fruity concoctions. Ask the waiter for detailed explanations of every item on the menu, feigning interest in the recital, and then order a cheeseburger platter. Ask for water repeatedly; pour this into the potted palm behind your table. Be loud and raucous. Carry a ghetto blaster. Send back the house wine. Send back the burgers. Send back the silverware. Send back the check. Casually remove articles of clothing throughout the course of the meal. Insult your companions. Insult the neighboring table. Insult the waiters. Insult the special. Belch loudly between each course. Vomit into the salad plate and announce that now you have room for dessert. Create a catastrophe. Fake a heart attack. Drop a plastic bug into the soup. Mace the waiter. Smoke several stogies after dessert. Pass around a joint while waiting for the check. Use a stolen credit card. Dispute the sales tax. Leave a food stamp for a tip. Use a rubber check. Write a mash note to the waiter on the bill: Be very explicit. Sign the credit-card voucher with disappearing ink. Misplace your coat-check ticket and then harass the coat-check attendant; demand immediate service. Expectorate as you leave.

· 5 ·

May

*T*he first thing I noticed about the waiting room was that everything was brown: the walls, the carpets, the lamps, even the file cabinets. Brown Hefty bags were stuck in the cracks around the windows for insulation. The desk top had a brown wood-grain Formica finish. Behind the desk I saw a photograph on the wall of a slightly different color: a purple-stained protozoan magnified to gargantuan proportions, a translucent two-eyed parasite identified in Gothic lettering as "Giardia Lamblia." On the desk a plastic embossed sign read, "PATIENTS: PLEASE NOTE PAYMENT IS REQUIRED AT TIME OF TESTING." A sticker on the door informed that MasterCard and Visa were accepted, just like a restaurant. How ironic, I thought. If anything, this was the inverse of a restaurant.

The fan oscillated quietly, and three pairs of empty specimen cups sat atop the file cabinet. I waited for the receptionist to register me. Maura, a light-skinned black in her early twenties, with dyed blond hair, assisted the gentleman lying on the couch. "How are you feeling now? Any better? Would you like me to call the nurse? If you want to throw up, feel free to now, if that would make you feel any better. The laxative has already—" I shut my ears. The man shook his head no and continued to lie there. Maura said, "Are you sure? OK," and then returned to her desk.

"Have you been here before?" she asked me.

"Once."

"Then you remember the procedure? Good." She searched through the file for my card. Last time I had tested negative. I had had the runs now since that night at the Stud. Oh, feckless youth!

"When was the last time you had a bowel movement?"

"Early this morning," I replied.

"Was it loose?"

"Just soft."

Maura measured a full dose of Fleet's phosphate-soda buffered saline laxative into a small plastic cup. Then she filled a larger plastic cup with water. "Now drink this. It tastes bad." She made a friendly face at me. Yuck.

"I still remember the taste from the last time." And that was months ago. I lifted the cup to my mouth. Cocktails from hell tasted like this. The laxative stang of sulfur and burning flesh. I took the first sip and wanted to stop. Imagine a cup of concentrated urine with some acid thrown in. I forced the rest down. This was a concoction one would throw out in chemistry lab or wash the sinks with after a failed experiment. Then I gulped down two cups of water, very fast, to wash away the taste. Some nausea was temporarily drowned, although my throat felt glazed with salt.

On the phone I had been warned to take no solid food for three hours prior to the test. Now I was instructed to have a hot beverage, preferably coffee, and something solid to eat. "No bananas or rice, because they are natural binders. Come back in an hour," advised Maura. "It usually takes that long to take effect." I felt like a walking time bomb, set to detonate in sixty minutes. I planned on returning within the half hour. I didn't want to take any chances. My symptoms were far less severe than the test, I thought. Some irregularity. Mild diarrhea. Occasionally, a well-placed fart capable of clearing out the gym in a second.

I went across the street and had my biannual cup of coffee and an order of fries at Cruiseburger on Christopher and Seventh. The burgers tasted like dried-out re-ground patties reclaimed from the trash can outside the White Castle on Eighth. But then food was never the attraction there; location was. Three stools faced Sheridan Square. On the third sat a gargantuan steroid mass of flesh: a hustler. He glared at his watch. The ashtray in front of him overflowed onto the counter. He seemed trapped to the spot, physically incapable of moving, literally muscle-bound. He muttered a curse, shifted his weight to the left, dug into a pocket for his wallet, and gracelessly stood.

I strode out quickly, tensing my sphincter muscles anticipatorially. I walked quickly past the Bagel And, a garish eatery on Christopher Street that really belonged in a mall in New Jersey. The Bagel And stood on the site of Stonewall, the bar where the gay-liberation movement started back in 1969. And what remained in its wake, its ashes? An overpriced deli filled with mirrors, fake-wood paneling, hanging ferns, and brown pillars that climbed to the ceiling to spread artificial branches in unnatural symmetry. I recalled the acute disappointment I felt when I found at Hollywood and Vine several desultory transvestites and a Howard Johnson's. Across the street from the Empire State Building sat a McDonald's fast-food franchise.

My destination was specific: a discount drugstore on Sixth to get a large economy-size bottle of Kaopectate, "the pleasant-tasting antidiarrheal," according to the misleading label.

After my purchase, there was just enough time. I felt a contraction and dashed back. I pressed the buzzer, pressed both buzzers, pressed all the buzzers for the entire building-complex in desperation. The door signaled it was open with a harsh squawk. I bolted upstairs, climbing three steps at a time, rushed into the waiting room, picked up my first specimen cup, and went to the bathroom down the hall. The floor tiles were cracked. Quickly I searched for an empty stall. The stalls were private, with doors that reached to the floor. Two were occupied. I heard no sounds. My knuckles were white as I forced my way into the third, unclasped my belt and dropped my pants in a single motion, shut the door with my foot, and placed the cup in optimal position. A stream of shit the consistency of soft frozen yogurt filled half the cup, which I carefully set on the floor to avoid making a mess. Another abdominal spasm and the bowl was clouded with a watery suspension that I quickly flushed. I dressed, wiped the container meticulously with a paper towel, and walked back down the hall to the closed Dutch doors where the actual lab was. I rang the small bell on the counter between the doors, a small bell one would find in a diner that the short-order cook would ring, indicating the plate was ready for pickup by the waitress. The upper door opened. The nurse who spent all day examining faggots' shit for amoebas and other parasitic dysentery took the cup in plastic-gloved hands. She had harsh Teutonic features. She reminded me of a high-school anthropology teacher who failed half the class out of spite; she felt doomed to pedagogy when her heart was in research. I tried to think of less appealing occupations. Cosmetician at a mortuary? Masseur at a leper colony?

"This is not the correct consistency," she scolded me. There was no pity in her voice, no kindness in those clipped terms. I saw out of the corner of my eye a paperback Dorothy Sayers mystery opened and flattened inside the lab, two-thirds of the way finished. The bitch. I suppressed the urge to toss the next specimen at the rapidly swirling fan to find out once and for all what happens when the shit hits the fan.

I went back to the waiting room and considered how appropriate the name was. I was there to wait. I decided the ubiquitous brown was a cue, a prompt, the visual equivalent of having the doctor run water to help a patient produce a urine specimen, seeking a sympathetic response. I rummaged through *People* magazines from the last six months. Bette Midler declared, "Give me some respect—I'm a screen goddess now." Since *10* premiered, Beverly Hills matrons had been phoning black beauty-parlors in Watts for appointments. Shelly Hack tragically dumped from *Charlie's Angels* on Valentine's Day. Gary Coleman was everybody's favorite child actor. Taking a cue from Hitler, a Nobel sperm bank had been set up in California to perfect the master race. Nobody knew who shot J.R.

Under the magazine table a portable radio played "Heartbreaker" by Pat Benatar. A fern peeked out of a large beige trash-can vase. A yucca tree sat in the corner. I fidgeted. The air was filled with tension. There was little talk in the waiting room. Embarrassed, the man who was lying down excused himself for the bathroom. After an hour of fruitless waiting I drank a cup of Great Mountain Bear water from the cooler and tossed the cup into the trash. I looked through the window, a large semicircle that extended almost to the ceiling. Wire hexagons were twisted into the glass. I wondered if they were there to prevent jumpers, like in an insane asylum. An uncovered rusted sprinkler hung from the ceiling. It was probably not proper to cruise from the second floor of the labs. I felt another tremor and automatically reached for a specimen cup. I was an earthquake with a series of ever-growing aftershocks.

"Good, that's much better," said my dyspeptic lab technician dressed in white. Great. I didn't know which was worse, to be insulted for your feces or complimented on them. Another half hour passed uneventfully. I dashed back to the bathroom, uncontrollable.

This time she said, "Fine, you're all done for now. Vuld you like a binder?" I was instructed to call my doctor tomorrow, after 3:00 P.M. "Ve are unable to give out information directly to the patients by law," she explained.

I took the subway home. By this time the contractions were practically simultaneous. I allowed myself to go to the bathroom at half-hour intervals, timing myself by the clock and not by need, since the need was constant. In between I went downstairs to the Korean vegetable-stand down the block to stock up on bananas. Now I was shitting French onion-soup in a continuous stream.

The pink Kaopectate left milky, stringy strands on the bathroom sink. By my twenty-fifth john run the shit felt like weak acid as it coursed through my fragile organs. If I drank so much as a sip of water, I'd be in the john in a minute. I was undergoing the China Syndrome in my bowels. At midnight I collapsed on the bed in my underwear. I wouldn't sleep naked tonight.

The following day I called the doctor from the student center. After my experience at the V.D. clinic I had determined that a private doctor was a necessity, not a luxury. Martin, the cute blond receptionist, answered. Martin, twenty-two, was just out of Vassar, where, according to him, a lesbian experience was required for graduation. Martin was slightly overweight and extremely neurotic. "Yes, who is it?"

"It's B.J."

"Oh, hi." His voice changed from office to evening, like a makeup mirror with four settings. "How *are* you, B.J.?"

"Fine. I just called for my results."

"What results? Just a minute, let me get your chart." His voice dripped with warmth. He started humming "Getting to Know You" from *The King and I*. "Ah, yes, here it is. Do you know what I'd like to do with you?"

"No." I really didn't want to sleep with my doctor's receptionist.

"I'd like to come over to your apartment and play Scrabble one night and let you win. Do you know what I'd really want to do with you?"

"No." I sighed. Wasn't anyone professional these days? Even if I were interested in Martin, I would *never* sleep with someone who had access to my medical records. How did I know he wouldn't leak them to the *Times?* I didn't want to read about my venereal diseases in Liz Smith.

A line formed behind me. A punk student was snapping his leather wrist-bracelet. "Listen, I don't have much time; I'm at a public phone."

"I'd like to bite off the buttons on your shirt one by one and then undress you with my mouth, pulling down the zipper of your pants with my teeth."

"You and five thousand other queens in Manhattan," I retorted.

"Could you give me my results? I have better things to do than listen to this horse manure."

"Positive," he replied, stung. I wondered why he had any interest in me, because he must have followed the course of my illnesses in great detail. "The doctor will phone in a prescription to whatever pharmacy you like." His voice was lifeless.

"Have him call Wedgwood."

"Fine." His voice lowered to a whisper. "B.J.?"

"Yes?"

"You won't ever tell Doctor Weinstein about this? He'll have my hide if you do."

"Don't even think about it."

"He's already given me a talk about flirting with the patients."

"I have to ring off. Good-bye." I hung up abruptly. The little twerp. Dejected, I went to my next class. It looked as if I was going to be out of commission for another extended period of time.

I went home and turned on my machine. "Hi. It's Dennis. You are out. [pause] Having fun. I'm here [pause] all alone. My plants are mad at me and won't talk to me. [long pause] Give me a call when you get a chance. Bye." Dennis. I was just crazy about him.

I met Dennis at a cheap Italian trattoria in the Village. "So what's doing, guy?" asked Dennis.

"Three more days and I'm finished with the medication."

"It's been a while, hasn't it?"

"Twenty days in all. One pill I had to take four times a day for ten days, and the other pill three times a day for twenty. I had to avoid alcohol and milk products initially and was supposed to take one pill on an empty stomach, either one hour before or two hours after a meal. It got so complicated I had to make up charts and set alarm clocks to remind myself which pill to take when." I scratched my nose. "So, what's this about your being down?"

"Oh, you know. I-I-I-I-I-I-I-I-I get a little anxious some times. *Je me depresse.* Even my mother sensed something was off last Sunday when I visited her." Dennis's father had died two years ago. His mother had lived with his sister for a while, but they fought constantly. Since she needed looking after and Dennis couldn't take her in at the college, they had to place her in a home. She was failing physically and had been declining mentally since his father died. Sometimes when she talked to Dennis it was as if he were still a child. "I have problems sleeping. You know, I have these—these—these *conflicts* I need to *resolve*."

"Dennis, have you been seeing a therapist?"

"How'd you guess? I went over to Identity House and they recommended one for me. I get shrunk every Thursday."

"Ann Landers always suggests to see your clergy or therapist. But a therapist for a clergyman? Isn't that redundant?"

"Every man in the town of St. Ives who doesn't shave himself is shaved by the barber. Now, who shaves the barber?" posed Dennis.

"Well, let's see. If the barber doesn't shave himself, then he does; and if he does shave himself, then he doesn't. I give up."

"It's easy. The barber's a woman."

"But what about her legs?"

"She uses Nair." Dennis chuckled. "Actually, my therapist *specializes* in gay clergy."

"No kidding? Only in New York. I wonder what's taking so long with lunch. I'm starving."

"So is my anteater." Dennis placed his left hand squarely on the tablecloth, five fingers curled as if he were about to play a piece on the piano. His hand slowly crawled across the table in delicate anteater movements, the central "fuck-you" finger extended, waving gently like an antenna sounding out the territory, or a snout searching for grub.

"So how do you like therapy?" I didn't think I would. Who had the time? Who had the money? Friends were for telling your problems. Why pay for it?

"OK so far. He gives me exercises for when I can't sleep. Things like imagining I'm at the top of a large staircase and slowly walking down each step one by one."

"I guess I have some problems, but they seem really insignificant in the scale of things. My neuroses are so commonplace, I fear I would fail to interest a therapist in myself and resort to manufacturing dreams for his amusement."

"I think ve can spend years investigating your problems," said Dennis. "Unfortunately, as the meal is being served presently, ve must vait." Sure enough, the waiter came a moment later with our plates. We devoured lunch. Dennis cut his veal assiduously into tiny squares and piled them into a pyramid that he then inhaled in a single gulp. I polished off the eggplant and soaked up the sauce with two pieces of Italian bread.

"Want any dessert? Do I see the word *chocolate* on the menu?"

"Actually, I have my eye on a slice of cheesecake."

"Be my guest."

Dessert arrived a few moments later, with coffee and tea. The cheesecake was gelatin based. Dennis toyed with his cannoli. He shifted the swirl of nondairy topping round and round. He had his traditional three sips of coffee. "Any more than that and I'm climbing the walls. I've had waiters follow me out of restaurants, asking if there was anything wrong with the coffee. It's so em-*bare-ass*-ing," said Dennis, getting maximum mileage out of the bad pun. "Good luck with your follow-up test."

Cocktails from Hell

The Macbeth: *A perennial holiday favorite. Mix one eye of newt with one toe of frog. Add wool of bat and tongue of dog. Puree in blender for thirty seconds. Serve straight up.*

The Day-Tripper: *Popular during the sixties, updated for the eighties. Start with a hit of MDA. Follow with a night of ecstatic dancing at 12 West. Take a hot hunk dripping with sweat, wearing a ripped T-shirt, home and serve with three Quāludes. Garnish with K-Y.*

Portnoy's Complaint: *Equal parts Maalox and Midori. Serve chilled in the WC. A prune garnish is optional.*

The Al-Anon I: *One cup black coffee in Styrofoam cup. Optionally, with one teaspoon nondairy creamer. Serve with a carton of unfiltered cigarettes. Use the unfinished cup as an ashtray.*

The Al-Anon II: *Equal parts self-pity, self-loathing, sanctimoniousness, and vodka.*

The Well of Loneliness: *Absinthe, straight up.*

The Kamikaze: *One part liquid helium, two parts prussic acid. Agitate with great alacrity. Toss in three tablespoons green bile. Add some ennui and angst and several shots of gin. Pour into a tall highball glass. Add one teaspoon urine from the tub in the basement of the Mineshaft. Pour into a Cuisinart. Pulse 350 times. Whip in a blender until smooth. Garnish with a fruit and a sprig of poison ivy. Stir and add ice and club soda to taste.*

· 6 ·

June

*L*eaving Mr. Mackenzie proved to be a rather involved task. His incredulous penis, having withdrawn prematurely, refused to subside, obstinate in its inflexibility, causing untoward difficulties in the resumption of vestments. Even boxer shorts were problematic at this juncture, for he faced a problem of gross dimensions, a member of mammoth proportions.

The hour was late, and I had to go. The air in Mr. Mackenzie's apartment had become so rarefied that I found it difficult to breathe. Moreover, my artificial plants needed watering, the stuffed dog on the mantel needed walking, the linoleum needed Hoovering. There were a thousand and one immaterial reasons to vacate the premises, not the least of which being Mr. Mackenzie himself.

Our eyes had met at a local watering-hole in the Village where show tunes are sung heartily by off-duty waiters and out-of-work chorines. I had just stopped in for a quick cocktail, figuring that the bar might be easier to approach with most of the patrons huddled around the piano in raucous song. I recognized Mr. Mackenzie immediately from the book-jacket photo that he wore smugly on his vest, Mr. Mackenzie being of course the noted author of the best-selling *Three Blondes in the Dumps*, a comic updating of Chekhov's *Three Sisters* set in present-day Malibu, which, according to the trades, had just been optioned for a movie. Farrah Fawcett, Bo Derek, and Raquel Welch were rumored to have expressed interest in portraying the cinematic triumvirate.

Having never met, much less slept with, anyone remotely famous, with the possible exception of rubbing shoulders at the Spike with a deposed Village Person who had been ejected from the band for public indiscretions at a time when the sexual orientation of the group had been deliberately left vague for maximum audience demographics, I immediately gravitated toward him. Mr. Mackenzie, a man not known for his direct prose, easily looked a decade younger than his age, which was forty-five; I had noted that his Library of Congress data facing the title pages of his earliest books included birth year and open-ended dash; the later novels omitted this salient detail.

I charmed him in short order. Without delay we sped by cab to his cooperative apartment on the Upper West Side. The building, formerly a Masonic temple, stood twelve stories. We took the elevator to the sixth floor and removed our shoes at the door. I followed on socks down the cold marble floor to the living room. An ingenious designer had installed identical white doors flush with the walls, giving no indication whether a given door led to the kitchen, the linen closet, the bathroom, the bedroom, the lady, or the tiger. A firm industrial-gray carpet covered the floor; black track-lighting lined the ceiling. Hands fluttering, Mr. Mackenzie disappeared briefly to an undisclosed alcove, returning with two vodka and cranberry cocktails, one of which he nervously handed me as he sipped his own, spilling a few drops on the glass coffee table, which he quickly wiped with the sort of paper napkin that novelists are so fond of transcribing novels onto in cafés and drawing rooms of private university clubs. On the table, discreetly placed so as not to call undue attention, lay a stack of preautographed books of his imprint practically reaching the ceiling, precariously balanced. My friend Gustave had once tricked with a well-known recording artist; throughout the sexual act, one of the singer's LPs flooded the bedroom in quadriphonic sound. At least books don't talk, I consoled myself, although Mr. Mackenzie did pepper his speech liberally with frequent quotes from his collected works.

We discussed the usual topics: his fame, his fortune, and his apartment. Halfway through our second drink he attacked like a hawk, the cavernous leather sofa almost swallowing me. I was towed into his bedroom. Mr. Mackenzie shed his clothes like a snake sheds its skin, in a single motion, and pinned me to the bed as he kissed me deliriously on the lips. Mr. Mackenzie, with dark-brown bewitching eyes and nipples one could hang Christmas-tree ornaments from, threw his head back in mock abandon. I toyed with his tits; my mind was elsewhere. Once we started sex the tension, almost palpable before, had dissolved, and with it my desire. My fickleness knows no bounds. I am so little in touch with my feelings that frequently I take opinion polls from my friends to determine my attitudes, opinions, and actions. At least that way it's democratic. I saw my confusion reflected in the diagonally placed mirrored tiles on the walls. The ubiquitous track-lighting focused at the confluence of our cocks.

The amount of equivocation and uncertainty on my part was overwhelming. Was it confusion or merely indecision? In the absence of experience, I had reached the point where I could cynically plot out an entire relationship—complete with dramatic fights and tearful reconciliations, couple therapy, and the use of prosthetic marital aids—all during the twenty-odd minutes in transit from barroom to boudoir. Why even bother consummating that which was destined to be a failed romance? I was too messy for him; he wasn't clever enough for me; my eyes were the wrong shade; his ankles were too thick.

As I performed my internal and infernal calculations, I abrogated all power to him and let him become the aggressor, the predator, perhaps to absolve myself of guilt. The atheist suppressed his sneeze, for fear of being blessed by the priest. My sins were my own, a cologne I covered myself with completely.

The door to Mr. Mackenzie's bedroom was shut, for the roommate who practically lived at the Sheridan Square Health Club was currently entertaining a gentleman caller in the shower. "My significant other," explained Mr. Mackenzie. Hidden behind another as yet undisclosed door was another bedroom. Two bedrooms, river view. I slipped back into my trousers when Mr. Mackenzie left the room, responding to an urgent plea for a glass of water. When he returned, he could barely conceal his disappointment that I was dressed. "It's time to go," I explained, "it's a school night." This was a euphemism, because the spring semester had ended weeks ago and I was working as a cashier for minimum wage at a midtown restaurant that summer. It was after midnight. There was no time to lose.

So a quick peck on the cheek and a mad dash down the stairs . . . to discover that my jacket had been left behind. Tossing a pebble at Mr. Mackenzie's sixth-floor terrace would be unwise, for I was perennial last pick on the high-school gym softball-team. Instead, I shouted like a loon in heat, a mad dog wailing, my late-night serenade. Soon he appeared at the window. I mouthed the word "jacket." He found it and tossed it down, matted into a ball, begrudgingly. I suspected he might have masturbated on it, for it was wet in strange places. Then I bid adieu, blowing a kiss to my Juliet at her sixth-story balcony, my Rapunzel in her high tower . . . to find that my keys were missing. I looked up. He had closed the window. I gingerly pressed the buzzer, embarrassed. Coolly, curtly, he afforded me entry. I stumbled into the elevator. It was indeed far too late to be up. He came to the door, eyes now mute, glazed, doubtless in the midst of fiendishly, feverishly jerking off. The last graceless exit, I swore.

"What is it *now*?" He knew I had returned only of necessity. The heaviness of my casual rejection had now sunk in.

"My keys."

Dutifully he searched first the bedroom, then the living room. The keys were discovered deeply embedded in the couch, in the crack between two pillows.

"Wallet?" he asked.

"Check."

"Wristwatch?"

"Check."

"Jacket?"

"Check."

"Subway token?"

"Check."

"Then out," he tersely ordered.

"B.J.? Did I wake you?" It was Dennis. He sounded desperate. I checked the clock, squinting through bleary eyes. Numbers swam into focus. Four-fifteen. "Did I wake you?" was the traditional opener for me. I was perennially subcomatose. Was it low blood-sugar or merely chronic depression? I hadn't yet determined.

"Yez-z-z-z-z-z-z-z-z-z-z-z-z-z?" My affirmative response mutated to a snore.

"B.J.? It's you? It's not too late?"

"Mrrrrrrrrp. 'Course not. Izit Sunday?"

"No. Tuesday."

"Oh. I was just—" A yawn unsuccessfully stifled, I forgot the rest of the sentence. I was walking down a long and elegant staircase, the type that Fred and Ginger danced on, one step at a time. Groggy, I started to lose consciousness again.

"B.J.!" shouted Dennis, a verbal slap of Aqua Velva to the cheek, and I was awake.

"OK. Just a minute." I patted the night table down and stumbled over my glasses. Suddenly the world came into focus. "What seems— what seems to be the problem?"

"Joseph."

"Who's Joseph?"

"You remember, I met him in Loops."

"Ugh." I shuddered. To my taste, Loops was definitely the creepiest place in all of Manhattan—a hustler bar on the East Side, filled with slimy bankers in their fifties and artificially animated whores in their late teens and early twenties. There was an adjacent restaurant with expensive, tasteless food, phony as *The Merv Griffin Show*, a denatured Las Vegas lounge after a lobotomy, replete with dim lights, mirrors, and a baby grand with a floozy drag with chalk-white skin and a flimsy silk pastel pantsuit lip-synching to a Streisand recording while stretched across the piano—Ann-Margret with a concussion, Deborah Harry with toxic shock, Patti Smith on horse. "Wasn't he a former student?" Dennis frequently ran into former students when he was cruising.

"Yep. He was at the college a few years ago. He dropped out. He was having problems at home. His parents kicked him out when they found out he was gay."

"Was he surprised to see you there?"

"I'll say." Sometimes Dennis pretended he had merely wandered into the bars and discos by mistake, or that he was with friends and didn't realize what sort of place it was.

"Why do you go to Loops anyway?"

"You know, professional interest. I find it intriguing, an interesting anthropological phenomenon of the latter part of the twentieth century in the megalopolis. It's just—"

"Sociological research," I finished for him. We both laughed.

"You sure you don't mind my waking you? I know it's kinda late."

"Oh, don't worry. I'll make some kawwwww-feeee," I joked, doing my best post-stroke Patricia Neal. "Now I remember. Joseph, he was the knockout, wasn't he?"

"Six two, eyes of blue, brown hair, a tiny mole on the right cheek reminiscent of many a male screen idol of the forties."

"And I bet he's even better in person than in black and white on the screen."

"In the sack, too," confessed Dennis.

"You slept with him?"

He hedged. "Not exactly. I mean—I mean—I mean, not on the first date or anything. Actually, they weren't dates at all. We just had *discussions*. That's it, *discussions*. You know. Problems. The great mysteries. The meaning of life. The purpose of existence. The search for values. And, you know, he was always fond of me. So one thing led to another. And. And. And. And. And."

"And you screwed."

"I prefer to use ze French term *faire l'amour*. We *faire l'amour*ed."

"Dennis. An ex-student," I chided.

"So I'm fallible."

"You and the pope."

"Shhhhh." Dennis checked the plants for electronic bugs. "We're safe. Actually, I think it must have been my irresistible appeal, *n'est-ce pas?* My joie de vivre, my esprit, and—and—"

"And your lousy French accent."

"Yeah, I kind of think it was that."

"*I* think he probably had a father fixation."

"Now, now, my son. We do not speak of such things lightly."

"Anyway, who *doesn't* want to sleep with a priest? I read a Linda Ronstadt interview in *Time* magazine, and *she* always had this fantasy of seducing a priest."

"Why not me?" suggested Dennis.

"Well . . . uh . . . er . . . Dennis, I think she's—y'know, *female.* And . . . uh . . . I thought—correct me if I'm wrong—but, gee, I could *swear* that you were—like—y'know, *gay.*"

"Oh, yeah, right. Gee, B.J., thanks for reminding me. I almost forgot."

"Don't do it again, and I'll let you slide just this once."

"Scout's honor."

"So let's get back to this Joseph. You met him at Loops, and an hour or so later you and he were at it like rabbits."

"I was offering him solace," corrected Dennis. "How could I refuse?"

"Where did you fuck?"

"*Chez moi.*"

"At the college? Don't the nuns listen in?"

"I've got it rigged up so it's practically soundproof. You know, since I'm a resident adviser, I've got a suite. So what I do is I go to the second room, the inner sanctum, and stack the extra mattresses against the door."

"I guess so long as you're careful," I said dubiously.

"Not to worry. Situation under control."

"So what's the problem? He's not underage. He's a *former* student.

He's not likely to rat on you to the archbishop. He's good-looking."

"B.J., he's *crackers*! He's *bananas*! Let me finish and you'll understand."

"I'm all ears."

"Well, after we *made love* the first time, things looked OK. Sure, maybe he's a little clinging. Maybe he says he's stuck on me. Maybe he doesn't want to leave. It's the weekend. It's cool. We spend Saturday together. We go into the city, visit the Whitney, and then I go back to the college; I've got classes to prepare for and two services on Sunday. I say good-bye and I think, gee, it would be nice to see Joseph again, but like you told me, I don't get involved until at least the second date.

"And I get back to the college, and there's already two messages from him on my machine. He wants to see me tomorrow. I call him back; I tell him I'm really busy; I say Wednesday would be the earliest. He says fine, hangs up, then calls me back in an hour and asks me what I want for dinner. He wants to cook me dinner. This is Saturday, and he's talking about Wednesday. So he calls me six or seven times each day until Wednesday. By then I'm kind of dreading seeing him. I mean, excitement is one thing, but this is bordering on obsession. I go over to his place; I pick up a bunch of flowers at the Korean deli on the corner. I'm hardly in the door, and he's all over me. I can hardly breathe. I still have my jacket on; I haven't even put down my briefcase. I could hardly eat dinner. He kept rubbing my knees and kissing me. We had a couple bottles of Chianti. Then we go to bed and make love three times. I'm so exhausted afterwards, even though I hadn't planned on it, I spend the night. He makes waffles in his waffle iron and serves them to me in bed, on a tray with a rose and a glass of fresh-squeezed OJ. Then he apologizes, but he has to go to work, so we leave together.

"On Thursday I talk to my therapist. He agrees there's something wacky going on with Joseph. I should never have slept with him. I don't want to see him again; I'm afraid he'll suffocate me. I don't want to just drop him. That wouldn't be ethical. But I'm scared of him. He's taller than me and a lot stronger. I don't know what he'd do. My therapist says let go gently. Go out and have dinner with him. Level with him. Explain the situation. It's like Joseph is starved for love. He needs help."

"It's probably some kickback scheme. He probably gets a payoff for psychiatric referrals," I groused.

"So I go out and meet him on the West Side for dinner on Saturday. We go to a quiet Italian place on Columbus, have spaghetti, and knock off a couple bottles of wine. I tell him I can't see him again unless he starts seeing a therapist. He gets upset when he hears me say I might not see him again. We talk for hours. We practically close the place. We leave; I go to the subway to say good-bye, and he jumps in after me. He's got his arm on my sleeve, and he won't let go. 'Just let me spend the night,' he pleads. 'Just one night.' He's begging me, 'Please don't leave me; let me come, too.' I tell him no, he can't. He doesn't let go of my arm. He's crying. I get off at Columbus Circle and go to the street. He follows. I run; he chases me. We walk across Central Park South. He's pleading; he's crying; I'm not talking. It's drizzling. I'm desperate. It's one in the morning. We've walked all the way to the Plaza. People are staring. I try to calm him down. I try to calm myself down. He's a leech; he won't leave. I take out my umbrella for the rain. He holds my arm tighter.

"Finally, I get this idea. I see a cop. We're at this taxi stand in front of the Plaza. I grab for the door of a waiting cab, and Joseph leaps to follow me. I shout to the cop, 'Don't let him come after me.' Then I hit him on the head with my umbrella to fend him off. The cop restrains Joseph. I escape to the cab. It's a twenty-two-dollar fare, but I ride straight to the dorm on Staten Island. I go home and barricade the door. I turn out the lights. I wake up at three in the morning. I hear a scratching sound at the door. It's Joseph. He's trying to pick the lock. What can I do? He followed me. I let him in. And you know the only way I finally got him to leave? I was crying. My tears sent him away."

"Christ, Dennis, what a story: 'The Trick That Won't Let Go.'"

"So then I called you."

"That just happened tonight?"

"Yup."

"Poor Dennis. What are you going to do now?"

"I don't know."

How to Get Rid of the Trick Who Won't Leave

Certain vintage Elton John albums are effective, as are acoustic Joni Mitchell, lesbian folksingers, Polish operas, and Bob Dylan's Self-Portrait.

When you shower after sex, be sure to give him a towel you have sprinkled with itching powder. As he dries, mention the case of crabs you're almost positive you're over.

Tell him he reminds you of your ex. Call him by the wrong name. Call him by different names. Ask him if you and he did it last week in a back room.

Ask him if he loves you.

Ask him if he would mind taking a personality test.

Talk to him in baby talk. "Does ootems want a widdle nap? Does ootems want to go sweep?"

Ask for reassurance every five minutes. Apologize profusely.

Stare into his eyes and say in the sweetest voice imaginable, "Penny for your thoughts."

Take up all of the bed. Sweat profusely. Fart under the covers. Spill poppers on the sheets. Go to the bathroom every fifteen minutes, climbing over him, explaining each time that you have a prostate problem. Leave the window wide open in winter; turn off the air-conditioning in summer. Start scrubbing the kitchen floor at three in the morning; when he asks, tell him it will take only a minute. Pretend you are doing this in your sleep.

Accuse him of stealing your food stamps.

Eat a clove of garlic in the bathroom in the guise of brushing your teeth; French-kiss him good night. Hide the toilet paper and turn off the water. Tickle him until he wets the bed.

Casually mention that your homicidal six-foot boyfriend is expected in fifteen minutes. Hand him his shoes, keys, and wallet as he races past you for the door.

· 7 ·

July

I'm sure we would have ended up lovers if Philip hadn't given me herpes. The precise etiology of this particular infestation remained in question, for Philip claimed that it was entirely conceivable that I had earlier been inoculated with the virus in a less virulent dosage, and that he merely served to raise it past a dormant threshold. In any event, this precluded the possibility of any meaningful relationship developing on the foundation of sex—for sex was what drew us together in the first place.

Our mutual attraction was so strong it didn't wither through a series of near-miss encounters. In February on the Number 1 local his bright brown eyes burned a hole through the crotch of my Levi's. Then at Twenty-third a pimply teen with a bright pink radio on her shoulder and seventeen crosses around her neck entered to block my sight-line. A Viet vet wheeled through the doors between cars while we were stuck between stops. Panhandlers preferred the IRT over the IND because you could hit several cars in a single stop; the doors between IND cars were locked. Philip disappeared at Forty-second Street, the door shutting behind him. I strained to see a piece of paper, an indecipherable phone number hurriedly scribbled with smudged pencil, at the filthy window. With a lurch, the train resumed motion.

Again, in April, we saw one another at Ty's, stuck with our respective since-forgotten dates. The term fuck-buddies would imply an element of intimacy otherwise lacking in these assignations. Our eyes met in swirls of smoke; then my companion jerked me out, preferring to piss in the alley to waiting for the john to clear out, while Philip's, clutching his stomach, started retching in the corner.

Then in June I saw him at the Gay Pride Parade. I was standing on the steps of St. Patrick's for the celebratory release of lavender balloons by Dignity; regrettably, Dennis couldn't make it. Sundays were taken. Philip's eyes darted everywhere. He was obviously in the parade to better cruise the streets. His shirt was off; his chest glistened with sweat. Every two blocks or so he would leave the parade to renew an old acquaintanceship or foment a new one. This time I didn't think he spotted me; he was too busy working the crowd. But then, surrounded by friends, he winked at me and shrugged his shoulders.

The fourth time was the charm. Central Park, a cool evening in July. The Philharmonic. I was wandering aimlessly, having decided to come at the last minute, certain I would pick out Rachel midst the two hundred thousand people picnicking on the Great Lawn. Babies squalled. Couples discussed cholesterol in loud voices. Teens surreptitiously sneaked joints. Lovers caressed on blankets. Mosquitoes buzzed through the air, swatted at distractedly. Homosexuals with their perfect dinner-sets poured Moët et Chandon champagne into fluted glasses and served seafood salad on white china with scalloped edges along with Brie and English soda-biscuits on white linen tablecloths complete with pewter candelabras. Rachel and her forbidden, *trayf* boyfriend were nowhere to be found. The police courteously directed patrons around the crowd-control barricades. And then I saw Philip.

Philip, alone on his blanket, a ratty beach blanket of gray flannel, stood up and waved me over. Philip was short, shorter even than I. He bought suits at Barney's in the boys' department for a hefty savings. His friends hadn't shown, or they were where I was, which was lost. I lay down, the stars above me. Philip offered a cup of Tropicana orange juice not-from-concentrate, and then a hit of *sinsemilla*. The music was almost beside the point, the concert acoustics muffled by the low hum of passing planes and police helicopters, the constant drone of conversations, lovers giggling on cheap burgundy. Afterward the fireworks exploded to an almost oblivious crowd, too drunk to care, parents ignoring children setting off tiny firecrackers.

"Do you want to come over for a nightcap?" asked Philip. Did I ever. He lived in splendor on Central Park West in an art-deco jungle. The entranceway, two frosted-glass doors with stylized stainless-steel margin, opened to an elegant lobby. The elevator had mahogany paneling. We entered his apartment to the purplish glow of plant-lights illuminating his Boston ferns and wandering Jews and African violets. Hood ornaments of streamlined nymphs bearing tiny globes stood as bookends to his *Architectural Digests*. A cat named Fred slunk past his legs as we headed for the bedroom. A mirror of beveled glass hung on the wall. We screwed into the morning, into exhaustion. The next day Philip dressed in his miniature Pierre Cardin suit, a Rolex on his wrist. We shared the subway downtown. He continued to the financial district; I got off at Fiftieth to crash.

The next few days I felt a curious tingling, itching sensation on my face.

That Saturday we met for a stroll down Christopher. My as-yet-unidentified acne was approaching its zenith in facial disfigurement; Philip had a few days' growth of beard covering an equally unsavory condition. Now, I was a moderately gregarious fellow. Still, for every hello I garnished, Philip received five. It took us an hour to traverse the prime blocks of Christopher from Seventh Avenue to the river. As we passed the PATH train-entrance Philip alluded to certain encounters that took place therein of which he was party. Reluctant to explain further, he indicated the johns as point of reference. Was I to infer? Yes. Again, I experienced some disillusionment, for Philip was not as I had imagined him to be. My definition of sleazy was someone who was sleazier than I. Philip fit the bill. A nice Jewish boy, a mild-mannered accountant who faithfully visited his widowed mother in New Jersey every Friday night for dinner (matzo-ball soup, boiled chicken, noodle *kugel*, stewed apples for dessert) and then went home via the Village tearooms. A predilection for those of a slightly darker persuasion: blacks, Hispanics, Italians, and fellow hebes like me. Along with a fondness for disproportionate members, with which he himself was blessed. "All meat and no potatoes," he had said that fateful night of reckless disregard, referring respectively to his mammoth shaft and the accompanying pair of minuscule testicles.

Now he was telling me about "Trick Towers," known as London Terrace apartments to the uninitiated. This complex on Twenty-third and Ninth was so large that every gay man in Manhattan had tricked with at least one resident. Hadn't I? I thought back and realized Philip was correct. We strolled down the Morton Street Pier. Squinting into the sunset, one could see the outline of the Statue of Liberty. Across the Hudson in Jersey was the Maxwell House coffee sign, the largest illuminated outdoor billboard in the world, so I was told on a Circle Line tour.

Somehow the topic of dermatology was broached. Here followed a series of grim accusations and counter-accusations resulting in the dissolution of tender romance. Our voices were never raised past the level of the neighboring boom-box playing disco; our tone was calm and terse.

"We should have waited," said Philip. "Another ten days wouldn't have mattered."

"Why?" I asked.

"The herpes," he whined—an obvious fact, at least to him.

"Whose herpes?"

"Yours, mine, and ours."

I touched my face nervously. "This?" I inquired.

"It's not exactly poison ivy."

"What do you mean? I don't have herpes."

"You do now," said Philip.

"I didn't before," I said slowly, the truth gradually dawning.

"Well, you must have picked it up right before you and I fooled around, because I didn't have any symptoms on Tuesday."

"That's not possible. It's been two weeks since I did anything."

"So maybe it's a recurrence." Now Philip was on the defensive.

"Don't you think I would be able to tell an initial outbreak?"

"Well, you didn't seem to know this time."

"Have *you* had herpes before?" I asked.

"Yes."

"I thought it was just genital. I didn't realize you could get it on your face. Where was yours?"

"Same place as now."

"Then *you* must have given it to *me*," I accused.

"That's not possible. I always get a warning—a tingling sensation."

"It's not transmissible earlier?"

"I don't think so," said Philip.

"Shit." We were sitting on the end of the pier, legs dangling over the water. I bent over, holding my forehead in my hands, a classic advertisement for aspirin or pain-reliever.

"Hey, don't worry. Sometimes it doesn't even recur," said Philip. "Just take lots of lysine. Whatever you do, don't scratch. It will spread. Keep it dry. Stay out of the sun. Take it easy. Avoid stress. Get lots of rest."

"Any more good advice?" I was boiling. "Avoid stress? My life is stress. Relationships are stress, even the ones that don't last past the first date. What should I do, go through the rest of my life with earplugs, dark sunglasses, and long underwear?" I moved my fingers to scratch where it itched and caught myself in time. "Should I wear a straitjacket? Get into passive bondage? Am I sentenced to a life of padded cells and plastic silverware, avoiding sharp objects at all cost? Speak softly and carry a big teddy bear. How am I supposed to avoid stress? New York City *is* stress. Should I drop out of grad school and move to Des Moines? Should I turn hetero?"

"What did I do, press a button or something? Slow down. There's no need to fly off the handle. I didn't ask for a song and dance."

"Any more advice you got for me?" I asked bitterly. "Wash behind the ears? Don't sleep with strange men? Eat my vegetables? Stay away from guys who have large urns suitable for umbrellas filled with numbers of tricks?"

"Listen," said Philip, "I think maybe I should go now, OK? I'm walking back up Christopher to the subway. I'll give you a call next week to see how you're doing."

"Thank you for the gift that keeps on giving. See you in the funny pages," I said to his receding figure, barely under my breath.

"What am I going to do?" wailed Rachel into the phone. "Christopher just walked out on me!"

"Calm down, Rachel. What happened?"

"He just packed a suitcase and left."

"Sit down. Breathe deeply a few times. . . . Better? Good. Now put down the phone and pour yourself a glass of scotch," I advised. She did as I told her. "Feel a little calmer?"

"A little."

"Now tell me all about it."

"Christopher had a bad cold. I was being extra nice to him— fluffing up the pillows, cold washcloths to soothe his brow, Vicks VapoRub on the chest, weak tea with lemon and honey, the works. So then I made him homemade chicken soup. You get some necks and gizzards from the butcher and boil them; it takes a couple hours. Christopher takes a sip, spits it out, claims I'm trying to give him a relapse. B.J., it was the first time I tried chicken soup, and I admit it was maybe a little too salty, I was experimenting, but he had no right to be so mean. I don't care if he was sick. He goes on to tell me that maybe I should switch to TV dinners. I'm not a bad cook, am I? I know sometimes I make things and they don't turn out exactly like the photographs in the cookbooks, but does that mean I'm a terrible cook?

"Well, that was last Thursday. Tonight, we're having veal scaloppine. So maybe the meat is a little overcooked. So maybe I should have pounded it a little more. Christopher, he thinks he's being funny, he asks for a Black and Decker saw to cut the meat. I don't have to take this crap. I graduated cum laude from Radcliffe; he dropped out of SUNY at Stony Brook after three semesters, and the only reason he lasted that long was because he had a great drug-connection on campus. I tell him, 'Fine, you want a cook, a launderer, a housekeeper, look in the classifieds section in the *Times*. I don't need any deadbeats around here. If you're not satisfied with the service, you can go elsewhere. I don't need the abuse.' B.J., I told you I just started a job; it's temp work at a law firm, just to get my feet wet. I might go to law school next year, and I wanted to find out if I liked it. So now I've got enough stress as it is. A new job takes a lot out of you, and I don't have to put up with Christopher's snide comments about my cooking in addition. So what does he do? He goes to the bedroom, packs a suitcase, and leaves. I throw a lemon soufflé after him; I miss and hit the wall. And now there's plaster everywhere," she sobbed. "What did I do wrong? Why did he walk out on me?"

"Rachel, you're better off without him. He was just dead weight."

"*How can you say that?* You never really knew him. Christopher is so smart. He's such a sweet guy; he'd buy me the cutest *tchotchkes*. So he's a little unconventional. I *need* that in my life. He knows how to make me laugh. Christopher would tell me all sorts of things I would never know otherwise. Like what the crazy old lady on the park bench in front of the Regency said that day. Or the best place to get bagels in Manhattan on a Sunday morning. B.J., I'm in love with him. Christ, how do I get him back?"

"Rachel, it's just not a good month for romance. I just got over my first herpes attack. And you know what's worse, Rachel? Guess who I ran into on the street at the height of my affliction? Carlo. I know, he's trash; I should forget about him completely. He's just an egotistical bastard who's full of himself, but still, I thought, maybe one of these days he'll change and become a better person, and then of course he'd realize that I was perfect for him and he was right for me. But do you think he'd ever want me after the way I looked that day? Not a chance. Talk about the scarlet letter, the mark of adultery. Me, I have the mark of venereal disease right on my face! Why do my ailments have to be so visible?"

"B.J., I really don't want to hear about it."

"Sorry, I just get carried away sometimes."

"OK." She removed her hands from her ears.

"So, Rachel, face it. Men. They're not worth it. You can't live with them."

"And you can't live without them. B.J., what am I going to do?"

"Christopher is such a flake he could show up anytime. Think long-term for a moment. You want kids, right? And marriage."

"Who doesn't?"

"Try Christopher."

"Oh, he wants his freedom."

"Don't you see an impasse?"

"B.J., don't try to reason with me. This is not a sociolinguistic research problem you can codify. This isn't a fucking mathematical equation with variables and constants. Love isn't rational, so why don't you lay off and help me?"

"OK. Have you ever considered using a gourmet deli or a part-time caterer?"

"B.J., not you, too!"

"Just kidding. Listen, Rachel, you're a feminist; we're all feminists. I'd burn my bra if I were a transvestite as an act of solidarity with the movement. So let's forget the food issue entirely. It's a nonissue. Let's concentrate on Christopher. He left. He's probably staying with friends for a few days. He may come back unexpectedly. He may even come back later tonight. He's unpredictable. I think you should calm down, wait a few days. No sense in making a mountain over a molehill. This whole thing could blow over in a few days."

"In the meantime, what do I do?"

"We'll go see a movie tomorrow. You can catch up on your reading. Finish the pillow in needlepoint. I don't know. Take an extra exercise class. Go shopping. Or I'll meet you in the park tomorrow at four; we'll try to get free tickets to Shakespeare in the Park— Linda Ronstadt and Kevin Kline in *Pirates of Penzance*."

"Christopher and I were supposed to see that next week," she moaned.

"OK, we'll stick with a movie. How about *Bringing Up Baby* at the Thalia?"

"Whatever. It doesn't matter."

"Just don't think about it," I advised. "I know, it's like telling someone not to think of the word *rutabaga* for five minutes. Or like saying stay calm or cheer up. But what can I say?"

Rachel took a deep breath. "I'll give it a try."

It was Saturday night. I was home. Another eighteen-year-old had stood me up. It ran in cycles: One month last year I had met three oboists who were working on their master's degrees in performance (Juilliard, Purchase, and N.Y.U., respectively); another month it was a spate of forty-five-year-old textbook editors with a penchant for leather. After Philip, I decided to steer away from accountants, word processors, and other office workers. I began to frequent the Ninth Circle, a chicken bar on West Tenth Street in the Village. Now I was inundated with eighteen-year-olds who lived with their parents in New Jersey and had aspirations of being flight attendants.

I had met Evan in the basement near the pool table. I bought him a beer, and we went out to the patio in back. His long blond hair was parted in the center. Deborah Harry was singing "Heart of Glass" on the jukebox. We walked through the amber-lit bar, the color of Budweiser, past the moose head bolted to the wall, and out onto the street. Evan came over to my place for sex. It was fantastic. He gave me his number, and I gave him mine. He warned me to be discreet because he lived with his parents. I called him on Wednesday and left a message with a man I presumed was his father. Evan called back on Thursday, saying he'd be in the city on Saturday and would give me a ring.

Evan had left an item of apparel, a rather intimate item. I mentioned it discreetly. "Oh, yeah, my cock ring. Don't lose it! I'm quite attached to it." I thought it was the other way around.

Now, at one in the morning, I snapped it and unsnapped it irritatedly. He hadn't called. Most likely he'd forgotten. I tried to think back five years. Did I have that short an attention span? Was I completely irresponsible? I debated calling his parents in New Jersey to leave the message that I had called, and does Evan want his *cock ring* back, and should I mail his *cock ring* to him, and how should I address the package, should I say, "WARNING: CONTAINS AN INTIMATE ITEM OF APPAREL (COCK RING)," or would he rather pick up the *cock ring* himself? Perhaps I could even send the *cock ring* to him care of his mother without even telling him. That would be a nice surprise. Everybody liked surprises. I particularly enjoyed surprises like waiting until one in the morning on a Saturday night for a phone call from an irresponsible eighteen-year-old who lived with his parents in New Jersey and had aspirations of being a flight attendant but was presently unemployed.

I was furious. It was one thing, just hanging out in the apartment on a Saturday night when everyone else in the world was out on a date, having fun. Unlike Dennis, I didn't even have any plants to ignore me. I was mad at Evan and even madder at myself. Why should I get so upset that some bimbo from Jersey wasn't sufficiently well-mannered to send his regrets? Why was I doomed to repeat my hopelessly insecure childhood at the slightest setback? Last pick, odd guy left out, stood up by Madeleine Garfinkel at the high-school dance. Instead, I had gone to a double feature of *Planet of the Apes* movies alone and felt like a pervert in a raincoat who talked to himself when the lights went on during intermission.

I couldn't call Evan. The evening was ruined. My only recourse was to perform the Elimination Ritual.

This is how it went: First I took the card with Evan's name, phone number, and address out of my Rolodex and tore it in half. Then, using the Bic lighter purchased solely for the Elimination Ritual, since I do not smoke, I set the card aflame in the ashtray, muttering caustic and obscure curses in Sanskrit. After the fire exterminated itself, I flushed the ashes down the toilet after a not-inconsiderable bowel movement.

All traces of Evan must be erased. I checked my date-book. I crossed out his name in indelible black marker. I scribbled over the name in ink twenty times in my pocket address-book. If Evan had lived in Manhattan, I would have torn out his page from the New York telephone book.

Why was the world full of shits? I curled up in a fetal position after the Elimination Ritual and waited for sleep to come.

The sun burned with steady fury on the gaggle of gays at the Rambles in Central Park. Perched on a slope of granite, I surveyed the crowd below. Bodies covered with sweat and Speedos were arrayed before me; I only had to choose. But the two men of my dreams were a couple, one rubbing baby oil onto the other's back. A possible suitor wearing a Walkman sang along intermittently much louder than he realized.

I sat on the rocky slope above Gay Acres, not wanting to stain my white shorts on the grass. I removed my shirt and neatly folded it beside me. The hours at the gym were not for naught, but I had to be careful: no more snacks until October. It was swimsuit season. Quite a few looked up the slope to check me out. A boy in lime trunks, reddening at his belly, gazed in my direction, upper torso propped up by the elbows, a plastic visor shading his eyes of indeterminate color. Then he turned with a flop, his belly following with alacrity, losing his only good angle.

I tan easily, being of Semitic stock. SPF 2 is all I ever need, and that for only the first few sessions. I decided I could do without suntan lotion if I didn't stay too long. A man came through the group with a cooler, selling beer and soda for a dollar a shot—out of my price range.

The air was stagnant in Gay Acres. I longed for a breeze, a giant fan to cool us all down—it felt like an outdoor sauna. A skinny blond in a blue-and-white-striped bikini sprayed himself with water from a plastic plant-mister. Two youths in loose cutoff jeans stood by the bench on the sloping path, evidently completing a drug transaction. Above me, a thirtyish man stood straddling his bicycle. Not bad. I heard salsa music below, under the trees. The man who sold beer was lying on a blanket in the shade, tattoos on his arm, the physique of a junkie. He joked with a woman friend wearing a peasant blouse and jeans.

I felt a shadow over me. I turned to see a familiar face.

"Hello" was his dry greeting. A long-drawn-out voice. He was pale; the portion of his legs between his socks and shorts was white. I knew him from somewhere, but I couldn't quite place him. I was sure I'd remember after a few words. I was too embarrassed to ask his name. Luckily he hadn't referred to me by name; I wasn't under any obligation to call him by his.

"Hi. It's been a while," I said, a fairly safe bet.

"You're looking good, B.J.," he replied.

Shit. He knew my name. Stalling for time, I asked, "What's the book?" He was carrying a large hard-cover.

"You don't want to know. *Management: An Introduction*. I thought I'd get some reading done while I caught some sun. I'm working on my M.B.A. I don't remember if I told you about that. I'm taking evening classes; it's only my first semester. It's quite a drag with a full-time job, but I figure once I get my M.B.A., I can switch jobs and get a significant raise in the bargain, although I'm not sure if it's really worth it financially, because classes at Fordham aren't exactly cheap, but anyhow my accountant says I can deduct it, so I guess it's all for the best. Been to any concerts lately?"

I was so embarrassed. *He* was the one from the Juilliard concert. Funny, I didn't remember him as having quite so flat a personality. But then, we didn't talk that much. When you're cruising, sometimes certain forms of communication are kept to a minimum. Now, *what was his name*? I could recall the apartment quite clearly. Like a hurricane had hit it. Papers everywhere. Synapses, don't fail me now. What the fuck was his name? "Not really. I caught the Philharmonic last month on the Great Lawn, but that's about it."

"Oh, I was at that concert, too. If you mean the concert on the fourteenth. If, however, you are referring to the concert on the twentieth, I was elsewhere. Did you enjoy the performance? Frankly, I felt it was lacking, rather uninspired. I don't know whether it was the amplification or just the outdoor acoustics, but the woodwind section sounded badly out of tune. The choice of selections was fairly pedestrian, don't you agree? The usual bombastic crowd-pleasers, culminating with an amateurish display of fireworks that was totally out of synchronization with the music. On the other hand, if you attended the other concert, perhaps the evening was more entertaining. Although I doubt there was that much difference between the two."

He paused for a breath. I rushed to cut in. My luck. To be bored to death in the Rambles by an ex-trick—a bad one at that, I thought, because I couldn't even recall his name. Wait a minute. Bob. That was it. Bob Broome. The man on the bicycle who had been looking intently in my direction remounted and pedaled away. No fair. I bet if Bob hadn't come—well, never mind.

"Listen, Bob, I was just leaving now." I grabbed my shirt and put it back on. "Which way are you going?"

"Oh, I'm going out by the Museum of Natural History. You *do* remember I live nearby," he said ruefully.

"Sure. Gee, I'm going to the Met this afternoon. I would have walked you." If he had said he was going east, I would have switched destinations and said I was going west. "Well, it was nice running into you," I said. "See you soon."

"Same here. Take care." With that, he stood and slowly lumbered his way down the patch. I walked toward the Upper Terrace. After twenty feet or so I turned to see his figure disappear from view. Bob Broome. The type of person who told shaggy-dog stories without punchlines. Bob reminded me of *Middlemarch*. I was force-fed everyone's favorite novel in college, and I despised it because on page fifty I already knew everything that would occur and I had another five hundred pages to go. Well, Bob was attractive and relatively pleasant. No harm in being friendly.

I gave one last look at Gay Acres, one final cruise. By the Upper Terrace I discovered a series of paths through the woods, snaking around rocks and edging the nearby lake. Elderly couples with binoculars were out bird-watching. Kids ran through, playing tag. A boy and a girl, arm in arm, ambled their way through the shade, stopping to sit on a bench and make out. But there was also a subtext. Half-hidden behind a tree, I spied the sexy cyclist. He wasn't alone. Someone was working him over but good. He muffled gasps of pleasure.

Sex in the great outdoors: the freedom, the liberation, the fresh air, and the concurrent risk of arrest. I looked around, more carefully this time, as if my eyes were adjusting to the dim light of a theater, and discovered more of the nether world. Shades were floating between trees, around clumps of vegetation. A group of them were on a boulder midst the darkest part of the forest. Furtive shadowy glances. Dark and brooding. Silent movements. An occasional cock slipping out of a pair of shorts, only for a moment. This was the St. Mark's Baths *en pleine air*, on a much more discreet level.

I stayed for a while, enjoying the unexpected benefits of my nature walk, and then returned home.

Helpful Hints for Alfresco Sex

1. *In the event that both of you get stung by a swarm of mosquitoes on a private part of your persons, keep handy a jar of calamine lotion large enough to fit two erections comfortably. A portable vacuum cleaner is most helpful for sand up the wazoo.*

2. *Avoid using shiny leaves as nature's lubricant. Poison ivy is a most unpleasant thing to have in your rectum.*

3. *Be prepared to share your climax with unexpected guests: a troop of Brownies, an elderly couple bird-watching, a mounted policeman, the film crew of a nature documentary for a public broadcasting station, your lover. Carry enough extra cash to buy a sufficient amount of Girl Scout cookies to placate the Brownies. Amyl nitrate may also double as restorative for the couple who have fainted or suffered heart attacks. Be sure to have proper identification, since no matter how hoary your appearance or ill-mannered your disposition, police officers will invariably ask you for your phone number and address. A small blow-dryer can come in quite handy for your cinematic debut (you do want to look your best). Your lover may be either invited to join making the beast with three backs, scolded for his tacky voyeurism, or safely ignored, depending upon the stage of your relationship.*

4. *Don't let the lack of sanitary facilities prevent you from maintaining proper appearances. Carry a generous supply of Wash'n Dri's. Floss for stray pubic hairs. Don't necessarily tuck in your shirt; the casual look is appropriate for alfresco sex, and afterward, you may want to hide cum stains on your shorts. Besotted hankies can either be draped decorously on tree branches or buried. A spare change of underclothing is desirable for those who value comfort. Be sure your fly is properly zipped. Use your mirrored sunglasses to check your hair.*

5. Realize at the outset that things will *be stolen* right from under your nose *during the course of your activities: articles of clothing, watches, jewelry, wallets, key-chains, recreational drugs, address books, and prospective tricks. Only the final item of the previous list will truly devastate. Unfortunately, there is absolutely nothing you can do about it.*

· 8 ·

August

*A*ugust was really the cruellest month in Manhattan. The mercury hovered around ninety, and so did the humidity. If you could leave, you left.

Women sat on fire escapes, drinking beer and fanning themselves with newspapers against the exhaust of Ninth Avenue. In Central Park a horse pulling a carriage buckled and collapsed of heat prostration. Below, in the dyspeptic belly of the city, the subway platform was twenty degrees hotter still. The train screeched in and I collapsed onto a seat; the windows were jammed shut, the air-conditioning was broken, a *Post* was stuck to the floor, footprints on a Brooke Shields ad for Calvin Klein jeans. I heard the whine of the Stones doing "Emotional Rescue" through someone's headphones. Five stops later I peeled myself off, sticky with sweat, and dragged myself up the flight of stairs and crawled out into the haze. A multicolored puddle at the foot of an Italian-ices cart wended its way toward the gutter. A tourist asked me directions to the Staten Island Ferry. I was annoyed; it seemed whenever *I* asked directions, I always got victims of dyslexia who didn't know right from left. I told him to ask the subway clerk. I walked home. My favorite junkie, a cute Hispanic with beautiful brown eyes, pupils perpetually dilated, unself-consciously scratching at his crotch (heroin addiction? crabs?)—even he was on vacation. The druggies had all gone to Coney Island for the day.

I entered my apartment and felt the heat of Gloria's Pizza Parlor below. The wiring in my prewar apartment-building didn't support air-conditioning, not that I could afford the electricity. A fan at my window blew over a block of ice molded in a bowl in my freezer. I panted like a sick cat. It was too hot to even masturbate. The park was unbearable. I set the alarm for eight A.M. Saturday morning and went to sleep, a glass of ice water by the bed. I took a sip in the middle of the night, felt something furry, turned on the light, muffled a shriek, and tossed the drowned cockroach into the sink. At around four I woke up, like every other night in August, the single sheet molded to my sweaty body like a plaster cast, crawled to the bathroom, took a quick shower, went back to bed without drying myself, and slept fitfully through the rest of the night.

At eight I rose and packed a backpack with a towel, *The Culture of Narcissism*, a copy of *After Dark*, and a sandwich. Today was a Jones Beach day. I called the weather to make sure it wasn't going to storm. Once, it rained at the beach and people ran for cover like in some Japanese horror picture, as if the giant crab from outer space were in hot pursuit. Because I was sick of the subways and it was only twenty blocks, I walked to Penn Station.

At Thirty-eighth a nice black lady asked me if I wanted a date. At nine o'clock in the morning? I was insulted. Didn't I look gay enough to drive away whores?

Manhattan was an island, and I had island fever. Penn Station was another medieval torture. I stood in the ticket line for fifteen minutes, sweltering. Even a tank top was too much clothing. Then I milled around. There was another line at the information booth, where a bored, efficient WASP matron with a shellacked hairdo was snapping out times and gates through a microphone. I bolted to buy breakfast, then rushed downstairs to the tracks, sweat dripping through my blue mesh T-shirt. The train awaited with closed doors. When they finally opened, people pushed in much like dough forced through molds in a cookie factory. My luck—the first three cars remained locked, reserved for passengers boarding in Queens. I had to trudge through the crowd to the sixth car. The fourth and fifth were already jam-packed, people standing in the aisles, body to body. The sixth car was for smoking, so I walked through to the seventh. I found a seat next to a man with seventeen chins, the monster who ate Chicago. I sipped my plastic cup of reconstituted orange juice and took a bite of my over-buttered pumpernickel bagel, smearing my hands. There were never enough napkins. The train lurched, then started, seemingly in the wrong direction, for my seat faced the rear. Compressed, I read the Saturday *Times* elbow to elbow. The paper was good for ten minutes. All was dark, then suddenly the train burst into the light of Queens.

For the first few stops, only the front three cars were opened for passengers. At the earliest opportunity I extricated myself from my seat and started making my way toward the front-most car, a Pilgrim's Progress, past the plastic coolers and the folded chairs, the raucous brats on summer vacation, the dental hygienist and her cousin from Weehawken, the grandmother reading *TV Guide*, the hot Italian who sold stereo equipment at Tech HiFi and his Puerto Rican girlfriend with acne on her forehead. A beach ball fell from the overhead luggage-tray. The train ground to a halt at Jamaica. The Fire Island queens got off en masse, discoing a conga line. These were the A-level fags, straight out of an International Male catalog— bodies to die for, glib and wicked, disposable income to burn. Jealous, resentful, morally superior, I stayed on with the rest of the proletariat. Three cars to go. I felt like a salmon swimming upstream to spawn as I pushed my way through the cars. After Jamaica it was less crowded. By Rockville Centre I was at the first car, casually edging my way toward the door.

At Freeport, the Jones Beach stop, was the mad dash for the bus. I sprinted out as the door opened, scrambled down the long flight of stairs, and discovered that the line for the bus extended back to the third staircase. Disappointed, I dragged myself to the end of the line. What was the point of rushing? I'd never get on the first bus. Five buses awaited across the street; one had pulled up in front and was loading. There were only sixteen thousand five hundred and twenty-three people in front of me. I searched for my ticket and ripped off another section, labeled "BUS TO:." In another fifteen minutes I was standing on a bus inching down the highway. The air outside was perfectly clear, though the windows were filthy. Two guys riding Peugeots passed us on the bike lane. We picked up speed and drove around a stalled car on the shoulder, a family having a consolation picnic nearby on the dried grass. Then the bus waited at the toll plaza, the entrance to the beach area. Now we were zooming over a bridge; sailboats were on the Sound.

I got off at the East Bathhouse. The middle portion of my Jones Beach Special five-part ticket was good for a locker at the bathhouse. I saw another long line. I headed for the sand. I peeled off my shirt as soon as I saw the ocean. I walked east on the boardwalk, past the last beach-umbrella rental, and for a dollar, bought a large cup of cola to last the day. At the picnic tables I removed my shorts. At the edge of the parking lot the sneakers came off, tied by the laces to hang on my backpack. A few barbecue grills were set up by the lot,

Lot 6. A mother screamed to her seven-year-old to wait half an hour before going into the water. Before the dunes were the kites, all exotic: a double box, a Japanese fish, and one made of seven different-colored diamond kites strung together. The seven kites dipped and looped as one. I walked down by the water where the sand was packed flat and firm, waves licking at my ankles. The farther I walked, the fewer mixed couples and families I saw. A plane flew overhead, an ad for Coppertone trailing behind on a banner. A few topless women, singly and in pairs, were scattered in the mainly male crowd. An immense woman in a black one-piece suit sat like a Buddha, surrounded by a group of disco clones.

I scanned the beach, looking for familiar faces and objects of desire. A tall blond and his red-haired friend cavorted in the waves, swim-suits around their necks. I stopped and looked at a life-size sand-sculpture of a nude muscle-man with a tremendous dick, grass for pubic hair, and creamy suntan lotion squirted around the crotch. By the dunes stood a purple concrete-block painted "6½," numbering the adjacent nonexistent parking lot. I had arrived at the heart of the gay section.

Sand castles had gone condo in this neighborhood. Brightly colored sashes tied to sticks as flags identified groups. Frustrated designers constructed elaborate beach retreats with driftwood, bamboo poles, and Laura Ashley sheets. A pair of muscle-bound behemoths sat in an inflatable raft on the sand. Grace Jones declaimed "Warm Leath-erette" on someone's tape deck. A twenty-year-old dancer manqué did isometrics on his towel, pretending to be oblivious to the stares he attracted. A man in glasses, hair slightly thinning, read Edmund White's *States of Desire* on his stomach. I heard a shout. "B.J.!" It was my friend Dave Johnson, from the Y. The N.Y.U. gym had been closed for the summer, so I joined the West Side Y. I'd met Dave on the Nautilus circuit. Slender and tightly muscular, he stood six foot two, with soft-blue eyes and sandy-blond hair. An appendix scar was lightly etched on his stomach above the Speedo. Dave motioned for me to join him and his companion. Dave had grown up in Charleston and had a slight Southern accent.

"This here is Paco, my roommate." Paco eyed me through blue eyes that were practically phosphorescent and gave me an evil smile through perfect teeth that I found very alluring. A pencil-thin mus-tache framed his upper lip, black as his neatly cropped hair. His skin was very dark. In lieu of a suit he wore a red jockstrap.

"Nice to meet you." We shook hands. "Are you Spanish? That's a great tan."

"Brathilian," he replied, fingers still clasped, etching a circle on the back of my hand with his forefinger.

"Hey, I'm a lousy hostess. Paco and I made Bloody Marys last night in this cooler. Would you care for a cocktail?" Dave poured me one into a Dixie cup. I looked around and noticed seven or eight scattered cups by their sheet.

"Thanks." I took a sip. "How are you doing, Dave?"

"Same old same old. Work, gym, sleep, and the beach on the weekend." Dave worked in the production department of a company that put on industrials, elaborate musical numbers for industrial conventions. He told me about his current project, sewing a zucchini costume for the vegetable finale at a frozen-foods convention.

"You been here long?" I asked.

"Honey, Paco and I got here at eight-thirty. We took the seven-ten train this morning." They lived up in Harlem, in an expansive five-bedroom apartment.

"You must have been up at the crack of dawn."

"Five-thirty. Ain't the sun great! Hey, catch the guy in the purple suit walking down by the water. See him? Between the red tank-top and the white bikini." We turned as one to stare.

"Not bad," I said. "A seven."

"A possible eight," said Paco. "I need to get a closer look at the bulge to tell for sure."

"Are you guys crazy? That's no more than a six, or my name isn't Miss Jessica."

"Hey, are we rating on a scale of one to ten or guessing how many inches?" I asked.

"The former," said Dave. "It *would* take a size queen like you to bring up a question like that."

"Not me."

"Well, then, what kind of a queen are you?"

"I'm no queen at all," I protested.

"Honey, everybody is a queen of some sort or another. Take Paco here, for example. He is, regrettably, a tearoom queen. I do believe his favorite is adjacent to Bloomingdale's, although he is partial to the one in Altman's on the fifth floor. I think it depends on the time of day, doesn't it, Paco?" Words spilled effortlessly from Dave's mouth, a lyrical singsong. He refurbished his drink and smiled.

Paco grunted a reply. He was on his stomach, trying to catch a few *z*'s.

"I've got it," said Dave. "You're a muscle queen."

"You mean I'm sort of a hunk? I think I've got quite a ways to go," I demurred.

"No, I mean you crave them muscles. I can see those pretty green eyes of yours bug out when you see some bulky, misshapen things at the gym that I would toss out of bed if they so much as asked for crackers."

"And what about you? Are you the generic queen?"

"Close. Honey, when you're from the South, you've got an early start on the rest. Remember, I've been at it since I was fourteen, with boys and girls and an occasional barnyard animal. No, I admit, I just threw that in to perk up your interest. My own personal tastes are fairly spread out. I suppose you could call me a mud-wrestling, white-trash, bridge-and-tunnel, face-sitting, coke-snorting chicken-queen. I might throw in dish queen while I'm at it, which is to say that although I am not one to spread reputation-ruining gossip from disreputable sources, I am not above circulating an occasional rumor about someone's minor fall from grace. I won't name names, that would be beneath my dignity, but I will say a certain black-haired youth currently wearing a red jockstrap"—he flipped his head in Paco's direction—"has been known to pick up as many as five men on a single night. I *do* wish he'd tell me his secret. Hey, B.J., your glass is almost empty. I think it's time for another cup all around."

Dave, garrulous, a bit tipsy, was a natural raconteur. We spent a long day drinking and cruising and dishing, smashed, playing musical swimsuits in the water, tossing and exchanging them. In drunken lunacy we had two execrable hamburgers and three orders of cold, greasy fries at the refreshment stand. Back at the East Bathhouse we prowled the corridors and showered in icy water. Paco had a changing room. We met there and had one last cocktail. Then we had the same series of lines to wait in in reverse. At the train station we got cones from the Mister Softee truck at the foot of the stairs. The train came miraculously in ten minutes, a short wait. Dave took a nap on the ride home. Paco told me about the monthly orgies he went to on the East Side and asked if I wanted to join in. He explained that there was an orchestrator—a man who sat in the corner positioning people, a sexual choreographer. I declined gracefully.

We split at Penn Station. I was back in the concrete cesspool for another week.

"I'm in love," said Dennis over a cup of cappuccino.

"Who is it this time?" I asked.

"His name is Nathan. We met at Man's Country."

"Where's that?"

"It's a bathhouse on Fifteenth Street."

I remembered seeing the billboard for Man's Country at Sheridan Square, above the tobacco shop: an unshaven man with curly black hair, fist in the air, a tattoo on his bicep. "Cheap" read the sign, both figuratively and literally. I didn't recall an address or any other further explanation. I always thought it was a private dance-club, a gay theme-park, or a macho gym. Dennis explained it was all three. Each floor had a different theme. One was a maze; another had a set of slings. On the sixth floor was an actual Mack truck. Nobody knew how it got there. A membership gym occupied the top floor.

"Are you sure this is love? Tell you what, after three months I'd like to meet him."

"Nathan's great. He's a singer. He's also a DJ. He hasn't gotten too many jobs yet; he's just starting. This is the real thing. No kidding."

"You've had five real things in the past six months, Dennis."

"He loves me. What can I say? The guy's got taste. Want a bite of my napoleon?" We were at Rocco's Pastry Shop on Bleecker. "Hey, watch out, guy. Looks like you're turning into the abominable cream-puff. You got some whipped cream on your chin." Dennis took his napkin out and dabbed me clean.

"You can dress me up, but you can't take me anywhere." I sighed. "Dennis, am I ever going to get a boyfriend? I feel my life has no direction. Sometimes I feel like I'm just treading water; I'm not really making any progress. I mean, at least you have been having a series of relationships with men. I don't seem to last past the one-night-stand stage. If I get interested in somebody, I scare them away, or they live in New Jersey with their parents and have aspirations of becoming a flight attendant or worse. I go to a bar, and trolls stick to me like I'm made of flypaper; I can't shake them, so I end up leaving early. My life is completely out of control."

"Ve should approach dis matter carefully." Dennis put on his Viennese-therapist accent. "Vat should ve discuss first? I know. Ve

94

discuss sex. Because dis matter is primal. Also because dere is prurient interest here on my part. Is basic to everyting. Also is smutty and dat vay I can get my kicks talking about it. You tell me you are attracted to men?"

"Yes, doctor."

"Vy do you tink dis is da case?"

"Well, I had a strong mother and an absent father."

"Go on."

"I played with dolls? My testicles didn't descend until I was twenty, and my voice still hasn't changed? My psychosexual development was somehow retarded due to a combination of genetic and environmental factors?" I was whining.

"You are teorizink here! Dis vill not do! I vant you to personalize your feelings!"

"Well . . . maybe because I like it?" I guessed.

"Aha! Ve are makink progress! Dis is called ze pleasure-pain principle. Ja vold. I think ve have it there."

"That's all?"

"Sure. Hey, B.J., you know, I might get out of the priesthood after all. Nathan is grooming me for stardom. I have a few jokes I'd like to present to the audience out there."

"Oh, my God, you're not turning into a lounge lizard before my very eyes, are you? I'm horrified!"

"OK, OK, I'll move right into the singing portion of my act." Dennis took out a Cloraseptic breath-spray and squirted his throat. "Mi mi mi mi mi mi mi." He started the worst rendition I had ever heard of "Moon River," forgetting most of the words. I panicked.

"Dennis. Enough! Waiter, check, please! Hurry! Dennis, people are staring!" I tried to use my napkin as a makeshift gag, but Dennis hit a high C, and I dropped it in horror. "God, that sounds like a cat with a hysterectomy in false heat. Will you please be quiet?"

"Whatsamatter, you don't like Art? I should introduce you to Ralph? Maybe I need a little more practice on my act."

"Listen, I'll take care of the check, OK? Just don't start singing again."

"Be my guest."

Some Queens

Drag queens, size queens, shrimp queens (toe-sucking), rice queens (Orientals), potato queens (Occidentals), Fire Island queens, circuit queens (Fire Island/gym/disco circuit), cha-cha queens (Latinos), rice-and-bean queens (Mexicans), Queens for a Day (married men from New Jersey who go to the baths), face-sitting queens, fist queens, dish queens, Astoria Queens, dinge queens, beanie-boy queens (Orthodox Jews), salami queens (Italians), salami-casing queens (uncut Italians), leather queens, opera queens, tearoom queens, smoke queens, popper queens, enema queens, personals queens ("likes long walks on beaches"), glory-hole queens, tattoo queens, butt-hole queens, Studio queens (Studio 54—similarly, disco dollies), snow queens (cocaine, or blacks who like whites), fag-hag queens, hyphenate queens (actor-model-dancer-waiters), stress queens, roller-derby queens (wheelchairs, etc.), alfalfa queens (macrobiotic), diesel queens (men who dress up like dykes), chicken queens, diva queens, screen queens, seafood queens (sailors), souvlaki queens (Greek action), crepe-suzette queens (French action), Perils-of-Pauline queens (thrill-seekers), blue-jean queens (Calvin Klein, Gloria Vanderbilt), teddy-bear queens, cherry queens (deflowering virgins), Crisco queens, smut queens, ice queens (diamond-stud earrings), banana queens (curved dicks), Jimmy Dean queens (Levi's, Elizabeth Taylor, and rebels without a cause), Lean Cuisine queens (perpetual dieters), mean queens (S&M), twisted queens (deranged), pee queens (water sports), teen queens, un-weaned queens (sucking on tits—also known as Dairy Queens), magazine queens (addicted to glossies and press releases), railroad queens, locker-room queens, Mile High Club queens (making it in airplane johns), rubber queens, dildo queens, beet queens (Future Farmers of America back in high school—see also "yam queens"), dream queens (GQ types), scream queens ("Faaabulous!!!!"), Palace queens (Leona

Helmsley), *tuna queens* (*male lesbians*), *pesto queens* (*into garlic*), *egg-cream queens, fashion-victim/style-police queens* (*beyond therapy*), *hostage queens* (*fantasies of being taken hostage in a foreign American embassy and being brutalized by idealistic young university-student revolutionaries*), *vanilla queens* (*into vanilla sex: basic sucking and fucking, no fantasies allowed*), *matzo-meal queens* (*Reform Jews*), Wuthering Heights *queens* (*hopeless romantics*), *skin queens* (*uncircumcised*), *peeled queens* (*cut*), *designer queens, steroid queens, beach queens, smack queens, Ma Bell queens* (*phone sex*), *Tom Thumb queens* (*small dicks*), *uniform queens, piano-bar queens, salad queens* (*rimming*), *bottle queens* (*alcoholics*), *flea queens* (*sex in run-down hotels*), *bullhorn queens* (*politicos*), *flab queens* (*a.k.a. chubby-chasers*), *evil queens* (*approximately ninety percent of the above*), *therapy queens* (*electroshock queens, Bellevue queens, couch queens, Valium queens, etc.*), *condo and co-op queens* (*the landed gentry in Manhattan*), *and closet queens.*

· 9 ·

September

Y ou could say we met cute.

Richard was having a panic attack on Fifth Avenue, clutching a lamppost with arms that bulged like tin drums. Richard stood five foot ten, slightly stooped. He wore a pair of translucent glasses and was covered with muscles—strong but sensitive. A short-sleeved blue Arrow shirt strained to contain a chest as vast as the Sahara. Below, he wore a pair of khaki pants and brown oxford shoes, riddled with the traditional tiny holes.

I was dressed in blue jeans and Nikes and an angry-red T-shirt with the cover illustration of Hunter S. Thompson's *Fear and Loathing in Las Vegas*. I was on my way back from lunch break to my emotionally satisfying and intellectually fulfilling job in the exciting world of data processing, as they say on the matchbook covers. I had dropped out of grad school at the beginning of the semester. It was inevitable. My thirst for knowledge had been slaked, surpassed by a hunger for cash. I had been living lean too long. I was tired of eking out an existence near poverty level on my meager assistantship. One day I walked into the dean's office, picked up my last monthly check, and had a memorable exchange with Miss Fenster, the dean's personal secretary, who had perversely reclaimed her maiden name after the death of her husband of thirty years. Miss Fenster had considered me her personal serf, screaming, "*B.J.! I need you this second!!*" in a gravelly voice strong enough to reach the second balcony in a Broadway theater while I hid in the supply closet, reading a detective novel under the pretense of taking inventory. A harridan with two-toned hair, fat ankles, and Harlequin glasses on a chain, Miss Fenster wanted me to go out for Cremora or sharpen a gross of pencils or test a pair of speakers in the audiovisual lab or perform some other demeaning task far below my mental capabilities. When word got out that toxic shock syndrome was caused by tampons, I anonymously sent her a box of Rely's, a symbolic gesture, since she was postmenopausal.

So I told her to take a flying fuck at a rolling donut and made like a banana and split from the academic world for the more lucrative private sector. In less than a week I was employed in the dissolute field of computers. I had just partaken of a hearty lunch at a health-food restaurant on Fifth. As I left to return to work, I spied this hunk across the street and resolved to have him.

Street pickups were delicate courting dances, comprising a complex interplay of attraction and feared rejection. Because they took place in the straight world, even more tact and discretion were required than, say, at the baths or the bars. I approached Richard in quantum leaps, but only when he wasn't looking in my direction. Richard first noticed me from across the street as he loosened his grip on the lamppost. He blinked and found me ten feet closer, casually inspecting my shoelaces. He disengaged and scratched the back of his neck. He looked up and scanned the sidewalk. I was nowhere to be found. He shook his head and began to leave. Then he spotted me, not more than fifteen feet away, leaning against an open-air telephone-stand, tapping my left foot in rapid staccato. He smiled. I returned the smile. He removed his glasses, wiped them on his shirt, and replaced them. In time-lapse trick photography, in cartoon alacrity, I was upon him.

"Hi." My standard opening.

"My name is Richard Wilson." He extended a beefy hand in my direction. We shook.

"I'm B. J. Rosenthal."

"You live around here?"

"No, uptown. I'm on my way back to work."

"So am I."

"I'm late."

"Me, too."

"You OK? I saw you hugging the pole for dear life."

"Oh. I just had a little dizzy spell," said Richard, eyeing the contours of my T-shirt. "Listen, I better go now. I went home for lunch, and I've got to get back to work."

"You have a pen so I can give you my number?"

"No. Do you have a good memory?" He recited his number twice, slowly. "Give me a call soon."

"OK."

"I'm free tonight," he said hopefully.

"Sure."

"Maybe we can get together," he added.

"Fine."

"Don't forget." With that, he was off. I repeated his number, turning it into a musical jingle of seven notes, cursing my pitiful short-term memory, wishing I hadn't smoked so much dope in college. I strode back to my office deliberately, avoiding all distractions, drumming the number into permanence, hoping I wouldn't meet a friend and get drawn into a conversation and forget the number. Back on the sixth floor of my office-building I wrote down the number on a pink "While you were out" message pad. Just to make sure that he hadn't given me the number of a mortuary and embalming school, I tried it out. I got a recording. The voice sounded right. I hung up.

I wasn't expecting much: the typical quick screw and subsequent one-way unrequited lust or passion or heat or romance. At this point I wasn't certain which direction the emotion would flow and from which direction it would be stanched. From my past experience, prospective boyfriends remained prospective boyfriends until roughly five minutes after the first orgasm. It was then that the former prospective boyfriend typically alluded to his own boyfriend, a factual item seemingly irrelevant before ejaculation yet now curiously apropos. A case of hemorrhoids was revealed; a sexual dysfunction was uncovered; more often, a mental entry was made in the trick reference-file, an exhaustive encyclopedic compendium to be published posthumously. So many men, so little time. I went over to Richard's for dinner. Instead we fucked. "I don't usually fuck on the first date," I said, referring to the anal method of intercourse.

"That's what you think," replied Richard. He kissed me full on the mouth, one hand at my back, the other straying to my behind. He forced his tongue through my lips as he lightly circled my ass. His tongue met mine. I felt a surge of electrical power. He massaged my ass. Jolted, I pushed his hand away. With both hands he began kneading my neck.

Sex for me was nonverbal. I rarely spoke to express preferences, preferring to use body language. In the intensity of passion, I assumed my partner knew my innermost sensations by touch, by my response, by the look in my eyes. I felt Richard had gotten my message. There was no need to fight to defend my ass. However dishonorable men could be outside sex, they rarely used deceit during the act. The first encounter was a sexual audition where each partner gave his utmost to ensure the other's pleasure, either in the hopes of a repeat performance or with the knowledge that there would be no recurrence; even in the event of an extended engagement the heightened intensity and emotion of the first time were rarely equaled.

If he was really into fucking, how could he ignore the invisible tattoo above my anus that read "Abandon all hope, ye who enter herein"? And why force me when there were so many other willing men? I had nothing to worry about.

We undressed rapidly and then resumed touching. His body was even better than I had imagined from his clothes. He was massive, monumental, lacking only the ideal washboard stomach. Richard was solid. A great dick, an inch or two longer than mine. Thick, with real balls, not just a set of marbles. I hugged him, then traced lines on his biceps, around his back, a five-finger exercise pianissimo. He pressed me tighter to him. I could feel his chest against mine, his heart beating next to me. Again his left hand went for my ass. I ignored it. No harm in that. I moved my mouth to his arm and licked his muscle. Richard brought both hands to his lips and then placed his wet thumbs on my nipples. I gasped. That wasn't fair. He had chanced upon my prime erogenous zone, rivaling only my dick, which, already hard, twitched at his touch. "You like that," he murmured into my ear, gently biting the lobe. My arms dropped to my side as I let him jerk me on the tits, alternately rubbing and pinching. He placed his mouth on one tit and sucked long and hard. I felt a direct line of current from my nipple to my cock. I could feel myself surrendering.

He bent down and licked the underside of my shaft, rubbing both tits with his fingers at the same time. An alarm rang in my hindbrain: "Sensory overload! Sensory overload!" I was flooded with so much pleasure at once I felt incapable of reciprocating; I was barely able to concentrate on enjoying it all. Effortlessly, Richard slipped a forefinger into my asshole. I clenched involuntarily. It felt good . . . and yet, it was wrong. I wasn't ready. I told him not today. Yet how could I deny him this token? So long as he stuck to his fingers. I grimaced at the feel of the first knuckle. Oral sex was less involving. Why bring an asshole into the deal? I was a slow learner. The desire may be primal, but the mechanics are learned.

It had taken me over a year to overcome my initial revulsion over cocksucking. Sure, it felt good having my cock sucked, but to put someone else's in my *mouth*? Who knows *where* it had been? Now, of course, I put fellatio right up there with chocolate truffles and *Annie Hall* and the Pacific Ocean and life's other great pleasures. There was nothing as satisfying as a big, hard, thick dick in your mouth, except perhaps feeling it get hard by virtue of your tongue. To be filled so completely. Perhaps I had never been successfully weaned. Was I, fed on formula from birth, fruitlessly searching for a suitable pacifier at twenty-three?

And what can beat sixty-nining on hash? Your two bodies were symmetrically linked, coterminous; you went down on him as he went down on you; in effect, by mathematical laws of reflexivity and transitivity you were sucking your own cock. An Oriental circle of yin and yang; no aggressor, no conquest. No hierarchy, no relationship of power. Anal sex was more intimate, deeper. You couldn't get any closer to someone than by fucking him. Two bodies melded into one. My inhibitions remained high there. Quite frankly, I was unable to dissociate my asshole from shit. As for rimming, even the thought of it was beyond the pale—especially after my amebiasis.

"Lie down," said Richard. "Let me give you a nice rubdown." I lay on my stomach, on his bed, a white gym-towel under my belly. I shut my eyes and pretended I had control of the situation. "Why am I so damned quiet?" I asked myself. He kneaded my shoulders, pounded my back, pushed his knuckles against my spine, working his way down. I felt more relaxed. Now he was spreading my cheeks, firmly kneading my buns. It felt good. He slapped my back, slapped my butt, then kneaded my flesh. I felt so warm and relaxed and lazy; I was drifting; I was dreaming. He put his finger in again.

"No," I muttered.

"It's OK," he replied. "I'll be gentle." It felt good. I didn't notice the knuckle this time. He poked around. I was still tight.

"Easy, relax," he said. He withdrew his finger, then replaced it, all the while kneading my shoulders. I realized he was kneading my shoulders with both hands. Which meant that all of his fingers were presently occupied. Which meant . . . well, it wasn't so bad. He was gentle. I wanted to like it. He stuck his dick in farther. I felt pain. "Relax," he intoned. I couldn't make myself relax.

"Maybe you better stop. I don't think this is going to work," I said in a conciliatory tone.

In a husky voice Richard asked, "You like poppers?" My other weakness, next to my tits. Without waiting for an answer, he took a deep inhalation, then placed the bottle before my nose. I sniffed it in both nostrils, then returned it to him. He took two more hits. His dick was still poking slowly. I felt white-hot. I wanted it. It still hurt a little, but I wanted it. He moved in and out. Slowly, maddeningly slowly. I wanted it deeper. I wanted him inside me. To fill the hole— I wanted him to fill the hole completely. I wanted to feel him all the way inside me. The inner music of my body took over. I was relaxed. I felt no more pain; I had no inhibitions; I just wanted him to fuck me completely; I wanted more. He gave me another hit, and a few seconds later I was back in the rhythm, feeling the beat. I started rocking with his dick, moving away as he pulled and then propping my ass up as he approached. He placed his hands firmly on my ass, holding me down. "Don't move." I complied. If I moved, he might stop. He was on top of me, taking slow, deep thrusts. He was all the way in; there was no more resistance. "Like a hot knife through a stick of butter," he said. I wondered whether I should clench, a viselike grip on his dick, to give him additional sensation. He was propped on his arms. He weighed a good thirty pounds more than me. He fucked me slowly, a steady rhythm, never speeding up. He dropped his arms, lay right on top of me, snaked his fingers under my chest, and played with my nipples while he fucked me. I reached back to grap his ass, trying to ram him into me. I sensed he didn't want me to force; instead, I pushed with him, riding the thrusts. His deep growls became incoherent. He came with a loud mixture of grunts and sighs. Simultaneously, silently, I came. The towel beneath me was drenched with sweat and cum. I had overshot onto the sheets. We rested for a minute or so.

I accused him, "You tricked me."

"You can't rape the willing," he said, a satisfied smile on his face, lying on his back. Richard lit another True.

"Have you been smoking for a long time?" I asked.

"Since I was thirteen."

"Have you ever tried to stop?"

"A couple of times. Once I joined SmokeEnders." Richard slipped on his underwear and walked over to the closet. He picked up a jar large enough to hold a fetus in formaldehyde. It was filled with water and cigarette butts. "Every time I smoked, I was supposed to dump the butt into this jar for a month. Not a pretty picture, is it? The smell is horrific."

Richard lived in a single-room occupancy, a holdover from the twenties, when Greenwich Village was filled with writers and artists. His apartment was on the sixth floor, in the back. He had two windows—one on the side, with a view of a few large trees and the neighboring building, and the other at the back, by the fire escape. A gentle breeze blew through the windows, lightly rustling the curtains. I could hear a brat screaming in the building next door.

"I'm hungry," I said.

"Let's get dinner ready." We dressed and made burgers in the kitchen down the hall. Richard filled me in on his background, an oral résumé as application for the position of prospective boyfriend. Richard was an orphan, adopted at nine months. He had just turned thirty. He had written a few plays in his early twenties; one of them had been produced off-off-Broadway to good reviews. For the past couple of years he had been blocked. Richard had a secretarial job at a nonprofit theater-development foundation. He had started drinking heavily during the success of his second play. He had been an alcoholic for five years before joining A.A. Five years ago he had attempted suicide, throwing the *i ching* and slashing his wrists in the pattern that the sticks fell. A particularly acerbic playwright-friend of his who had visited him in the hospital told him that to do it right, you had to cut along the veins, not across them. Now Richard was stabilized on tricyclic antidepressants. As a side effect, he found it difficult to urinate in public. Richard had gone home for lunch that day in order to pee.

I was heartened that Richard was so forthcoming with me. I wanted to reciprocate in kind, but I had hardly any outlandish stories to tell about myself. The usual difficulties with my mother. A father's death when I was nineteen. A history of mental illness on both sides of my family, leading me to the conclusion that I must never have children (but then the doctors had told me that I was physically incapable of bearing children, due to a serious lack of ovaries). In short, an average upbringing, quite undramatic in many respects. I was a timid child. I always buckled my safety belt and drove below the speed limit, stopping for school buses, pulling over for sirens. My drinking capacity was two beers. I voted in every primary. I always mailed my rent check on time, along with my phone and utilities bills. I called long distance after eleven P.M. I used exact change on the bus. I didn't talk to strangers. I brought my trick-or-treat candy to the school to check for razor blades and pins and strychnine. I gave a quarter every week from my allowance to the United Jewish Appeal cans at Hebrew School. I practiced the piano for an hour every day. How would I ever be worthy of a relationship with someone as marvelously fucked-up as Richard?

We quickly settled into a routine. I'd go over to his place once or twice during the week and on Fridays and Saturdays. We made recipes, doubling the ingredients from *Fearless Cooking for One*. Richard did his Julia Child French-chef imitations, basso profundo. "Mince two cloves of garlic."

"I hate that word, *mince*."

"Fry in a pat of butter. Now, for the sauce, we add a little flour and just a touch of wine." Richard mimed pouring in a jug of Gallo.

"C'mon, you wore the apron *last* time. Isn't it my turn?" I pleaded. We alternated active and passive roles in fucking, according to the imaginary scorecard above the bed. We usually used poppers. About oral sex Richard was halfhearted. He was mildly amused at my extreme attachment to his chest. "Hey, Richard, whatsamatta you? You a homosexual, right?" I swaggered in my best Stanley Kowalski. "So how come you ain't sensitive?" With that I flicked his nipple. "Jeez, what a waste!"

"I'm an ass man," he said evenly, "and you're into tits."

I had fantasies of walking arm-in-arm with him through the Shopwell on Sixth Avenue, merrily prancing through the aisles, lingering far too long in the fresh produce, debating over zucchini or cucumbers, bickering in the meat department, making up at the ice-cream case. Instead, after work my stomach was always growling. Richard hated the six o'clock crowds, so we spent as little time there as possible.

Richard sent me postcards with out-of-context headlines affixed in saucy counterpoint, my billets-doux. "Moon over New York" read one, a photograph of three construction workers atop the World Trade Center, bending over for the camera. I bought him a copy of *Anal Masturbation* magazine in honor of Yom Kippur.

He came over to my apartment only once. He didn't like it. Ninth Avenue was too noisy for him. Richard thought I should invest in indirect lighting, maybe paint the walls peach, make it a little cozier. Sure I was a slob, but he wasn't much better. He didn't spend the night.

Sleeping with Richard was complicated because his bed was a

single. Filled with the optimism that only newlyweds have, we walked over to Fourteenth Street and bought a foam mattress that Richard stored beneath the bed. On the nights I stayed over, he'd take it out and place it on the floor next to his bed. We'd cover it with a sheet, a joint domestic chore. I'd sleep on the floor because Richard had a bad back. He'd dangle his hand down at his side, and I would hold it for a while. I made jokes about being his faithful Indian companion, sleeping at his feet.

Once in a while we'd go to the roof and Richard would set up his telescope, a heavy red globe with a small stalk for a viewer. "Look at the stars, so vast, so far. Imagine, it takes light-years to travel here from the nearest galaxy," Richard rhapsodized.

I tried, but I couldn't focus clearly with my glasses on, and without them, the sky was a blur.

"There's Jupiter, and there's Saturn," I bluffed. "And look," I said, goosing him on the ass, "there's Uranus."

"We're just a blink of the eye in the time scale of the universe. We're really inconsequential. There are so many planets out there, some of them habitable. Do you think there's any intelligent life in the universe outside of on Earth?"

"Just rubber checks. That's where all the bounced checks end up. Flotsam and jetsam of the universe. Also farts. They rise through the atmosphere. Everything that rises must converge."

"Flannery O'Connor."

"Check."

"You are a cynic, aren't you?" asked Richard.

"Damned straight. The world is flat for all I care. What difference does infinity make to us? Are you absolutely sure that the stars aren't just pinpricks in the sky, a black sphere illuminated by a high-wattage light-bulb? What bearing does the creation of the universe and the nature of entropy have on us? Let's just go downstairs and screw." Since our relationship was primarily driven by lust, I didn't want to let philosophy get in the way.

"What about right here?" Richard began to knead my backside.

"On the roof?"

"Sure, why not?"

"Congratulate me, B.J. Tonight's our anniversary." Dennis and I were dining at the Big Wok on Seventh Avenue.

"What do you mean?"

"Me and Nathan. Three weeks. It's our third anniversary."

I made retching noises.

"Sauce gotcha?" asked Dennis. "Perhaps you need some real sauce to wash it down?" With that he took out his flask with a flourish.

"No, just the sentiment. I'll get over it."

"So how come it's been so long, B.J.? You've been neglecting me," Dennis accused, shaking his forefinger at me like a metronome, making clucking noises.

"I've been spending a lot of time with Richard."

"So when do I get to meet him?" asked Dennis, twirling his sesame noodles on chopsticks as skillfully as if they were spaghetti, starting to crochet a pair of baby booties, then thinking better of it, aiming for the mouth and piercing the void, filling the hole. This was the hangar, and this was the plane.

"I don't know." Richard was at his home away from home, the Sheridan Square Gym. Dennis and I were going to meet Nathan later.

After dinner we walked down Christopher to the West Side Highway, an elevated fossil of a roadway scheduled for imminent demolition.

"So how's Rachel doing?" queried Dennis.

"She's a mess. I keep telling her she's better off without Christopher, she's worth a hundred of him, and then she breaks into sobs. I tell her she should start dating, go out and have a good time. She just stays at home with that infernal *Joy of Cooking*. For a while I was afraid she was going to commit hara-kiri by eating one of her own concoctions. Amazingly enough, her culinary skills have improved since he left her."

"That's a shame. I really like Rachel. Poor thing."

"What's odd is that she seems twice as well-organized as before. I mean, she puts in overtime at work, her apartment is always immaculate, she goes to exercise class twice a week. I don't know how she can do it. Last month she took the L.S.A.T.'s and almost got perfect scores. She applied to four schools. Hopefully, she'll start in January."

"Well, if it gets her mind off Christopher, I guess it's just as well."

"I guess."

Dennis stopped. "Here we are," he said.

"What's this place called, anyway?" I asked.

"The Cockring," replied Dennis.

"You mean the 'Ring," I whispered, sotto voce, reluctant to pronounce the first syllable in public, even though we were in the heart of gay Greenwich Village. Across the street, outside Badlands, a group of men stood drinking their beers. We walked in and paid the nominal cover. Nathan was nowhere to be found. The Cockring consisted of several bars, smoked mirrors, strands of white lights along the walls, and a sunken dance-floor. A disco ball revolved slowly above the empty dance-floor. It was nine-thirty, early for a Friday night. The crowd was ethnically mixed. At the bar at the entrance a pair of nondescript men in jackets and ties morosely nursed their vodka gimlets. Briefcases at their feet, they had come hours ago directly from work. A Latino in an abbreviated muscle-T danced alone with uninhibited grace.

Nathan appeared, a light-skinned black. "Hey, good to see you," he said, kissing Dennis on the lips. "Sorry I was late. I was just talking to my friend Pedro in the DJ booth. You two must have slipped in while I wasn't looking." Dennis introduced us. Nathan gave me the once-over. I returned the gaze sharply. His features were delicate; he had the bone structure of a professional model. Nathan's body was linear, willowy limbs unfolding like a measuring stick. We shook hands. Nathan took out a joint, lighted it, and offered it to me and Dennis. I looked at Dennis. He shook his head. I did the same. Nathan shrugged and took another hit. Dennis sipped his traditional Dewar's on the rocks. I was drinking Heineken.

We went to the dance floor and danced together, the three of us. Irene Cara shrieked "Fame" through the sound system. After a few songs, hot and sweaty, I took off my shirt. Dennis followed suit. Nathan remained clothed. Sweat flowed across my chest. Dennis departed to take a leak. "Tiny tanks," he explained. I danced with Nathan alone. He moved to hold me. Our bodies accidentally collided at the hips. Next to us two short white clones danced, mustaches glistening, eyes dark brown, ablaze. One held the other at the waist, alternately bumping and grinding into his ass with his pelvis, simu-lating humping him. The guy in front passed his companion a hand-kerchief soaked in ethyl.

"You're a real cute guy," said Nathan. I was annoyed. If I were taller, people wouldn't say I was cute.

"Thanks," I said noncommittally.

"Let's get together some time," said Nathan. He slipped a piece of folded paper into my pocket. Dennis rejoined us.

"Glad to see you're getting along so well," said Dennis.

I wanted to tell him Nathan was a mistake. Instead, I kept my eyes on the dance floor. In my head I prepared the condolence speech I would deliver in two or three weeks when their affair was over. Nathan was attractive but certainly not compelling enough to risk my friendship with Dennis. Maybe if he was my dream date, my exact physical type, I'd do it once on the sly. No. It wasn't worth it. "I feel pretty tired. I think I'd better go now," I told Dennis. "I've got a lot of errands to take care of early Saturday morning. Oh, look. Someone must have given me his phone number when I wasn't looking."

"Can I have it for future reference?" joked Dennis.

"Naah, I'll just toss it." For Nathan's benefit I tore it into a thousand pieces and scattered it over the dance floor like confetti. "It was nice meeting you," I said to Nathan's hands. "Talk to you soon," I said to Dennis, and I departed.

A History of Insanity on Both Sides of the Family, or Why I Have Always Been Attracted to the Mentally Ill

Call me a Venus's-flytrap for emotional cripples. Social work was my destiny. As young as nine I counseled my sister's rejected Barbie dolls. Their nude, inflexible bodies before me, I held seminars on self-esteem for their benefit: My sister Sheila's fickle desires had nothing to do with them personally. I encouraged them to denounce the callow subjugation of women and switch from heels to flats. They stood there lifeless on tiptoes. Sheila, aged eleven, had gone on to bigger and better things, an E-Z-Bake oven with a one-hundred-watt light-bulb as the heating element. Late at night, when Sheila was asleep, I stole into her room and baked hash brownies for our consciousness-raising sessions in it.

At the school playground the nerds and geeks would cluster around me as I lectured on spiritual disenfranchisement and the virtues of nonconformity. They applauded enthusiastically, knocking together the slide rules attached to their belt loops in their excitement, toppling the glasses precariously balanced on the bridges of their noses.

My sister, my father, and I sat in Sheila's room on Saturday mornings, curtains drawn, lights out, and watched the cartoons in rapt attention. It was always my father who laughed the loudest. I attempted to explain the semiotics of George of the Jungle, feckless would-be Tarzan, forever crashing into the nearest tree. My sister shushed me. My mother, looking in scornfully, unable to understand my father's fascination, ridiculed his interest, trying to entice him to a household chore such as mowing the lawn or oiling the particle accelerator my father had set up in the backyard in the hopes that one of us kids would grow into a physicist. My mother, a stickler for neatness, insisted that Father change the screens every two weeks. Sheila and I were responsible for polishing the brass and crystal chandelier that hung over the dining-room table.

Once a month we took the family jalopy to visit Aunt Ida in the Cooperstown Home for the Criminally Insane. She had always been envious of cousin Sylvia's flaming-red hair. When Clairol had proved ineffective, she had set the boardinghouse in which she had lived on fire. At twelve I explained R. D. Laing's theory of insanity as a normative process. She listened patiently, playing a composition of her own invention on the spoons. When I finished, she had no questions. Afterward we'd go to the Baseball Hall of Fame across the street.

My father complained of worms when I entered high school. There were worms slowly slithering through his brain. Sheila, who had changed ever since she had gotten her first period, wanted to sleep late on Saturday mornings. She put the pillow over her head and lay hidden under the covers as my father took his customary position to watch the Saturday-morning cartoons. "For chrissake, can't you get your own TV?" she snarled as Father guffawed. My mother was chasing a bat down the hall with a broom and could not be disturbed. Then Father clutched his head and moaned softly.

Gleefully I sat on the floor of the dining room, next to the rusted piano, systematically making my way through the Encyclopaedia Britannica. The soft light of morning made rainbows through the crystals of the chandeliers. I was on Volume 12, "PSYCHOTHERAPY" to "RAVING LUNATICS, FAMOUS." I replaced my earplugs with fresh beeswax, licked my finger, and turned the page.

· 10 ·

October

One of the six thousand seven hundred and forty-three things wrong with our relationship was that Richard and I were never able to have commonplace, run-of-the-mill orgasms. It was always Sturm und Drang, with periodic flashes of lightning and the Valkyries on the stereo. How could Richard insist on Wagner when he knew I was born Jewish? Sex was always a big production, with Busby Berkeley choreographing a multimillion-dollar extravaganza with the June Taylor Dancers, climaxing with Ann Miller tapping on an over-size Campbell's soup can at six hundred beats to the minute.

What ever happened to casual sex? In my dreams I lazed through *Cosmopolitan* for beauty tips, eating chocolate-covered cherries, while Richard ploughed me without apparent enthusiasm—me, a firm believer in retaining my sense of irony at all costs, even during the most intimate of acts. The problem was, I was used to fast-food sex, and the sudden change to gourmet French (or to be precise, Greek) perturbed my system.

Richard, needless to say, demanded complete fidelity.

"I can't even sleep with Carlo if he lets me?" I pleaded.

"You little shit, are you talking about Carlo Montagna?" Richard was irked.

"You know him?"

"That filthy whore is a slut on wheels." My ears perked up. "Miss Montagna slept with my last boyfriend," he hissed.

"So what's wrong with that? Hasn't every male homosexual in Greenwich Village slept with everyone else at one time or another?" And why not with me?

"The timing. Miss Montagna defiled the conjugal couch while I was asleep in the bedroom."

"Oh." I suppose Richard had a point there.

"So if I ever catch you've been with Carlo," said Richard, "you can say good-bye to your balls."

I looked down, grimaced, gave up. "You win. No Carlo for me."

I fucked Richard for a while from a standing position; he bent over, hands against the wall for support. I withdrew and we switched positions, me on my stomach on the bed, he from behind. One hand gripped my neck as he slowly entered me. It was always difficult at the start. Another snort of poppers and I craved him. The pain became pleasure after four inches (this I knew from the measuring rod along my anal canal). I tried hard not to come first; after I ejaculated, I lost all interest. I tried not to move much; Richard warned me he would lose his erection if I did. Afterward we showered together. I accused Richard of not being clean "down there." "What do you expect, rose water?" he replied.

Nonetheless, it was good practice, sex on a regular basis. After a few weeks I realized that I had made love with Richard more times than with anyone else in my life. Back in California, where I came out, I was lucky to get a one-night stand. In most cases I'd have an afternoon quickie, and that was all.

Richard was much less inhibited than I was. I'd call him on the phone at eleven. "I'm beating off; I'll call you back in a few minutes," he'd grunt into the phone, and then hang up. If someone ever caught *me* masturbating on the phone, I'd never admit to it. I'd furtively continue my anguished jerkings, stealthily coming, all the while carrying on a conversation about the most banal subject: the weather, the endless hostage crisis, the presidential debates.

Richard had fantasies of prison rape, barracks sex, copulation with freshly murdered El Salvador troops—the usual. I balked at them all. I closed my eyes and imagined I was in a far distant universe a long, long time ago.

One day Richard broached the topic of S&M.

"Give it a try, B.J. It won't hurt—much, at least. You might like it. Here's some rope. Do what comes naturally."

I looped it and tied it together and started playing cat's cradle.

"Wrong," said Richard.

"*How dare you even think of S and M with me*, you evil cradle-snatcher, despoiler of infants!" I shrieked. "I am uncorrupted youth. Richard, I'm only twenty-three. Do not molest what's left of my innocence. Listen, I've got it all charted out. At twenty-eight I become a tired old jaded queen and get into light S and M. At twenty-nine

I graduate to heavy stuff: fist-fucking, slings, the works. By thirty I'm dead. Let time take its natural course. Don't try to speed things up." I finished my speech with worldly exhaustion.

"C'mon, B.J., it's no big deal. It's just theater in the mind. Role-playing. Let's pretend. It doesn't mean anything."

I remained resolute in my refusal.

Richard shrugged his shoulders and gave up.

When you finally found your perfect bodybuilder, what did he want to do? Go to the gym and work out. Once Richard had done his best to get me to drop most of my friends, he returned to his gym with a vengeance, knowing he no longer had any competition. Our schedule changed. He wanted to see me only once during the week aside from weekends. More than that would conflict with his work-outs. Richard was bulking up, working on his lats, his tris, his abs. My desire for Richard remained constant. I craved him for sex continually. I dropped over uninvited, to be rebuffed. "I'm in training tonight; I can't," he explained. Crushed, I spent the next few hours barhopping, eventually ending up with a sleaze-bucket who lived on the hideous Upper East Side. He enticed me over to his apartment with the promise of MDA. "I'll show Richard," I thought. How did he expect me to remain completely monogamous if he wouldn't satisfy me himself? I had never taken any drugs more exotic than hash except for three years ago, when I had split half a tab of acid with my straight friend Bob in Pasadena, California, the night before the Tournament of Roses Parade.

My overeager and underweight sleaze-bucket was named Dominick; he designed windows at Henri Bendel's on Fifty-seventh Street—partially clad mannequins tearing off each other's negligees. Dominick wore snug, green khakis ripped at the back pockets, with an assortment of key-chains, handkerchiefs, and handcuffs; his shirt, opened to the waist, revealed a matching set of nipple rings. This reminded me I needed to replace my shower curtains. His apartment was a tasteful disappointment, clashing with his tawdry appearance. Autographed publicity stills of famous fag-hags now reduced to guest spots on soap operas (a friend of his did wigs for TV, he explained) decorated the entranceway. A framed labia by Georgia O'Keeffe was on the wall. The bulletin board in the kitchen overflowed with invitations to discotheques, including opening night at a new club called The Saint in the East Village. We sipped our cans of Bud and waited for the MDA to hit. We went to the bedroom too soon: I didn't feel

the effects. The closet bulged with an assortment of costumes: policeman, utilities repairman, and fireman. I saw a strapless black gown
in the corner, a pair of stilettos discreetly hidden on the floor.

He opened the drawer of the captain's bed, which was filled with
toys that he proffered. I refused. The sex was messy, unsatisfactory.
I was extremely disappointed. It was like the time I was in college
when I went home for Passover and three Jewish friends and I went
for a furtive midnight donut-run. The donuts turned out to be lousy.
Wasn't sin supposed to be fun?

We didn't exchange numbers. My body started to tingle as I walked
home across the park. That night I didn't get to sleep until three; the
following morning I came down with a bad cold, severe enough to
miss a day at work at my new job.

When I saw Richard the following Saturday, my cold was practically gone; nonetheless, I unwittingly gave him my remaining germs.
His cold turned to flu; he stayed home from his hateful secretarial
job for a week. Guiltily and at the same time resentfully, I tried to
nurse him to health—guilty because I got the cold while tricking and
Richard would skin me alive if he ever found out, resentful because
Richard wasn't the best of patients and I doubted he would reciprocate. When I had another outbreak of herpes, he didn't even see
me for five days. Florence Nightingale in blue jeans, I stopped over
during lunch and made him Progresso chicken soup and grilled-cheese
sandwiches, burning my forearm on the skillet in the process. Richard
lay in bed, pale, weak, a tray on his chest, playing game shows on
television with one hundred million other housewives. I cursed the
frying pan.

"I'm bored," he complained. "I'm sick of being sick. Could you
scratch my back a bit?" I removed the tray with the half-eaten sandwich and the untouched soup as he turned around. I scratched between the shoulder blades. "Harder," he implored. I did my best to
satisfy him.

"Is there anything I can get for you?" I asked on my way out,
lunch hour over.

"You're leaving me alone so soon? Don't go just yet. Give me a
hug." I went over to him, kissed him on the forehead, and gripped
him tightly. "Could you pick up a carton of Trues? I'll pay you back
next Friday on payday."

"I can't buy you cigarettes," I said. "That would be like buying an addict heroin. I won't be a party to your self-destructive

habits. Besides, won't they card me at the newsstand?" I had never bought cigarettes for anyone and had no intention of getting them for Richard.

"Come on, just this once," Richard whined.

"Don't make me do it."

"OK." He relented. "How about some toilet paper, some milk, and a loaf of bread?"

"Sure."

"And could you get some cookies? The Archway oatmeal kind?"

"No problem."

"And maybe some Häagen-Dazs? Strawberry, please. If they don't have that, then vanilla."

"I'll see what I can do."

"And I think I'm running low on coffee, too. Maxwell House, drip grind. Get two pounds, if it's not too much trouble; I think you can save money over the one-pound can."

"I'm on my way," I said before Richard could add to the list. Another errand to run after work before I came over to make Richard dinner. I hated errands. At least it was Friday. The weekend would be easier. I didn't want to be late for work. It had been only a month. I was afraid my boss would discover that I was completely incompetent and justly fire me. I felt this way with any new job. Everything I did seemed to take too long. I was writing computer programs in a structured, high-level language. The work was slow and meticulous. I ran my jobs over and over again, trying to get them right. Eventually I discovered bugs that in retrospect were invariably obvious: a missing semicolon, a misspelled variable name, an uninitialized constant. It was infuriating. After another slow afternoon I dutifully trudged over to the local A&P, filled a shopping basket with Richard's list, dinner, and a surprise or two. I faced the endless line at the checkout counter and read about suspects accused of shooting J.R. on *Dallas* in *The National Enquirer*. As a joke I actually bought it for Richard to thumb through.

Someone let me in at the front door of Richard's apartment building. I figured I could surprise him. He heard me approach through the hallway. "Honey, I'm home," I said, miming standard television sit-com fare. Richard was lying in bed, resting, when I peeked in. "I'll just unpack the groceries and put on dinner," I said.

"What was that?" asked Richard, aroused from a deep sleep. I came over to give him a hug and noticed a cigarette still burning in the ashtray on the desk. Beside it was a carton of Trues. "Oh, hi. Weren't you . . . weren't you going to start dinner?" he said groggily. Richard was completely covered; the sheets were up to his neck.

"Are you cold? Should I bring the comforter?"

"I'm OK," he said. I smoothed the blanket over him and felt something hard at his feet.

"Richard, I think I'd better help you make the bed. It looks like your shoes are in it." I ripped off the covers. As I suspected, Richard was fully dressed.

He giggled. "Had you fooled, didn't I?" He walked over to the desk, flicked the ashes, and finished his cigarette.

"I spent twenty minutes in line shopping for you, and you're all right?"

"I guess I got better this afternoon. You wouldn't get me my cigarettes, so I went out and got them myself. I realized I was feeling better. But since you seemed to like coddling me, I decided to pretend this evening. You didn't give me time to change into my pajamas. You should have called at the corner."

"You filthy bastard!" I was furious. "That's it! I'm walking!"

"Hey, wait a minute," said Richard. "I'm well now. You know what that means?"

"I couldn't care less what it means. You owe me twelve dollars and forty-three cents."

"It's nookie time!" Richard patted me on the ass.

"You think you can bribe me with your sexual favors, you cheap hussy, you," I spat out. "I'm incorruptible. You owe me an apology *and* dinner *and* twelve dollars and forty-three cents."

"Sit down," said Richard.

"You're not getting out of this one that easy," I said.

"OK, I'm sorry! I was just kidding. It was only a joke. Here!" He gave me a coffee jar filled with dimes, nickels, and quarters. "It's yours! Come on, be nice now. I'll make dinner. I'll make . . . I'll make burgers." Richard looked at me with sad Keene eyes, brimming with what I suspected were artificial tears. His eyes were lethal weapons, retouched studio-portrait eyes. "Please don't leave me. I'm sorry for what I did, and I won't do it again. I just got so bored sitting here, alone, waiting for you to come home. I hate being sick. Please don't go. Stay."

My heart melted like the polar ice-caps would during a nuclear attack. "Hey, don't get so upset. Everything's going to be all right.

I'm here; I'm with you," I said, hugging Richard, rocking him against me as his tears flowed freely. "Everything's going to be all right," I said, holding him, looking at the wall, the reflection of his back in the mirror, the books on his mantelpiece, focusing on Sigmund Freud's *The Psychopathology of Everyday Life* and *The Interpretation of Dreams*. What was to become of us?

"I'm in love," said Dennis on the phone.

"Again? Who is it this time?"

"His name is Christian. We met through the ad in the *Voice*." After breaking up with Nathan, Dennis had once again placed his ad. "I just have this feeling this one's going to last."

"I think I heard this one before."

"So how's Richard doing?"

"I don't know. Already it seems more difficult than I would expect. I know they say you have to work at a relationship, but this is definitely hard labor."

"The good old Protestant work ethic. Stick with us Catholics. We got guilt; we got confession; we got just about everything."

"I'll stay with the atheists, thank you."

"Suit yourself. You don't know what you're missing."

"Maybe my problem is I want the honeymoon first—you know, months and months of marital bliss, followed by inevitable compromise, concessions, adjustments, and change. I know some guys who bail out after the first sign of difficulty and easily slip into a new relationship. I don't think being madly in love is too much to ask for, do you? But I really don't have any long-term relationships to compare it to. Do you have any advice?"

"Have you checked out Ann Landers's pamphlet on the subject, *Love and Sex and How to Tell the Difference*?" asked Dennis.

"I already know; they're mutually exclusive," I said matter-of-factly. "With Richard, I wanted moonlit dinners, and what did I get? Sodomy on the roof, that's what."

"Doesn't sound too bad to me," said Dennis.

"Anyway, enough about me and Richard. Tell me about what's-his-name."

"Christian."

"Yeah, Christian—what's his story? For starters I figure he's not a son of Abraham and Moses."

"Correct. As I was saying, we met through my ad in the *Voice*.

We had a nice quiet dinner at Trilogy. He said he wasn't into the gay scene. Chris is blond, slender, wears thick glasses and a diamond pinkie-ring that's more Jersey Mafiosi than gay hairdresser. We had a long chat and got to know one another. He's kinda sweet, you know? He's pretty shy. I did my napkin tricks, he broke up, the ice was broken, but still, he was a little reserved. It was like he had this secret from me he was afraid to tell. What could it be? Barnyard buddies? A penchant for women's lingerie? At this point I was half smitten, charmed by his childlike motions and the fact that he was nervous, sweet, and innocent. After dinner we walked to his car. He'd parked under the West Side Highway. It was a Cadillac. We sat in the car, and he told me he had a confession to make." Then Dennis started laughing. "I'd been expecting something all along. Naturally I was the perfect person to unburden one's soul to; you know that." Dennis guffawed. "So Chris told me—" Dennis, laughing, lost his place. "Chris told me—" He could barely breathe by now. "Chris told me that he was a church organist. Most guys he met thought this was too far out, positively antediluvian. They couldn't handle it. They thought it was ridiculous. They dropped him. So that's when I told him I was a priest."

"On the first date?"

"On the first date."

"You didn't with me," I said resentfully.

"Every rule has an exception. It's been nothing but wine and roses since. I want you to meet him. Maybe we'll get together this Saturday."

"Better Friday. That's when Richard works out."

"OK, on Friday then. I know you'll really like him, B.J." As it turned out, when I met him on Friday, I didn't particularly, but if he made Dennis happy, what was I to say? It wasn't anything specific I disliked about Chris other than his name, his Cadillac, and his pinkie ring. It was just that we didn't have that much in common. Secretly I was disappointed. I thought Dennis could do much better. I felt like his mother, rejecting prospective suitors as unworthy of his affections. But I sensed they were getting along fine and easy—sharing private jokes and the like. Chris was eager to meet me, afraid to disappoint, trying to please me, shy yet jealous, knowing Dennis and I shared a past.

I silently gave them my nonsectarian, nondenominational, antireligious blessing. "Be fruits and don't multiply."

*   *   *   *

"I need a cat," said Richard one day.

"I understand. I'm a cat person myself." I imagined Richard, my massive hunk, sheltering a tiny kitty in the cradle of his arm. Ferdinand the bull sniffing flowers in the field. We were in bed; Richard was smoking his postcoital carton of Trues. "You could probably find one by checking for notices in the neighborhood. Someone is always giving away kittens."

"I want to get one at the Humane Shelter, one they're about to destroy."

"Have you had cats before?"

"Sure. A couple. When I was growing up, we had a tiger-striped tabby called Isadora." I pictured a cat entangled in a long, trailing silk scarf, springing into action, pouncing dramatically in modern-dance poses.

"Our cat was named Sandy. My sister, Sheila, liked to pick him up by his forepaws, like he was standing, so his feet barely touched the ground. He'd go crazy trying to scramble away, his cute little feet doing circles in a furious dance. 'Look,' she'd say, 'Sandy is doing bicycles.' I got a camera from a comic book for a dollar ninety-five when I was eleven. It was supposed to be the smallest camera in the world! You could fit it in the palm of your hand. Film and processing were expensive, of course. I took pictures of Sandy constantly, hundreds it seemed. They all faded away."

"My greatest regret in life was abandoning Amanda, my calico. I was with my first lover, Marty."

"The one who drove you to drink?" I questioned, having heard parts of the story, but always confused when it came to names. I could barely keep the names of my ex–potential boyfriends straight, and Richard had averaged one ex-lover a year for the past nine years.

"That's the one," concurred Richard, "my first lover. Marty wanted to go to England and France for a few months. I was between jobs. I couldn't find a place for Amanda to stay for a few months. Then Marty suggested putting her to sleep. I was torn. I was in love with Marty, and I had always wanted to go to Europe. I wrestled with my conscience for a week. Amanda would feel no pain; she wouldn't even know what was happening. So—so I did it. I went to the Humane Society. I felt terrible. I couldn't sleep for weeks afterwards. She surfaced in my dreams, that little sad face, the whiskers, the eyes looking at me, forlorn." Richard stopped. He couldn't go on.

I took the back of his hand and patted it, saying, "There, there, Richard, everything's going to be all right."

"I really need a cat," said Richard.

"Fine. We'll get you a cat."

"Uh . . . I'm a little short on cash now. Could you lend me the money, just until payday?"

I bristled. "Now, Richard. You already owe me eighty-five dollars and seventeen cents."

"Make it an even hundred fifty."

"You know money is a touchy subject with me. I'm still suffering the aftereffects of two years of abject poverty, otherwise known as graduate school." When I was growing up, my family had funny ideas about money. We never got an allowance. My mother said she would give Sheila and me an allowance if we cleaned our rooms up every day for a week without her asking us. We never did. My record was four days in a row. My father would slip us a few dollars if we asked for it, but we'd have to tell him exactly what we wanted it for. They grew up in the Depression. My mother reused tea bags, drying them out on a plate first. Once we complained the milk was sour. She tried to slip it into the butterscotch pudding, but we could tell. "Let me think about it," I told Richard.

"I need a cat now!" said Richard.

"Just give me a little time."

"OK, forget it," he said. "Forget I even asked you. I tell you the most painful thing I've done in my entire life, and you're counting pennies. It would be my luck to be stuck with a boyfriend who's a tightwad."

"Why don't you come out with it and accuse me of being a cheap Jew?"

"Oh, now he gets on his high horse and accuses me of being an anti-Semite! Let's just drop it. I don't need your money. I'll find a way."

"Jesus, look at the time. It's ten o'clock. I'd better go home now," I said to Richard, hopping into my pants.

"There's the door. What's your hurry?" said Richard in a jaded Bette Davis *Whatever Happened to Baby Jane?* imitation.

The next day Richard got a cat. He named her Jessica.

"I am not a junkie!" insisted Richard to the pharmacist. Richard held in his left hand an empty container of Valium, which the druggist had just returned to him.

"I'm sorry," said Mr. Johnson (I read his name from the it's-a-pleasure-to-serve-you nameplate on the lapel of his white chemist's jacket) in a voice that was the audio equivalent of a bottle of Maalox, smooth and slightly nauseating. "This prescription is for a controlled substance. It was filled three days ago, and it should have lasted a week. I'm not allowed by law to refill it." Mr. Johnson was balding; the top of his head glowed in the reflected light from the ceiling tubes.

"You're treating me as if I were an addict!" shouted Richard, near hysterics.

"His cat ran away three days ago, and he's very upset," I chorused in.

"I'm sorry for you, but there's nothing I can do. Good day, sirs," said Mr. Johnson, turning away to his vials and his scales.

"But . . . but . . . " Richard sputtered. I took him by the shoulder and guided him out.

"No use trying there anymore," I said.

"That's the last time I ever go to Rexall's," asserted Richard. "They treated me like a common junkie."

"It's OK. We'll just get that prescription for Valium filled somewhere else."

"It's no use," moaned Richard. "If they won't refill it, no one else will. What am I going to do? I'm never going to get to sleep!"

"Don't worry, I'll think of something," I hedged, running out of ideas.

"Warm milk and toast? A bedtime story? I know I'm going to be up all night worrying about Jessica," said Richard bitterly.

"I'm sure she'll turn up any day."

"I should never have left the window open. I just wanted to leave Jessica some air. She must have jumped to the fire escape."

"Richard, I've heard this a thousand times in the last few days. Don't blame yourself. It was an accident. Just be patient. She could be waiting outside your door this very second."

"So long as I find her before the super."

Cats and other domestic pets weren't allowed in Richard's apartment building. When the super came around to empty the trash cans, Richard stuffed Jessica into the closet. On Saturdays the coast was clear. He gave her full rein of the hallway. Jessica raced up and down, bounding with the full force of twelve pounds of mischief. She tore through the halls four or six times and then lethargically slunk back into the room, having exhausted her energy for the day, ready to curl up on the bed for a nap.

Jessica chose to eat a spartan diet of only dried cat-food. Richard tempted her with Nine Lives and other canned treats; she sniffed at them and then walked by, aloof, in a distinguished, dignified gait. She simply wasn't interested. Sometimes she'd jump to the window box of wilted flowers, animatedly watching the sparrows in the adjacent tree. As she leapt, Richard's heart would lurch. It seemed a physical impossibility, her massive body bounding with the grace of a ballerina. He couldn't comprehend how such an ungainly lump of feline irascibility could retain her balance and not overshoot to the depths below. Richard offered Jessica food from his own plate, seeing if she favored anything. To his surprise she was found to be partial to peas. Sweet Pea became a nickname, along with Weasel, describing how she would weasel out of your arms when you lifted her to pet her, Potato, recalling her physical bulk, and The Poop, for the enormous amount of shit she produced. "She's a regular poop machine," remarked Richard.

"If you'd empty out the box daily, I'm sure it wouldn't seem as bad," I suggested. "Like in restaurants, how the waiter constantly empties your ashtray to give you the impression that you're not chain-smoking."

When we took Jessica to the vet's for shots in a corrugated cardboard box, she clawed her way out, panting, scratching at everything in sight, slashing me on the chest.

"If she has rabies, I'll have her destroyed," I said to Richard. "Look at this; she's ruined my tan."

"Not on your life," replied Richard. When he had first seen her at the animal shelter, he had felt an immediate bond. They were both rejects, he told me. Richard had been passed from one set of foster parents to another until he was ten. No doubt Jessica had experienced comparable treatment.

"What I don't understand," I once said to Richard, "is how you can claim to have inherited alcoholism from your parents when you were adopted."

Now she was gone. Sadly, Richard and I had burger-deluxe platters at a grease-encrusted coffeehouse on Sixth. I paid the tab, and we made our way home. There was Jessica at Richard's door. "Jessica!" said Richard excitedly. "Sweetie! My little pumpkin! You're back!" Jessica, ever disdainful of public or private displays of emotion, allowed Richard to lift her, remaining limp, and let him pet her briefly before scrambling away. She had better things to do. She sauntered in as he opened the door, settled on the bed, and promptly went to sleep. "She's back! I'm so happy!" So was I.

How to Tell When Your Relationship Is on the Rocks

1. He forgets your birthday. He forgets your anniversary. He forgets your name.

2. He changes the locks. He neglects to notify you of a change of address. He gets married without sending you an invitation.

3. He is oblivious to changes: your new hair color, your pubic trim, your untimely overnight metamorphosis into a large cockroach.

4. You don't bother changing sheets before he visits. You don't bother changing sheets after tricking before he visits. You don't bother changing sheets after tricking with someone into wild scat scenes ten minutes before he visits.

5. He comes home five hours late, smelling of the cologne that the Barney's tie salesman was wearing and with a different tie.

6. He tells you at the last minute he can't make it bowling on Wednesday. He begs off from a movie on Saturday. He cancels a New Year's Eve engagement with you on December 30.

7. He complains he's too tired for sex.

8. He mentions your breath in public.

9. The poppers run out, and you know that last night the bottle was full.

10. He suggests a threesome and forgets to invite you along.

11. He never visits you at your apartment.

· 11 ·

November

The way I figured it, our relationship had been on the wane for the past six weeks and it had started only two months ago. Something had to give. As with any difficult action, we split up in stages, using the method of successive approximations. One day I told Richard that I didn't know if I was capable of love. He burst into tears. "This doesn't mean you're leaving me?"

"Of course not," I reassured. Now that he thought of it, Richard wasn't sure whether he was capable of love, either.

I was angry because Richard never came to my apartment. I felt I was being used, I was giving more than he was, I was tired of lying completely motionless while he fucked me, I wanted a little more involvement, I might just as well have been practicing yoga as he pounded away. I had lent Richard a total of one hundred twenty-six dollars and eleven cents and saw no prospect of ever getting back a penny.

Our "child," Jessica, treated me with increasing indifference. She was now sleeping with Richard at night, curled up into a ball on the pillow by his head. Jealous, I felt she had usurped me. On the sly, I tricked with two more faceless, failed fantasies. Guilt overwhelmed sex. What was the point of having a boyfriend if you couldn't cheat on him? Why even bother with unsatisfactory adultery? It was hard for me to move from my rapid-fire version of serial monogamy, in which each affair consisted of a single twenty-minute encounter, directly to sustained monogamy. Richard would say, "Don't leave at the first sign of trouble; don't be so fickle. Try to take things more seriously. Show a little bit of compassion."

My father, deranged also, had given me the same advice the day he tried to teach me pool downtown at the Veterans Administration Day Treatment Center. I was fifteen. My father, a manic-depressive, was stabilized under the drugs; the other guys there just seemed like genial crazies to me. My skin crawled as my father introduced me to his gimpy friends, one in a wheelchair, one with a stalactite of drool forming at his chin. I smelled Borax and medicinal residue intermingled with traces of vomit and urine. I only wanted to go home, back to my room, shut the door, and read *The Grapes of Wrath,* which bony Miss Constantine had assigned last week and was due in two days.

"Try to be a little more compassionate," said my father, painfully aware of my aversion. I scratched the back of my neck, picked up the cue stick, and tried an easy shot. As if in slow motion, I watched the white ball slowly rolling toward the nearest sack, teetering on the brink, then sucked in.

Breaking up is hard to do. I wanted to do it subtly, without hurting anyone's feelings—an anonymous telegram, a notice buried in *The New York Times* classifieds, a brief announcement on the news: "Richard Wilson and B. J. Rosenthal have severed all ties—details at eleven." Watching television, Richard and I would look at one another, shrug our shoulders, and dissolve the relationship, blameless both.

Methods of indirection were preferable by far to the direct, gaping-wound approach. I felt I had to wait for the right time to tell Richard. How could there be a right time? "I have some bad news. Better sit down. It's terminal cancer. No, just joking. We're only breaking up." Then Richard informed me that he dropped me the week previous. Curious. I must have been in a psychological coma from the effects, an amnesiac fog for a week. Relieved yet confused, I tried to reconstruct the actual event.

Then it all came back to me.

Richard sat on his chair. "We have to talk," he told me. "I feel guilty. I can't give you what you really need. You make me feel guilty by constantly asking me to come to your place. And you're not exactly what I had in mind, either. I think we should call it quits."

"Fine," I said slowly. And then it dawned on me. "But I thought that . . ." I didn't realize that breaking up would mean that we wouldn't be seeing one another. "Does this mean that we won't be seeing one another?" I'd lost a friend and a lover in one fell swoop.

"Not for a while, at least."

"Oh." Stunned, I got up, then sat down again. Tears started welling up in my eyes.

"I'm sorry I had to do this," said Richard. He was crying too. We hugged, and I departed. My brain felt cauterized. I started bawling full blast when I got to the elevator. The door opened; two people got out; I got on. How dare he dump me! I should have orchestrated this on the phone in my apartment. Now I had to take the subway home, and my mascara was running. Like Jessica, I had this thing about public displays of emotion: crying in public, bleeding in public, draining cysts and abscesses in public, picking noses in public. Surreptitiously, I stuck boogers on the ends of my fingertips and then tossed them onto the third rail of the subway. I didn't know that I would be rejected, *feel rejected,* when we broke up. I always wanted the people I hated to hate me too. I guess I just didn't expect it.

I called up Rachel, and she said, "Listen, you're better off without him. Want to come over and try my salmon mousse?" Dennis told me to cheer up and threatened to sing me a medley. I had leftover hamburger in tomato sauce on a bun, sloppy seconds, and turned on the stereo and listened to James Taylor.

The saddest moment in the world was when I realized I had run out of prospective boyfriends: The last possible boyfriend I had been courting turned out to be impossible; the would-be was a has-been, and the rest of the also-rans had already fled the country; the one on the griddle had not panned out, and there were no new ones lurking on the horizon. The future looked bleak and barren. At this point the best thing to do was join a new gym, move to another city, change jobs, or get a new 'do. Experiment with drugs. Go to Europe to forget. Redecorate. Try on some lingerie. Cry me a river. Then, go to the baths.

"You know, B.J.," said Dennis, spearing his asparagus with the proper fork, "a funny thing happened last week when I went to visit my mother at the nursing home. She's a little daffy now. Sometimes she thinks I'm my father, and sometimes she thinks I'm only ten years old. Anyway, I pull up a chair by the bed and say hello. She lifts her head, turns to see me. Her skin is glowing, almost like she has a fever. She asks me how my girlfriend is. Of course, I play along. I say, 'Just fine.' Obviously, she doesn't remember that I'm a priest. And she's really happy for me; she has a big smile on her face. You know, somehow I think she must have picked up on Christian—the fact that we're together and everything is working out. I kind of feel she approves." Dennis dropped his fork and swallowed the lump in his throat. "Hey, I got another. Are you ready for this?"

"Ready for anything," I said.

"OK, here goes. What do you get when you cross a donkey with an onion?"

"I give up."

"You're sure?"

"Come on, out with it already."

Dennis paused for dramatic effect. "You get a piece of ass that brings tears to your eyes." Dennis provided his own laugh track as he daintily dabbed at his cheeks. "Heard anything from Richard—ooops!"

"The love that dare not speak its name? Not a word. I guess it's all for the best."

"Yeah. Gee, I'm sorry how things ended up between you two."

"Well, that's the breaks. Looks like this year will end with at least you having a boyfriend. One out of two ain't bad."

"Now, B.J.!" Sliding his glasses down his nose an inch or two, Dennis peered over the top and gave me his "dumb fuck" look. "Don't give up! We have all of December to work on you." Dennis opened the left side of his tweed jacket like a hawker of stolen wristwatches on Forty-second Street. "Have I got a date for you!" He pretended he had an assortment of cards with names and addresses of suitable suitors. "Just tell me what you want. Tall, dark, and handsome? Short, pale, and grotesque? Gentile? Jew? We got 'em all. Take your pick! Name your dream date, and for a small nominal fee, a tiny donation to the charity of my choice, I hook you up."

"I prefer to sulk and moon for at least another week. And by then it will be time for the annual pilgrimage upstate. Familial duties. Thanksgiving."

"OK. Come December, you'll have prospects out of your ears."

"Thanks, Dennis. I don't need a yenta. I mean a pimp. I mean a marriage-broker. I mean a Miss Lonelyhearts."

"Up to you. Whatever you say. So I guess I won't see you until after your birthday?"

"I guess not."

"I'm thinking of getting you a dog."

"Don't you dare! I loathe the canine species!" I'd been bitten at least three times by dogs in my childhood. Once I was riding my bicycle to the local branch library. A collie on a leash nipped me on the heel, going through the skin. This was right after I'd read an article in *Life* magazine about a reporter who had been bitten by a bat and forced to go through a painful series of rabies shots. I didn't tell a soul.

"This one you'd like. He's really cute."

"Cease and desist with these threats!"

"OK, I'll lay off. Well, have a nice time up in Rochester."

"I'll survive."

"B.J.? Thank God you're home." Rachel sounded hysterical.

"What's wrong?" Now it was my turn to ask.

"You haven't heard? Turn on your radio for the eleven o'clock news. Some maniac went into a gay bar in the Village with an Uzi machine gun and went crazy."

"You're kidding." I sat down and breathed deeply.

"Would I lie about a thing like this? It's called the Ramrod. Six guys got shot, and it looks like two are dead already. I was so worried that you might have been there."

"There's nothing to worry about. I never go down to bars on West Street." Those bars were too low-rent for my taste. Right on the river across from Paradise Alley, they didn't exactly attract the type of guy who read Proust in his spare time. The only time I'd ever been to the Ramrod was on Gay Pride Day, and that was just to use the john.

"B.J., promise me you won't go back to that awful steam-bath place. I get worried when you tell me about going home with strange men." I was fiddling with the tuner, trying to get a station with news. Pat Benatar did "Hit Me with Your Best Shot." Finally, I found the right frequency.

"They've caught him. The streets are safe."

"They're never safe. B.J., I want you to promise me never to go to the Ramrod."

"Rachel, he's just a freak. It's not going to happen again. I can't live in fear."

"Better scared than dead."

"OK, I promise."

"I wish the world wasn't so mean." I could hear Rachel taking a bite of her dietetic brick candy.

"So do I, Rachel, so do I."

*   *   *   *

There was absolutely no possibility of sex for the duration of the annual pilgrimage. This was but one of the many restrictions I would face in the next four days. I bid a fond farewell to the stack of porno mags beside my bed. No need to bring one with me and secrete it under the pillow for my mother to "discover" when she made the bed. We'd already been through that once. I locked the windows, pulled down the blinds, turned on the answering machine, made sure I had my wallet, my keys, my toilet articles, my vitamins, my contact-lens paraphernalia, and I was off. As usual, I forgot to pack the shaving cream and bring tissues for the trip. My overstuffed backpack contained two magazines, several paperbacks, some socks, some underwear, a few T-shirts, a dress shirt, a pair of suitable slacks, a sweater, and a spare pair of glasses. Before leaving, I made a feeble attempt at straightening things up: tossing stray articles of clothing into my laundry bag, clearing the dishes from the sink, paying the bills that were visible among the heap of papers on the desk, dumping the garbage out back.

Laden with luggage, I trudged down the stairs, made one last check for mail, and then walked ten blocks south to Port Authority. I stopped first at the Citibank automated teller-machine to get eighty dollars for plane fare and incidentals. I was always tense, afraid I would miss the flight. The whores came on to me, but I walked past them as if I were wearing blinders; transformed from city-dweller to traveler, I thought the hustlers would mistake me for a tourist, a mark. Bristling, I strode briskly into the bus station, picked up a ticket for New Jersey Transit's express bus to Newark International, and took two escalators to the packed waiting-room. I was wearing my terrorist pants with twenty Velcro pockets and a red knit-acrylic ski-cap. Beneath my bomber jacket was a nasty Sex Pistols T-shirt. Nobody would dare talk to me in this getup.

At the airport all was chaos. I was taking People Express, a cut-rate airline that was cheaper than Greyhound. Long lines of people with mournful faces sat on their suitcases in the aisles. A woman screamed at a ticket clerk because her bags were routed to Cleveland by accident. I looked around for attractive men—a futile search. Why would one go to Rochester? I got my boarding pass and wedged myself between a mammoth, cigar-smoking gentleman and someone's Aunt Irene, serenely knitting. We boarded like cattle in somber groups. I grabbed a chair by the window over the wing, took off my coat, and bundled it on my lap. I left the overstuffed backpack on the floor, wedged between my feet. I tried to look as forbidding as possible to discourage anyone from sitting next to me. Since it was Thanksgiving, I had no such luck. I glared at the woman who sat beside me and put on my shades.

The flight was mercifully brief.

My sister picked me up at the airport. My mother, a basket case behind the wheel, rarely drove. She was home, cooking the turkey.

"Benjy! I'm so glad you're here!" She hugged me. I felt her large breasts larger still from estrogen: She was on the pill. Sheila wore oversized purple sunglasses. Her hair was streaked blond. Sheila, an inch or two shorter than me, was zaftig in her violet corduroy pants and blue fiber fill jacket. "She's on the warpath again." "She" was my mother.

"What's wrong?"

"What's always wrong? The way she treats Alexander is what's wrong!" Alexander was my sister's boyfriend, with whom Sheila was currently living in sin. Four years ago, my father had found the two of them in flagrante delicto. He had no recourse but to toss Alexander out of the house (the clothes soon followed). Alexander was persona non grata in the Rosenthal residence. I had been sure an accommodation would be reached after a year or two of probation, but my father died six months after the incident, suddenly, of a heart attack. Consequently, my mother felt it her duty to remain keeper of the flame. Firm and resolute, she refused Alexander entry to the house, forcing him to pick my sister up at the curb. My mother had always wanted Sheila to marry Howard Goldfarb, a nice Jewish boy from the suburbs who had aspirations of becoming an accountant. "*You* try to talk some sense into her," said Sheila. "She listens to you! I can't stand her attitude! She's so nasty to the man I love. She won't even invite him to dinner on Thanksgiving, and we've been going together for practically five years."

My natural inclination was to play devil's advocate. In arguments and disputes I tended to take the role of the proxy, the person who was not present. "But what about when Dad caught the two of you?"

"For godsake, that was *years* ago! I was a child! I made a dumb mistake. Do I have to spend the rest of my life paying for it? You were away in college. What did you know?" I had gone to school in Boston, and my sister had stayed home and gone to the local community-college, which was where she had met Alexander.

When Sheila was twenty, she drank like a fish and smoked like a fiend. "She's just a party-girl! All she wants to do is go out!" complained my mother in her shrillest voice. "Every night of the week! When is she ever going to get any studying done, I ask you. Look at her grades—pathetic. She's got potential; she's just lazy. When she grows up, she should have such ungrateful children! She doesn't know how I suffer." My poor mother, whose entire life was suffering. Her father had died when she was four, in a fire. Mom grew up during the Depression, always doing without a new dress. When her friends went to dancing lessons, she stood behind the counter of Schirmer's music store downtown and sold sheet music. Sandwiches on day-old bread for lunch, accompanied by bruised fruit, all in a recycled paper-bag. My poor mother, the "KICK ME" sticker permanently plastered to her behind.

"Benjy, when Dad died, you just came home for the funeral and went back to Boston the next week. I was stuck here. I really helped her out when she needed it. Did I get any thanks? She treats Alexander like shit. She always liked you better! Don't give me any recriminations! Did she disown you when you told her you were gay?"

I was living in California at the time. I found it necessary to place a continent between myself and the institutions of family and education before I could come out. I went to the Gay Pride Parade in Hollywood one year and mentioned it in a letter home, describing the silly pom-pom boys and the disco floats. The crowd for the parade was mixed, gay and straight. I wasn't necessarily saying anything. In my sister's next letter she wrote that Mom was hysterical, that she thought I was gay. I had no recourse but to inform her that her conjecture was correct. Mom had always taught me to be scrupulously honest. I can't say that what I did was completely devoid of cruelty—a way of striking back at 5,740 years of Jewish guilt. My letter was not the sort of letter you spent months writing and re-writing; I didn't recommend the appropriate literature, local counseling groups, or hot lines; I simple wrote back, "You're right." My father, safe in the grave, was not informed. I promised not to embarrass her in front of the rest of the family. When they asked at weddings if I had a special girlfriend, sometimes I tossed in Rachel's name to shut them up. "No, darling, I prefer to take it up the ass," I'd mutter to myself.

"You're not going to boycott Thanksgiving?" I asked Sheila, instantly regretting my question, for putting the idea in her head.

"I just might!" she said indignantly.

"For my sake, please don't. Thanksgiving is bad enough as it is for me. I don't think I could face it alone, without you to make it bearable."

She softened momentarily, then barked back, "Then don't give me any recriminations!"

I apologized. "OK, OK, I just wanted you to maybe understand her point of view a little. She's very conservative, you know. She's from a different generation, a different background, than you or me." Grimacing, I noticed my voice was attaining characteristics of the hideous local accent—the horrifying, flat, Rochester nasal. This was an entire community of speech-pathology. The mayor should have declared it a national disaster-area to obtain federal aid for emergency elocution-instruction. Also, I was no longer making any sense. How could I claim that my own mother came from a different background, the mother that raised me? For every day I stayed in Rochester, my intelligence quotient dropped another ten points. If ever I stayed too long, I feared I would become so stupid I would be rendered incapable of purchasing a ticket out of the place. In Rochester, Alzheimer's disease struck in the late teens.

Sheila dropped me off at Mom's. Alexander's car was in the shop, so she had to go pick him up after work. "You're not coming in, not even for a minute?" I asked.

"I'm late as it is."

"Well, thanks for picking me up at the airport. See you tomorrow, I guess."

"Your guess is as good as mine." With that, she backed down the driveway and was off, squealing rubber. I entered through the back door, which slammed behind me.

"Hi, Mom, I'm home," I announced.

"Hi!" she said brightly, waddling into the kitchen. Four foot ten, she stood on tiptoe to kiss me on the cheek. Mom was on a perpetual diet. She hid the sweets from herself in the kitchen cabinets. Mom wore large bifocals with Sophia Loren frames and a pastel polyester pantsuit that stretched over her abdomen. She had gone through seven lean years; this was evidently one of her full ones. She turned to present a soft cheek for me; I bent over to kiss her in return, skin gentle as down. Foundation, blush, and a trace of Chanel Number

Five blanketed her face. "So Sheila picked you up? You didn't have to wait too long? Is Sheila coming in, too? I thought I heard a car pull out just now."

"She has to go pick up Alexander."

"Oh," said Mom, tight-lipped. Subject closed for now. "So, how was the trip? Did they feed you on the airplane? Do you want me to make you a sandwich? You look good, Benjamin. Are you wearing your contacts much?" Two years ago she had prodded me into getting contact lenses. To improve your self-esteem, she had said. Subliminally, I felt she thought I was gay because I had low self-esteem. And with contact lenses, who knows? I might be cured.

"Not on the flight, Mom. I'm afraid the cabin pressure might mess me up."

"So, are you hungry? Do you want me to heat up some corned beef? It won't take a minute. How's your job? Did you get anything new for your apartment? Do you want me to get a dill pickle for you? I've got a jar in the refrigerator, already opened. It's no trouble. I've got fresh skim-milk, and there's some soda on the way to the attic."

"Mom, I just got in. I'm going to put my things down in the bedroom first." I walked down the hallway, dragging my backpack behind me, to my old bedroom.

That evening we sat together in the living room with the TV on. I was on the couch, thumbing through old *Time* magazines addressed to my late father. My mother had renewed several times without bothering to change the name.

My mother extracted information from me like teeth. She liked to talk. I didn't feel like opening up. In Rochester, among the heteros, I was always pretending on some level, always faking it. I couldn't really talk about the things that really concerned me: my recent disastrous relationship with Richard or my friend Dennis. Rachel was the only safe topic I had. My mother pummeled me with questions, tried to draw me out. I responded with curt answers tempered with moderate annoyance.

My poor mother, living alone. Would she ever remarry? So much to say and no one to say it to. When my father died, he was instantly canonized from "You crazy fool, keep it up and I'm going to have to send you back to Canandaigua," the local loony-bin, to "My dear wonderful husband, Solomon, may he rest in peace, who never gave me a moment's grief."

Suddenly, she burst into tears. "Right under my nose," she blurted, weeping. "Why couldn't they at least leave town? Why is Sheila so goddamned disrespectful to me?"

Always uncomfortable around tears, I sat on the couch, mute.

"It's like spitting in my face: living in sin with him, right under my nose."

Foolishly, having not learned the lesson with Sheila earlier that afternoon, I tried to elucidate, explain. "She's twenty-five years old, Mom. She's an adult. She can do what she chooses."

"Can't you see how much it is hurting me? She could at least have the decency to move to another town, but no, she has to insult me right under my nose."

"Are you worried about what people will say? They don't matter." I didn't understand what difference moving to another city would make. "Who cares about gossip? It's just petty people with nothing else on their minds."

"I don't care about the others. She's doing this to me." My mother dabbed at her eyes with Kleenex. "If Solomon were still alive today, he wouldn't allow it. He'd make them get married. It's disgusting! Like animals!" She spat. The vehemence of her distaste shocked me. "He's no good for her anyway. They go out to Bob's Big Boy and split it dutch treat. It's not right. When is he going to get a decent job? He'll never amount to anything. She has no respect for me!" My mother continued sobbing. At this moment I realized I would never be able to tell her about my personal life. If shacking up grossed her out, I was sure she didn't want to hear about sodomy on the roof.

"They're in love," I said.

"*Feh!* What do they know about love? All she knows is to hurt! It's bad enough they're living together, right under my nose!" At this key phrase that she repeated like a cue, on went the faucets. "He's not even Jewish!"

"You hardly go to temple yourself," I said, not able to contain myself.

"You, too, taking her side! Nobody ever takes my side! I'm all alone in the world!" My mother burst into another set of wracking sobs. "Well, go back to New York City. I don't need you here! Go on! Desert me! See what I care!"

"I didn't mean it," I apologized.

"Nobody ever takes my side. Everybody is against me. When you have kids . . ." At this there was another eruption.

(In Rochester, "gay" was never discussed, never alluded to. After my brief coming-out letter, about a week later I had made the regulatory, uncomfortable follow-up call, only because I'm human. "You got my letter?" I asked. "Yes," she said tersely. "Do you want to talk about it?" I asked. "Bad news," she said bitterly. "You always get bad news in the mail," she said softly, resignation in her voice. She realized there was no possibility for change, no hope for altering the future. This was not a phase. That was the last time we had ever referred to the matter of my sexuality.)

"Could you pick up Grandma?" asked my mother in the kitchen. The kitchen drawers and counters were littered with coupons and scraps of papers, dull pencils and soft, plastic pens from insurance companies; the doorknob held a year's supply of rubber bands. Several kettles were on the stove, simmering. The turkey basted itself in a paper bag in the oven. The silverware was in a jumble on top of the cabinet.

"Sure, just toss me the keys," I said.

She nervously rifled through her purse. "It's been making a funny noise. Be careful. Remember to warm it up before you leave, Benjamin. Last week it stalled again at the corner."

"Thanks," I said. I went out and hopped into the car, a luxury sedan that dwarfed my mother. First I had to push back the seat. Mom had moved it all the way to the front and placed two pillows on the seat so she could see over the dash. I waited for the car to warm up, fiddling with the radio. The weather forecast was for overcast skies, like three hundred and ten other days of the year in Rochester. I pulled out of the driveway and headed for Grandma's.

I parked across the street. She was sitting on the front porch, waiting, with gloves in her lap. Grandma was in her late seventies, slightly doddering, short and squat, with deep bags beneath her eyes. She wanted me to eat an apple dipped in honey she had wrapped in waxed paper. "Are you kidding? Mom would kill me! That would spoil my appetite for Thanksgiving. I just had lunch."

"It wouldn't hurt, just a taste," said Grandma. Born in Lithuania, she retained a heavy accent, although she had immigrated to the States when she was fifteen. I held her arm as we walked down the front steps slowly, one at a time. "No sense in rushing," she said. We plodded down the walk, and then I had her wait by the curb. I pulled up, opened the door for her, made sure she was buckled in. Her support stockings bunched up around her knees.

At home I took off her heavy red coat and placed it on Sheila's bed, our makeshift cloakroom. "Can I help you in the kitchen?" Grandma asked Mom.

"Look at you!" my mother said. She straightened out Grandma's stockings, then applied lipstick to the meek face. "Go sit in the living room and let Benjamin entertain you. Oh, Benjy, we needed some cranberry sauce, but I called and asked Aunt Maude to bring some. Tell Grandma about living in New York." Mom bustled in the kitchen, wiping off the table. The food was ready; she just had to clean up now.

Grandma walked to the living room. "I wanted to help. She said she doesn't need me," she moaned. "Oh, well."

"Make sure she sits in the chair with the good back," shouted Mom from the kitchen.

"Here," I said, pulling out the appropriate chair. The TV was on, *Miracle on 34th Street.*

"Do you like it in New York? It isn't too big for you?" My grandmother asked the same three questions. "You have a steady girl? Do you make enough for spending money with your job?" Animatedly, she thumbed through the advertising circular I gave her, a catalog of women's clothes. My grandmother didn't read English, only Hebrew and Lithuanian.

"My job is OK, I guess. I'm not seeing anyone special now. I'm doing fine."

"Oh, Benjamin, could you do me a favor? Come here," shouted my mom from the kitchen. I came. "Could you call Sheila and find out what time she's coming?"

"What time should she come?"

"I don't know. Four, maybe five? What do you think?"

My mother didn't want to call and risk speaking to Alexander. She took only incoming calls from Sheila.

I made the call. "She wants to know when I'm coming? When I feel like it. When I'm ready," said Sheila, and she hung up.

The relatives came one at a time, starting at 5:30. Aunt Maude came with two shopping bags: one with several cans of cranberry sauce and a salad in a Tupperware bowl, the other containing a pumpkin pie from Snowflake Bakery. Next was my cousin Bertha, whom I had had a crush on when I was in sixth grade and she was in fifth; now there was no love lost between us. She brought her friend-who-is-a-boy-but-not-a-boyfriend, Sid. He was far from svelte. One look at Sid and I calculated he would eat a third of the turkey. My uncle Reuben, always late, arrived at 6:30 with hurried excuses. "So how's New York?" asked Aunt Maude. She had grown up in Brooklyn and swore she would never set foot there again. Her son, Herschel, who lived in rural Michigan, was conspicuous in his absence.

At seven my mother felt she could wait for Sheila no longer. The table was set. In the kitchen she carved the turkey that ate Cleveland and several neighboring suburbs. Aunt Maude, offering to help, was relegated the busywork task of transferring condiments, filling up the pickle-and-olive tray. Soon we were all seated at the table, laden with turkey and salad and candied yams and the fruit-and-Jell-O mold and a string-bean casserole garnished with canned onion-rings. Sheila sauntered in wearing slacks and an artificial-silk print blouse with a bow at around 7:30. My mother, up and down like a top, constantly moving back and forth from the kitchen to replenish plates, saw her first at the door. "You couldn't wear a dress or makeup?" she hissed. Sheila tossed her hair and said that Alexander preferred her natural. "Thank God you were at least considerate enough to wear a bra. Go on, sit down; I'll fill your plate."

The relatives talked about food and illness, pregnancies and operations, cancers.

"Did you hear about Leona Meltzer? Cervical cancer."

"She's so young. It's such a shame. Pass the pickles, please."

"Could I have some of the juice?"

"What's the recipe, Selma?" Aunt Maude asked my mother. "It's really tasty!"

"It's just pink lemonade and cranberry juice from concentrate."

"The turkey's great! Could I have some more stuffing?"

"So, Benjy, you live right in the heart of the theater district? I bet you see a lot of shows."

"Some, Aunt Maude."

"Do you ever see any real stars walking down Broadway?"

"Woody Allen, once."

"Woody Allen! No kidding! Gee, that must be exciting."

"We have quite a lot of culture here in Rochester, what with the new Civic Center," said my mother. "There's the symphony; there's

Rochester Stage; we get Famous Artists, a different play every month. I saw Ann Miller in *Panama Hattie* a few years ago; she was superb."

"And it's not crowded like in New York."

"You've got the country just a few miles out if you want it."

"Could I have some more Jell-O?"

"Watch out! You almost spilled the salad dressing."

"It's Good Seasons," said my mother.

"Pardon my reach."

"While you're at it, could you pass me the margarine?"

"Does anybody want more rolls?"

"I'm really sorry that my boyfriend, Alexander, couldn't make it," said Sheila, "but he has a touch of the flu."

My mother, pouring gravy, glared at Sheila. The gravy overflowed onto the tablecloth.

"Shoot! Gosh darn it!" my mother cursed.

"Here," said Aunt Maude, passing her a napkin. "I'll go and get some seltzer water from the kitchen to clean it up."

"That's all right; I'll do it," said my mother, a Christian martyr of Hebraic origins.

"You're sure you don't need any help?"

"Sit down!" barked my mother. "I'll do it." She bustled into the kitchen and came back with a roll of paper towels.

For a moment there was an embarrassed silence. Sheila stuffed a pickle into her mouth. Uncle Reuben chewed unenthusiastically. I could hear my grandmother's dentures making sucking noises as she worked on a turkey leg. Then cousin Bertha announced that she and Sid had to leave after dinner; they were meeting friends for drinks.

"The stuffing is delicious, Mom," I said. A small light-brown spot remained from the gravy spill; she'd have to wash the tablecloth later that night.

"Cherry cheesecake! My favorite!" said Bertha when Mom brought out the dessert. Aunt Maude's store-bought pumpkin pie got second billing.

"It's no big deal. You just follow the recipe," demurred my mother, proud of her accomplishment yet unwilling to take undue credit. We all complimented her on the cheesecake.

"Delish," said Sheila. Thankfully, she didn't ask to take home a piece for Alexander.

Aunt Maude took "just a sliver" of both pies, then seconds of the cheesecake, begrudgingly. We all settled around the television set in the living room. Grandma yawned and asked, "If it's not too much trouble, could someone take me home now?" Every morning she got up at five; eight-thirty was late for her. Bertha and Sid left with Grandma, then Sheila, then Aunt Maude and Uncle Reuben. I asked my mother how to make the cheesecake. I was shocked to discover that Cool Whip was a key ingredient. I took another piece out of the refrigerator, trying to dislike it with my newfound knowledge, horrified at my evident lack of taste, my indiscriminate palate. Hard as I tried, I kept going back for more.

Friday was overcast, perfect weather for a visit to my father's grave. The local weather was always funereal. Dad died in '76, the year of the Bicentennial, the week that Howard Hughes kicked the bucket. Aunt Maude had called me at school with the news. "Sit down, Benjamin, I have terrible news. Your father died early this morning of a heart attack. It was quick. He didn't suffer." At Logan Airport, numb, waiting for my plane to Rochester, I tried to get drunk, thinking that this was what was expected of me. I felt I was impersonating a human being.

The ceremony was bitter and pointless to me. A pallbearer myself, wearing my two-toned pimp shoes with the six-inch heels, I tripped over a root while carrying the coffin. With six of us, the casket was lighter than I had expected.

Now I looked at the headstone, kicked a few rocks, tried to experience a feeling of loss. Nothing. Instead, I found myself looking at wreaths on neighboring graves, dried-up flowers that should have been tossed or replaced long ago.

On the way back to Mom's, I dropped by to say hello to my grandmother. She made me a chicken sandwich, toast from the fifties toaster on the counter, lettuce from the glass salad-bowl in the refrigerator. For dessert, homemade applesauce that was not to my taste. A piece of *kichel* buried in honey, not fresh, probably left over from Rosh Hashanah. I got the three questions again: "How's New York? Are you seeing a steady girl? Do you make enough for spending money?" She slipped me a dollar bill from her change purse. Then home for another dose of TV, Mom vacuuming in the background.

On Saturday I flew back. "I don't understand why you're not staying till Sunday," complained my mother.

"I've got things to do, you know," I said.

"Are you going to visit Grandma on the way to the airport?"

"But I just saw her yesterday!"

"She's not getting any younger, Benjamin. She's not going to be around forever."

"Come on, Mom, you know how nervous I get before plane trips." I had to be at the airport at least an hour early. Of all places, I didn't want to be stranded in Rochester. "Sheila is picking me up at two, and my plane leaves at three-thirty. There's not enough time! I've already seen her twice in three days; what do you want?"

"She's going to be dead for a long time," said my mother flatly.

Jewish guilt-trips could be tolerated up to a point, but here my mother passed the limit.

"No," I said quietly.

"OK," she said, the battle lost. Mom packed me some turkey breast for sandwiches in New York. We'd finished the cherry cheesecake between the two of us. At Sheila's honk in the driveway I gave Mom a peck on the cheek, thanked her for the hospitality, and left through the back door to Sheila's car.

The flight home was nothing to speak of. The New Jersey Transit bus approached the Lincoln Tunnel, curving to the right in a U loop. For just a moment I caught a glimpse of the New York City skyline to my left, shimmering light against the clouds and stars, a dramatic view of Emerald City. My heart leapt. I was home again.

Overwhelmingly horny, that night I picked up a burly cabdriver at Crossroads. The sex was less than satisfactory; after he came, he zipped up, not waiting for me to finish. "Got to run," he said. "The better half is waiting." I decided that given him and virtually any other person on this planet, the other would always be "the better half." On his way out, he took care to insult the apartment. "What are you, a high-school student? Get rid of the stuff on the walls. Get some throw pillows, indirect lighting. Work on this place. You're sitting on a gold mine!"

"I didn't realize you were a decorator, too," I said snittily.

That night I slept uneasily.

I had a nightmare so commonplace and realistic that it scared the shit out of me. I went to sleep with the window open, curtains fluttering in the breeze, light cacophony of horns and sirens, my midnight lullaby. At around two in the morning I could sense a shadow. An intruder stood over me, waiting. I was naked under the sheets. He had a wrench hanging from his belt loop. He hovered over me. I stared at him through closed eyes. He swayed in the wind and bent over.

He was going to rape me.

He was going to rob me.

He was going to maim me.

He was going to murder me.

I opened my mouth to shout for help, but nothing came out. I was paralyzed. I waited. He waited. Nothing happened. This was the scariest part.

I forced my eyes open and woke up. There was nothing. A shadow of a streetlight. The window was open. Everything was exactly as it was in my dream. Was it a passing truck? A lunar eclipse? I was frozen with fear. I felt as if I had been violated in the dead of night. I could not go back to sleep. I stayed up until dawn, reading Lévi-Strauss's *Tristes Tropiques*.

What to Do on Your Annual
Holiday Visit When Your Family
Disapproves of Your Sexual Preference
or Orientation; or You Haven't Yet
Told Them in Explicit Terms,
but You Suspect They
Would Disapprove, with the
Possible Exception of Great-Aunt Mary
and Cousin Harold, the Perennial
Bachelor; or You've Told Some
of Them but Not Others,
Perhaps Only Your Immediate Family
and Your More Attractive Nephews,
and Your Mother Has Warned
You That Grandpa Jake
Has a Weak Heart
and You Don't Want to Be
Responsible for a Coronary; or You
Suspect They Already Know, and
Although They Don't Approve
of It, They Tacitly Condone

Your Behavior on the Condition That It Never Be Brought Out into the Open; etc.

1. Avoid the issue. Change the subject. Talk about less volatile topics: religion, politics, money. Express an interest in Cousin Herb's stamp collection. Leave the room when marriage is discussed.

2. Invent an imaginary love-interest of the appropriate sex and species. Carry a wallet-sized photo of your "beloved" at all times. Usually, photo frames from Woolworth's will come equipped with suitable pictures. You may obtain snapshots using scissors and your favorite glossy magazine. Avoid, however, the photojournalistic rags under the mattress with the nude pictorials.

3. When pressed for details of your amorous life, claim debilitation through war wounds. Be frank. Tell Aunt Felicia that you haven't had an erection in seven years. Offer to show Uncle Manfred your scar. Carry gauze tape. Mention the sebaceous secretions that make it necessary to change the dressings every twelve hours.

4. Whenever possible, retire to the backyard or the attic to smoke dope.

· 12 ·

December

"*There* are vultures hanging over us," said the immense dowager seated in the last row of the Winter Garden Theater. This Margaret Dumont look-alike was accompanied by a handsome young man—an acolyte, perhaps, or a nephew; more likely a hired companion from an escort service.

For reasons of economy, Rachel and I had gotten standing-room tickets to see *42nd Street*. We were celebrating. Rachel had just received an acceptance letter from N.Y.U. Law School; she was to start in the spring. I had passed the three-month probation period at work and no longer had to worry about being summarily dismissed. We were the vultures, standing directly behind Mme. Dumont, with her sequined purse and overly ample bosom. Rachel carried a flask of brandy to sip from discreetly. This made standing less of a trial. I was tempted to spill some down Margaret's immense cleavage, a crevice rivaling those found in Alpine glaciers, but Rachel, with her strong sense of propriety, immediately vetoed this. I wadded up some tissues into a ball and absentmindedly dropped it into the abyss below. Rachel's reflexes were sharp; she snatched it midair, saving us from Madame's rage.

After a few moments the lights dimmed, the crowd hushed, and the show began. It was the classic theater legend: Grande dame breaks a leg before opening night; ingenue takes over with scant notice and receives rave reviews; show turns into a colossal hit. It was pleasant enough: a bit too lowbrow for my cynical taste, but no matter. The spectacle of a Broadway stage filled with dancers tapping their little hearts out for the audience was so resolutely anachronistic that it succeeded for me.

Afterward, Rachel and I went uptown to her apartment for cocktails and after-theater mints. We chatted about the three necessities in life: an apartment, a career, and a boyfriend. With law school, Rachel was well on her way to success in a career; her apartment was deluxe; and although there was a hurt after Christopher had left, Rachel was beginning to heal. I had put the boyfriend idea on hold for a while. After Richard I needed some time to recover. My apartment, I realized, was a bargain; the neighborhood couldn't help but improve. My job was fine. I had developed a very congenial relationship with my boss, who I discovered was gay also. During our interview he had supplied me with a few key clues: He had spent two years in San Francisco, he told me; after the job-related questions he remarked that the company was repainting the offices and asked what I thought of the proposed color-scheme. For a month or so I'd had a little crush on him, which I wisely kept to myself. In time it passed.

I left Rachel's at around quarter past eleven, walking down Broadway to Ninth. Passing Roosevelt Hospital on Fifty-ninth, I saw a big commotion—an ambulance flashing lights, a slew of TV reporters and cameramen at the entrance. I figured some notorious Mafioso had been shot. I wasn't the type to cross the street and ask questions. In general I followed the New York dictum Don't Get Involved. Indeed, I found it grotesque the way people clustered at fires, car crashes, and suicide attempts from twenty-third-story ledges. If the ambulance was important, which I doubted, I'd read about it in tomorrow's *Times*.

At home I opened my mail. Christmas season had started with a vengeance. I had three appeals in today's batch alone. One started, "In the time it takes you to read this letter, three people will die of hunger." Suppose I hadn't opened it promptly? Suppose I suffered from a reading disability or, worse yet, was illiterate? Did this make me personally responsible for more deaths? Irritated at this attempt to sway me by emotion, I tossed it and the other two, unopened, into the trash.

Christmas was just another occasion for me to feel left out as a disenfranchised, atheistic, former Jew. Christmas was everywhere: radio jingles, television specials, holiday lighting-displays on the streets, an orgy of consumerism culminating with mass hysteria in Bloomingdale's and Macy's the week before the holidays. There was no escaping it. If only Madalyn Murray O'Hare had set up a radio station, WGID, for "God Is Dead," that ignored the heathen celebration. When someone said to me, "Merry Christmas," I'd reply, "Sorry, I've made other plans."

I called Dennis. Things were fine with him and Christian. We chatted for almost an hour. I was ready to go to sleep when the phone rang. It was Rachel. "B.J., I've been trying to reach you ever since you left. I turned on the news. John Lennon's been shot. He's dead." Dazed, I told Rachel I'd be right over.

I had grown up on the Beatles. I remembered seeing them on *Ed Sullivan,* then trotting six blocks to the drugstore to get the lyrics to *A Hard Day's Night,* just to be the first kid on my block. Back in eighth grade it was a big deal when John Zaccarelli gave Christine Bonaventura the "White Album": In junior high, giving someone a double album was tantamount to getting engaged. The next year we all recorded "I Am the Walrus" on our portable tape-recorders and tried to play it backward for the secret message. Belinda Davenport cried in the cafeteria when she first heard the rumor that Paul McCartney was dead, around the time of *Abbey Road.* Miss Constantine, from eleventh-grade English, taught our class "All You Need Is Love," using a study guide from some enlightened, offbeat equivalent to Monarch Notes. We all hated Yoko Ono for breaking up the Beatles. We thought it would last forever.

And now it was over, forever, with a bullet.

I walked uptown to meet Rachel. The Dakota, where John Lennon lived and was shot, was only a few blocks away. We went there to join the scattered assembly: flotsam and jetsam of the sixties, die-hard hippies in their thirties, listeners to album-oriented rock, a young girl with long blond hair who looked like a runaway, a professional couple in down jackets hugging each other, a bald man in a trench coat with tears in his eyes. The police stood on the sidewalk on Seventy-second Street in front of the Dakota; a few were mounted on horses. They'd set up sawhorses marked "POLICE LINE: DO NOT CROSS." Rachel and I could see the bloodstains on the pavement.

It was one-thirty in the morning. About eighty to a hundred people had gathered to pay their respects. Stragglers kept joining in ones and twos. No one could go to sleep that night. Someone started chanting Lennon's "Give Peace a Chance." Soon the entire crowd was chanting together, swaying slowly, some with arms linked, off-key, a horrible dirge.

In second grade my class was sent home from school for the afternoon when John F. Kennedy got shot. Our teachers sobbed as we left, unable to contain their grief. At first I thought it was an enormous practical joke. Then, in '68, when Arthur Wallowitz told me at the school-bus stop that Martin Luther King, Jr., had been assassinated, I knew it was true; my skepticism hed been replaced by a deeper cynicism. Later in the year, when Robert Kennedy was killed, I felt grief that such sorrow had struck twice in the same family. I was living in Los Angeles when I heard the news that Harvey Milk and George Moscone had been assassinated in San Francisco by a rabid homophobe. I felt sadness, despair, and a bitter rage. The world was enveloped in a thick black cloud. My limbs had grown heavy. I could barely move.

I felt that John Lennon's death would be the last murder that would affect me this deeply.

On Sunday I joined hundreds in Central Park for a moment of silence in his memory. The mood somber on the grassy knolls, I stood, feeling like an observer, detached from the group, defeated. That night I went to St. Mark's Baths for the solace of the flesh, but all I could think of was John Lennon. At a loss for something to say when I enticed a stocky, brown-haired bodybuilder, my first words were "Isn't it terrible about John Lennon?" He nodded and then moved on. Disgusted with myself, frustrated, I left, vowing not to return. What was the point? The St. Mark's Baths was ultimately depressing: always a matter of waiting for such fleeting satisfaction that afterward my mood would only worsen. I had been there maybe five times since January, generally out of desperation. I no longer wanted to admit that desperation inside of me. I would bury it like a stone in a deep, deep well.

PART II

1986:
LEARNING HOW
TO CRY

Prologue

Studies in San Francisco show that in January 1986, up to 80 percent of the gay men have been exposed to human T-cell lymphotropic virus type III (HTLV-III), known by its French discoverers as lymphadenopathy-associated virus (LAV). This virus is classified as a lentivirus, a slow-acting retrovirus that causes disease. HTLV-III/LAV is thought to be the primary causative agent of acquired immune deficiency syndrome (AIDS). In New York City it is estimated that in January 1986, 50 percent of the gay men have been exposed to HTLV-III/LAV; however, it may be as high as 90 percent. The incubation period of this virus can be as long as five years or more.

The two most common opportunistic diseases currently seen in AIDS are a rare form of skin cancer known as Kaposi's sarcoma (KS) and a protozoan lung-infection known as *Pneumocystis carinii* pneumonia (PCP), with PCP accounting for approximately half of the AIDS-related deaths so far reported to the federal Centers for Disease Control (CDC). Fifty percent of the People With AIDS (PWA's) have died within two years after diagnosis. Of those diagnosed with AIDS in 1981, 90 percent are now dead. As many as one million people are infected with the HTLV-III/LAV virus in January 1986. Of those infected with the virus, it is estimated that between 20 and 50 percent will eventually come down with AIDS-related complex (ARC) or AIDS. By December 30, 1985, 15,948 cases of AIDS have been diagnosed according to the CDC's criteria. Most doctors and clinicians believe AIDS to be universally fatal. At present there is no cure for AIDS.

I sit at the desk with my calculator and figure the odds. My hands are trembling; my palms are sweaty; my fingers stick to the keys. Around me are crumpled balls of paper, wadded up. My head is pounding. I take off my glasses and massage my forehead. I can't think clearly.

Distressed, I disconnect the calculator, lie down, and stare at the ceiling. Shapeless, transparent blobs rise and fall, flicker in the periphery of my vision, as my eyes involuntarily twitch. My breath is shallow, my arms lifeless at my sides.

By the time you read these words I may in all likelihood be dead.

· 13 ·

January

I'm twenty-nine, and I still don't have the slightest idea of what to do with my life. After five years I still work at Amalgamated. My job consists of memos and directives. From nine to five I hide in a large private office with the door closed and compose memoranda of increasing complexity designed to create the appearance that I am doing my job effectively. Upon closer examination, beneath the convolutions of syntax and rhetoric, my memos are virtually contentless.

My boss at Amalgamated works out of Jersey; I'm lucky to see him twice a month. My boss, a dashing, multilingual middle-European in his mid-forties, wears four-hundred-dollar suits. On each visit he's greeted with a sheaf of memos which he tosses, unread, into the cavernous file-cabinet bulging from my exertions; I merit an entire drawer. He mutters nondescript praise and convivial pleasantries and then rushes to a power lunch at a three-star restaurant in mid-Manhattan with an important client. For the most part he leaves me to my own devices.

At work there are various battling factions. Daily I fire off three to five obscure directives like projectiles aimed at different departments, with the general aim of building a protective smoke-screen of obfuscation. My memos are spitballs in the face of the faceless monolith where I work. As I stride down the endless, gray corridors, armed with a folder of memoranda to Xerox and distribute, my fellow staff shrink in fear at the sight.

Through corporate machinations I do not claim to understand, I've been twice promoted in the past three years, most recently to the nebulous position of "manager." Between eight and twelve people work directly under me. For the most part, my department runs itself. The cogs turn with little need of lubrication on my part. My job would be a breeze were it not for a certain Miss Caroline Yamamoto.

I decided long ago that Caroline had crawled out from under some igneous rock from the forest primeval of ooze and muck and that her primary purpose in life was to exasperate me. Caroline is in her late forties; she resembles a five-foot potato with black tufts of Raggedy Ann yarn for hair. Four years ago she was hired at the same level as I. With each of my two promotions, her resentment toward me grew. The invisible powers-that-be decided to keep Caroline directly under me; I am unable to transfer her to another sector.

While assuming a pose of utmost civility and cordiality, Caroline is relentless in her campaign to undermine me. She stirs up antagonism, bullying members of other departments in the guise of working on my behalf. Naturally, their anger falls upon me. Willfully, Caroline misinterprets every instruction and assignment I give her, as if I were speaking in a foreign tongue. Caroline cannot decipher the simplest directive without endless explanation; yet she is sufficiently touchy that were I to commit the sin of repeating that rare instruction that she *did* comprehend, she would accuse me of patronizing her. For some time I seriously considered sending her to classes in English as a second language.

Her reluctance to correct her mistakes and her sluggishness once she accepted the tasks necessary to correct them are so infuriating that half the time I end up fixing them myself. In my department Caroline is the one cog that doesn't fit. Powerless to grind her to size, I seek to circumvent her.

Other than Caroline, the job is a breeze—a job punctuated by lunches and dinners, weekends and vacations, where the bracketings are more important than that which they sandwich.

At twelve-thirty I leave the office and go to the deli for a grilled cheese and a soda. I walk over to Washington Square Park. The bottles and cans of former years have disappeared since the state passed a bottle-refund law.

I sit on a bench in the sun and spread out my lunch on my lap. Today is a rare warm day in winter, in the mid-fifties. The park is swarming with half the student population of N.Y.U. On the next bench a group of unshaven men in their sixties, white stubble on their faces, sit in silence. One coughs, long and wheezing. My flesh crawls. I see germs everywhere. Whatever happened to manners? He could at least cover his mouth. Another takes a sip from a flask in a paper bag. I pick up the *Daily News* next to me, headlines screaming the latest development in the New York City municipal scandal. Koch's administration is crawling with corruption and graft. Every day a new official is linked to another scheme: the Parking Violations Bureau, the Queens Borough president, the Bronx Democratic leader. Across from me a man with several jackets in tatters, stinking of urine, lies down, taking up an entire bench. A couple to the left gets up to leave.

I overhear two girls talk in utmost seriousness and gravity about the gross inequities in the grading system. One has long nails painted blue; the other wears a felt hat with a feather. I feel old. The students, barely out of their teens, look like children to me—girls dressed pointedly retro in black wide-net stockings and psychedelic mini-shifts, boys in leather motorcycle-jackets and razor-blade earrings, skinny legs stuffed into stovepipe jeans. Now Blue Nails and Felt Hat are talking about relationships. Blue Nails imparts her worldly wisdom, trying to impress Felt Hat with her depth and spirituality. Felt Hat blows a bubble with her gum. I finish my sandwich quickly and toss the wrappings into the trash. I leave the refundable soda-bottle on the bench to make it a little easier for the vagrants.

When I was just out of college, I used to have a recurrent examination nightmare. I arrive late at an auditorium filled with row upon row of molded-plastic lecture-chairs. Thousands of students are diligently filling out final exams with Number 2 pencils. I dash to the one vacant chair and start. I realize I haven't studied for this test; I'm not sure if I even attended any of the classes. The questions make no sense at all. I sweat and panic. The buzzer rings, loudly. Proctors begin collecting the answer booklets. Mine is completely blank. I hear a louder buzzer. Six armed proctors surround me and demand I surrender my blank examination-book. I struggle with them, thrashing around, and wake up to the alarm.

These days the examination in my nightmare is a physical. The doctor and his assistant probe me with harsh, cold, metal instruments, all the while asking questions of an extremely intimate nature, far beyond professional bounds. "What was the size, shape, and texture of the last penis you sucked? Describe in detail your last bowel movement, leaving out nothing. I will need to have you take your rectal temperature with this thermometer every twenty minutes for the next three days," the doctor says, producing an implement the size of a baseball bat. I am reduced to a morass of symptoms, an amalgamation of indications and manifestations that together bode only ill. The doctor shakes his head. His eyes, sharp as lasers, are etched with the truth. He leaves without speaking. His assistant hands me the diagnosis in a sealed envelope and also departs. I sit on the edge of the padded table, naked, and stare at the envelope. I cannot bring myself to open it.

"What's new, terrific, and exciting?" asks Gordon.

"Now that's a novel conversation-opener," I reply. I'm at the office, doodling my version of the Sistine Chapel on some computer printouts.

"I picked it up from this boring salesman that I interface with at work. Come on, B.J. What's new, terrific, and exciting?"

"Nothing much on this side. How's by you?" I had met Gordon last fall in Central Park. He was speeding through the big loop on his bike; he was in training for a triathlon. I was slowly jogging alone. He passed me once. As he was about to lap me, he turned around and squirted some water from his water bottle at my face. "You look like you could use a drink," he said, and sped on. Later, he told me he spoke to me because I was wearing last year's Gay Pride benefit T-shirt.

"Have you read Judith's latest?" he gushes. "I was on the subway, and *everyone* had a copy of *I'll Fake Manhattan*." Gordon writes fiction on the side. He loathes most of the blockbuster novels that get on *The New York Times* best-seller list. Gordon is in customer support for a large computer company so heavy in middle management that he hardly ever works. We speak on the phone practically every day.

"I'm sure you've got the title wrong. I think it's *I'll Fake Orgasm*."

"You sure? Didja hear Judith is already planning a sequel? It's about an alkie. It's called *I'll Take Another Manhattan*."

"Gordon, you shouldn't be making alkie jokes. Isn't your boyfriend one?" Gordon's lover, Jonathan, is an editor. When I met Gordon, a six-foot blond Adonis whose only flaw was some minor acne scars on his face, I had the hots for him, but I figured his marriage was too ideal to wreck.

"Hunh!" he ejaculates. "You're right! Gee, I'd better stop now!"

(I had found out that Jonathan was an alcoholic from Timothy, a mutual acquaintance. Gordon was away on a sales conference. Timothy had told me that he hoped Jonathan would stay on the wagon. It just slipped out; Timothy assumed that Gordon had told me. A few months later, when Gordon finally told me about Jonathan and his meetings, I mentioned it to Gordon. "No, I'm not mad. I don't care that my friend Timothy, an *ex-hustler*," he emphasized, "told you that Jonathan was an alcoholic." "Tim used to be a hustler?" I asked. "I thought you already knew," Gordon had replied.)

"Did you catch the news last night?" I ask Gordon.

"Yeah."

"I thought it was obscene the way they kept showing the clips of the shuttle disaster with Christa McAuliffe's parents watching."

"It wasn't exactly in the best of taste."

"Pissed me off. Trust the stations to make a disaster even worse."

"Listen, I gotta go now," he says. Frequently, Gordon has to hang up abruptly. Sometimes his boss is making a rare appearance. Other times his breakfast bran-muffin has just hit.

"OK. I'll check in tomorrow."

"Bye," he says.

Wednesday night Dennis and I meet at a quiet French restaurant in the Village run by a gay couple from Provence. His hair had gotten grayer in the past five years, his features gentler. If anything, Dennis is more comforting in appearance and bearing. His mother died back in 1981. Since then, every once in a while he would drift off, staring into space, a wistful, sad look in his eyes. That year he had come out to his sister and her family; the following year he had officially severed ties with the Mother Church. Now he led services for the Metropolitan Community Church, a Protestant gay denomination, and he was also involved in counseling gays. He had gotten a new job teaching philosophy at Rutgers. Dennis had a very busy schedule with all of these commitments. Still, we managed to squeeze in a lunch here, a dinner there.

After Dennis had met Christian, I felt a little like a third wheel. It was nothing that Dennis had said or done specifically. I just didn't want to feel I was intruding. In a way I let him go. I mean, I'm still as close to Dennis as I was before. It's just that we don't have all the time in the world to spend together anymore. There's an asymmetry: I'm single, and he's married.

Domestic life with Christian suited him well. Christian had been promoted to vice president of the bathroom-fixtures wholesalers where he worked. Christian's parents had moved to Florida a few years back, leaving him and Dennis their home in Saddle Brook, New Jersey.

I enter the restaurant and spy Dennis at a corner table, nursing his traditional Dewar's on the rocks.

"B.J., it's good to see you."

"It's been too long." We hug. "Where's Christian?"

"He couldn't make it. He had to work late tonight."

"That's a shame." Secretly, I'm glad to have Dennis all to myself.

"We're doing a wedding together this weekend. It's for a former student of mine. I'm performing the ceremony, and Chris will be playing the organ."

"A regular set of traveling minstrels, you two." I pick up the menu, gaze blankly, set it down. "What should I get?"

"I recommend ze cassoulet," says Dennis. "Eet eez exquisite."

"What's it like?"

"It's *délicieux*. 'A delicately spiced white-bean stew with luscious pieces of pork,' " he says, reading the cursive menu verbatim. "Yikes! I forgot! Pork!"

"That's OK; I don't keep kosher."

"I mean—I mean—I mean—I didn't mean to offend you—I know how touchy you can be."

"Well, according to the *Greenwich Village Gay News,* I shouldn't be eating pork for health reasons." When the *G.V.G.N.* started five years ago, I was overjoyed. Responsible gay reporting had finally come to New York City. As the years went by, however, it degenerated into the mouthpiece of its crazy publisher, with screaming headlines you'd expect from the *Post*.

"Are they still doing the swine-flu bit?" asks Dennis.

"Yes. Swine *fever,* actually. The publisher is relentless."

"A maniac," agrees Dennis.

"For the past three years he's been shoving this pet theory of his, that African swine-fever virus causes AIDS, down our throats, and he shows no sign of giving it up. You know, they could come up with a cure for AIDS and totally eradicate it, and I bet he'd still be pushing swine fever."

"I hope they come up with something soon."

"So do I. Well, that made up my mind. Cassoulet it is."

"So you haven't told me how Sherlock is," says Dennis, feigning grumpiness.

Sherlock is the stuffed dog Dennis had given me for my birthday the year I met him. Sherlock sits on my bureau, watching me with forlorn eyes as I dress. I give him a pat on the head, but it makes no difference: He's still depressed. "Oh, same as usual," I say.

"You remember to feed him and walk him every day?" inquires Dennis.

"He's been acting rather sullen the last week. I've decided to try a different dog-food."

"He's partial to caviar," suggests Dennis. "Make sure you serve it very cold."

"I'll give it a try."

"Hey, I got a joke for you. It's really good. My friend Joseph told it to me. Ready?" Dennis is already chuckling.

"Shoot."

"OK. This matronly woman goes into a restaurant and says she wants a virgin turkey. Nothing else will do. The waiter shrugs, figures how is she going to tell the difference, says 'Fine, we'll give you a virgin turkey.' In half an hour he delivers a succulent specimen on a silver platter. She takes one look at it, frowns—here's the good part—then she sticks her finger in the ass, twisting it like a corkscrew, and says, '*Shtup!*'" Dennis demonstrates, finger twisting in the air, laughing. "I love that sound. *Shtup!* When Joseph told it to me, I cracked up. Anyway, she says, 'This is not a virgin turkey. Take it back and get me a virgin turkey.' So the waiter comes back with another turkey half an hour later, and she does the same thing: '*Shtup!*'" Dennis demonstrates again, practically falling over himself in laughter. "That's my favorite part. *Shtup!* Once again she determines it's not a virgin turkey. She tells the waiter, 'Now don't try to pull a fast one on me again. Don't try my patience! Get me a virgin turkey.' Finally, he comes with a third turkey."

"She goes, '*Shtup! Shtup!*' I know, I know. So what's the punch line?"

Dennis is laughing, head held back. He takes a deep breath and continues. "She goes, '*Shtup!*' She says, 'Yes, this is a virgin turkey.' The waiter is amazed. She was right. He had gotten her a virgin turkey. Totally mystified, he asks, 'How did you know?' And then she says . . ." Dennis pauses. "She says . . . damn, I forget what she says. Gee. Let me think. It was a good joke." He frowns. "*Shtup! Shtup!*" He starts giggling again. "I remember the *shtup* part, but I can't for the life of me remember how it ended. Oh, well. The *shtup* part was funnier than the punch line. Trust me." Dennis shrugs.

"I guess I don't have any choice but." I sigh.

"Hey, B.J., you down in the dumps again?"

"It's nothing. The job's a drag, but you know that. Caroline is a pain, so I put up with her."

"Perhaps you need ze spice in ze love life?" says Dennis.

"Come on, Dennis, you know me, a mass of symptoms. I've got enough AIDS anxieties as it is. You're lucky. You found a boyfriend. You've been involved in a monogamous relationship for five years. I've tricked around enough to be worried. It was just dumb luck that I stopped going to the baths in '81."

"Perhaps you should be seeing someone."

"Gee, thanks a lot. Just find me a regulation boyfriend, and everything will be hunky-dory."

"I was thinking more in terms of therapy."

"Me in therapy? What a joke. I think I'm too advanced for therapy. You know, Dennis, people have this overwhelming compulsion to try and fix me. Strangers on the street straighten my collar, point out the fact that my socks don't match. Little old ladies tell me to work on my posture. Even lesbians tell me that I need a haircut. Am I such a mess? What is it about me?"

"The little-boy-lost look," suggests Dennis. "Well, therapy did me some good."

(Dennis had been in therapy for about a year. When it was over, he announced to me that he had graduated. "There was a ceremony and everything," he told me. "I even got a certificate of mental health," he said. "Suitable for framing?" I asked. "Come on, you're pulling my leg." "Actually, I got over most of my crises and couldn't afford it anymore, so I had to stop," he had admitted.)

"I miss Richard. I wish he were still in New York." Richard had left for San Francisco abruptly last fall. After we broke up, we had become close friends, in a way even more intimate than before, during our relationship, although I had realized this only after his departure.

"How is Richard doing these days?"

"He's still in the halfway house."

"The one for gay alcoholics?"

"No, that was last fall. This one is a halfway house for people with emotional disturbances."

"How's his health?"

"Richard's indestructible. After all he's been through, I'm sure he'll outlive us all." To me, it was difficult to separate his physical problems from his emotional ones. "He got a shot for pneumonia in December.

They have a new vaccine out. He won't ever get it again. I'm sure it was just the foggy weather in San Francisco, the sudden change in climate."

Dennis stirs his cocktail contemplatively, then downs the rest in a single gulp. "Why don't you go out there and visit Richard?"

"That sounds like a good idea," I reply.

Our cassoulets arrive in porcelain pots, filling the air with a wonderful aroma. The meal is sumptuous. Afterward, Dennis says, "Let's do this again soon. Don't let the time go by without giving a call."

"OK."

"Speak to you soon."

"Bye."

Dennis heads for the liquor store on Greenwich to get a bottle of white wine for Christian. I start mentally planning my trip to San Francisco.

Some Symptoms

Dry mouth. Peculiar breath. Ringing in ears. Cold hands or feet. Numbness. A tendency to fall asleep during interviews, sexual acts, and other stressful situations. Loss of interest in personal grooming. Anomie. Itching or crawling sensation on the skin. Excessive sweating. Sudden and unexplained hair-loss. The inability to enter a room that does not have indirect lighting. Blurred vision. Heart palpitations. Internal trembling. Muscular twitching or cramps. Chronic indigestion and/or diarrhea. An inability to eat without reading-material (the Daily News, The Diaries of Evelyn Waugh, or the ingredients printed on the side panel of Cap'n Crunch cereal); similarly, an inability to go to the bathroom without an issue of a magazine that has New York in its title. Lack of appetite. Fondness for intravenous feedings. A craving for sweets. Violent mood-swings. Ravenous hunger between meals. A taste for dirt or chalk. Bulimia. Anorexia. Hypoglycemia. Diabetes. Fainting. Blackouts. Exhaustion. Depression. Anxiety. Constant worrying. An obsession with certain twentieth-century French philosophers. An unjustified fear of being laminated in plastic. Nervousness. Shortness of breath. Restlessness. Insomnia. Nightmares. Smothering spells. Persistent cough. Uncontrolled flatulence during professional encounters. Any sore that does not heal. Progressive changes in size or color or feeling in a wart or mole. Involuntary twitching. Facial tics. Uncontrollable blinking of one or both eyes. Night blindness. Hallucinations. Speaking in tongues. Persistent hoarseness. Uncontrollable sighing and yawning. Gasping for breath. Staggering. Vertigo. A compulsion to ride in glass elevators in Marriott hotels. Lack of coordination. An inability to insert the correct protuberance into an appropriate orifice during the sexual act. Indecisiveness. Mental confusion. Difficulty in concentration.

Forgetfulness. Feeling light-headed. Frequent migraines. Loss of mental proficiency in accurately calculating logarithms. Irritability. Extreme sensitivity to noise and light. Hot flashes. Pink eyes. Purple bruises. Sudden cravings for tofu products after midnight. Moodiness. Temper tantrums. Feelings of "going crazy." Suicidal tendencies. Trembling in the hands. Convulsion. Deathbed conversions.

· 14 ·

February

This is what happened to Richard since we broke up:

His mother died of a fall in the bathroom. He called me and cried; I took him out to dinner at a Chinese restaurant. He took a six-hour bus trip to Oneonta for the funeral. He stayed with his aunt and uncle. His father, who lived in a trailer, was drinking heavily. After a few hours Richard felt he couldn't take it any longer, and so he took the next bus back to the city. He missed his mother's funeral.

Despondent, Richard called in sick at work for two weeks. Then he went back for a week and found he could no longer take the petty office politics. Richard quit his job. A week later he begged for it back. The next week he quit again. This cycle went on for another month. Finally, he got them to lay him off so he could get unemployment.

Richard became bored with nothing to do and complained to me over the phone. He went to the gym twice a day, two hours at a time. He had a few one-week affairs with preppy college-students. Richard started cooking with wine. He allowed himself a half glass of wine to go with the meal, which he prepared in private. Pretty soon he was drinking again. He went back to A.A. Richard tried to get on disability when the unemployment ran out. I lent him some money for the last time. I didn't want to see him starve.

Richard saw a shrink, who gave him a prescription for anti-depressants. He had his doctor check a swollen lymph-gland under his arm. He canceled his checking account because he couldn't afford the fees, and I ended up cashing his checks for him. He became more depressed. He put on weight. He stopped going to the gym. He could no longer concentrate. He went to the hospital for tests. They took a biopsy. The swollen lymph-gland was benign.

Richard called his father for a loan so he could go to bartending school. I didn't think this was such a good idea, but Richard explained to me that some of the best bartenders are former alcoholics. For six weeks he mixed colored waters in varied proportions. The placement office of the bartending school got him a job at a restaurant on the Lower East Side that did poor business. Richard quit the next day because there was nothing to do.

Richard told me he felt like he was back to square one. He needed a vacation, a break. He needed time to think things through. He developed periodic night sweats. The sheets would get soaked; he would have to change them in the middle of the night. This eventually passed. I lent him some money for the last time. Richard had been through a lot. I felt he deserved a rest.

Richard got a fungus on his toes that he couldn't get rid of. He had difficulty swallowing. The doctor diagnosed this as thrush. It went away with medication. He asked his father for a loan so he could go to word-processing school. After the six-month course he got a job at Citibank. He was happy for a few weeks. Then it soured. He went to another shrink, who prescribed another set of antidepressants.

All through this time he had a never-ending stream of boyfriends. It never ceased to amaze me how he could do it. He would pick them up at A.A. meetings, in the gym, on the street. He had perfected the twenty-second pickup at Uncle Charlie's on Greenwich. He would see an attractive boy and start talking to him. "It's pretty crowded here. I don't like all the smoke. Let's go for a walk." He lived only a block away, and he'd invite them up for coffee. One thing followed another. I was amazed at his success, forgetting his unique attraction—a combination of sweetness, vulnerability, and muscular physicality. I saw him too well beneath the surface.

The last boyfriend was named Bart—a Teutonic god he picked up at the Sheridan Square Gym who was majoring in finance at Hunter College and selling clothes weekends at an expensive men's haberdashery on Fifty-seventh Street (he had once waited on Jackie O. for her son, John, Jr.). I don't know whom I was more jealous of: Richard or Bart. I hung around Richard, hoping Bart would notice me. After a few months of coddling and supportive behavior, Bart gave up on Richard. "I can't have a boyfriend who's afraid to ride the subways," he said one day and left.

Things got rough at work. Richard's shrink added two more drugs, a tranquilizer to help him sleep and a mild muscle-relaxant for the side effects of the antidepressants, dry mouth and difficulty in urination. Richard asked to be transferred to another department at work. His doctor found that his T-cell ratio was abnormally low and diagnosed him with ARC. Richard was distraught. He took a psychiatric leave from work, which he extended. He started going to A.A. meetings twice a day. After the expiration of his leave he did not return to work. Once again he was low on cash. I lent him some money for the last time. I called Richard every day to check up on him. His voice sometimes sounded high and funny.

Richard gave me his tranquilizers so he wouldn't be tempted to abuse them. For two weeks I dropped off his daily supply of pills on the way to work. Jessica hid under the bed. At my arrival Richard would perk up. He'd be sitting at his desk, scribbling indecipherable notes to himself in pencil on a yellow legal-pad. The glass of water for his pills would be waiting at the sink. I finally told him I couldn't be the Keeper of the Pills anymore. I was losing my favorite half-hour of sleep in the morning.

A week later he accidentally set his apartment on fire. A combination of medications had lowered his blood pressure drastically, causing him to lose control over motor functions. I took him to the emergency room at St. Vincent's. I checked him in overnight so they could monitor the effects of drugs on his system. They transferred him to the psychiatric ward. At this point he could have voluntarily checked himself out at any time, but he had to wait a forty-eight-hour period before being released if the doctors advised against it. He spent three weeks in the locked ward on the sixth floor. I looked after Jessica and visited him every other day. He had plenty of other visitors. He stayed with me for a week after he was released.

One day Dennis came over. I decided we would do a group project: making lobster-avocado salad together, a recipe I had clipped out from the Sunday *Times Magazine*. We stood there terrified as the water boiled—three faggots, two lobsters, and one tiny pot. Dennis dropped the first one in, muttering a benediction beneath his breath. Richard refused to touch the contents of the brown paper-bag from the A&P, since the remaining lobster was thrashing about. I had to stuff the second lobster in the pot, which was too small. The three of us shrieked hysterically as one lobster tried to crawl his way out up the sides. I batted it with a broomstick handle and slammed down the cover, which lurched and shuddered. Our hearts were palpitating.

Dennis peeled the avocados and sliced them while Richard cut up the lettuce. Dennis told Richard, "I think you should be cutting the lettuce in slightly smaller pieces," and Richard screamed, "Can't you see I've only been out of the hospital for five days?" He stopped shredding and started crying. Dennis soothed him, guiding him into the living room and showing him my stash of porno magazines.

Richard moved back to his apartment. His landlord had retiled the floor, repainted the walls. Most of Richard's paperbacks had been ruined from water damage. He needed new curtains. I lent him some money for the last time. Richard's landlord wanted to throw him out and had started eviction proceedings. Richard got legal advice from a friend at the gym. His friends rallied for him, and with their help, he was able to keep his apartment. For his birthday, since he was out of work, I gave him a year's membership at his gym.

Three weeks later Richard told me he was moving to San Francisco. I told him that this was ridiculous; he had never even *been* to California. How could he just pick up and move there? I offered to loan him money to go for a two-week vacation there and see if he liked it. I was torn between altruism and self-interest. I didn't want Richard to leave, and here I was helping him. I still loved him. He was my best friend. I would miss talking to him. Whom would I tell all my secrets to, my misadventures and misalliances? Whom would I completely confide in? But I wanted only what was best for Richard. And maybe in California the crises would be less frequent. At least I wouldn't feel as responsible for his well-being if he were three thousand miles away.

I reminded Richard that he had just fought for his apartment. I told him it was too difficult to find an apartment in New York for him to just chuck his. The next day he said he might use the money just to have some more time to think; he didn't want to get a job just yet. He was confused. Then he went to his shrink, who told him it was a fine idea, going to San Francisco on a visit to see if he liked it. Richard hadn't had a vacation in years. He went there and stayed with a friend for two weeks. Then he called me collect from a phone booth on Polk Street. "I can't really talk; I need money," he said. Nothing had worked out in S.F. Everything was a mess. His friend wasn't very sympathetic. He had stopped talking to Richard. He hadn't been taking him out much and had left him on his own and didn't know that he was recently recovering from a deep depression and planning on moving to S.F. and didn't have a job. Richard missed me, and he missed his cat, and he wanted to come back to New

York, and he was running out of money, and he was two weeks behind in rent at his apartment, and he also needed plane fare back to New York.

I said, "I just lent you money two weeks ago, and the money was so you could fly back if you chose and keep up on the rent in the New York apartment."

He said, "Sure, you can talk. You've got a job; you've got money coming in every two weeks, but what about me?"

I said, "I can't possibly lend you any more money now."

He said, "Thanks a lot, my fair-weather friend," and hung up on me.

Two days later he was back in New York. He was staying with a guy he had run into on the street, the roommate of a former trick. Richard called me and asked me over for dinner and told me it was a long story; he couldn't go into it over the phone. He told me that his luggage was lost—they lost it at the airport—actually, he was off the plane, and he realized that he had left his Valium on the plane, and he told the employees that he had to get back on—it was a matter of life and death—and after an hour or so of arguing he finally got back on the plane, but the bottle was missing; it must have been in his luggage all of the time. He panicked. He went to the luggage belt, but by that time it was late and they had closed it down for the night. They told him that he had to come back to Newark and pick it up himself. He called them up at the airport and said that he was a cripple, a paraplegic in a wheelchair, and that he had pneumonia and couldn't possibly come to pick it up, so they said they would deliver it. I gave him a five to tip the porter. I went out and picked up some Chinese takeout while he waited; he had been waiting all day for the luggage to be delivered; he had called and called, and they kept on saying it would be over in the next hour; he felt like he was a prisoner of the apartment.

That was when he realized he had a severe drug-addiction problem. He knew he had to get off the pills. Richard went from hospital to hospital, trying to check himself into a drug detoxification program, but there was a long waiting-list everywhere, and his condition wasn't serious enough to warrant immediate attention. The doctors at the various emergency rooms suggested that he detox himself by lowering the dosage over a period of two weeks. He tried Roosevelt Hospital and New York Hospital and St. Vincent's and St. Luke's and Beth Israel. To no avail. He told me the only way he could get checked in to a hospital was by attempting suicide. Two weeks later he flew back to San Francisco because they had a great public-health system. For the first six weeks he was in a detox program. Then he moved to a halfway house for gay alcoholics. He didn't like it, he told me, collect, on the phone. It was full of screaming queens. After three months he moved to a halfway house for the emotionally disturbed. Richard had gotten pneumonia once right after he got to San Francisco, but he had recovered. When he was in the hospital, they did extensive AIDS tests and determined that his T-cell ratio had stabilized and at present his condition was normal.

And that's where Richard was now.

I still rely on Rachel for advice. I call her up at work. She's on Wall Street, a financial analyst. Neal, her secretary, puts me on hold for a couple of minutes. I listen to a brief passage from one of the Brandenburg concertos and work on the *Times* crossword. Caroline has called in sick, so today will be a relatively stressless day.

"Oh, hi, B.J., sorry to keep you waiting. I was on the other line with a client."

"How are you?"

"Busy, busy, busy. Went to the networking party at the Palladium yesterday. What a drag. Alice is coming over for dinner. I'll have to stop off at Pasta and Cheese on the way home. It's Ida's birthday this Sunday. I've got to get to Fortunoff. She's had her eye on a pendant for some time. I thought I'd surprise her. The fur is still at the cleaners. I don't know what's taking them so long. I'm going to Palm Springs next weekend. I'm taking Friday off and making a mini-vacation out of it. I haven't been to exercise class in ages. It's a good thing my job keeps me going. Last week I was so busy I worked straight through lunch twice and didn't even realize it until I got home that night. How are you? Neal, wait a minute. I'll just sign these. Good, now you can send it out. Excuse me, my secretary just stopped in with some paperwork. So is anything new with you?"

"I was thinking of going to San Francisco for a week or so—check up on Richard and all."

"No, no, listen, get out of aerospace. After the shuttle explosion everything in the industry took a dive. Oh, sorry, Bert came in. He wanted some advice on Grumman Industries. What was that you were saying? San Francisco? It's kind of cold this time of year. Isn't this the rainy season? I know a great restaurant in Berkeley, Chez

Panisse. It's pricey. See if you can put it on an expense account. Beth, can it wait a minute? I'm on the phone with a friend. Sorry."

"So do you think it would be a good idea?"

"Are you talking about a vacation in San Francisco or Richard?"

"Both."

"B.J., you want to go somewhere tropical in the winter. Aruba. Key West. San Juan. You don't go to Anchorage, Alaska, in the winter, and you don't go to San Francisco during February. As for Richard, take my advice and cut your losses. It's not going to rally or turn around. It's strictly a bear market. You get my drift?"

"You really think it would be a mistake?"

"Listen, B.J., I gave you my evaluation of the situation. You can either follow it or ignore it. I'd like to talk, but someone's ringing me on the other line. Let's have lunch next week. No, make it the week after that. Call me and we'll set a date. Take care of yourself. Bye."

It rains nonstop from the moment I step off the plane. The *San Francisco Chronicle* features daily articles about the flooding in the Russian River region and outlying areas. I stay with my friend Allan, a flaky architect I had briefly been infatuated with in 1983. Allan lives with his lover, Eric, and their two neurotic Doberman pinschers, Marie Antoinette and her sister Josephine, in a Victorian house near the Haight. Allan, with crinkly-around-the-edges blue eyes, looks perpetually dazed. He whines constantly about the weather for the duration of my visit. "Marie Antoinette would like to go for a walk today, but it's too damp for her, the poor thing," says Allan. "Eric wanted me to get her altered after a hysterical pregnancy she suffered last August, but I wouldn't let a gynecologist touch her with a scalpel. I think I'll stay at home and knit her a wool raincoat. You go out and have a good time." Allan is around five six. To look at him you'd never guess he is in his thirties, let alone thirty-five. To listen to him you wouldn't think he had escaped puberty.

"B.J., you go on out and see your demented friend Richard. I have to stay home and clean out my foreskin," says Allan as I visibly blanch. "An enormous amount of smegma has gathered there since I last touched it in the privacy of my own bathroom. It must have been weeks." Allan had recounted to me the story of his foreskin on several occasions. When Allan was born, his father decided that he wouldn't let his son be circumcised. When Allan was old enough, his father explained that they were going to take away enough from him in this life and he might as well keep that.

I flee from one lunatic asylum to another. Richard's halfway house is about five blocks away. Any further and I would have been smart enough to take an umbrella. When I leave Allan's, it is only drizzling; by the time I get to the bottom of the hill, it is pouring. I knock on the purple door with a white Safeway yin-yang sign in the center. An overweight man with bifocals and a rope for a belt answers the door, knocking against the stained-glass wind chimes in his hurry. "You want Richard? He's upstairs, making dinner. I guess you can come in, for a minute. We're having discussion groups after dinner, so you'll have to go by then." I am completely soaked.

I ascend the stairs. A woman with braids around her head drifts by listlessly. A stocky blond man is slowly dealing himself a hand of solitaire on a card table in the living room. Richard and an olive-skinned woman are in the kitchen. "Hi, B.J.," says Richard, his hands full of lettuce for the salad. He wears an extra-large blue Hawaiian shirt missing the top two buttons.

"Richard, you know, I think you should be cutting the lettuce into smaller pieces."

"Can't you see I've only been out of the hospital for five days?" he replies. "Waaaah! Waaaah!" He roars like a baby prematurely withdrawn during breast-feeding. It has become a set piece between the two of us, another routine. "You just get in today?"

"Yep."

"I wish you could stay here with me, but we aren't allowed to have any houseguests. They have a lot of rules at Tomorrow House. You get demerits if you miss a meeting or come late to dinner without calling beforehand. Ten demerits and you're out."

"Sounds like prison."

"Sometimes it's a little restrictive, but I really need some structure in my life. Things are moving along here. I can see some progress."

"Can I stay for dinner?"

"I guess so. Wait here a second; I'll ask the resident." Richard hands me a dish towel and is off. I am left with his friend, who is slicing tomatoes. I've run out of small talk. She has her back to me and doesn't seem particularly sociable. Richard returns after a short while. "Oh, I'm sorry, I forgot to introduce you. Maria, this is my friend B.J. from New York."

Maria turns around. She gives me a quick smile, then returns to her tomatoes. Her shirt sleeve falls open at the cuff as she turns back, and I see the razor marks on her wrist. Richard takes me aside and whispers, "Maria's a little shy; don't mind her. She's from Nicaragua. I can't get into it any more now. She's very nice. She's one of my closest friends here."

"That's fine."

"Oh, dinner's OK. I've got two meetings tonight right after dinner. I'm going to be leading the first one. We're exploring interpersonal relationships."

"You can bring me along as exhibit A."

"Silly you. The second one is an A.A. meeting. I guess I'm going to turn in early tonight."

"Do you want to get together tomorrow?"

"Tomorrow's pretty bad for me. I do volunteer work at the Y downtown in the weight room. I was planning on going down to the Castro afterwards and seeing if I could volunteer for the Gay Games. How's Wednesday for you?"

"I guess that's OK," I say. What am I going to do tomorrow?

"Oh, my God, the spaghetti!" Richard turns off the burner and empties the spaghetti into a huge colander. He picks up a piece and bites it. "Not exactly al dente, eh?" Richard takes a limp strand and places it next to my arm. "Just a few more pull-ups and I bet we could build you up to this."

"Sure, with massive steroid doses and a personal trainer and a membership at Definitions."

"It's nothing a good sauce can't hide," says Richard to himself, surveying the overcooked spaghetti. "What do you think, Maria?" Maria runs from the room. A few moments later I hear a door slam. "Hey, Maria, it's no big deal. It's not your fault. Shit."

At dinner Richard introduces me as his best friend from New York City. The conversation is awkward, moving in fits and starts. I leave shortly after dessert, applesauce spooned from two twenty-pound bomb-shelter-sized cans.

Tuesday I kill time. I wander in and out of bookstores on Haight Street. I look for packets of sourdough-bread starter in health-food stores. Rachel has sent me on this impossible errand. She claimed that San Francisco was the only place where you could get it. I spend a half hour at a hologram store. I stroll down the street and stand on the corner of Haight and Ashbury. Nothing. Just like the first time I stood at the corner of Hollywood and Vine. Why should I expect anything?

A man dressed as a condom walks down the street, followed by a man and a woman who hand out safe-sex leaflets and prophylactics. Allan is at work at his store, an upscale Bowl and Board named Beyond the Forest after some campy Bette Davis movie. I buy a T-shirt that says "San Francisco" at All American Boy on Castro Street and go to a gym to work out. My actions are reflexive, without thought. Janet Jackson bemoans, "What have you done for me lately?" over the PA. I shower and return to Allan's for a tofu-and-sprouts dinner.

Wednesday morning I call Richard at nine-thirty.

"I can't talk," he says in hushed tones.

"What do you mean? What's the matter?"

"Just give me the address, and I'll be over in half an hour," he whispers. I recite the address. Richard says to someone else, "I'll be done in a minute, OK?" Then he hangs up abruptly.

Allan stays home, wanting to meet Richard.

"I have to personally introduce Richard to Marie Antoinette and Josephine, my gorgeous girls, or they'll rend him limb from limb. I've always wanted to meet your demented friend Richard. Where is he? I don't know *what* to do. I *could* take Marie Antoinette and Josephine out for another walk, but they just did number two half an hour ago, and I think they want to have a nap now. When did you say Richard was coming? That was at least forty-three minutes ago. Oh, well, I'll just tie Marie Antoinette and Josephine up so they don't rend Richard limb from limb. It's time to open the store. I can't wait any longer. Give him my regards," says Allan.

Richard shows up about an hour late. "I got reprimanded for using the phone after nine," he explains. "We're supposed to be out of the house during the day from nine to five. I didn't have your number written down, so I couldn't leave. Jesus, are those Dobermans?" The two dogs are sniffing Richard's pants.

"Don't worry, they're harmless. I was spooked by them initially, but they're friendly, and they wouldn't hurt a flea."

"Dobermans turn against their owners," says Richard evenly, a tinge of suppressed terror in his voice. "Let's get the hell out of here."

We take a trolley at the corner, which enters a tunnel and turns into a subway. "I think this is close enough; I still don't know the transit system here that well," says Richard. We get off and walk about seven blocks in the downpour.

"You're just doing this to me because you got soaked and misery loves company," I grouse.

"I know someone who hasn't had breakfast yet." Richard still remembers the time I went over after work for dinner and demanded that he make white rice instead of brown rice because white rice takes twenty minutes and brown rice takes forty-five and I was starving. I tend to be very short-tempered on an empty stomach. I have been waiting two hours for breakfast, and I am dripping wet. Richard and I get a table at Richard's favorite breakfast hangout on the Castro. I don't feel like talking until the waiter takes our orders. I glare at the menu.

"Well, if you're going to be nasty, I guess there's no sense in trying to have a civilized conversation," chides Richard. He takes out a paperback from his knapsack, a nineteenth-century novel, and begins reading. It looks like Trollope to me, upside down, but I don't feel like asking him. I know it would come out as a snarl.

My waffle arrives after ten minutes of silence. I dig in. Richard gets a second refill on his coffee. His western omelet comes with hash browns on the side and a superfluous garnish of an orange slice and parsley. He douses it all liberally with salt and pepper and wolfs down two forkfuls.

"Better now?" asks Richard.

"Yes," I reply sheepishly, ashamed of my immature behavior.

"So tell me, how's Jessica?"

"I don't know. I haven't seen Paul in a while." Richard had left his cat with Paul, his downstairs neighbor. I ran into Paul occasionally during my Village strolls. "So what's the story with the halfway house? Do two halfway houses make a whole?"

"Sort of like the sound of one hand clapping."

"You mean two people doing it at the same time?"

"No more amputee jokes, please."

"So, Richard, do you have any plans for the future? Are you coming back to New York?"

"I don't know, B.J. I really miss my friends in New York. It's so hard to get close to people here. It's true what they say about people being superficial on the West Coast. You remember in New York I could get a boyfriend just like that?" He snaps his fingers. "It's not that easy here. It's such a small community; everybody I meet knows someone who's died of AIDS. It's a whole different attitude. Plus, the fact that I'm living in a halfway house and don't have a regular job yet may contribute to my difficulties in meeting friends."

"It's always hard in a new place. Every time I moved it took me at least a year to settle in."

"I know, B.J., but I'm lonely here. I miss my friends, and I miss my cat, and I miss the neighborhood. And then when I think of the transit system and the health-care system in New York and all of the people and the crummy weather, I'm glad I left. It's a trade-off. Some days I think I should just pack it in—that this whole move was a mistake. I want to go home. Other days I remember what I hated about New York. I don't know."

"Give it time. I really miss you, too."

"Me, too."

"So what about now? Any employment opportunities looming in the near future?"

"A job? Don't say that word!" jokes Richard. "Me, with a job? Who are you kidding! No, seriously, I thought I might try something in horticulture. I really like growing plants. The solitude. The peace. You remember my window box? Jessica sitting on the edge in the sun, with all the flowers in bloom in spring? I was thinking of working in a greenhouse. Or maybe at a gym: a personal fitness-adviser, a trainer, something like that. I haven't defined it yet, but I'm thinking about it. I'll never go back to word-processing. One thing's for sure: I'll *never* go back to Citibank. That's what got me depressed in the first place. That's why I ended up taking those antidepressants and then that horrible mess with the apartment when I set it on fire, and then later I became addicted to the tranquilizers. Never again!"

How does he survive without gainful employment? I wonder to myself as I pick up the tab for breakfast. The deal was he'd leave the tip—only he doesn't have any change, and could I help him out with it just this once? I have my horrifying job at Amalgamated eight hours a day, five days a week, fifty weeks a year, an endless grind of toil stretching out for the foreseeable future. If I can stand it, why can't Richard? He's sensitive, I guess. Still, sometimes I wish *I* were the one on the public dole, and *he* were the one facing Caroline, my nemesis at work. Since Richard left for California last fall, my bank account has grown by leaps and bounds. Did this explain my ambivalence at his leaving me?

Richard and I go shopping on Castro Street. I am running out of contact-lens solution, so we dash into Walgreen's. At the back is an extensive display of lubricants, both with and without nonoxynol-9, a chemical shown to be effective in killing the AIDS virus in vitro. This is the sort of display one would find only at the Pleasure Chest back in New York. We spend half an hour at Crown Bookstore. Richard picks up *Jane Brody's Good Health* in hardcover. I dawdle in the magazine section, amused to find *Blueboy* and *Mandate* in a chain bookstore with branches in malls. We walk by the Castro Theater, a gorgeous deco movie-house with a large pipe-organ inside. Richard tells me that a resident organist plays "I Left My Heart in San Francisco" before every evening performance. I get a T-shirt for the Gay Games at a boutique filled with T-shirts, shorts, and swimsuits. There's a stack of free *Bay Area Reporter*s, the local gay newspaper, at the door. I grab a copy.

Richard takes me to the Country Club, an A.A. hangout, a cross between a lounge and a coffeehouse. Alcohol is not dispensed. Richard goes up to the counter to get me some apple juice and a cup of coffee for himself. I flip through the *Bay Area Reporter*. Near the middle are six or seven AIDS obituaries. Throughout are ads for recorded phone-sex, a series of 976 numbers that when dialed, for the nominal charge of two dollars plus local tolls, play back messages changed twice daily: fantasies of sexual congress with handymen, high-school gym coaches, illegal aliens, leather men, bodybuilders, blonds, and vacuum-cleaner accessories, among others, in toilet stalls, cooperative apartments, department stores, swimming pools, gym locker-rooms, produce stands, airplane johns, abandoned warehouses, ski lifts, truck stops, and elsewhere. The phone numbers have suggestive mnemonics such as 976-SUCK, 976-DICK, 976-HEAD, 976-FIST, 976-MEAT, 976-LOAD, and 976-RODS.

Richard and I sit at a table by the window and watch a steady stream of people flow into the Blue Whale across the street, a popular video bar with a large aquarium.

"So, how's your health these days?" I ask Richard.

"Pretty good. I still get tired sometimes. When I had pneumonia last fall, I was terrified. I was in the hospital for ten days."

"Are your lymph nodes OK?"

"For the most part. They're still a bit swollen but no worse than a year ago."

"That's a relief."

"And what about you?"

"Well, I'll always have my herpes, I guess. It only comes once or twice a year now. My stomach still bothers me occasionally. I used to tell my doctor about it, but he'd always insist I take the amoeba test. I'd put it off for a week or two—"

"It's hideous," put in Richard.

"And then finally I'd take a day off from work and take it. Once I tested positive again. I can't imagine how, unless I never was completely cured from years ago. So now I just let it slide."

"It's probably no big deal. Well, how do you like the Country Club?"

"The name sounds like a drying-out clinic in Poughkeepsie or something. It's OK."

"It's pretty low-key. I like the fact that you can come here to hang out for a few hours and nobody will bother you. The people are nice. I wish New York had a place like this, a bar that didn't serve alcohol. It's true; it can get boring after a while. A lot of the same crowd comes here every day." The room we are in has a Persian rug and tiny tables and chairs. It is a converted living room of a Victorian with bay windows. In another room are sofas, armchairs, and a coffee table stacked with magazines.

"Home away from halfway house," I comment. "Richard," I ask, "there's something that's been bugging me ever since you left. Do you mind if I ask you a question?"

"Sure."

"Why did you leave?" I ask, omitting the implicit object of the sentence, me. I know I won't get a satisfactory answer, just a rehash of previous explanations. I don't even know myself what would constitute a satisfactory explanation: Richard admitting he was foolish to leave so abruptly? Richard apologizing for not taking my feelings into consideration?

"You know why, B.J. I was addicted to Valium. I couldn't get into any treatment centers in New York."

"I'm not talking about the second time you left. I mean the first time."

"I already went through this with you. I couldn't take New York anymore. I wanted a new start. I hated the crowds, the weather, the dog-eat-dog attitude. I had been living in New York for more than ten years. It was time for a change."

Why did you abandon me? I ask myself silently. This is the sort of question I wouldn't even consider asking aloud. Too cliché. Too pathetic. Too much of a whining baby. I don't speak in those terms.

"You know, B.J., we've worked out much better as friends than as boyfriends."

"I know."

"I'm serious. Boyfriends have come and gone, but you've stuck by me through everything."

There have been times when I just want to drop the whole relationship, but I can't admit this to Richard. I don't want to hurt his feelings.

"Yeah."

"I want to thank you for your support of me. Times have been hard. I'm hoping things will pick up any day now."

Aren't we all?

"I just want to tell you that I've always loved you and I always will."

"Me, too," I reply, hoping we'll pass out of the maudlin stage of this conversation soon.

"Well, I guess we'd better be going." We split up at the subway stop, after a hug.

The next night Allan and I go to a vegetarian Vietnamese restaurant. Allan complains about the rain, the fact that he never got to see me, his lover, his dogs, everything. "I think Josephine is going through menopause now, and I can't understand why; she had a hysterectomy before I got her. It gets me depressed. My dogs are down, and so am I. Can I have a bite of your spring roll?" says Allan. "The store keeps me busy, and I have to wake up at five in the morning for my crew team. I told you I rowed with a crew team three times a week—I'm the only gay guy on the team—it's really fun, except when Eric wants me to be a dazzling socialite and we go out, I'm always falling asleep in the second act of the ballet. I mean, I don't snore that loudly; I don't see why he gets so upset." Allan yawns. "What do you say we get the check and go home and catch a few z's? If you want, you can stay up and see something on the VCR. I've got *Mildred Pierce* and the American National Bodybuilding Championship on tape." Allan picks up the tab, I say thank you, and we head for his Volvo.

"Richard, what on earth are you doing out here?" I ask.

Richard is walking down the street without an umbrella. Rivulets fall from his rain hat. "I couldn't take it anymore. I decided to go for a walk. I'm in the doghouse again," says Richard.

"Richard, this is my friend Allan."

"Hi, pleased to meet you," says Richard, extending his hand.

"I've heard so much about you," says Allan.

"I got another infraction today at the halfway house. Three more and I'm out. I was late to a meeting tonight. Since they already started and I was bored with the whole thing, I went out. Can you believe this weather? Rain, rain, rain. Nothing but rain. San Francisco doesn't look so hot to me now. I'll give it another week. I don't know; maybe I'll go back to New York. Hey, I'm getting soaked. I better be on my way."

"Can we drop you anywhere?" asks Allan.

"No, thanks, I need the exercise. I'll be on my way," says Richard. He casually strolls down the hill.

"So that's your deranged friend Richard," says Allan.

"You don't have to say that in front of him."

"He's well out of earshot; it's OK. Gee, why would anyone go out for a walk on a night like this?"

"Beats me. He probably feels cooped up there at his halfway house."

"I don't know," says Allan. "These are the actions of a deranged individual."

"Shut up already. You're no picture of mental health."

"*I* know that. I think it's Marie Antoinette and Josephine's fault. They've been driving me batty this past week, constantly whining to go out, and I can't let my daughters get soaked, can I? Everybody is on edge, you know?"

I grunt a reply. Is Richard really planning on returning to New York? Who knows?

The return flight is a nightmare. I sit in the last seat of the last row of plastic chairs in the waiting area, scan the *Examiner,* put it on the empty seat to my left for someone else to read, and then pick up a copy of *Esquire* and start flipping through the pages. "Is this seat taken?" snarls a woman in her early twenties with seven earrings in one ear and half her head shaven. Without waiting for my reply she picks up the paper, tosses it onto the floor, and sits down. There's a swatch of blue dye in her hair. She unnerves me. I wonder if my apartment has been ransacked in my absence. I think back to the month when I was mugged three times, January 1983. I riffle through my *Esquire,* practically ripping the pages out at the seam. I look up. The Zulu Warrior has a copy of *Tess of the d'Urbervilles* in her hands, lips pursed in concentration. She glares at me. "Could you *please* stop rocking the seats? It's *extremely* disturbing."

"Sorry, I'm kind of jumpy. My doctor OD'd two weeks ago, and I'm on the last of my diet pills, and I don't know how the hell I'll be able to get a new prescription for them, and I really hate flying, and on top of all that, it's my period."

She breaks into a grin, rummages around in her purse, and offers me some Midol. "I empathize *completely,*" she says. "I've been on the psychological rag for the last *twenty-three years.*"

We don't start boarding until midnight. I sit next to an immense, wheezing man who takes up two full seats. Unfortunately, I am in one of them. The wheezer's nose is red, as are his knuckles and the skin between his fingers. "I have a respiratory condition. Do you mind if I use your air nozzle?" I am in no condition to refuse. His lobster-red elbow digs into my arm as he stands to adjust the nozzle. I barely survive the flight.

Home, I play back my messages. Someone had an extra ticket for *Song and Dance* and wanted to know if I was free, a week ago Thursday. Two hang-ups. A solicitation from the United Negro College Fund. A breather. Another hang-up. I am asked to subscribe to Brooklyn Academy of Music's "The Next Wave" series. An unidentified gentleman provides an explicit description of his testicles and scrotum, accompanied by an invitation to perform a sexual act illegal in twenty-seven states and the District of Columbia. A solicitation from the National Gay Task Force. Another two hang-ups. A call from Dennis, remembering midway through that I was in California. An invitation to dinner from Rachel. Another hang-up. And something disturbing from Dave Johnson, my old Jones Beach buddy from the West Side Y.

"B.J., I've got some bad news. It's Bob. He's in the hospital with PCP. It looks like he'll pull through this time. If you have a chance, could you stop by and visit? I'm sure he'd appreciate it. He's at Lenox Hill, in Room 332. Thank you."

Bob. Bob. Bob. Who do I know named Bob? There's Robert Walker. Bob. Bob. Was he the one—? No, that's someone else. Arthur. Think. It'll come to me. Bob. Bob. Broome! That's it. Bob Broome. Wait a sec—he was the one from the Juilliard concert, wasn't he? Shit, we tricked. It must have been four, five years ago. What did we do? I knew I shouldn't have tricked with him. Sloppy seconds. I shouldn't have tricked with anyone, but that's beside the point. Who knew back then to take precautions? When was it? Five years ago? Six? I wonder exactly what we did. Should I go and visit? I hate hospitals. I wasn't that close to him. So we tricked maybe once or twice. That was all. When you come down to it, I didn't even like him that much. Didn't know he was such a slut. Wait a minute. He wasn't any worse than me. For all I know. Bob was a bit dull. Shouldn't use the past tense. Bob *is* a bit dull. What did we do? I met him at the concert. We talked. We went over to his place. After that I get a blank. Later, we met at the gym and had pizza for brunch. Did we fuck? We couldn't have. I haven't fucked with anyone except for Richard in the past five years. Well, there was Bill in August of '83, but we used condoms, so there's nothing to worry about. *What did we do?* I could check my calendar. Why bother? Nothing but names and numbers. As if I listed the sexual acts along with the associated risk-factors back in 1981. Stars next to names, writing "s-f-s-x" for "safe sex." I actually started doing that last year. Shit. Why am I thinking only of myself? I wonder. Does Dave know that Bob and I tricked? Does he realize the implications, the ramifications of the situation? I need a drink. I *should* be feeling sorry for Bob. Poor Bob. Perhaps I have an asymptomatic case and transmitted the virus to him. No. That's pretty unlikely. I'd probably be dead by now. What am I doing? I'm getting upset over nothing. I'm just driving myself crazy. It's not nothing. Bob is ill and will probably die within the next two years. Jesus, did we do poppers? That's always been my weakness. They're cofactors to worry about, according to the latest medical data, although two years ago they were dismissed as unrelated. I'm sure we must have deep-kissed. That's not that risky, at least not this week. Did we suck cock? Is that risky if you don't come? Chances are I did. Why am I thinking only of myself? Precum has a negligible danger. Poor Bob. My gums have been bad; I should have flossed more often. They bleed once in a while. Sometimes I get a canker sore. They say it's another form of herpes. If they were bleeding when I did whatever I did with Bob . . . shit. This speculation isn't doing anybody any good. Chances are I've been exposed to the virus that may or may not cause AIDS. And. And. And if I last five years with no symptoms, I'll be fine. Home free. Maybe. But have I already developed any symptoms? Don't my lymph nodes swell when I get a cold or a herpes attack? That doesn't mean anything. Does it? All I have to do is wait until February of 1991. Jesus. What should I do? Should I call him, send my regards? I don't want to remind him. That might make him feel guilty. He's probably not thinking about all of the tricks he may have infected. Does he even want to know that I know? I guess he does. But what am I to do about Bob, the possible instrument of my death, the agent of my demise? No, how can I be so cruel? How can I even think of that? How can anyone assign blame? If I have the virus, it's my responsibility, no one's fault but my own. It's fate. It's irrelevant where it came from. But the problem of Bob remains. What should I say? What should I do?

After I Was Mugged

After I was mugged three times in January of 1983, I started shaving every day. My hands shook as I slowly ran the razor over my face, cutting through the cream in even swaths. Each time I broke in a new razor, I'd cut myself on the chin, bright-red blood seeping through white shaving-cream like maraschino-cherry juice on whipped cream.

I used Q-tips on my ears. I flossed daily. I wore a tie to work. I ate three balanced meals. I started the day off with a handful of vitamins, milk, juice, toast, and bran cereal. I had a regular bowel movement at precisely ten o'clock. I slept for seven hours each night. I went to the gym every other day. Each night I would apply moisturizer with care, making sure not to miss any spots.

Much later I realized that I went through these routines as if they had some mystical significance. On some superstitious level I believed that if I maintained the pattern, I would remain unharmed in the future.

But nothing guaranteed that the phone wouldn't ring in the middle of the night with bad news.

· 15 ·

March

"*B*ut doesn't everyone take notes during therapy?" I ask, pencil poised above my personalized notepad purloined from the office. Neil Wollowitz, Dennis's former therapist, assures me that this is not the case.

I am in a crisis situation. Bob Broome has AIDS, and I don't know how to deal with it. In desperate straits and full of misgivings, I decide to seek therapy. Rachel tells me not to go to a gay therapist. She thinks that I have already isolated myself enough in the gay subculture. But who else could understand AIDS anxiety to the extent that I had it? My friend Gordon takes the opposite approach: He sees a lesbian, someone as far from the AIDS crisis as possible.

I have several therapists to choose from. Stephen Petersen, a slender dandy from Boston I met in the half-price ticket-line in Times Square, used to commute to New York three days a week; he continues to see his Greenwich Village therapist, Laurence Mansberg, after Stephen's consulting job ended, flying into Manhattan once a month for a double or triple session. On the other weeks, he does it over the phone on the WATS line at work. Dennis tells me I might like Neil Wollowitz, his former therapist.

"I thought he only treated gay clergy," I say.

"You really believed me?" Dennis laughs. "It was a joke. Get it?"

From Stephen's description of Dr. Mansberg I know I would suffer a painful case of unrequited love and spend most of my sessions trying to seduce him. With Neil Wollowitz, however, sexual transference is out of the question. Short and pudgy, comfortably stuffed into a plump, high-backed leather-chair on coasters, Neil has the sex appeal of a head of Bibb lettuce. He reminds me of Mr. Whipple on the Charmin commercials. Neil wears tortoise-shell glasses. He has a gym teacher's brush cut; his hair is gray. The white shirt under the gray suit-jacket is stiffly starched; the tie is held in place by an alumnus tie-tack.

Nervously, I have written down the address on a blue three-by-five index card. Neil is booked after work; I am seeing him during my lunch hour. Early, I duck into a deli on Spring Street and have a candy bar. I check my watch. It is time for my appointment. Then I can't find the address. I wonder, "Is this subconscious?" I empty out my pockets, upend my backpack on the sidewalk, and search frantically through the contents: today's *Times,* an overdue library book, some bills I am meaning to mail, my gym lock, a pocket address-book, my emergency tie. No card. Sweating, I thumb through my wallet and find it, neatly folded in the billfold.

"Hi, my name is Neil," he says at the door. "And you're"—he looks down at the appointment book in his hands—"you're Benjamin Rosenthal."

"B.J.," I correct.

"Step in." I walk with him down the hall to his office, a modestly furnished room.

"Take a seat, please."

The couch has been recently reupholstered. A stiff plaid pattern covers two thick foam-rubber pads. I sit, and the couch doesn't respond.

"My friend Dennis referred me to you."

"Ah, yes. And how is he now?"

"Pretty well."

"So. What brings you here?"

I look around nervously: an uncluttered desk; an answering machine, the light flashing; a window hidden behind slats of venetian blinds; above the other couch, similarly sterile, a mounted Mondrian print. Neil's chair is the only comfortable piece of furniture in the office.

If I wanted antiseptic surroundings, I would have gone to a psychiatrist.

"I'm nervous. I'm depressed. I have a friend who has AIDS, and I don't know what to do. He's been in the hospital for two weeks, and I'm afraid to even visit. . . . I have to use the facilities. Could you show me where the bathroom is?" I ask tentatively, a student raising his hand, waiting for the appropriate interval to interrupt an endless lecture without appearing disruptive. I fumble for the light inside, a switch on the wall. I'm not about to ask him for help. I turn on six hundred watts of illumination. The sink and the faucet are spotless. I wonder what happened to the paper hymen on the toilet. I check my hair in the mirror. A mess. I flush. What is wrong with this picture? Me.

"Exactly what is your background?" I ask, returning to the room.

"I'm a certified social worker. I follow the teachings of Paul Goodman. It is generally referred to as Gestalt therapy. However, my approach is eclectic. Whatever best suits the patient."

Certified social worker. I checked with our office manager at work. Our health-insurance plan covers psychiatrists, psychologists, and CSW's. When I made the appointment on the phone, Neil said that sessions were sixty dollars. Our health plan pays for fifty percent up to a thousand dollars. Making a quick mental calculation, I determine that means a maximum of thirty-three sessions before I have to pay the entire amount. Well, I *should* be cured by thirty-three sessions. . . .

I notice that Neil's lips have stopped moving. He is evidently waiting for me to answer a question. "Could you repeat that?"

He pauses, puzzled. "I said that you may find the book *Gestalt Therapy* helpful. It's available in paperback. The authors are Frederick Perls, Ralph F. Hefferline, and Paul Goodman."

"Oh, thanks." I dutifully scribble down the title and authors. "I'll pick it up tonight at Barnes and Noble." Back in high school, I'd take home a lockerful of books each night. Typically, I'd bring the lot of them back without opening a single one.

"You're hunched over, tense. Many of my patients prefer to lie down. You may find it more comfortable."

"That's fine," I say. "I'd rather sit." I straighten my back, hearing my mother's voice telling me to have good posture at all times and to keep my hands out of my pockets. Lying down at this early stage? I'd read Michael Korda's *Power*. I understand the relationship of domination and submission between someone sitting and someone lying down. I'm not ready for it yet. What is this, Vienna?

"Here we will examine habits and behaviors that formerly may have been appropriate adaptations and adjustments to situations but no longer retain that function." I write this down verbatim, for much the same reason I took notes in college. My boredom threshold is next to nil. I take notes to stay awake, to retain information through muscular memory. It's just another dodge, an excuse to avoid eye contact, a way of staying focused, concentrated—alternatively, a way of avoiding the issue.

Neil smiles. "In most cases the therapist is the one taking notes on the patient, not the other way around."

Is this sarcasm? Is he baiting me? "But doesn't everyone take notes during therapy? It's expensive. I would think this would help one retain more. Later, I can go over this." I know at that moment that the book on Gestalt therapy I would buy would sit on the shelf, unread, for a year or longer before being tossed in the trash.

"A few of my patients at times, but none to this extent." Is he saying that I am acting peculiar? I don't care.

"I make lists all of the time to remember things. Take this appointment." I tell him about my frantic search for the index card with the address. "I write things down so I understand them."

"You may find your recall improving if you *don't* write things down," he says. This I transcribe word for word. "If you focus carefully on what people say," he says slowly and clearly, "and don't rely on external cues, you may find it easier. We can try an experiment. First, let me explain the concept of an experiment so we understand our terms. An experiment is merely . . . ."

He goes off into a little spiel. I drift off. I know science and technology. I had chemistry and biology in high school. This clearly isn't science proper. It is as if I were back in college, taking Philosophy 101, and the professor was talking about "the meaning of 'meaning.'" To me it was immediately apparent, a tautology, a verbal redundancy. I'd tune out. Subsequently, I'd flunk the final. I know I should be making an effort to follow what Neil is saying.

". . . trying to integrate the self . . ."

Sure, I saw that in a porno video once; this guy who was hung like a horse was integrating himself. Damn it, I should cut out the sarcasm for once. It's such a reflex I wonder if I could stop if I tried. I wish Neil were a little cuter. I know I am too lazy to comparison-shop for a therapist. He'll do. I'll cooperate. I wish he weren't so fat. He can't even control his basic bodily urges, and I should trust him to tell me how to run my life? What did therapy ever do for my father, who was *certifiable*? He saw a medical doctor three days before he died of a heart attack and passed the checkup with flying colors. Well, no sense in blaming Neil for *that*. That wouldn't be fair to him. I should give him a chance. I don't want to hurt his feelings. How can I reject him?

"I would first like to find out your background, your family, to help me know you better."

Jesus. What relevance does the fact that I was weaned at the age of fourteen have to do with my present state of terror? That I suckled a prosthetic breast for five years without knowing it? That the first time I saw my father naked was in a blue movie at an adult cinema downtown? What's the point in blaming it all on Mom and Dad?

When I turned twenty, I decided to take full responsibility for myself. So a week later I attempted suicide. Maybe it was too much at one time. I should have eased in gently.

I can tell Neil the basics and leave out the lurid stuff that might offend my family. I don't see what the point is, but I'll play along. I give Neil a brief rundown: the crazy father, the awful apartment, the horrifying job, Miss Yamamoto, my friend Richard, the whole song and dance. This takes almost half an hour. Neil listens attentively. Once in a while he jots something down.

"So your current crisis is your friend with AIDS. Tell me what you feel about him."

"I'm scared. I'm afraid he's going to die. I never knew firsthand anyone who had AIDS. It's been just a statistic until now—friends of friends, stories you read in the paper. But nobody that I knew personally." In the biblical sense, I add to myself. "I figure if Bob has it—I mean, he wasn't the Whore of Babylon, by any means—I might have it, and it scares me."

"Have you exhibited any of the symptoms of AIDS?"

"Not yet. I mean, I get a lot of little things that go wrong with me—a high fever once in a while, a cold, swollen lymph-glands— but it goes away, and I haven't lost a lot of weight suddenly. I had this purple spot near my ankle for a week. I went to my doctor, and he said it was just a bruise. Afterwards, I remembered I had dropped a large weight on my ankle a couple of months ago. I was afraid that maybe the trauma of the bruise had lowered my immune system and activated a dormant virus. I thought it might have been KS."

"There are several groups I could refer you to that meet once a week. They're for the Worried Well. I can give you a number to call if you're interested."

"I don't think I could face a group of people. I think it would only serve to reinforce my fears. I think my anxieties would only increase."

"I just wanted you to know it's an available resource. Well, our time is about up. Do you plan on coming back for regularly scheduled sessions?"

"This is it?" I think to myself.

"I guess," I tell Neil.

"Good. We will be meeting once a week. If you are unable to attend a session, you must notify me at least twenty-four hours in advance, or I will have to bill you for the session. Is this a good time for you?"

"As good as any." I don't really care. Neil writes down my name in his appointment book for the following week, same day, same time. "How long do you think this will take?"

"Some of my patients are here short-term, a few months. Others have been coming for years."

He writes "DSM II 300.02, generalized anxiety and depression" on my claim form under the diagnosis. So that's what I have. Now I have a finger on it. Now I know what is wrong. The next step is for him to fix it. I place my trust in Neil.

Some of the People I Distrust

Doctors, lawyers, accountants, electronic repairmen, door-to-door salesmen, insurance salesmen, Jehovah's Witnesses, third-world terrorists, paper delivery-boys, psychotherapists, clergymen, stockbrokers, hitchhikers, people who pick up hitchhikers, people who ring your bell and ask to come in to use the phone because their car has broken down, boys who live in New Jersey with their parents and have aspirations of being flight attendants but are presently unemployed, stereo salesmen, hardware-store salesmen, members of religious cults, the Internal Revenue Service, the President of the United States, International Business Machines, American Telephone & Telegraph, my mother, my boss, my underlings, my coworkers, the cashier at the gourmet delicatessen on University Place who always overcharges me, the butcher with his thumb on the scale, the taxi driver with the meter off, my dead father, mental patients dumped on the streets, the Centers for Disease Control, The Advocate, The Greenwich Village Gay News, Larry Kramer, the mayor of the city of New York, prospective boyfriends, Richard, meter maids, Larry Hagman of Dallas, Joan Collins of Dynasty, Vanna White of Wheel of Fortune, my landlord, the United States Postal Service, the man in the moon, Ivan Boesky, Steve Rubell, Richard Nixon, John Belushi's dealer, queens over thirty, queens under forty, anybody from New Jersey, the Citibank automatic teller-machine when it says, "I'm sorry, I can't give you a record now," the person who selects the sayings on Celestial Seasonings tea-boxes, critics in general, three-card monte dealers in Times Square, the Los Angeles Police Department, prostitutes, gamblers, thieves, Bob Dylan during his Christian-

revival phase, Tylenol caplets, my therapist, anyone I've slept with in the last ten years, the entire staff of Trilogy restaurant, any employee of the city of New York, the Central Intelligence Agency, the Federal Bureau of Investigation, Rupert Murdoch, the Union of Soviet Socialist Republics, every country that has the bomb, and myself, among others.

· 16 ·

April

The Talking Heads wake me up with "Psychokiller" on the radio alarm-clock. Can't disk jockeys be more compassionate at 7:00 A.M. on Monday morning? I scratch my nose, get up, switch off the radio, turn on the stereo, and wander, blinking, into the bathroom. I piss, flush, remember I should have waited until after my shower to flush because of the water pressure, curse, wash my hands, check my face for purple spots in the mirror. None today. I hop into the shower, hoping the hot water will work today.

I turn on the left faucet full force and wait. At the first sting of heat I turn on the right. I shampoo, rinse, work in some conditioner, soap up my body, rinse out my hair, rinse off my body, check for swollen glands in the crotch, under the arms, at the neck. None today.

I give myself a second cleaning with pHisoHex. I rinse off and stand, dripping, on a towel. I scoop up the hair clinging to the drain and toss it into the toilet, which is still flushing involuntarily. Naked, I jerk the chain stiff, and the rubber ball is sucked into place. I wipe off the mirror and shave briskly. I dab at the cuts with toilet paper. I step on the scale to check for sudden unexplained weight loss. None today.

Back in the kitchen, I scarf down a bowl of granola and skim milk, then pop twelve assorted vitamins into my mouth and wash them down with a gulp of orange juice. I go to the closet and put on some socks and underwear and a pair of slacks. I rinse the cereal bowl and leave it in the kitchen sink for tonight. I go to the bathroom and brush my teeth. I put the back of my hand on my forehead to check for fever. None today.

Back at the closet, I select a striped shirt and slip it on. I slip the noose of an already tied tie over my head and tighten it at the collar. I call 976-1212 to find out the weather and hang up in the middle of the recording, after I find out it will be in the mid-fifties this afternoon, with a chance of showers later in the evening. I put on a tweed jacket, grab my keys and my wallet and my backpack, and I'm off.

At the corner I discover that I've forgotten my belt. I pick up the *Times* and the *News* at the newsstand on Broadway and Fiftieth, walk past the scaffolding on the United Artists Twin Cinema, turn at the abandoned Howard Johnson's at Forty-ninth. Across the street the *Sperminator* is playing at the World—an unintentional AIDS title: death by sperm. The plump man who stands at the landing of the subway stop every day and asks for change with an empty coffee cup is wearing a Puerto Rican Day straw hat. Crowds surge through the stairs, forcing me to step against him. I stare at the ads on the R train. *"Para dolores hemorrhoides, Preparation H."* Poor Dolores, she's got hemorrhoids. She sits on her ass eight hours a day, she drives a cab, and the last thing she needs is hemorrhoids. After seven years of New York City subways I can read Spanish well enough to translate ads for *cupones de alimentos* (food stamps), *arroz Carolina con pollo* (chicken with Carolina rice), and *acercate con Certs* (breath mints). I'm ready to switch to another language, Italian maybe. I'd consider writing Mayor Koch with this suggestion, but he's up to his ears in graft, corruption, and municipal scandal. Meanwhile, opportunity is knocking. One can learn to be a cashier in six weeks and obtain gainful employment in such exciting venues as boutiques and grocery stores. I'm waiting for the ads to learn to be a street drug-dealer in six weeks (government loans available).

Today is the day I have decided to meet with Caroline and discuss the problems in our working relationship—Caroline, the albatross around my neck, my Achilles' heel, an animal-trainer who reads Kant, a large blob of protoplasm masquerading as a human being. Last week she came to work an average of three hours a day, claiming she was using up her comp time from last month's fiasco of a production job. I've been dreading this day for weeks.

Saturday I woke up livid at six in the morning, brooding over Caroline. I wrote down six thousand reasons to fire her: because she takes my suggestions grudgingly, like castor oil—she stuffs her fingers into her ears and rolls her eyes; because when we have meetings in my office, she plays with rubber bands, drums her fingers on *my* desk, bends paper clips, brushes a stray hair from her face and gets it caught in her granny glasses; because she is always asking me,

"What do you *mean?*" as if I am speaking Urdu or Xhosa and she left her phrase book at home; because she uses my phone to make personal calls when I'm out of my office and the phone she shares with two others in her office is in use, and she always replaces the receiver backward, so the cord snakes around; because she wears light-brown polyester pantsuits and pearl-white nail-polish; because she is the objective correlative to fingernails scraping on blackboards and bamboo under the nails; because she works at the rate of continental drift; because she's shorter than I am; because she projects an aura of electrostatic confusion and atmospheric imbalance, and the hair on the back of my neck stands on end when she is within five feet of me; because she always borrows tissues from my office by the handful; because she is as slow as molasses and stubborn as a mule and crazy as a loon and stiff as a board; because she brings out my latent misogyny to an extent surpassing even that caused by my own mother.

I try to ask my boss for advice on what to do with Caroline, but he's in Brazil this month, and I won't be able to schedule an appointment with him for another three weeks after.

I call Rachel and hear phones ringing in the background, bells and buzzers. She's in the middle of three deals. She barks some orders to her assistant and gets back to the phone. "B.J., try to separate the personality difficulties from the ones directly relating to job performance. Have a meeting with Caroline and discuss the objective factors of her performance that you are dissatisfied with and give her concrete suggestions on improvement. Present everything in a positive light. Say that you appreciate her contribution. Listen, B.J., I wish I had more time, but I've got American Express on line two and Citibank on line three. We'll have lunch next week, OK?"

Dennis tells me to calm down, take a deep breath, and count back from a hundred. Then I can fire her.

I talk to Gordon.

"Maybe she's a lezzie," he says. "Maybe she doesn't like men."

"Caroline a lesbian? You've got to be joking! If I found out she was a lesbian, then I'd never to able to fire her. Amalgamated has a very liberal policy on minorities. If they got wind that Miss Yamamoto was a lesbian, they'd probably promote her above me."

"J.k." Gordon chuckles.

" 'J.k.'?" I ask.

"Just kidding." Gordon and I work in the acronym-laden field of computer systems. Gordon has invented his own auxiliary language of abbreviation. I usually forget what they stand for. "J.k." is "just kidding"; "s.b.t." is "sad but true"; "t.t.g." is (drunk) "to the gills"; "f.o.s." is "full of shit"; "p.i.t.a." is "pain in the ass"; and so on.

"Check," I reply.

"Did you ever have one of those days where nothing went right?" asks Gordon in his plain, stuffed-up-nose voice.

"I'd say every day of my life."

"Let me tell you about yesterday. The system was down when I got in. I was all set to catch up on my correspondence; I was really pissed. I can't write anymore without using word-processing software. So I decided that I'd balance my checkbook instead. I was in my cubicle, and I was just about to start, when I get this phone call. My boss wanted me to go out to New Jersey and install a system. I told him I had an appointment in the afternoon in Brooklyn. He thought it was work related, so he said he'd try and get someone else. So I was supposed to meet this bike trainer this afternoon in Brooklyn, right? I take the BMT and get stuck in the tunnel for an hour. By the time I'm in Brooklyn, I'm half an hour late. I called the trainer at his home. He was out; I left a message on his machine. I took the next train back to Manhattan. It was a totally wasted day."

"Sorry."

"So you were telling me you had problems motivating Caroline to work?"

"I have a feeling you're the wrong person to discuss this with."

"Yeah, maybe you're right. Well, I'm sure you'll do the right thing," says Gordon.

"Thanks for the help."

"A.t."

" 'A.t.'?"

"Anytime."

Caroline stumbles in at eleven. "Could I see you in my office?" I ask.

She's just settling in, taking her coat off, putting it on the back of the chair. "Oh?" she asks, startled. "Can it wait a minute?" she asks, pointing to the steaming cup of coffee on her desk next to the Danish.

"Fifteen minutes," I say tersely, and leave. She comes in at 11:20 with a pad in her hand and a puzzled expression on her face.

"Good morning," she says.

"Good morning," I reply gruffly.

"I guess Herman is chomping at the bit again." Herman, the monster upstairs who runs his office like a Marine barracks, frequently gives us assignments, always marked "URGENT!!!" Herman's staff turns over at a rate comparable to that of a McDonald's restaurant, mainly a result of his gestapo tactics, which include monitoring bathroom breaks, never allowing staff vacations during August, and forcing the keyboarders who use Walkmen to play ergonomic tapes he obtained from Muzak. The keyboarders particularly hate him, pounding out anger with every stroke. I had made the mistake of grousing against Herman in the presence of Caroline; since then, she blamed Herman for everything.

"Not exactly." I don't know how to present this. "It's not Herman; it's you. We have to talk."

"Oh," says Caroline. "Well." She pauses. "Talk," she says coldly.

"Although your work has been consistently good, I've been having problems with your hours," I say with a trace of a nasal whine.

"Oh?" she asks. "What seems to be the problem?" she says, her voice totally devoid of emotion. The pupils of her black eyes contract.

"Well," I begin awkwardly, "you've been coming in rather late for quite some time."

"I have flexible hours," she says, proclaiming her inalienable rights, guaranteed by the Constitution and the employee handbook. "I don't see why it makes any difference when I come in, so long as I work seven hours every day."

"Well," I continue cautiously, "there have been several occasions when I've wanted to see you early in the morning. I've gotten in at nine A.M. and had to wait up to two hours to see you." Why am I on the defensive?

"I certainly don't want to hold you up," says Caroline, "but the way I understand it, I can come in as late as eleven."

"According to the memo I sent to personnel, *ten* is the cutoff."

"But a year ago you told me this memo was merely a formality," she insists.

I feel like a fool. Caroline is right. But why is it written in stone? "It's just not working out for me," I tell Caroline. "In the future I would like you to be in by ten every day."

"You're the boss," she says grimly.

"OK?"

"Ten o'clock it is." Caroline keeps late hours. I feel bad about cutting into her social life; I feel that I've withdrawn a privilege for no reason save malice. "I don't suppose there will be a grace period?"

"Pardon?" I ask.

"According to the employee handbook, workers who are supposed to arrive by nine o'clock are allowed a fifteen-minute grace period before being marked as tardy."

"Oh. Uh, let's say ten minutes," I compromise, instantly regretting my words.

"That seems fair to me," says Caroline.

Now in her mind she must arrive by 10:10, and I expect her to arrive up to ten minutes later at least every other day.

"Is there anything else?"

I look down at my yellow pad. I've written some notes for our meeting. Number one is tardiness. Number two is her combative nature. Number three is her slowness to accept and complete projects. Frankly, I'm exhausted from this confrontation. "No, I think that's all for now."

"OK. I'll go now, then, if that's OK with you," she says.

"Sure."

She saunters out and goes back to her office. I'm sure she'll be calling her friends, telling them what an inhuman boss she works for. I close the door and let out a sigh of relief. Nothing has been solved, but at least I've taken the first step.

Bob Broome returned home for the last two weeks in March. Unfortunately, he came down with another bout of pneumonia and went back into the hospital.

After work I go over to Lenox Hill Hospital to visit him. For a while they were afraid he was having a recurrence of his *Pneumocystis*. Luckily, the doctors determined it was only pneumococcal pneumonia. It's frightening that one can be *thankful* for ordinary pneumonia.

I've always hated hospitals. I loathe the antiseptic smell, the long, sterile corridors, the overhead fluorescent lights reflected in the freshly waxed floors below. The cool, harsh, efficient nurses who jab with their thermometers in the middle of a sentence and mechanically snip closed the IV tubes with saline or glucose solutions. The moronic attendants who, afraid of being in the same room as an AIDS patient for fear of contagion, leave dinner trays at the door. The painfully slow elevators, whose speed can be measured in millimeters per hour. The anguished bronze statuettes of Jesus on the cross on the walls of every room of Catholic hospitals.

The fact that the rooms are full of the sick and dying.

I went to see Bob once before today, with Dave Johnson, who had told me Bob was sick. Since I switched gyms, I saw Dave only occasionally, usually at Jones Beach. Dave's old roommate, Paco, died of AIDS late in 1984. Dave lives with his lover, Jerry, in the Village. They both work in showroom display.

At Lenox Hill I jog up three flights of stairs and find Bob Broome's room, which overlooks Park Avenue. The flowers are in bloom. At the door is a sign instructing all visitors to wear a mask and gown to avoid contaminating the patient. Bob gives me a weak smile. His hair is ratty; he hasn't shaved in days. His face is gaunt. He's connected to an IV. I smile nervously beneath my mask, then realize he can't see my facial expressions. My breath clouds and condenses on my upper lip. My glasses fog up at the bottom; I'm wearing a portable sauna. I walk over to the window and comment on the flowers. I try to think of nice ways to comment on his appearance without saying he looks like shit. According to the Duchess of Windsor, one can never be too rich or too thin. Well, here's proof positive she's wrong. Bob has lost over twenty-five pounds since last year.

Instead, I talk about Caroline and my difficulties at work. I talk about a rash on my arm that looks like an allergic reaction but is in fact the heartbreak of psoriasis. I tell him about a paper cut I got Xeroxing memos at work. I tell him about Michael Jackson and his $25,000 hyperbaric-oxygen sleeping-chamber. Then, when I tell him about some of the more attractive men at my current gym, he nods appreciatively. Bob perks up as I describe a twentyish blond in detail. "He's too stupid and beautiful to be a common whore. I think he's just kept." Bob seems to be engaged in this conversation. I figure I'm on the right track. I dish the dirt for half an hour and then leave him. I promise to call the next day to find out how he's doing.

Later that night I feel compelled to go out to the bars. I head for the Spike. Every major city has two gay bars, the Spike and the Eagle. A neon spike in the window announces the bar in lieu of a sign. Inside, bartenders wearing leather harnesses serve beer in cans to an assortment of brutes, heathens, and opera buffs. A large American flag is nailed to the wall above the red digital-clock that tells military time. At 23:45 several unsavory types with beer guts cluster at the doorway beneath, waiting to use the can.

I lean against the cigarette machine and watch the men play pool, sipping my Bud. Fully a third of the patrons are leather grannies, wizened creatures whose skin can no longer be distinguished from their vests and jackets. The sound system plays "Sledgehammer" by Peter Gabriel.

I wonder what draws me so urgently to the Spike tonight. The criminal's compulsion to return to the scene of the crime? The microbe's urge to return to the site of the infection?

After seeing Bob Broome, I don't want to be left by myself tonight. I'm afraid to be alone.

I call my friend Lucy from work the next day. We discuss therapists.

"Each week mine comes up with a new diagnosis for me," I complain. "One week he said I had no sense of self. What does that mean—when I look in the mirror, all I see is what's behind me? The next week I was hypoglycemic. I don't know when it will end. I thought I was suffering from generalized anxiety and depression. He makes me feel even crazier than I am."

"Is that possible? At least yours still listens to you. I think mine just sits there and writes down grocery lists."

"Or solves quadratic equations."

"I owe my therapist so much money I think he only sees me for entertainment: white noise while he does his taxes, a break between the patients he cares about, the ones he listens to, the ones whose balances are marked 'Paid in full.'"

"Don't you hate it how when you're just getting hot, he always tells you that time is about up?" I ask.

"They must have a class in that: Advanced Deprivation at the Carl Jung Institute for the Criminally Insane."

"Do you think yours is crazy?"

"I don't know. He never says anything to me except 'Our time is almost up' and 'I see from my records you now owe for twelve sessions.' I might as well be using a tape recorder."

"I think mine is dyslexic. When the bank returned the check he endorsed, I noticed the N was backwards."

"Mine just uses a paw print. Oh, my gawd!" Lucy does a fabulous Valley Girl imitation, even though she grew up in Rhinebeck, New York. "It's time we got together for brunch, isn't it?"

"Yeah." Once every few months I have lunch with the girls, genuine biological females, every one of them. I suppose I am the inverse of a fag hag. It never ceases to amaze me that they can be as foul as us guys. "I'll call Rosemary and Belinda, and you can ask Maxie."

"OK. Sunday at two?"

"Sounds good to me."

"Better get back to the salt mines. Miss Houlihan is breathing fire today, and I don't want to be responsible for her ulcerated duodenum."

"Catch you later."

"Bye."

It could just as well be me at Lenox Hill Hospital. I am painfully aware of this fact. It could just as well be me.

Six years and three gyms later, I run into Carlo Montagna from N.Y.U. at the Attitude Factory, a three-story gym in Chelsea. My former heartthrob has put on weight. Inside every perfectly proportioned muscle queen is a chubbette screaming to come out. Carlo gives me his famous half-smile, half-smirk, and for the first time I realize he stole it from the Mona Lisa. "Hi, B.J. How are you?"

"Still skinny," I think to myself. "Also, still unable to come up with something resembling intelligent conversation in the presence of someone who turned my knees to jelly six years ago."

"In therapy," I say to Carlo.

"Oh." He pauses. Once again I've thrown him for a loop. Why can't I just act normal and have a sane conversation for once, with anyone? He's probably thinking, "It's about time."

"I haven't seen you here," he says.

"I joined a few months ago. I had to leave my last gym. It was just a septic tank. I usually come late at night, after the crowds. It's pretty intimidating around six o'clock."

"Oh, these girls won't bite. They're all looking for husbands just like you and me. Well, I think I'll go back and finish my curls," says Carlo, abruptly finishing the exchange. He returns to his bench and starts lifting a thirty-pound dumbbell.

I look at Carlo. I was in love with this? How the mighty have fallen. I walk over to the mats and do my stretches. Five are for loosening up; the other ten are for getting rid of incipient spare tires. Eternal vigilance is the price of freedom from love handles. For the hell of it I do an extra set of bun-twisters on my back, a perennial crowd-pleaser.

In the age of anxiety gay men go to the gym five nights a week, just to keep out of trouble. On weekends it's home with the VCR, watching porno, "Masterbates Theatre." In between checkups and hospital visits there are Front Runners, the Central Park Ramblers, the Times Squares, the bowling league, Sundance, and a host of other gay athletic-groups. For the religious-minded there's Dignity, Congregation Beth Simchat Torah, and the Metropolitan Community Church. There's an endless list of twelve-step programs that meet at the Gay Community Center; people take on alibis at Adult Children of Alcoholics (ACOA), ACOA Al-Anon, ACOA Gay Men Incest Survivors, Alcoholics Anonymous, Cocaine Anonymous, Debtors Anonymous, Narcotics Anonymous, Overeaters Anonymous, Sexaholics Anonymous, Sexual Compulsives Anonymous, and Sexually Abused Anonymous. The socially conscious volunteer at the Gay Men's Health Crisis, the American Foundation for AIDS Research, the AIDS Network, the American Run to End AIDS, and so on. Any way to sublimate desire; anything to avoid sex.

I see the Dynamic Duo leaving the warm-up mat to go upstairs. I haven't figured out whether they are lovers or trainer and trainee or just a run-of-the-mill S&M couple. The younger one leads arrogantly, never looking back. The older follows, eyes lowered. There is a striking physical resemblance; the older has the body that the younger will grow into in ten or fifteen years. Both wear scanty T-shirts. Two dried raisins of nipples peek out from the older's spaghetti straps. He is far too pale to be wearing this little. I've overheard their strained conversations, with sentences carefully measured so as not to tax each other's intellectual capacity. They chat in monosyllables in the middle of the floor yet glare protectively when anyone dares to approach the station they are planning to work at next.

I've decided that most of the boys are actually blind. *That's* why they ignore me completely. Their Walkpersons are in actuality radar sensors cleverly disguised, I theorize. The weights are marked in braille with irregular bumps that to the uninformed would appear to be defects.

Gwen Guthrie whines over the speakers that nothing's going on except the rent. Upstairs, a six-foot brunet with perfect teeth and a sheepish grin lumbers by wearing the Annie-Hall-Got-Raped-in-Central-Park look, layers and layers of ripped and torn clothes: a faded, unzipped sweatshirt; a pair of sweatpants that the dog must have gotten to, hanging down so low I can see the Fruit of the Loom underwear hiking up toward his waist; several oversized pairs of socks stuffed into a pair of Converse basketball sneakers with the rubber on the soles peeling away. A compact, well-muscled man in his fifties carefully rearranges his shoulder straps so only one pencil-eraser nipple is displayed at a time, depending on the exercise. A singer-slash-accountant in a pair of black Lycra biking shorts chats with an actor-slash-hairdresser wearing aquamarine surfer jams covered with blue, yellow, and white frolicking porpoises. I take a long drink at the water fountain, wondering what virus I might catch. I count the gulps and stop at an even multiple of four. I check out the bulletin board: an ad for a used PC, Spanish lessons, muscular massage, Dancercize, psychotherapy, fearless dentistry, several shares for Fire Island Pines this summer, and an AIDS bereavement seminar.

Near the pull-down machines I get a lecture on body parts from a guy who looks like Mel Gibson on steroids. This is usually the least effective way of flirting with me. However, this stud could fascinate me by reading price quotes from the Dow Jones Industrials in a monotone. "I hope you don't mind me telling you all this," he concludes.

"I hope you don't mind me ignoring all this," I reply to myself. Predictably, he walks away after completing his set and disappears down the stairs.

I have rules for the gym. Never take advice from anyone less developed than I am. Avoid lifting multiples of thirteen. I try to convince myself I'm not being superstitious when I skip from 120 to 140 pounds on the leg machine; I tell myself I'm just pushing myself. Besides, I don't know offhand of any apartment buildings with a thirteenth floor; this is hardly unprecedented behavior. Another rule is avoid Mondays. The gym is always crowded after the debaucheries of a weekend; everyone has to work off the Lucullan feasts and Dionysian libations comprising the Sunday brunch. Because of the widespread knowledge that Mondays are always crowded, however, more people are skipping Mondays and coming on Tuesdays. If this trend continues, in fifteen years Fridays will be the most crowded day.

When interrupting someone's solitary set, always ask, "Mind if I work in with you?" When finishing a shared set, remark as you depart, "It's all yours." Try not to curse when the girls are gossiping at the water fountain and all you want is a drink. Avoid the protein drinks that come in shampoo bottles. Don't try to wear the trashiest outfit; someone is bound to find a sleazier costume.

After my workout I go downstairs for a shower. I look around, checking for purple spots. A peroxide-blond is meticulously shaving his body. Is there no decency? Has he no shame? I decide he doesn't, remembering his Lycra bodysuit from the gym floor, which left nothing to the imagination: I could tell that he wasn't circumcised, shaved his pubes, and had one solitary pimple on his ass.

I go to the steam room. The music is drowned out by the jets of steam. I pretend that they took out the speakers in preparation for the renovation. They'll be placing video monitors with MTV in the steam room and the sauna. No, there will be video cameras in the steam room transmitting to the monitors in the sauna and vice versa. The mirrors are too poorly laid out for optimal cruising. All but a few seats have a partial view. A month ago the steam room was locked, an explanation on the door: "Because several members have abused the equipment and other members, the steam room will be closed indefinitely." Two weeks later, someone posted an angry rebuttal, alluding to a private party allegedly held by the management after hours in the steam room. The next day both signs were gone and the steam room reopened. I expected there would be a new sign: "No lifeguard on duty. Steam at your own risk." The two remaining bathhouses in New York, the Wall Street and the East Side Sauna, have "Lifeguards," whose duty is to be Big Brothers peeping through keyholes, watching to make sure that everyone wears rubbers and no bodily fluids are exchanged. The Health Department closed down the St. Mark's Baths last December.

In the changing room Ed Gumm tells me he'd like to talk with me. I met Ed at my last gym in their cesspool of a sauna. Ed has jet-black hair, a pronounced overbite, a pleasant disposition, a nice body, and a huge dick. He is one of the few circuit queens (hot discos, Fire Island Pines, trendy gyms, and Metropolitan Opera, Metropolitan Museum, and Metropolitan Movie House) I know who actually returns phone calls. I lusted after Ed years ago, but since we never got together for sex, the tension was gone.

"Sit down," he says in a low voice. We're on the bench. I'm watching another unattainable blond goddess dry his hair and hoping his towel, knotted around the waist, will fall.

"What's the poop?" I ask, only half-listening. He's finally free for Friday night? He's three years too late.

He gives me a somber look and begins. "I haven't been around the gym much for the past month. I wanted to tell you what's been going on. My lover died two weeks ago. He had three inoperable brain tumors. He got sick; it was very fast. I just wanted to let you know."

"God, I'm sorry."

"That's OK."

"You'd been together for long?" I didn't even know he had a lover.

"Thirteen years."

"Jesus, I'm sorry."

"It's been rough."

"Are you all right?"

"I'm doing OK."

"Let me know if you want to do anything." I don't know what to say. I leave the gym, enveloped in a thick black cloud of despair. I'm reeling. I wish there were some way to stop the dying.

I meet the biological females for brunch on Sunday at a gallery/restaurant in the East Village. This month's artist has covered the walls with portraits of animals in heat. I arrive at quarter past two. As expected, Rachel canceled at the last minute. Maxie, the Zulu Warrior I met at the San Francisco airport, is sitting at the bar, chewing on the plastic stirrer in her vodka tonic. Her hair has almost grown back. Today she's wearing only four earrings. She greets me with a smile and pulls back a chair for me. "Damn it, where's Lucy?"

"Late as usual. You haven't been waiting long, have you?"

"I got here at two o'clock on the dot. At least someone here cares about being *punctual*," she says, spitting out the last word like an olive pit. She upends a worn copy of *Lady Chatterley's Lover* on the counter. "So, how are you, B.J.? Long time no see. Don't you think I look *pretty* in my black-leather miniskirt and matching jacket and genuine yellow fishnet stockings? I'm not *fishing for compliments*, mind you. I just want an honest appraisal."

"Are those shoulder pads?"

"No, dummy, they're *false titties.* I just store them on the shoulders for ease and comfort. Who else is coming?"

"I think it's Belinda, Rosemary, and Martha. Hey, watch out on the sauce," I say, pointing to the sign behind the bar, warning pregnant women that drinking alcohol can cause birth defects. I wonder why they bother with this sign at the Spike.

"What do you think, I'm *preggers?* Do I look like I have a *bun in the oven?* Am I *positively glowing?* Am I blossoming into a *woman?* Do I appear to be in the *family way?* Am I *eating for more than one?* In other words, am I *about to drop a litter?*"

"You do look in the bloom of health."

"It's Chernobyl. I'm glowing because I just had chicken Kiev. Look, there's Rosemary."

The last time I saw Rosemary she got mad at me because I told her she looked perky à la Mary Tyler Moore in *The Dick Van Dyke Show* in her new haircut. Where Maxie can be a bundle of nervous energy, Rosemary's a lesson in languorous subversion.

"Why, I do believe I'll join you," says Rosemary, sidling up to a stool.

"I think we've passed the critical mass necessary to get a table," I remark.

"Well, then, let's '*Please wait to be seated by server,*'" says Maxie, reading from the sign at the steps to the main dining-room.

Stopping short of blowing kisses, I give Rosemary a brief hug. "I'm afraid of intimacy. I found that out from a test in *Cosmopolitan* last Tuesday at the supermarket," I explain sheepishly.

"Don't worry. I was so afraid of commitment that it took me years to even get a magazine subscription," says Rosemary. "Where's Lucy?"

"Fashionably late."

"Shall we make wagers?"

"I think we should all get the brunch special."

"Oh, I see Belinda and Martha. No, that's Kathy."

"Martha couldn't make it," explains Belinda, seating herself. "PMS?"

"No, she's out shopping for a bridesmaid's dress with her mother."

"This is my friend Kathy."

"We've already met."

"Hi."

"I bet Lucy won't be here before three."

"What are we betting?"

"Sugar in the Raw? Sounds *obscene* to me," says Maxie, reading a paper packet of sugar.

"Stop playing with the silverware. Can't take you anywhere."

"Can't even dress me up."

"Where's the waiter? I'm famished!"

"What's the brunch special?"

"Let's see. There's Spanish omelettes, western omelettes, three-cheese omelettes, smoked-salmon-and-chives omelettes, steak and eggs, and eggs Benedict."

"Don't they have anything else?" I whine.

"Now, B.J., for *godsakes* don't give us that *egg-paranoia* speech again," admonishes Maxie. "Poor little pussy! He's afraid of a little *ovum*. Can you believe it?"

"Fruit salad for him," suggests Belinda.

"Now, girls, let's not be nasty," says Rosemary.

"Show us why you spend all of your time at the gym, B.J. Make a muscle for us," demands Maxie.

"Come on, B.J., let's see," chorus in Belinda and Kathy.

"Not here," I whisper. "I'm incognito. If anyone sees me flexing my bicep, my cover's ruined. I'll be deluged with sycophants and admirers and whores ripping off articles of apparel for souvenirs. They're uncontrollable. And there goes our quiet brunch."

"OK, we'll skip it." Maxie relents.

"What's taking Lucy?" asks Kathy.

"The poor thing lives in Brooklyn. It's probably subway delays."

"Jumper in front of the train. Had to scrape him off, takes at least an extra hour."

"Killer mutant rats in the tunnel under the East River attacked the engine."

"Hey, guys, do you think I'll ever get laid by someone whose IQ is higher than a *turnip's* in this lifetime?" asks Maxie.

"What do you expect, working at the Reggae Lounge?"

"You don't think I'd actually go out with the *scum*, the *vermin*, the *dregs of humanity* that hang out there? Just because my hair was trendy for a while, *everybody* was offering me joints and pills and crystal and acid, and you know I don't do drugs. I'm *pure as the driven snow*, and besides, the dope was shit. By the time you strained all the seeds there was nothing left. I'm talking about Scotty."

"Maxie, you're worth ten thousand Scottys. Just forget him."

"Get over him," says Kathy.

"Oh, great," says Rosemary as the waitress delivers a pitcher of Bloody Marys. "Let me serve," she insists. A head shorter than everyone else at the table, Rosemary distributes the contents of the pitcher without spilling a drop. "Dear." She pauses. "I forgot the parsley garnishes. Oh, well!"

"Did you save some for me?" Lucy breezes in. "Hi, guys, sorry I'm late." She takes off her black-lace gloves one at a time. Lucy wears a matching hat and a pale-blue prom dress she bought second-hand on St. Mark's Place that has an indelible port-wine stain on the back under her white shawl.

"Subway trouble?" asks Belinda.

"An all-night date, and if he doesn't call me by tomorrow, I'll tell him I have herpes," says Lucy.

"But you don't now, do you?" I ask.

"No. He'll find out eventually. Scare tactic."

To think that *herpes* is so upsetting to the straights.

"Maxie, where did you get that miniskirt?" demands Lucy. "I want one just like it!"

"You've seen it before, the night we went to Heartbreak."

"I was so drunk that night you could have been wearing the carcass of Jacqueline Bouvier Kennedy Onassis wrapped around your throat and I wouldn't have noticed."

"Can you believe that woman over there in the polka-dotted muumuu?"

"Don't stare."

"She looks like a *Glamour* Don't."

"Remember *Glamour* Dos and Don'ts? They'd have a photograph of Sally Teenager sitting in a skirt with her legs wide open and a ton of mascara, and there would be this black diagonal slash through the photo, like on a 'No Smoking' sign."

"Hey, has anyone been to the Egyptian restaurant next to the Pyramid? There's a gorgeous waiter there. I've gone there at four in the morning and had five cups of cappuccino just to get him to wait on me," says Lucy.

"Him?" Maxie bends her pinkie. "I had him. He gets the *limp-dick-of-the-year* award. Everyone thinks he's so *hot*. He couldn't even get it up, and there wasn't much to start with, anyway."

"That omelette looks like a Today sponge."

"Did you ever get one stuck in you? You practically have to get a fishhook to get it out."

"I used a plumber's helper."

"Did you get the *worst* yeast infection?" asks Maxie.

"Did you have to dial the 800 number to get it out?"

207

" '*Stay calm,*'" says Maxie. "This matron would come on the line. You know she's postmenopause; she must be sixty. She's spent the past twenty years as a guard at the state penitentiary. You can tell she doesn't have a lot of sympathy for you."

I clear my throat. I feel uncomfortable. I don't want it to look like I've staged this luncheon just to get pledges for the AIDS Walk. I hate to ask for favors. I tell the biological females about the AIDS Walk next month, a sort of March of Dimes, with proceeds going to Gay Men's Health Crisis. All five of them sign up. Lucy calls herself "Lucy Brook Astor Ziti" on the pledge sheet.

"Now all you have to do is figure out the check for us, and we're set," says Lucy.

6:12 P.M.

At three o'clock I decide that I am dying. Five years ago I could have attributed my sore throat to strep, clap, or sheer stretching in the act of fellatio, but now I know that it is candidiasis, a.k.a. thrush, a.k.a. a logical precursor to AIDS, which means that I will be dead before the year is out. I am at work, shuffling papers and solving crises with mild-mannered telephone calls and drop-dead memos. Suddenly, it all seems existentially absurd, even more meaningless than yesterday.

At four o'clock I begin to make plans for disposing of my worldly goods. I'll give the lease to my rent-stabilized apartment to my friend Philip, who gave me herpes years ago. I figure that will really make him feel guilty, and at least I'll be remembered this way. The books and magazines will go to the hospital across the street with the AIDS unit. I hope the nuns don't mind the pictorials from Power Tool. There are no plants, because I refuse to allow any other living organisms in my apartment—OK, Jessica can get the cockroaches. Dennis can take what's left of the Dewar's. I'll give Gordon the unreadable novel I wrote in college. I can already hear him smirking to his lover, Jonathan, "It's a tour de force." The nude photos of me can go back to the photographer so he can sell a limited-edition printing of maybe twenty million poster-sized beefcakes, proceeds to be donated to the AIDS foundation of his choice. The swimsuit of most recent vintage goes back to the salesperson who drooled when I tried it on, the gym apparel to my sleazy health-club. I'd like to be burned or buried in the Fortunoff watch.

At four-thirty I contemplate possible methods of suicide. Pistols? Can I make an appointment with destiny or, saving that, one with Bijan on Fifth Avenue to get one of his designer gold-plated pistols? Naturally, I'll charge everything from now on. Who needs an I.R.A. these days? I'd prefer a purse-sized pearl-handled revolver. Maybe

209

pills. I would leap in front of the IRT express to get back at the subway system once and for all (imagine the mess), except I know how distressing it would be for the passengers. I can already hear the garbled message over the loudspeaker: "Attention, passengers, there will be a slight delay in service due to mrfxgggggl xrffffffff gggggggggg rrrr hmmmmmmmmmmmmmmmmmm." When I was in college, a humanist-feminist professor of contemporary literature, who once had the effrontery to accuse me of having an unresolved Oedipal complex when I had interrupted one of her student conferences to demand the return of some odious papers I had written the previous semester so I could bury them, suggested to our class once that should suicide ever be the only rational solution, the best thing to do would be to take some tyrant down with you, to die in a kamikaze blaze of glory. She suggested Qaddafi or Idi Amin; I wonder whether I could set up an interview with William F. Buckley at The National Review.

At five o'clock my throat burns like a flame as I take the subway to my doctor. I take a seat. My senses seem hypersensitive, acute. I notice every detail. A woman sitting next to me is picking her cuticles, then shaking her floor-length, fake-fur coat. The train is stuck. I move down the car. I can't take it. I am dying. I sit again. The woman across from me makes loud popping noises as if she is cracking her knuckles. I look closely and see it is her gum she is snapping. Why are these sounds so magnified? Why is everything so loud and horrible? An attractive man stands by the door, glasses and a brown mustache, reading Barbara Pym. I decide I am entitled to one last cruise. I am going to die. I might as well look.

At six o'clock the doctor says, "Yes, your tonsils are inflamed. You appear to have a sore throat." He recommends lozenges. I'm ready for a prescription. "You can try Sucrets or Luden's cough drops. You can find them at any drugstore."

My voice is a whisper. I can barely say it. "It's not . . . it's not thrush or anything?"

He looks at me, puzzled, then sighs. He looks at me calmly. He thinks about his house in Maine. He says quietly, reassuringly, "Oh, no. Thrush typically produces white spots on the palate. You have nothing to worry about. It's quite painful. You would know it if you got it."

At 6:12 A.M. I leave the doctor's office with a new lease on life. But for how long?

· 17 ·

May

I meet Bob at his apartment. It's Friday, prime date-night. But, hey, I'm no teenager. How can I say no to a dying man? Bob's been out of the hospital for three weeks. He was hoping to go back to work part-time; he tried for a few days and became exhausted. His doctor recommended he rest and wait a month or so before trying again. I wish he had an elevator in his building. He lives on the fourth floor, and it's quite a climb for him.

We take a cab down to the Village. At six the French bistro is quite empty. We deposit our jackets with a young woman whose silky black hair is done up with two knitting needles. She presides over the cloakroom, which is in a hallway under the stairs of the adjacent building. Irritated, she gives us a check and returns to her Virginia Woolf paperback.

The dining room is small and efficient, with walls of polished bronze, mirrors, and tiny paintings of impressionist landscapes. There are only four couples dining at this hour. The busboy rushes to refill my water glass after every sip. The menu is modest. Bob skips the preprandial cocktail. "Once you get *Pneumocystis,* you're never rid of it," he explains to me. "I have to take this medicine twice a day for the rest of my life to prevent recurrent bouts. I'm not supposed to be drinking any alcohol."

"Well, I might as well skip my gin and tonic."

"Oh, don't on account of me," says Bob.

"That's OK; I wasn't feeling like it," I lie.

I have roast chicken, and Bob orders the broiled flounder.

"Does it taste good?" he asks.

"Sure, it's great. Would you like a piece?" I offer to cut a piece of my chicken, hoping he won't take it. If he does, I will accidentally drop my fork on the floor afterward, so the waiter will replace it with another. I know it's impossible to catch anything from sharing silverware. Still.

"No, thanks, I was just asking. I couldn't tell myself. I seem to have lost a lot of my sense of taste. It must be the medication," drones Bob in his inimitable monotone.

"Everything is cooked to perfection here."

"That's good to know." Bob takes a pill after the meal. I don't ask what it's for.

"Well, are you up for a play?"

"I suppose so," says Bob. "It's still pretty early. It's not that far, is it?"

"Just around the corner."

We walk to the Gay Community Center, a renovated high-school on Thirteenth Street. We take our time. At the door we find out the play is on the third floor. Bob balks at the steep stairs. I tell him to take it easy. He ascends, huffing and puffing, stopping at each landing. It's a struggle. The play, a TV-sitcom farce, is moderately amusing. Afterward, going downstairs is easier than going up was.

"I guess the Palladium is out for tonight."

"I guess it is."

"Hey, Bob, you don't have it so bad," I say, flagging a cab at the corner of Thirteenth and Sixth. "Do you realize that I don't have a date for tomorrow? That will make three Saturdays in a row!"

"You poor thing," agrees Bob in his depressingly laconic voice. "I haven't had a date since July of last year."

"Well, you have an excuse, don't you?" Did I say the wrong thing?

"I suppose so."

"Gee, I'm sorry. I hope I didn't hurt your feelings."

"That's OK. I never had any. I work in the exciting world of data-processing, where emotions are optional."

"How could I forget, being in the same profession? Jeeze, I could kick myself. Well, I had a nice time tonight."

"So did I. Let's do it again."

"OK. Take care of yourself." The cab drops me off on the way to Bob's. I hand him my portion of the fare. I give him a firm grip on the shoulder, and then I'm off.

I wake up at seven on Sunday morning, the second day of the infernal Ninth Avenue International Grease Fair, serving oils and hydrogenated fats from a panopoly of nations: Italian sausage drowning in its own fat, Pennsylvania funnel cakes that absorb grease better than Bounty, Vietnamese spring rolls that can and do soak up to ninety times their weight in saturated oils. Every year I threaten to flee to Southern California or the Jersey shore during the Food Fair, and every year I find I cannot leave, due to extenuating circumstances. For about twelve hours each day, a cacophonous din approximately equivalent in decibels to a Boeing 747 jet taking off from Shea Stadium during a Ted Nugent heavy-metal concert greets me at my second-story window.

This year I can't leave town because of the AIDS Walk. At eight I make my way up Ninth Avenue, the street a Jackson Pollock canvas of spray-can plastic colored strings, this year's fad, along with green-foam Statue of Liberty crowns. Last year it was animal-snout masks, and the year before, antennas on springs. Up at the plaza across from Damrosch Park, tables line the perimeter for registrations. I'm meeting Philip Moscowitz, who still to this day denies that it was he who gave me herpes. He's moved to Jersey and bought a four-story Victorian house in an unsavory neighborhood to renovate in the first wave of gentrification. Philip is late as usual. I sit, perched on the concrete ledge facing the rows of green benches in the band-shell area.

I had done fairly well collecting pledges. I even tried to sign up Bob Broome, explaining that this would be trickle-down supply-side economics in practice; he'd eventually get it back. But then he started an interminably involved explication of zero-sum theories and the inherent fraudulence of pyramid schemes; cutting him off, acknowledging his superior powers of reasoning and his ability to bore a man comatose, I conceded. At work I pondered the morality of marshaling my many minions to sign up, but then my eminently practical friend Rachel, who has enough common sense in her pinkie for Ann Landers, Dear Abby, Ask Beth, and Doctor Ruth, advised me against it. So instead I went through my little black telephone-book and amassed almost two hundred dollars in pledges. This netted me one ticket to the gala celebration next month at the "fabulous Saint nightclub," as it was referred to in the pledge brochure—which I would probably skip.

"Hi." Philip stands at my feet. "Sorry I'm late. I was almost out of the door when Fred threw up, and I had to clean it up." Fred was his cat. "He *always* does it on the carpet. You'd think for once he'd miss and get the linoleum in the kitchen. Traffic was fine through the tunnel, but it still took me a while to get a parking space. Should we get a seat?"

"I think the opening ceremony is going to start soon."

"I'd really like to look around a little first, see who I know." Trust Philip to go cruising at an AIDS benefit.

"Tell you what; I'll save you a seat in this row."

"Great." And he's off making the rounds, exchanging heavy brown-eyed stares and an occasional phone number. I read through the program, looking for wealthy single benefactors in the list of sponsors. The director of the event comes to the podium, and the canned music stops, Ethel Merman in the middle of "Everything's Coming Up Roses." After a brief speech on the background of the event and GMHC, he introduces Mayor Koch. The crowd responds with a mixture of applause and hisses. Philip stumbles over my feet to his chair, whispering, "Excuse me." Our benevolent mayor lists his administration's positive accomplishments in the fight against AIDS. He wishes us the best and pledges his full support until this deadly disease is conquered, and then he dashes off for another public appearance to give another speech to another set of constituents.

"He'll do everything within his power to stop AIDS, so long as it doesn't cost anything," I grumble to Philip. "Compared to San Francisco, Koch hasn't done shit."

"Remind me to move to the West Coast when I get symptoms," says Philip.

We listen to a few more speeches. Peter Allen accompanies himself on the piano for a song. Then we are instructed to leave Damrosch Park single file. More than six thousand of us are expected to squeeze through a tiny exit one by one, shepherded by marshals with green arm-bands. Crushed, we slowly ooze through the opening to the sidewalk. In twenty minutes Philip and I are out the gate. Gradually, over the course of five blocks, the march elongates and thins. After the second stoplight the walk is pleasant. Facilitators at corners play crossing guards, giving directions for turning. They gossip, collect dates, compare notes, cruise the crowd.

"I was feeling a little damp last night," confesses Philip. "You know, and I was getting scared. I figure you don't get night sweats all at once. It comes in stages; maybe it starts with just feeling a little wet." Philip's nasal whine should be patented; hairdressers wouldn't need to comb hair up before cutting it because his recorded voice would make it stand on end.

"Don't worry. You'll *know* when you get night sweats. Last month I discovered a bruise on the side of my ankle; it cost me eighty bucks to find out it was just a healing contusion. There's no sense in getting paranoid," I reply, eating my words as I speak them. Intellectually, I'm convinced. The only thing to fear is fear itself. Psychologically, I'm a basket case, but there's no sense in alarming Philip.

We stride up Madison on the East Side and make a left turn a few blocks past the north end of Central Park. "I've never been this far north before. Are we in Harlem?"

Philip grabs his shucked T-shirt, tucked in the back pocket of his shorts. "Cotton comes to Harlem?"

"Nosebleed territory."

"Well, some people think anything north of Fourteenth Street is upstate."

"This is practically the North Pole for them."

We continue tramping across, back to the West Side. At Riverside Park we head south. A family picnics in the grass. The father asks what the march is for. Someone shouts, "GMHC," four unassuming initials. A guy wearing a spike earring in his left ear and a torn pair of shorts with a large key-chain on his belt-loop—along with a pair of handcuffs and a red hankie in his back pocket—shouts, "AIDS."

"Oh," says the father.

"Now I suppose he's going to grab his wife and children, run for cover, rush home, lock the doors, close the drapes," the guy in the torn shorts spits out disgustingly. "Stupid breeders," he mutters. "You can't catch it by casual contact, so don't worry," he yells at the father, but he's out of earshot.

Soon enough we are back at our starting point, about two and a half hours after we set out. Philip drifts off to some friends to say good-bye. He has some yard work to do today. I stay for the closing ceremonies. The emcee announces that we have raised close to $700,000 today. The march has been an enormous success.

That night an army of street-cleaning machines invades Ninth Avenue from the north, mowing down anything in their paths. The Food Fair is over. They march down Ninth Avenue in concert, a team of bulldozers scrubbing the road clean. A few follow gracefully some yards behind, dancing in ever-widening curves, waltzing in circles at the curbs. The next morning the only remnants are a few indelible plastic strings ironed into the pavement.

*   *   *   *

My life is a scene from a Jackie Collins novel. The bitch. The stud. The cunt. The slut. You Hollywood wife, you! The world is filled with divorced women. *The world is filled with married men.* I am jealous. Bob has invited me to dinner with his friends Gary and Patrick. After one look I am head over heels in love with Patrick, who, naturally, has a lover.

My life is a series of restaurants and meals. My mother's letters are always filled with buffets and dinners, wedding spreads and Jewish Home Volunteer banquets. When I go on trips, I consider sending her menus in lieu of postcards. Gallagher, a tobacco-chewing transplanted Texan whom I met in California, has a basic philosophy about food: Fill the hole. As for me, any orifice is open and waiting—like the pegs and the board, the blocks and the hole. Bend over and fill the hole.

I am the last to arrive at Fellini's, an Italian restaurant on Columbus. Bob Broome is in the middle of his Thanksgiving story. When I enter, he starts from the beginning again.

"My aunt had invited me for Thanksgiving dinner. She said to be there around four P.M. I was still in college. I didn't really like my aunt that much, but I decided that I might as well go. After all, she was my aunt. The rest of the relatives I didn't care much for at all. But I assumed that since they were relatives, they would be happy to see me. I was pretty depressed that semester. I thought it would be a nice break to go there for Thanksgiving dinner. Think again. Anyways, I ended up taking a Greyhound bus for four hours. The bus broke down on Interstate 90, and I ended up getting to the station an hour late. I thought I still had time. I took a cab from the station to Aunt Mary's. When I got there, I didn't expect everyone to come up and greet me. But I thought at the least Aunt Mary would come over. She did, eventually, and said, 'Oh, since you were late, we ate without you. We ended up eating at three; the kids were hungry. Here's your place. I kept the food warm on the stove.' Now, I had traveled four and a half hours on a bus just to have dinner with the family, and they had eaten without me."

I chew on a toothpick and start peeling the label off the bottle of Heineken. I know that Bob has just told the entire story to Gary and Patrick. We make a few jokes. "But, Bob, that happened forty years ago! Get over it, Mary," says Patrick.

"It was only twelve years," he says grudgingly.

"Listen, are the dinosaurs still mad about the climate change?" asks Gary. "No, they're extinct. And what about the caveman that invented fire? Is he still pissed that he didn't take out a patent on it? Nah, he doesn't care. Is Yma Sumac still angry at that reporter who ruined her career by claiming she was Amy Camus from Brooklyn instead of a Peruvian princess?" he continues. "She forgave. You got to move on, Bob."

"Oh, well, I suppose so."

This is at least better than Bob's stories about the twenty-three-year-olds who stood him up on Saturday-night dates. A few years back, at the West Side Y, every time I talked to him he went into this half-hour monologue about the latest inconsiderate twenty-three-year-old he had met at the gym who was initially pleasant and cheerful and after two months even gave Bob his phone number and a few weeks later agreed to go out on a Saturday night but then on Saturday at five called Bob to tell him that something had come up: an extra opera ticket, a pulmonary bypass operation, an unexpected visit from a maternal relative, or a particularly embarrassing haircut that made him cover the mirrors, lock the doors, and refuse to leave the apartment for at least ten days, let alone be seen by friends. Why did Bob persist in attempting to rob the cradle? Was something going wrong with his brain?

Gary has a tightly trimmed black beard. His cologne reads subdued but intense sensuality. Gary wears regulation Levi 501 jeans and a Ralph Lauren polo shirt. If he didn't live in Chicago, I'd probably be making a move toward him. But I can't keep my eyes off Patrick. Patrick's voice is comforting, like warm oatmeal, the flat *a*'s of a South Boston accent. He has the kind of appeal that makes you realize that he will always be in a long-term relationship: If he ever were to split up with his lover, they'd be lining up around the block just for a chance to snap him up. His Irish good looks and twinkling green eyes are part of it; so is a slight thickening in the waist, which makes him attractive like Gary Trudeau's *Doonesbury* characters, where the women all have twenty-three-inch Scarlett O'Hara waists and the men all have reassuring love-handles. Patrick is always expressing what is on everybody's mind, clarifying nebulous, unformed thoughts into common sense. I wonder if his lover ever takes vacations without him.

"I just joined the Y," says Patrick. "It's sort of exciting seeing naked penises in the showers after eight years of nothing but Bill, my lover."

"How is the Y these days?" asks Bob. He hasn't been back since he'd gone to the hospital.

"It gets pretty crowded in the evenings. It's a change for me. A lot of time I feel I'm just getting into a rut, stuck in the same routine. Go to work, go home, make dinner for Bill and me, feed the birds, veg out in front of the TV, go to bed, and so on. It's kind of boring."

I want to add some excitement to Patrick's life. Why does he have to be so married? Gary is returning to Chicago on Monday. He and Bob will probably go to see a foreign movie at the Cinema Studio tomorrow. I wonder how Bob can be so dull on the surface and have such interesting friends. Maybe he used to be fascinating. Is he hung or something? When Bob goes to the bathroom, Patrick comments on the twenty-three-year-old stories that Bob is always telling. "I don't know why he doesn't get the message. I guess that's just his dream date, a twenty-three-year-old blond who looks like a model. But, I mean, he *does* have floppy ears, and let's face it, he isn't the most attractive man in the world. I don't know why he kept on trying. It doesn't make any sense to me."

"My ideal date is Irish and has green eyes and a Boston accent," I say, looking straight into Patrick's eyes. He laughs, as if to cover his nervousness, but then I can see he isn't bothered at all. "Married, too. I don't know, married men have that 'je ne sais quoi' appeal."

"You mean they're unavailable?" asks Patrick.

"I guess that could be it," I respond.

"Do you think we should split now? I don't want to tire Bob out," says Gary.

"He looks pretty good now," I say.

"Let's just ask him what he wants to do," says Patrick.

"Is someone discussing me in the third person?" asks Bob, back from the john. He's wheezing a little from the steps. "If so, I hope it's flattering."

"We were just wondering what you were up to."

"I thought we might stop by the Works for a nightcap," says Bob.

"Sounds good to me," says Gary.

"Sure you don't want to go out dancing?" I bait.

"Not really. I'm a little tired. Actually, I don't want to end up staying out too late. Things don't get moving until two in the morning, and that's way past my bedtime," says Bob.

We pay the check and walk up Columbus to the Works. A year or so ago they played continuous porn videos on the TV sets. You would walk into the bar to find everyone staring at the screen above your head. No one would ever talk, let alone meet there. Now they play music videos and comedy clips. We have a beer, stand in the back by the pool table, and cruise the crowd. I feel tired. Patrick wants to stay. Gary and Bob are leaving, so I decide to go, too, even though part of me wants to stay and try to seduce Patrick—a hopeless cause.

"Exactly why do they call these fun runs?" I pant to Joey Romano, two miles into a four-mile run in Central Park with Front Runners.

"I'm having fun. Luis over there is having fun. So is Tom up ahead. Aren't you having fun?"

"Gee, I think I'm having *too much* fun. Maybe I should stop and walk back. I don't know if my heart can take this much excitement."

"Don't be silly. Come on, B.J., I know you can make it. Just take it nice and easy. I'll see you back at the restaurant."

"I guess."

Joey speeds up and zips off into the distance. He's running six miles today. He's training for a triathlon out on Montauk this summer. I concentrate on my breathing. Running's easy, just one foot in front of the other.

Last week I decided to start running again, figuring maybe I could tack on a few hours to my life expectancy. The way I see it, the only life insurance I could get these days would be term, renewable every two weeks, with a mandatory physical each time. All the stuff I do at the gym is purely aesthetic, just for looks. Is that why so many of the guys at the gym are superficial? I try and meet the intellectual types at bookstores, but all the attractive men tend to congregate in the porno sections. What else can I do? Found a homosexual chapter of Mensa?

A few of my friends belonged to Front Runners, a gay running-group named after a pulp novel by Patricia Nell Warren. The gay protagonist gets shot in the end. I figured I might as well join. I worry about cholesterol, because my father died of a heart attack at an early age. I've got to start doing something cardiovascular. Somehow,

I don't think amyl nitrite fits the bill. So I went to the Athlete's Foot (why would anybody name a store after a foot disease?) and got a pair of running shoes that came with an owner's manual, and I thought this was getting too serious. I met Joey Romano, a tall, skinny Italian from Brooklyn, at the start of the Wednesday run in Central Park. He said he'd run with me to show me the course.

Joey is all legs. I look around and notice that my legs look like toothpicks in comparison with the rest of the runners present; but then, I'm the only one who isn't flat-chested. I start out at a brisk trot. Joey tells me to slow down. I figure I can keep up with the best for at least a hundred yards. Afterward, I can take a taxi back to the restaurant. So after Joey takes off, I somehow manage to complete the four miles. I feel like retching in some corner. I'm soaking with sweat.

I follow the crowd back to a coffee shop. Joey gives me a big smile and tells me to join him at his table. He introduces me to his friends Paul and Mark. And somehow we get to talking about who's a virgin at the table. OK, I admit it, I was the one who asked. "Are you a virgin, Joey?"

"What sort of a question is that?"

"You know, have you ever done it with a girl? I, of course, have never been so defiled," I boast.

"Me neither," says Paul.

"I had a girlfriend in college, so I guess I'm disqualified," says Mark.

"Are you asking if I have ever had sex with a girl?" asks Joey.

"That's the question."

"How do you define 'having sex'?"

"Come on, I just want a simple yes or no."

"Well, I put it in a girl in college, but she said, 'Take it out, it's too big,' " brags Joey.

"I think that constitutes sex."

"I didn't come or anything, if that's what you mean."

"I guess I'd say it's sex if there's either penetration or ejaculation."

"Hmmmmm. If two guys are masturbating together but not touching, and one of them comes, is that sex?"

"I'd say so."

"I think so, too," agrees Mark.

"I don't believe that really happened," denounces Paul. " 'Take it out, it's too big!' "

"No brag, just fact," says Joey.

I can't believe Joey is saying this. Although I'm mildly attracted to him physically, if he is capable of such deceit, I'm immediately turned off. On the other hand, if he isn't lying, then . . . We finish supper and I walk home, running the conversation through my head.

Joey calls me up on Sunday. "I just had sex for hours."

"Man or woman?"

"Man, of course. I was blowing this guy for hours on end."

"What do you mean?"

"You know. You put a dick in your mouth, and he puts your dick in his, and—"

"I know that, but were you wearing rubbers?"

"Are you kidding? Of course not. It's not the same."

"That's not safe."

"We didn't come in the mouth, of course."

"But what about precum?"

"Listen, you jerk it long and mean until you know it doesn't drip. And you're OK."

"So why are you telling me this?"

"I thought you'd be interested. You practically jumped on me when we met. The first words out of your mouth were sex."

"I was just making conversation."

"I saw you staring at me change in the restaurant."

"You were just in my field of vision."

"I'm telling you because I feel bad."

"*You* feel bad! I've given it up for Lent, and Lent looks like it will last for maybe the rest of my life, and you're calling me and telling me you feel bad?" I try to remember the last time I sucked dick. I think it was last June. I had taken a vow of abstinence from dicks as of last June. I know: Warren. It was a mistake—somebody's boyfriend, a perfect body from the gym. He was white, tanless, in residency to become a therapist. Warren came over to my place. He was so beautiful I couldn't resist, but then he practically sat down on my hard-on. I had to pull him off; I wasn't wearing a rubber. It was my fault. I asked if he liked poppers, and he brought some out, which he just so happened to carry with him in his backpack at all times. He had just come off the night shift at the hospital, then he went to the gym, where I picked him up. We took a cab to my place.

Afterward, he rushed home to his boyfriend to go to sleep. The trials of adultery.

Before him was horrifying Jeff, with his monster of a penis. How sad to discover that you are a size queen at twenty-eight. Thank God he ditched me before I was too far gone.

"Listen, I don't want to hear about it, Joey. Let me tell you the parable of the Bavarian-cream pies. Bill loved Bavarian-cream pies. He loved them so much he could subsist on nothing but Bavarian-cream pies. He could eat them all day long and all night long. One day he goes to his doctor, and his doctor tells him that he has diabetes and must never again eat even the thinnest slice of Bavarian-cream pie or he will die instantly. Then, after he has resigned himself to this fact (now he is eating saltine crackers and unsweetened granola bars out of desperation), one night his friend Tom calls him up. Tom calls to complain about his stomachache. It seems that Tom has just eaten sixteen Bavarian-cream pies and loved every minute of it; yet afterwards, he felt bloated and empty. Do you want to hear the end of the story?"

"Sure. What happens next?"

"Bill decides to go to the bathroom and drop the phone into the bath. The resulting shock travels through the wires and instantaneously electrocutes Tom."

"That's a nasty story, there."

"Well, I don't want to hear about you feeling sad and empty after sucking someone off for five hours. It's not safe! You could get AIDS! And what's worse, I want to have oral sex real bad."

"Now, now, my dear friend B. J. Rosenthal, I won't get the dreaded AIDS virus, so don't you fret. I'm perfectly fine."

"So don't tell me about this unsafe behavior."

"There's nothing to fear."

"I don't want to hear it."

"I shall spare your virginal ears the details of my latest debaucheries if that would make you feel better."

"It would."

"Fine with me. I don't see why you have to get so upset."

"I don't see why you're so calm."

"Anyways, good-bye, my dear friend B.J."

"Bye." I hang up.

222

Safe Sex in the Age of Anxiety

Cover your mouth with adhesive tape and then do the same to your partner. Insert sterilized butt-plugs in the correct orifice and tape over. You may, if you prefer, use duct tape instead (obtainable at your local hardware outlet). Insert each penis into an opaque, reservoir-end, prelubricated prophylactic. Be sure to coat generously with a water-based, nonoxynol-9 lubricant. Secure with a strong adhesive. For added security, a Hefty industrial-strength Steel-Sak may be taped over the rubber.

Foreplay should commence in the shower. The water temperature should be at least 180 degrees Fahrenheit. Soap up with an antiseptic, antimicrobial, sudsing skin-cleanser such as Betadine or Hibiclens. Alternatively, use pHisoHex, provided that your physician has supplied you with a prescription. Inspect your partner carefully for lumps, bruises, swollen lymph nodes or glands, sudden weight loss, and night sweats.

After a thorough scrubbing, retire to the bedroom. Plastic washable sheets (obtainable at your local surgical-supplies outlet, in the bedwetting aisle) should tightly grip the mattress. The room should be brightly lit with direct overhead lighting, so should any symptoms suddenly manifest themselves (shortness of breathing, a rapid, irregular heartbeat, a temporary hearing loss, or visible bruising), both partners can immediately cease activity. To pace yourself evenly and avoid overexcitation, it is suggested that a metronome be set to sixty, loudly.

At this point a final precautionary measure is necessary. In moments of passion trussed-up participants have been known to remove their adhesive bindings. Not only does this lead to unsafe sex; it can also cause temporary bleeding at the point of removal. To prevent this, first tie your partner's hands behind his back, preferably using

200-pound-tested mountaineering rope (obtainable at your local sports-supplies outlet). Then insert your own hands into a carefully pretied set of ropes. Hook this over the bedpost and pull to tighten.

Enjoy.

Afterward, immediately flush area with ammonia-and-peroxide solution. Use separate sterile, disposable washcloths to clean up. Then wait for your roommate to come home to unbind you.

· 18 ·

June

"Oh, no," says Philip Moscowitz over the phone. "They're showing Reagan's asshole on TV again." President Reagan was recovering from his fifty-third polyp, another nonmalignant tumor. "Quick, turn on channel eleven."

"You know I don't have a TV."

"I forgot."

"I told you a thousand times. When I turn thirty, I'll get a TV, buy a co-op, get a job with Citibank, and become lovers with the first person who calls me on the phone. In other words, I'm going to sell out."

"Look at what you're missing. There is a cancer in the presidency, just like John Dean said during Watergate, and here it is, live on the eleven o'clock news."

"It's true; I am denying myself. How's Fred doing?"

"The same." Fred, his cat, was suffering from the same cancer that was wreaking havoc on our fearless leader in the fight against Communist domination. "He threw up yesterday. I swear, he ran up two flights of stairs just to vomit on my new oriental rug."

"What does the vet say?"

"A matter of weeks."

"Gee, that's a shame."

"I know. I'll probably put him to sleep when the pain gets too bad. He doesn't seem to be suffering now. Some days he can't keep anything down. Other days he's OK."

"So are we doing the parade again?"

"Sure." The Gay Pride Parade is coming up in a few weeks. For the past five years Philip and I have marched together. After he moved to Jersey, one year he held the banner of some New Jersey gay group. He got tired and persuaded me to carry it for a few blocks. I was mortified. Suppose the photographers from *Time* magazine got a shot of me. Then the entire world would think that I was a homosexual from *New Jersey*. "I'll call you the night before."

"OK. Take care."

"Oh, no! Another person died of AIDS!" says Gordon melodramatically. We're both at work. We are reviewing our respective copies of the *Times*. "That makes two!" he says sarcastically.

"Come on, I'm sure I've read about others."

"Yeah. Toxoplasmosis. Complications due to pneumonia. Obituaries that list aunts and parents as survivors. In lieu of flowers, donations may be made to the New York City Opera. But they never come out and say it, AIDS."

"Well, there was Rock Hudson."

"Sure, he was page-one news. They couldn't very well lie about him."

"Perry Ellis?"

"You horrible gossip! Spreading rumors about one of America's most famed designers! Imagine what would happen to the stock in his company if word got out! Shame on you!"

"Oh, did you see, the *Times* is using 'Ms.' now for women? I think it only took the feminists twenty years to get them to use it instead of 'Miss' or 'Mrs.' I bet they'll use 'gay' instead of 'homosexual' by the year 2000."

"B.d."

"Bondage and discipline?" I ask.

"Big deal, silly."

I hear a crunching sound. "Are you eating again?"

"Just a carrot. Is this loud enough?" He chomps down right by the receiver.

"You're always eating."

"Us triathletes have to get our four thousand calories a day," he says.

"I'd be as fat as a blimp if I ate as much as you."

"You wanna hear something funny?" he asks.

"What?"

"My company is the target of a takeover bid."

"Really?"

"You wanna hear something else?"

"Sure."

"You sure?"

"Sure I'm sure."

"I found out about it in today's *New York Times,* page D-ten."

"Really?"

Gordon laughs. "The people here are so screwed up that they didn't even know. I called my boss on Long Island, and *he* hadn't heard about it."

"Does this mean big changes?"

"Yeah, like I might have to actually do some work." Gordon sighs. "Looks like the country club won't last forever."

Gordon's daily schedule is like this: He wakes up at seven and goes to the Y and swims for an hour. Then he takes a relaxing sauna. He goes to the office at around ten. If Joyce, his office-mate, has bothered to show up, he goes out for breakfast with her; otherwise, he has two or three Egg McMuffins and a fruit salad from the Korean deli. He spends the morning taking care of important business: personal phone-calls, paying bills, reading the paper. By noon he's on his way to the gym again. He runs five or six miles in Central Park during his lunch hour and showers at the gym. He picks up a two-pound salad at the salad bar for lunch back at the office. He stops at the receptionist for his messages. During the afternoon he takes care of personal correspondence and his reading. He is working his way through the novels of E. M. Forster. Occasionally his boss has him set up systems and transport personal computers. Gordon usually tallies up his expense account and overtime every day at 3:30 so he can be out of the office by four.

Gordon told me about some of his tricks. His favorite is the steaming-coffee routine, where you leave a cup of coffee on a hot plate so it looks like you just stepped out for a moment, when you've actually left for the day.

"Do you think you can handle a job where you actually have to work?" I ask.

"Dunno. It's been so long. I think the last time I worked was when I was in college."

"Yeah?"

"I had this minor disagreement with my father, see, so I ended up working through college." Gordon hasn't spoken to his father in ten years. "I was a porter at this hotel. They worked me ten hours a day, and it was hard work. Funny, isn't it? The more you get paid, the less you have to work."

"Eventually, I'm hoping to get a job that pays a hundred thou and requires no work whatsoever," I say.

"Maybe you can be my replacement if they ever get rid of me here."

"You can't lose your job, Gordon. I won't let you. Who else would I call every day? I guess I could hire an assistant to comb the papers for AIDS articles every day, but it wouldn't be the same." I guess I feel that if I'm completely on top of the news, I can exert some control over it, I can feel a little less powerless than I do.

"You could always promote Miss Caroline Yamamoto," he suggests.

I gag. "C'mon, Gordon. Seriously, I'd miss you." It's funny how close you can get to someone on the phone. Living in Manhattan is such a whirlwind. Sometimes I feel like I'm stuck in a high-speed revolving door. All I ever have time for is working, eating, sleeping, going to the gym, going to therapy, and visiting Bob Broome. When do I have the time to see friends? Rachel is married to her job; she's always busy. Dennis has his lover and his jobs, and besides, he lives in New Jersey. Once in a while I'll see Gordon on a Sunday night, when his lover, Jonathan, is at one of his meetings. But it's mainly just talking on the phone. And we talk practically every day. I certainly tell him more than I tell my therapist. I certainly *trust* him more than I trust my therapist.

"No, I think you should consider Caroline," Gordon continues, blithely unaware of my concern.

"Consider her for what? Extermination?"

"I don't know. For your personal assistant, I guess. You know what I think, B.J.?"

"No. What?"

"I think that Caroline is irreplaceable. I don't think there's a single person in the world who can duplicate her talents, poise, and personality. I think she's unique."

"Maybe *you* can hire her?"

"No, I wouldn't *dream* of taking her away from you. You've earned her."

Thanks for small favors.

I'm sitting at Jones Beach with some friends I met through Ed Gumm, whose lover died of AIDS a few months ago. Nicholas is British and balding. He has the dry wit and biting sarcasm that go hand in hand with his elegant accent. His shoulders are getting red. I tell him to put on some sun-block. Peter is a professional homosexual. He is barely stuffed into a colorful Speedo with zigzags of red and green on blue. Peter is built like a Mack truck. Fitness instructors go to *him* for advice. Peter is the only guy I know under forty who calls everyone "girl" and uses camp like a dishrag. Cognitive dissonance is his appeal. You wouldn't expect a bodybuilder with a craggy face to shriek "Mary!" and dish the dirt continuously. Peter's an old-school gossip queen, and he's barely thirty-one. When I arrived at their group, he remarked, critically appraising me, "Same suit as last time."

"So what are we going to do at three? Today is the day for Hands Across America," I say, secretly hoping that Peter will let me hold his hand.

"I don't know about you, but I don't want to hold hands with someone who was holding hands with someone who was holding hands with Archbishop O'Connor or President Reagan," says Nicholas.

"Think of it as conceptual art, like Christo.'s 'Running Fence,' only with people instead of materials," I offer.

"Oh, girls, let's do hand-jobs across America instead," says Peter, cracking his gum.

"How rude," replies Nicholas.

"I would have bought the T-shirts if they didn't say 'SPONSORED BY CITIBANK' so prominently on the front," I say.

"Oh, it's just some massive PR job. Do you think the homeless and hungry will ever see a cent? It will be like the Live Aid concerts, where the food ended up rotting at the docks in Ethiopia because they didn't think to get trucks, or the army will commandeer it." Nicholas turns over onto his stomach.

"Imagine what would happen if there was a thunderstorm in Kansas," I speculate. "I can see it in tomorrow's *Post*: 'Lightning strikes Hands Across America. Eight hundred volts of electricity surges through ten miles of human chain, electrocuting thousands instantly.' "

"Let's not be morbid," says Nicholas.

"Honey, I don't have time for any of that at three. I've got to go and chitchat with my devotees." Peter strolls off, heading toward the bushes. He returns about an hour later, coming from the beach to the left. He's just come in from a dip; he's still dripping.

"Hey, girls, I'm back," he says, shaking like a dog, spraying water on Nicholas and me.

"Well, I hope you didn't do anything I wouldn't do," says Nicholas.

"Just got a blow job in the dunes," he replies matter-of-factly.

Half an hour later, Peter decides to take another walk. I tag along. "You were just kidding about the blow job, weren't you?" I thought he was talking cheap.

"No," says Peter. "He wanted it. Am I supposed to refuse?"

"He didn't swallow, did he?"

"Of course he did." Peter is annoyed.

"That's not safe."

"Listen, he took the risk. He knew what he was doing. See that guy on the beach over there?" He points toward an attractive man in his twenties, wearing loose white boxers. "Don't stare. Listen, his name is Anthony. My new boyfriend, Raul, used to be his boyfriend last year. Everybody's connected. It's a human chain. It's a little too late for damage control."

"Repeated exposure to the AIDS virus can increase one's chances of coming down with the disease," I parrot from the latest pamphlet from GMHC.

"That's bullshit for now. If you have it, you have it, and there's nothing you can do about it." My respect for Peter drops several notches. "It's too late to stop infection. If you're gonna die, you're gonna die."

I can't be a fatalist. There must be something I can do.

"Could I speak to Mister Rosen-Penis, please?"

"Joey, that's not what you said to the receptionist, is it?"

"Don't worry, dick-face, your secret is safe with me."

"Don't you ever do any work, Joey?"

"Listen. It's four o'clock, B.J. I just felt like unraveling my immense and profuse member from the manifold folds and crenellations of my elephantine pants and playing with it for a while."

"Joey, I'm at work. I can hardly continue with this gutter-talk," I say.

"So am I. You have a private office, and so do I. Just do as I say. Close the door. Is it shut now? Good. Now spread those legs across the top of your desk while I give you some dick-tation."

"Joey, how come you never sweet-talk me in person? It's always on the phone, when I'm at work, when you *know* that sex is the furthest thing from my mind."

"You little whore, you. Sex is never farther from your mind than my dick is from your heinie."

"C'mon, Joey, tell me why when I flirt with you at Front Runners, that you—the Whore of Babylon, a raving nymphomaniac, a slut on wheels—to my chagrin, repulse all of my advances."

"That's different." Joey sniffles. "That's *in front* of other people. You're just teasing. You're so mean to me. Everybody's mean to me. I'm going to stop having sex anyways. I don't want to ever have it again. What good is it? *Splort splort*. That's all. All that buildup for a little *splort splort*. B.J., I am the trashiest person you've ever met, and I am sick to death of it."

"You are not," I counter. "My friend Grimaldi was even worse. He'd go to Forty-second Street to the peep shows and wouldn't surface for days. He practically lived at the Metropolitan on Fourteenth Street. He is pure, unadulterated trash. There is no reason that you should want to be as trashy as that."

"OK, you're right. I'm the *second* trashiest person you've ever met. You know, you have a good cocksucking mouth. You should trim your mustache a little. You don't want to cover it up; there's no need to hide those cocksucking lips of yours."

"Joey, you just said you were going to stop talking trash for a bit."

"Oh, yeah, I forgot. You know what my problem is? My big problem is that after I have sex with someone three times, I no longer have any interest in them. And if anyone shows even the slightest bit of interest in me, I immediately lose any attraction to them. Do you know what I mean?" whines Joey.

"So what? Don't you think everyone has that problem? You know what you should do? You should either try to have safe sex continually until you are so sick of it that you stop entirely, or you should stop completely now, and when you *do* have sex, it will mean something. I know what I'm saying. I haven't read every Ann Landers column since 1943 for nothing. How often do you have sex now?"

"Oh, three or four times a week."

"Somebody's exaggerating. Somebody's not telling the truth. I wonder who that someone could be? Honey, have you ever heard of Sexual Compulsives Anonymous?"

"Shut up about that. I want to tell you why I called. You want to know what happened yesterday?"

"Shoot."

"I got a phone call."

"Let me guess," I say. "You got a phone call from someone you didn't know, and he told you that someone else had just died of AIDS."

"He got my name from this guy William's black phone-book," concurs Joey. "How did you guess? The service was this afternoon. B.J., I don't even know who William was."

"You sure?"

"Positive."

"Maybe you slipped him your number once at a party, at the baths or something, three or five years ago."

"I don't know."

"So what are you going to do?"

"I'm never going to have sex with anybody again."

"I'm sorry."

"B.J., what is the world coming to? Listen, I've got to go. Linda just handed me a shit-load of work. See you at the run on Saturday."

AIDS is beginning to sound like a broken record in my life.

I wait for Philip at the plaza in front of the Gulf & Western Building. Men and women stream out of the Columbus Circle subway-stop and line up on Central Park West for the Gay Pride Parade. I count seventeen heartthrobs passing by and debate whether it is too early to take off my shirt. The sky is overcast. At the foot of the park a rainbow of balloons marks the start of the parade. Philip pops into view. "Which group should we go with this year? Dykes from Hoboken? The Staten Island Fairies?"

"Ooooh, he looks nasty." We stare at a man from the Gay Male S/M Activists who single-handedly is responsible for the slaughter of a herd of cattle. "Leather is so outré in summer." Philip is wearing shorts and a blue muscle-T. We make our way up the street. On the side streets up to Sixty-third, other groups are forming. One block has religious groups; another has political groups.

"Where are the student groups?" I'm wondering if my Boston college is represented today.

"Look for NAMBLA, and they won't be far ahead." NAMBLA is the North American Man-Boy Love Association.

Everybody's favorite group is the Parents and Friends of Lesbians and Gays. Why isn't my mother up there? A close second is GOAL, the Gay Officers Action League. They attract the most groupies.

"Hey, look," says Philip. " 'Gays for Grain,' " he reads off a banner. A man wearing a bright-green tank-top and purple parachute-pants is chatting to the man holding the banner. His well-built hairy chest is peeking through in a few strategically placed holes and out the sides. His tits would launch a thousand ships.

"I'd give up meat for him," I pledge.

"What do you think they are?"

"Lacto-vegetarians? Homeopathic? Cybernetic? Macroeconomic? Oh, I've got it. 'Macrobiotic,' that's the word."

"I've never heard of them before."

"I think they just got two new recruits," I say.

"I don't know. What do they do for fun? Chew their cud in Central Park?"

"They're yuppies. They graze. I read about it in *New York* magazine."

The parade starts fashionably late, only half an hour after schedule. The grand marshals, a couple who have been together for more than forty years, lead, riding in a '57 Pontiac convertible. Dykes on Bikes rev their motorcycles and do figure eights in full regalia. A short man leads the gay chorus with clipped motions, reminding me of a German goose-stepper. The Times Squares clap their hands, change partners, and do-si-do. Black and White Men Together are strictly paired. Someone from the Spartacus League, a radical political group, hands out leaflets from the sidewalk. Gay Cable Network has a float with videocams and several of our favorite television personalities: the rambunctious sports-reporter, the bitchy culture-commentator, the even-headed anchorperson. A woman sells buttons with pink triangles. I see a man whose silk-screen shirt bears the cover of a recent *Daily News:* "GAYS YES; CONTRAS NO." The New York City Council passed the gay-rights bill the same day the House of Representatives voted against a bill for aid to the Nicaraguan contras. The Front Runners stop periodically and then run a twenty-yard dash, to the applause of bemused spectators.

Across from St. Patrick's Cathedral a group of twenty or thirty religious protesters behind police barricades mill around with placards and signs. "GOD LOVES HOMOSEXUALS BUT HATES HOMOSEXUALITY" reads one. A trio of six-foot transvestites blow kisses in their direction. The protesters shout, "Shame, shame, abomination." A hundred policemen stand arm to arm in front of the cathedral, which is blocked off by police lines. No one from the parade is allowed to climb the steps. I go back looking for Philip, but I can't find him. Someone from Hudson County Gays claims he just left. The parade seems endless. The streets are lined with celebrants. Kids sit perched on lampposts, drinking beer. The Ramblers pass a soccer ball back and forth, a display of agility and grace. We follow the lavender stripe down Fifth Avenue. In the Village, below Eighth Street, a party salutes us with plastic wine-glasses from the second story of a co-op apartment. "Join us! Join us!" shout members of the parade. At the end is the Disco Kazoo and Tambourine Marching Band, with industrial speakers on a flatbed truck.

After the parade there are speeches and entertainment on West Street. I stay for a short while, looking for Philip. He's disappeared into the crowd. I walk up Christopher Street, a mass of congestion for the annual street-fair: piña coladas, Italian sausage, raffle tickets for the Harvey Milk High School, Gay Pride T-shirts, and so on. Most of the groups from the parade have information booths.

The People With AIDS Coalition has "Hug a Person with AIDS." I plunk down a dollar and confront my deepest fears. He has no visible lesions. He looks reasonably healthy. I give him a hug and am joined by the facilitator in a therapeutic bear-hug. After it is over, I thank them and wonder why. What's next? Rim a person with rheumatoid arthritis? Dry-hump a person in an iron lung? Damn it, I can't even stop *thinking* sarcastic comments. Maybe it's the only way I can cope.

Dave Johnson calls me at 7:15 in the morning. "B.J., did I wake you?"

"Um, uh, yeah. Gee, thanks a lot for saving me from Madonna in the morning. Hmmmmmmph, might as well turn off the radio-alarm."

"I wanted to get you before you got to work."

"You heard a new Natalie Wood joke and just had to tell me the first thing in the morning."

"A space-shuttle joke. Where was Christa McAuliffe's last vacation?"

"I give up."

"All over Florida."

"That sucks."

"So does the fact that Bob Broome can't move his legs."

"What?" I take a deep breath.

"He'd been telling me how tough the stairs were getting. One day last week I called him. He casually mentioned that he hadn't been out of the apartment in three days. I asked why, and he said he just didn't feel like it. I went over that night after work. Oh, Bob, he's the great pretender. He was just sitting in the chair when I got there, in front of the TV, playing with the remote. It's a good thing he gave me the extra keys. So then it develops that he has difficulty moving. He tries very slowly to stand up and get to the kitchen to give me some instant coffee. He collapses. I say, 'What's wrong?' He says, 'Oh, they do that sometimes. Nothing to worry about. I think it's getting worse.' It started on Friday. I saw him on Wednesday. I got him a walker. He can barely get around with that. You got to go over and see him, have dinner with him, get him to eat. Do you think you could do it twice a week? I'm trying to organize a group of his friends so we can get someone over there every night."

"Jesus. It's the beginning of the end." I figure when your legs go, you're on the way out. I don't want to commit myself to playing Mother Teresa twice a week. Yet I don't know how to say no. I really identify with Bob: his pain, his helplessness. It could easily be me. I am sucked into his disease. My therapist tells me I have a problem with boundaries, I have no sense of self. I can't identify my own needs and separate them from others'. Half a year ago I barely knew Bob Broome, and now I'm supposed to be his personal nutritionist and nurse twice a week. "I'll go over tonight. I don't know what to say."

"Get him something tasty."

I pick up some take-out Chinese and half a pound of Mrs. Field's cookies. Bob buzzes me in. I climb the four flights and tell him to take his time at the door. He hobbles over on his walker, sweat streaming down from his forehead. "Hi," he says. "Good to see you."

"Hi, Bob. What's new?"

"Oh, nothing much." Painfully, he makes his way back to the couch and plops down in relief. "What's that?"

"I got you some Chinese for dinner, sesame noodles and beef with broccoli."

"I can't really eat spicy food. It burns the roof of my mouth. I suppose you can put the noodles in the refrigerator for Marcy. Didn't I tell you? My friend Marcy—I used to work with her at Manufacturers Hanover—she's coming over for dinner."

"Oh." I guess I wasn't needed after all. "I brought some Mrs.

Field's cookies. Maybe you can eat them for dessert. I know you have quite a sweet tooth."

"Why don't you have one or two? I lost my taste for sweets some time ago. I think it's the Bactrim, one of the side effects."

"I might as well." I take an oatmeal-raisin cookie. The sugar rush lasts minutes.

"So how's work?"

"I've got a way of dealing with Caroline. Every time she does something annoying, like calling in sick after jury duty because she claimed she was too upset emotionally to work, I write it down. When the list gets long enough, I'll give her another warning."

"You can't just give her the boot?"

"Now, that wouldn't be fair, would it?" I have never acted decisively in my life, and I'm certainly not going to let Caroline push me into action. "And when she doesn't do something annoying, well, that's reward enough in and of itself, isn't it?"

"Well, it's your life," says Bob.

I go to the refrigerator to put in my cartons and cookies. "Bob, when was the last time you cleaned out the refrigerator?" I am appalled, and that's saying something. For years I had prided myself on being the most slovenly of all of my acquaintances, yet I couldn't hold a candle to Bob's mess: in a dented tin saucepan, six pieces of dried-up chicken in chicken fat with several molds; on the second shelf, two bowls of lime-green Jell-O shrunk to half the original size, a transparent membrane lining the upper half of the bowls, hard as industrial rubber; a carton of milk left open, completely curdled, with an expiration date of January 10; an opened can of cling peaches rotting in their own syrup. I toss most of this in the garbage.

"You'll have to come over more often. What a treat," says Bob, "cleaning out the icebox. I've been meaning to get around to it for a while. Thanks."

A few of the plates and dishes are so deeply infested that I can't clean them. I add them to the burgeoning Hefty bag. "Once back in California I got food poisoning from canned mushrooms," I remark. "I had opened a can, left it in the refrigerator, and not drained it. A few weeks later I was making lasagna à la Rosenthal with mushrooms. I saw there were some white spore-colonies in the water, so I just poured out the liquid and added them to the pasta sauce. I shat green for days. I couldn't get out of bed. I called a doctor. His nurse told me to flush my system with water. I drank so much that my urine was crystal clear and I was afraid that I had washed away my entire endocrine system. I called back, panicked, but the nurse told me that was perfectly normal. Ever since, I've always thrown out stuff when it gets the slightest funny smell."

The buzzer rings. Marcy is on her way up. "Could you get the door for me?"

"Sure. No problem." At the door we briefly confer in whispers. I tell Marcy the score; she knows what I know already. She seems pretty cheerful. I'm not sure if it's just an act to cheer up Bob or her natural state. I leave them after exchanging pleasantries, taking the garbage downstairs with me.

It's like some horrible forties movie with Bette Davis going blind and George Brent keeping up her courage. Except it's real life, and Bob Broome is getting weaker every day and there's no cure. It's only a matter of time.

How to Stay Celibate in the Age of Anxiety

1. Acquire unattractive personal-grooming habits. Floss your teeth in public: at the opera, in major metropolitan museums. Better yet, use wooden toothpicks. Chew tobacco and spit. Clean your nails with a bowie knife in trendy restaurants. Blow your nose by holding one nostril shut and forcing the mucus to shoot out the other. This is particularly effective at cocktail parties. When questioned on this, remark upon the disgusting habit many Americans have of wrapping up their mucus in cloth and carrying it around in their vest pockets.

2. Avoid bars and cocktail lounges. Instead, patronize brightly lit all-night delicatessens. If you must drink, do so to excess. Hopefully, this will leave you in a state of lustful impotence. The resulting humiliation should serve to strengthen your resolve. Alternatively, order grasshoppers, pink ladies, and Shirley Temples in leather-and-western bars. Insist on extra maraschino cherries.

3. Subscribe to the Centers for Disease Control's Morbidity and Mortality Weekly Report.

4. Redecorate your apartment in hospital chic. Install a pay phone in your kitchenette. Change your linen daily. Dress in disposable pajama-tops with a motif of repeated fleurs-de-lis. Wear a plastic wristband printed with your last name and social-security number. Place a rolling metal IV support-stand next to your bed along with glucose and miles of plastic tubing.

5. Hang up on jerk-off calls.

6. When introduced to an appealing stranger at a party, immediately launch into an interminable monologue about your last seven therapy sessions.

7. Eat onions. Onions and lots of garlic.

8. Abandon your public. Leave the answering machine on all of the time with the message "The number you have reached is no longer in service, and there is no new number." *Cancel your subscription to* Muscular Development. *Read* Goethe. *Unearth your old high-school chemistry set. Cancel your gym membership. Adopt a dog that cannot be housebroken. Apply deconstructionist theory to Emily Brontë's* Wuthering Heights. *Sublimate. Bake complicated all-day recipes, like a Mocha-Mousse Linzertorte Orange Applesauce Raisin Chunky-Apple Walnut Chocolate Hazelnut Glazed-Lemon Cake. Toss out the results when you finally succeed. Practice your Italian with a foreign-language translation of Woody Allen's film scripts. Cancel your membership to the video club in the Village with the wall of gay pornography in the back. Write a novel, burn it, and then try to reconstruct it from memory.*

9. When your mind wanders toward fellatio (and it will, it will), remember the time when you were seven years old and ate an egg-salad sandwich without taking it out of the Baggie on a dare at school. First you squeezed it to see if it would break, but you only left four fingerprints on the Wonder bread, and the filling pressed against the wrapper. Then you bit through the plastic and tasted it. Some of the plastic got stuck between your teeth. It was sort of fun. Then you decided you weren't that hungry anymore, and you placed the sandwich on your paper bag and proceeded to pour your half pint of homogenized, pasteurized, and fortified-with-vitamin-D milk on the sandwich, which you then tossed at the guy you had lost the bet against. The cafeteria aides came, and you were placed in detention for an hour that afternoon.

Now, think back to last year. You wanted to eat a gourmet oatmeal-raisin raspberry-crunch bar. It was in a shrink-wrap cellophane coating, and the seal was impermeable. No matter how hard you tried, you couldn't get it open. You wondered whether the seal should be submitted to the Patent Office or added to the Periodic Table of Elements, somewhere after Einsteinium, as the strongest element. You thought, Christ, if Tylenol had only used the same process, no one would have been poisoned; they would all have died of ruptured spleens or heart attacks or sheer frustration as they tried to open the bottles. In disgust, you tossed the snack in the trash.

Now, consider performing fellatio with a condom. Don't you have something better to do?

· 19 ·

July

"*L*ook at the headlines in the *Post*, B.J.: 'PIT BULLS ON CRACK!' " Philip Moscowitz passes me the paper. We are milling around in Sheridan Square, waiting for the July 4 sodomy rally to begin.

"Remember last week, when Alfonse D'Amato went up to Washington Heights, dressed as a U.P.S. worker, to buy crack? Forget the cover story. I know for a fact *he too* is secretly addicted to crack."

"Good Lord! What's the world coming to?"

"Nuns on crack," I suggest.

"Girl Scouts on crack," offers Philip.

"Mormon Tabernacle Choir on crack," I say.

"That's pushing it. How about 'GRANNY CRACK-RING BUSTED BY FED DRAGNET'?"

"For the ring of authenticity, I think you have to give them a place—BedStuy, Loisaida."

"Jersey City?"

"Let's hear it for the home-boys." I pat Philip on the back.

"Tell me again what we're doing here," whines Philip.

"We're protesting the Supreme Court's decision upholding the constitutionality of sodomy laws—Hardwick versus the state of Georgia."

"I *know* that. I mean, what are we doing at a rally? I could be doing housework or gardening. I could have gone to the beach today. What good is coming to a rally?"

"Philip, we are here to be counted. Hopefully, there will be some rabble-rousing speakers, but more likely than not we'll just get bored. That's not the point. This isn't an entertainment. We're just here as bodies. We're hoping to get media coverage. That's all. We're just taking up space. Imagine tomorrow's *Daily News* cover-story:

'HUNDREDS OF ANGRY GAYS PROTEST SUPREME COURT SODOMY RULING.' "

"Who are you kidding? Tomorrow everybody is going to be reading about four hundred Elvis impersonators gyrating for the Statue of Liberty centennial."

"Oh, my God, he's here."

"Who?"

"Don't stare. Remember Gays for Grain from Gay Pride?"

"The one in the green tank-top with the hairy chest?"

"The same."

Philip sneered. "The short blond is with him again. I bet it's his boyfriend."

"No harm in looking."

"He's too hairy for me. Hey, don't mind me, but I think I've found the object of *my* affection."

"Which one?"

"Dark hair, glasses, white polo shirt, standing against the street-post over there."

"Too skinny."

"Not for my tastes."

"I'm so glad we don't have the same taste. I would feel terrible about stealing your prospective boyfriends from you."

"Not likely that you could if you tried. Shhhh, I think he's looking this way."

I give Philip a look. "Do you want me to walk away, so he doesn't think we're boyfriends?"

"Don't be silly. Oh, no, he's seen a friend. A new friend?"

"Do people pick up each other at a rally?"

"This is a sodomy rally. It's the politically correct thing to do."

"Like we're supposed to be practicing homosexuals."

"Until we get it right, we are doomed to practice, practice, practice."

A man mounts the platform. I hear the crackle of static, a mike being tested. "Looks like they're finally starting now."

"I don't know about you, but as soon as they start singing 'We Shall Overcome,' I'm splitting," says Philip.

We stand and listen to speeches for more than an hour. The tall ships are sailing down the harbor for the Fourth. It's hot. Philip takes off his shirt. One speaker calls the Hardwick decision the Dred Scott case of the eighties. A popular grass-roots councilwoman gives a few words of encouragement to much applause. Right after Gay Pride Day the Supreme Court announced the Hardwick decision. I'm angry. I feel like a dog kicked in the teeth. Sure, it's easy. Get 'em while their defenses are down.

A bearded man wearing a leather vest and jeans announces we are marching downtown. The crowd cheers. A legal facilitator cautions us that we may engage in a civil-disobedience action and that the police may arrest us. Philip says, "I'm all marched out, B.J. We did the AIDS Walk together and then Gay Pride, but I'm going to have to sit this one out. Besides, I can't get arrested. I could lose my job!" He leaves.

The police escort us as we march down Seventh Avenue. At Houston Street we are jeered by a group of Brooklyn punks. We carry signs and placards. Rally organizers with colored arm-bands link hands, forming a human chain at the crosswalks. We stop at the Municipal Courthouse and sit down en masse, chanting slogans. "We Shall Overcome," that dreadful standard, makes its inevitable appearance.

After we have been sitting for maybe fifteen minutes, a rally leader starts chanting, "Battery Park, Battery Park." The police block us with their nightsticks. Evidently this was not in the agreement made beforehand. We have been marching without a permit. A representative confers with the police. It is decided we can go as far south as Trinity Church. Jubilantly, we rise. Canal Street is blocked off for the Statue of Liberty festivities; no traffic will be allowed all weekend. The streets below Canal swarm with Middle America. An ugly, unsupportive crowd greets us, not at all like those standing on the sidewalks and perched in windows, cheering the Gay Pride Parade. We make our way through the masses to the church and sit down again. "Battery Park, Battery Park," the chant begins anew. The police will not let us take one step farther. A compromise is made. We cannot march together to the park. Instead, we will separate and make our way downtown in ones and twos. We will regroup at a statue of an eagle.

Families curse us as we gather. They have been waiting for hours to see the tall ships, and we're blocking their views. It's a zoo. We hear briefer versions of the same speeches we heard earlier at Sheridan Square. David Pleasance Gray mounts the granite eagle, and I groan. He hides his beady eyes behind Coke-bottle-thick wire-rimmed glasses.

His spindly arms grab on to the statue, and he hoists himself up higher. I've heard the same speech from him so many times I could die of boredom. He's even recycled it in print. Let's see, last year he announced that he had been together with his lover, Vincent, for nine years. That means *this* year he is going to announce that he has been together with his lover for ten. Sure enough, the first thing he does is introduce his lover of ten years to the crowd.

I wonder why he thinks we demonstrators are so interested in his private life. I mean, you expect an increment of one every year. What's the big deal? David Pleasance Gray asks the assembled crowd to raise our hands if we've been in a relationship for more than a year. What does it prove if we can mimic straight behavior? Why should we try to justify ourselves according to the breeder standards? Maybe this is sour grapes on my part, the fact that my longest-standing relationship was three months of living hell with Richard. Maybe I'm pissed that David Pleasance Gray pointedly ignored me four years ago at Ty's, on Christopher Street, but would I carry a grudge that long? Probably.

"No more lies!" shouts David Pleasance Gray, referring to the homophobic hate spewn by the media.

"Liar, liar, pants on fire," I mutter to myself. Why does he even bring up the relationship issue? Between the two, he and his lover have slept with half of the Eastern Seaboard, safe-sex exclusively since 1982.

"We're all fired up!" chants the crowd. "Gay, straight, black, white, same struggle, same fight!" I see Gays for Grain again. The crowd is too thick for me to approach. I catch his eye; he smiles and continues with his chanting. Now that we've made it to the heart of Battery City Park, it seems like we've accomplished our goal. Yet we all want to do something more. We're full of anger and energy. There's nothing to focus it on.

A rally leader shouts, "The *Post!*" We decide to march to the *New York Post*. We wend our way through the most crowded portion. I feel safer away from the people who jeered us at the statue. We march up the East Side. I overhear Gays for Grain talking to a friend and decide he is too disco-oriented for my liking.

By South Street Seaport a drunken crowd heckles us—Middle America: Mom, apple pie, bigotry, and hatred. "Shame, shame, shame," we shout, pointing our index fingers toward the rabble. Someone tosses a beer and douses me. Angry and disgusted, filthy and sticky, I decide it's time to disperse myself. The rally has been going on for practically five hours, and I'm tired.

I get a chicken-salad sandwich at a luncheonette and take the subway home. "The roaches were so bad, we couldn't even hang out toothbrushes," testifies a middle-aged, lumpy-faced woman for Combat roach-control system on an ad. How I miss the Miss Subway posters. Even a hemorrhoid poster-child would be more tolerable.

"Well, it looks like they've found a cure for AIDS," says Gordon.

"What?" I grab my *New York Times*. My door at work is closed; I can talk as long as I want.

"Page C-twelve. There's one small catch, though."

"Identical twins." I sigh. A man in France had fully recovered his immunity after receiving blood transfusions from his identical twin.

"I think I'll call my mother and ask her if she gave up my identical twin-brother at the hospital for adoption and forgot to tell me about him."

"Chances are he'd be gay as you."

"I know, but it's worth a try. So how's your friend Bob doing?" asks Gordon.

"Not good. He's back in the hospital. They're trying to figure out why he can't move his legs. He's been undergoing tests for more than a week."

"They haven't found anything?"

"Not a clue."

"What do you think?"

"I don't know. It could be toxoplasmosis spreading through his spine. It could be anything."

"It's horrible."

"I know. Do you ever get scared you have it?"

"I'd say about once a month. You know my acne scars?"

"Surely your only visible flaw."

"You haven't seen everything."

"I've heard tell."

"So every morning I check my face for purple blotches," says Gordon, ignoring the last exchange.

"It's the latest craze. Everybody's doing it!"

"That and crack."

"I hear you."

"And about once a month I'll find something that looks peculiar."

"And you'll make an emergency appointment with your dermatologist."

"And it'll turn out to be another false alarm."

"A couple months ago I paid my doctor eighty dollars to find out that I had a healing contusion on my right Achilles tendon."

"Well, that's about what I pay my therapist."

"Yeah. And I felt a lot better after seeing my doctor than I usually do after seeing my therapist."

"How's it going?"

"I don't know," I confess. "He gives me these strange exercises. Last week I was supposed to chew some meat at a meal until it liquefied. I was supposed to concentrate on the meat. You know, turn off the stereo, get rid of any reading material. Just concentrate on chewing. I don't know what the hell that was supposed to prove."

"Did you do it?"

"Nah. I tried it with some pasta and ended up swallowing after it got boring."

"My therapist is pretty helpful."

"How can you talk to a lesbian about the most intimate details?"

"B.J., your problem is you can't even trust your therapist, let alone anyone else."

"Correction. *One* of my six thousand eight hundred and forty-three problems is that I don't trust anyone."

"We talk about everything."

"Including what they do in bed?"

"Including what *I* do in bed."

"Hmmmmmm. Think she'd sell me her session notes?"

"B.J., you're an incurable gossip."

"I know. Does yours want you to cry?"

"What do you mean?"

"My therapist is big into crying. You know, public display of emotion, psychological stress breakdown on the IRT, that sort of thing."

"He wants you to cry?"

"I think so."

"Do you want to cry?"

"You know I haven't had an emotion in the past fifteen years!"

"Not for want of trying."

"Does lust count?"

245

"No, that's just biological."

"That's what my therapist keeps telling me. Crying is just a biological release. But how am I going to cry on my lunch hour and go back to work? I'd be worthless for the entire afternoon. I can't face Caroline and her gaping maw with tearstains on my face."

"Guess what?" asks Gordon.

"What?" I ask.

"Last week I had a breakthrough."

"What was it? She raised your rates to an even hundred a session?"

"No. We figured out that I was depressed because of the AIDS crisis."

"No shit, Sherlock."

"I know it's obvious. It's just that once you vocalize these things, they become more readily apparent."

"Well, congratulations. I haven't found out anything as useful as that from my therapist."

"You've got to level with him. You've got to stop pretending it's a game. You've got to realize it's not like he's a doctor who will cure you without you doing anything. Therapy is a two-way process. I mean, how are you ever going to experience personal growth?"

"Why is it whenever I hear the term 'personal growth,' I think of warts and tumors?"

"Get off it, B.J. Don't you want to change?"

"I'm not sure whether I can." I get defensive. "So what's wrong with me, anyway?"

"You want a list?"

"Sure. Shoot." I place the paper-napkin blindfold over my eyes and wait for the bullets to fly.

"OK. One. You deflect everything serious with sarcasm."

"Don't you?"

"Not all the time. Two. You constantly complain about your life: your job, Caroline, your family, your lack of a boyfriend, and you don't seem to do anything about it."

I cringe. "You don't seem to like your job that much, either."

"Listen, we're talking about you, B.J., not me. I've got my own problems, too; I'm not denying it. You sure you're listening? You're sure you want to hear this?"

"Yes," I say in a dull monotone.

"Three. You keep everything bottled up inside of you. You never let anything out."

246

"Is that all?"

"Just one more. Four. You seem to be going through life aimlessly, without any purpose."

I don't know; I just can't take criticism. Why is everyone trying to cut me down? Even my friends. "Get hip! I'm an existentialist. What *is* the meaning of life? There certainly isn't any God. At college there was a graffito on the physics building that said there's no gravity, the earth sucks. Come on, Gordon, would God have allowed the Holocaust? Would God have let AIDS kill all of these people in their prime? There *is* no meaning to life. You make it up as you go along. Sure, you could join a cult, find God, accept some external purpose. But I can't. That would be dishonest. What is the meaning of life? Sucking nipples? Orgasms? Is pleasure enough? Intellectual stimulation? Making art, music, literature? Ultimately, isn't that all just pseudointellectual masturbation? Maybe the meaning of life is making babies, propagating the *specious*. No. It's enough that the world has to put up with *one* B. J. Rosenthal. Maybe it's science. Improving the lot of mankind. Something noble. But who has the talent for that, the genius? Hardly anyone. Well, what about love? Is *that* what we're here for, to pair up with significant others? It always seemed arbitrary to me, the number two. Why not four? Why not seven? And what about us inveterate spinsters, us permanent bachelors? Gordon, I've been burned by practically every man I've met. And what's the point of it anyway if we're all going to die soon? Why even bother? You know, we're all living under the shadow of death, every one of us. It's a struggle just to stay alive. It's all I can do to drag myself through the paces of every day."

"B.J., if you let yourself go, if you stopped fighting against yourself, things would be a lot easier for you. You're like an emotional black-hole. Nothing ever comes out. You're such a source of negativity. I mean, it's obvious you don't like yourself that much. How do you expect anyone to want to get closer to you if they can't get to know you, if you won't show them yourself, your feelings, your emotions?"

"Maybe there's nothing to show. Maybe I don't even know what I feel. Maybe beneath this hard veneer is a vacuum."

"Don't be ridiculous."

"It's like I accumulated a protective coating, a ball of string, and now it's as large as the room, like a Magritte painting of a rock filling a room."

"Well, I think it's time you started unraveling it."

"I don't know. I'm safe this way. You know, nothing can harm me. I've got distance. I don't know if I could take life without protection. Aren't you scared of AIDS?"

"I'm terrified."

"I'm afraid of change. Maybe change isn't even possible. Maybe nobody changes. Maybe your personality is completely formed by the age of twelve, and you're stuck with it for the rest of your life."

Gordon pauses. "You know, I changed. I used to be a disco dolly. I used to be your typical Fire Island clone. I used to spend the weekends at the bathhouses fucking my brains out, or what was left of them after all the drugs I took. But I changed. It was pointless. Now I can barely believe I was like that. When I see Marshall Douglas on the street, I can barely speak to him. He was my boyfriend for six months, and we had absolutely nothing in common except for sex. He was a thirty-year-old pharmacist, and he still hadn't cut his mother's apron strings. He dragged me to the opening of the Palladium last year. He was like a throwback to the old days. The only reason we lasted so long was that I was lonely and needed someone, anyone. I'm so glad I found Jonathan. You know what we do? We read to each other at night." He sighs. "He's reading Virginia Woolf's *To the Lighthouse* to me."

"That's sweet." Frankly, I would be bored to death after fifteen minutes if someone read to me.

"We run together. He's been doing marathons the past three years. He's coaching me; the farthest I've ever raced was ten K in the park. And I'm teaching him cycling."

I have to admit they make a perfect couple. "You're lucky."

"I guess so. So why are you even bothering with therapy if you don't think you can change?"

"I don't know. I can get really depressed." I'm not sure exactly why I'm in therapy myself. "My therapist thinks it's silly for me to take so many notes. He says that if I feel more comfortable writing things down, that I could, as an experiment, write about my problems."

"Why don't you write about your egg paranoia?" asks Gordon. "That should get him going."

Gordon clears his throat. "Well, B.J., I've got to run now."

"Don't tell me you're actually going to do some work?"

"No, of course not. It's almost noon. I'm going to go to the Y and run in the park."

"OK. Talk to you tomorrow."

"Bye." The phone clatters into the receiver. I have five more hours until I have to visit Bob Broome at Lenox Hill this evening.

Dave Johnson leaves a message on my machine. "Be at the hospital on Thursday at six-thirty. I'm trying to organize a birthday party for Bob." I get to Lenox Hill at 6:15, straight from therapy. I bring Sherlock, the stuffed dog that Dennis gave me, as a gift. I bound up the stairs. Marcy, his friend from work, stands in the hallway with a bundle of flowers. Roxanne, who lives across the hall from Bob, clutches her husband, Ernie, on the arm. Ernie carries a gift-wrapped box the size of a coffee tin. Dave pops out of the hospital room, shushing the assembled group. "Be quiet. He doesn't suspect a thing. He was just complaining that nobody remembered to send him a card. Now, I want everyone to come in at six-thirty on the dot singing 'Happy Birthday.' OK?"

"Where's Patrick?"

"He couldn't make it. He and his lover have gone to the Island for a long weekend," says Dave. "He did send a telegram this afternoon. That was pretty sweet of him."

"He's been here almost every day," says Marcy. "He's always here when I come to see Bob."

"Should we wait for Jerry?" I ask. Jerry is Dave's lover.

"Shit, you're right. Jerry's picking up the cake," says Dave.

"Is he getting candles? It'll take a while to light up thirty-five of them," says Roxanne.

I didn't know Bob was thirty-five. The age Dante's traveler entered the inferno in *The Divine Comedy*. Halfway through the road of life. In Bob's case the road led to a dead end.

"After twenty you usually use just one candle," I say.

"Jerry's going to put a sparkler on the cake. We didn't want him to feel bad if he couldn't blow out a regular candle." Bob's breathing is not the best. Some nights he uses an oxygen mask.

"There he is," says Marcy. Jerry comes down the hall, carrying a bakery box by the string on the top.

"I guess it's about time."

"OK, let's go."

We file into the room one by one, with grins on our faces. Jerry leads with the cake. Bob's room is at the end of the hall, in isolation. The intern told Dave that plastic masks and gowns were no longer necessary, although Roxanne straps on a mask because she has a minor head-cold. We start singing "Happy Birthday."

Bob is obviously touched. Pale, weak, small in his bed, he forces a smile as a tear rolls down his cheek. "You didn't have to," he says.

"C'mon, open your presents," urges Jerry. Bob presses a button, and his bed rises in the back at a slant. He fumbles with the ribbon on Roxanne and Ernie's box, which turns out to be a tin of Amaretti di Saronno biscuits. He struggles with the top. Ernie helps him open it. Bob passes the tin around the room. Marcy puts her flowers in a vase on the window. I wish I had had time to wrap up Sherlock.

Bob tires easily. Ten minutes later he says there are too many people and asks if some of us wouldn't mind leaving. I look up quizzically, and he says, "No, B.J., you stay." Marcy takes the train back to Mineola; Roxanne and Ernie take a cab home. I stay with Bob, Jerry, and Dave. We chat for an hour and a half. I'm starving by the time we leave at nine. Jerry and Dave give Bob a hug good-bye; I give him a handshake. I feel bad that I can't get physically close to Bob; I *should* do more, but how can I express physical affection for Bob without being a phony? Afterward, we go into the bathroom and wash with Hibiclens.

I go down to the Village and have dinner with Jerry and Dave at Blazing Salads, a tiny health-food restaurant on West Fourth in Sheridan Square. They come to see Bob every other day, right after the gym, and usually stay for a few hours. The doctors still don't know what's wrong with Bob's legs, but they're afraid it's spreading.

We sit, drinking wine and eating pasta salad, with the tacit knowledge that today is Bob's last birthday.

Egg Paranoia

I have dreams of eggs. Nightmares. They are marching toward me
in formation. Six by six, they spring out of cartons in perfect unison,
not a single one cracked or blemished, no yolk dripping like yesterday's semen dried at the crotch of a crumpled pair of Fruit of the
Looms. Row upon row of eggs confront me. I cannot see the horizon;
they fill the landscape to the vanishing point. When I wake, the sheets
are stiff with sweat and albumen.

I have always been afraid of eggs.

My sister fears revolving doors. This I understand obliquely. I saw
an art movie called Koyaanisqatsi three years ago at Radio City Music
Hall, part of the New York Film Festival. My seat was so far back,
in the seventh balcony, that the screen was dwarfed to the size of
my mother's midget television on the kitchen counter between the
toaster and the blender. To the background of Philip Glass, revolving
doors, shot in time-lapse photography, whirled at close to the speed
of light. Caught in the fictive centrifugal force, victims circled at a
maddening pace, unable to leave the curvilinear quadrants of glass
and steel.

I dread subway entrances far from the surveillance of token-booth
clerks. The pinball slots indicate their probabilistic nature. Each time
I gamble against odds that my token will be accepted, that the bent-
metal walls won't grind to a rusty halt midway, leaving me in limbo.
Even seemingly innocuous turnstile-exits with interlocking horizontal
bars give my sister pause, however. On several occasions she has
been hurried through them by impatient attorneys and by irate psy-
chopaths on their way to methadone-maintenance clinics. She can
easily imagine being forced through the bars, which are serrated,
razor-sharp in my dreams, sliced into seven or eight neat portions at
equal intervals.

My mother is afraid of cars. One afternoon, backing down our seventy-foot macadam driveway as my mother, nervousness palpable, sympathetically watched for oncoming cars, neck darting like a bird of prey, yet hunched down in the back seat, careful not to obstruct my view, I asked, out of pure speculation, inventing an anecdote I knew nothing of, "When you were seventeen, were you sitting in the front seat of a Pontiac, next to Bill Meyers, with Sue and Tommy in back, driving down Erie Boulevard on the way to the bowling alley— Bill with his right arm around your shoulders, the radio playing Your Hit Parade, *Kate Smith holding C sharp longer than anyone thought was humanly possible—and did Bill reach into his breast pocket for a Camel and then suddenly lose control of the car, causing it to careen into the center divider and stop dead against a telephone, with you flung through the windshield, twenty-seven stitches on your forehead, luckily just above the hairline, so it doesn't show?"*

My mother, stunned, replied, "I was sixteen, and his name was Philip."

My father was afraid of being alone. Today, as I passed the bus stop on the way to work, a man said with booming false familiarity, "Hey, how are you?" I muttered something nonresponsive. Problem is, he reminds me of my father between medications. We have nothing in common. I met him five years ago at a municipal V.D. clinic in Chelsea. The nurse in starched white uniform gave me a prune-piss smile and instructions to avoid intimate relations of any nature for the next fifteen days. The man on the sidewalk and I share only a shameful past and perhaps a strain of gonococcus. I'm not ready for his unmitigating friendliness, his relentless cheerfulness. I don't want to speak with him. He lives, of course, in my neighborhood. I suspect, due to his gregarious nature, that in all likelihood he went to the clinic out of sheer conviviality. He was probably asymptomatic. I think he went just to talk and be social, like the disease. Who would sleep with need as strong as his, with loneliness of such fathomless depth? But I'm projecting. It's only because he reminds me of my father, who was crazy and is now dead.

My father died of eggs—three eggs over easy every day. He inhaled his meals, engulfed them in a matter of seconds. That morning he woke up holding his chest, thinking it was heartburn. Perhaps he asked my mother for a glass of water. They slept in twin beds. He snored. My mother is a light sleeper, with headlights in her dreams. It was his first and only heart attack. Two days later I saw him in the coffin, upside down; I couldn't bear to look at him face to face. His cheeks were white, made up. His lips looked red, as if he had eaten too many pistachios. I checked his fingers for the red dye, but they were clean, folded on his chest, lifeless. I looked away.

About a year ago I met someone nice at a guppy, as in gay-urban-professional, bar. We talked over Saratogas about neutral, nonsexual topics. I noted he didn't smoke. His eyes were bright and clear, full of promise. We left and went to his place. We were careful, cautious. We took a shower and examined for bruises. We dutifully soaped up and cleansed ourselves. He pulled down the shades and turned on soft classical music. Our lips brushed, but our tongues did not mingle. It was too early in the relationship for penetration of any sort. We had sex safe as Plexiglas. We rubbed bodies and came. We took another shower and fell asleep, barely touching. The next morning I awoke to the sound of butter sizzling on the grill. He stood in the kitchen in a cotton bathrobe, back toward me. "Good morning," he said. My eyes widened in horror. Egg after egg cracked on the rim of the stainless-steel bowl. "I'm making omelettes. Is three eggs enough for you?" I made my escape through the window, the fire escape. I left without making a sound.

· 20 ·

August

"Well," says Gordon, "the most hated homosexual in America has just died."

"You know, I hate to say it—not that *anyone* deserves it—but it's almost poetic justice, Roy Cohn dying of AIDS."

"He said it was liver cancer," says Gordon.

"I mean, after all of the fag-baiting he did with McCarthy back in the fifties. Did you hear about the interview he did with Barbara Walters? He denied he had AIDS; he denied he was gay. He denied he had ever been guilty of professional misconduct, and he was just about to be disbarred in New York. I'm surprised he didn't deny that the Holocaust had ever occurred."

"You know, last year, when I was at the opening of the Palladium with dumb-ass Marshall"—Gordon spits out the name of his old boyfriend with obvious distaste—"there were these guys picketing outside. They had signs that said not to sleep with Roy Cohn because he had AIDS."

"You're joking."

"U.n."

"What?" I ask.

"Unfortunately not."

"Well, who would sleep with that scum-bag anyways?"

"Whores."

"And that's who they were warning?"

"Yep. I bet he kept on screwing whores without any protection right up to when he died."

"He was a sleaze-bag."

"You've got the paper?" asks Gordon.

"Sure." I buy *The New York Times* religiously. It's almost a compulsion. The first thing I do is check the obituaries. Then I scan the contents for AIDS articles. Every Monday I get the *Greenwich Village Gay News* and I try to make my way through most of the medical articles, but sometimes it's just too depressing. I buy the *Advocate* for additional news. I'm practically a newsprint junkie at this stage. I didn't get a chance to read the paper on the train to work this morning; it was too crowded, and the *Times* is too bulky to read standing up. I'm pissed ever since they moved the news summary and index from page B1 to page A2. Before, at least you could skim the contents on the subway.

"Turn to page B-six," instructs Gordon. Dutifully, I open the *Times* and flip through to the second section. "You see it?"

"God." A man has gotten AIDS from a single sexual episode with a twenty-two-year-old after twelve years of celibacy.

"Talk about bad luck," says Gordon.

"My father had a friend from the V.A. named Bill Dexter. Bill was a virgin. In France during the war he went to a whorehouse. A few days later, he found out he got the clap. Well, that was the end of sex for Bill."

Gordon pauses. "Are you sitting, B.J.?" Gordon asks suddenly.

"What's wrong?" I panic. More bad news? I'm not sure I can take it.

"A friend of mine, Peter Quigley, committed suicide last night. He was just diagnosed, and he didn't want to go through it." I hear Gordon's awkward laugh over the phone.

"How could he? That's horrible. I don't think I'd have the guts to do it."

"Me, neither. I mean, there's always hope for a cure in the future."

"I'd probably mess it up anyways. If I tried to overdose on sleeping pills, I'd end up swallowing a bottle of Flintstones vitamins by mistake," I feebly joke.

"And I'd try to slash my wrists using a safety razor."

"Are you OK? Are you in shock?"

"It hasn't hit me yet. I think I'm living in a state of shell shock. Nothing much affects me immediately anymore. I usually get a delayed reaction."

"I'm beginning to feel like a Jew in Nazi Germany. People are dropping like flies."

"How's your friend Bob doing?"

"Worse. I told you he can't move his legs? Well, it spread. Now he lost control of his bowels."

"That's terrible."

"I've been calling him up, trying to cheer him up. I tell him about everyday things: the tape-drives at work breaking down, the latest in the never-ending Caroline saga."

"How is that model employee of yours? I don't see why you don't give her a raise."

"I'm waiting for hell to freeze over first."

"So when are you going to can her?"

"A couple weeks. Soon, maybe. I don't know. My therapist is on vacation."

"Welcome to August."

"Is yours in Maine, too?"

"Vermont."

"So what are you doing with your spare time?"

Gordon chuckles. "Ever run out of things to say?"

"Not really."

"Well, I'm writing down these dreams in case I don't have anything to say during our sessions."

"Are you dreaming a lot now?"

"No, silly. I'm making them up."

"Cheater."

"I'm making them very symbolic—a lot of trains going into tunnels."

"You know the flying dream?" I ask.

"Where you can fly?"

"Yeah. Well, a couple of years ago I had a half-assed version of it. I wasn't exactly *flying*; it was more like I was levitating. I was about two inches above the sidewalk back in Rochester. During the dream I was irritated that I couldn't get any higher." Even in my dreams I'm repressed.

"That's great. I bet my therapist will love that one."

"That's *my* dream. You can't use it."

"Did you get it copyrighted?"

"Oh, hell, be my guest. But do me a favor and tell me what your therapist says it means."

"OK."

The sun is shining brightly the day Bob finds out from his doctor that he is dying. "What do you think you will be doing three months from now?" he asks Bob.

"I suppose I'll be home in bed taking medicine. Or perhaps I'll be in the hospital again, undergoing tests."

"And what about six months from now?"

"The same, I guess."

"Any other possibilities?"

"I don't know. Maybe my condition will get worse."

"Yes?" he gently prompts.

"Oh. I see." Bob sighs. "I think I understand what you're trying to get at."

I am outside in the corridor. The doctor motions me in as he leaves.

"Heavy pizza," says Bob solemnly.

"What?"

"That's an expression in the Midwest for a very serious conversation."

"The doctor just gave you some news?"

"In a manner of speaking."

"Not good?"

"Bad news. The worst possible news." He tells me.

I wish I weren't the person to be there that day. I feel the burden to comfort Bob, play the adult, say the right thing, and I haven't a clue. It should have been someone closer to him. Denial is a powerful mechanism. The rest of us knew that Bob wasn't going to get any better. When I heard that he had lost control of his legs, I thought it would be only a matter of weeks.

David and Jerry get Bob a VCR. The room is filled with flowers. Bob's friend Marcy from Long Island visits every Sunday. I call Bob every day, in the morning. We chat about data structures, my increasingly nonexistent love-life, the yarn effigies I make of Caroline and stick with thumbtacks when I get particularly annoyed. I am relentlessly cheerful. I dread the phone calls. One day Bob says he doesn't feel like talking and hangs up on me. I feel some relief. The next day he calls and tells me to stop being such a cheerleader, to stop putting on an act and just be myself. One less barrier.

Occasionally, I run into Patrick at the hospital. His eyes gleam bright green. My heart quickens when I see him. He complains about his unappreciative lover to Bob. I needle him constantly about moving in with me. "You'd sleep on the sofa, of course."

"Sofa, *schmofa*, you'll pounce on me in fifteen minutes flat." Patrick laughs.

"Is it my fault that I can't conceal my undying love for you, dearest?" We keep up the banter for Bob's sake and ours. He is mildly amused.

"I think it's time to start your leg exercises," says Patrick.

Bob groans. "Not again!"

"C'mon, Bob, they'll atrophy if we don't exercise them." Patrick performs physical therapy unhesitatingly. Bob's legs are thin as toothpicks.

Slowly, at the knee, Patrick lifts the left leg. "Ouch! Ouch!" grimaces Bob. Then, just as slowly, Patrick replaces it. After five repetitions he does the same with the right leg. I look away. I talk about my friend Richard in San Francisco. He got thrown out of the halfway house for an overdose. He's living in a hotel with his friend Maria, a Nicaraguan who had been raped by soldiers years ago. She's agoraphobic; he has to accompany her to the supermarket and to public assistance. They share a room in the Tenderloin district.

Now Patrick rotates Bob's feet at the ankles, five revolutions in each direction. I'd like to help, but I can't. I don't want to touch Bob. Suppose he sweats? I feel guilty. Last month my therapist asked me if I would help Richard if he were ill, and I said, "Of course. That's different. We're very close." Therapy is a little like programming. You make mistakes, and when you find out what they are, nine times out of ten they're so obvious you could kick yourself.

Sometimes the bed smells, and the sheets need to be changed. Patrick or I ring for the nurse. After a long interval an attendant comes, wearing elbow-length, pink-plastic gloves. She and Patrick roll Bob to one side, and she strips and replaces the linens. I usually leave when this happens. Forty-five minutes is long enough for a visit. I promise Bob I'll call the next day and visit again in a few days. I say good-bye to Patrick and go. Usually, I walk home next to Central Park, down Fifth Avenue.

Blimps proliferate at Jones Beach. One day I see five, amassed in the distance: the Goodyear, Fuji, *Daily News*, McDonald's, and Citibank. The blimps move down the beach single file. About a mile away from me they change course and turn back slowly in graceful, wide curves. They drift off lazily to the west for a short distance. They return, turning again. This time they are less than half a mile away before they circle back. A third time they approach like a slow, silent threat, shadows moving swiftly across the sand.

The last time I saw Bob his lips were chapped bright red. A nurse coated them with Vaseline at my request. I showed Bob the new bull's-eye subway token, a copper center in a brass ring. The hospital smelled of ammonia and feces. The air was filled with spirochetes.

Dave Johnson calls me at 6:45 A.M. on Tuesday morning. "B.J., I was in the shower, and I just remembered a joke. Wanna hear it?" He is in the john, calling me from a cordless phone.

"Sure."

"What do NASA, Tylenol, and walruses have in common?"

"I give up."

"They're all looking for a tighter seal."

"That's disgusting."

Abruptly, in the same cheerful voice, Dave says, "I talked to Bob's doctor yesterday, and he said that the best thing to happen to Bob would be to die."

Whoa. I'm not ready for that. "What? Could you rephrase that? Is there a more delicate way of putting it? You just woke me up."

"He's not getting any better. He's not going to get any better. Whatever degenerative disease he has is attacking his central-nervous system, likely through the spine, and it's only going to get worse."

I'm not ready for Bob to die yet.

"Bob is dying," I tell Dennis.

"I know. It's rough," he says. He looks down and stirs his coffee. We've met for dinner at the Chelsea Gallery restaurant on Seventh.

"I've been thinking a lot about death lately. They pull the plug. Lights out, and that's it. Nothing. *Nada.* No trumpets, no angels, no gates of heaven designed by Rodin, no fiery pits, no ninth circle of hell. Just a box. The end of the line. Then dust. Dennis, I'm scared. I wish I could believe there was something. I wish I could hope, but I can't."

"Faith is a leap, B.J. You can't rationalize it." Dennis takes off his glasses; his eyes drift out of focus; he scratches the tip of his nose; he breathes in and sighs. "Everybody dies, B.J. It's a fact of life. We live on in memory and love. To me it's inconceivable that the spirit could disappear. I just can't accept that."

"And I'm torn up that I can't accept a God invented out of necessity, out of need. Richard used to tell me about the stars, billions of miles away, so bright. He said that the history of man was just a blink of the eye on the cosmic scale. I used to think about the universe a lot. Is it finite? Does it end six zillion miles east of Poughkeepsie? Is there, like, a brick wall at the end of the universe marked 'POST NO BILLS'? Or does it go on forever? How can you even think about infinity? Either way, I can't grasp or comprehend it. And what's worse is I don't even care anymore. I couldn't give a fuck. Remember how Andy Warhol dyed his hair white when he was young so he wouldn't have to ever grow old? I think I killed all of my emotions. I'm already dead; I'll never die because I'm already dead."

Dennis jerks out of his reverie. He puts on his glasses so he can tip them down and give me the dumb-fuck look. "What are you talking about, B.J.? Have you finally gone off your rocker? You're feeling all of the time. You're filled with emotions. What is this, depression and irrationality brought on by sugar deprivation?"

I smile ruefully. "Could be." I had taken my therapist's suggestion that I might be hypoglycemic and tried to avoid sugar products.

"I don't see how you could ever give up chawk-lit. How could you? Ouch! B.J., look at the menu. You skipped out on mud pie."

"D.K., those initials are apt, aren't they?" Dennis's last name is Kelly. "Decay. Here you are, trying to tempt me, trying to break my resolve."

"What do you expect? I told you the name Dennis comes from Dionysus, the Greek god of w-i-i-i-i-i-ne. Hey, it's up to you if you want to forsake Milky Ways and Dove Bars. I'm not trying to persuade you either way. All I'm saying is that, with life so rough, does it make any sense to deliberately deprive yourself of its pleasures?"

"So this is the voice of the church?" I ask.

"This is the voice of compassion, B.J. This is the voice of your *friend,* damn it." Dennis looks into my eyes and puts his hand on my shoulder. "Waiter," he says, "I think we'll be having dessert after all."

"I'm not so sure," I begin.

"Yes, that will be one hot-fudge sundae and, hey, this'll do the trick"—he starts laughing—"one Death by Chocolate."

There's nothing for me to do but try to enjoy.

"Hmmmmm," says Joey Romano over his coffee. "It says here that Rebecca Stein, famed lipstick-lesbian and noted critic, suggests that homosexual males, in the interest of safe sex, should content them-

selves with licking the shaft." Joey is reading the *Advocate*. We met
at Rumbul's on Christopher Street for dessert.

"I don't see how I could verbalize that during a sexual encounter,"
I reply, toying with the crumbs from my pistachio cake.

"Why not say, 'Let's do what Becky says.' "

"Like Simon Says."

"Yeah, only a little kinkier."

I pause to consider the ramifications of this suggestion. "I don't
know. Wouldn't that be a bit forward? Even in code it's just so much
sleaze."

"Don't you like sleaze?"

"Not really."

"I adore Boyd McDonald. He is God to me."

"That asshole? He writes those letters himself, doesn't he? They
all sound the same to me." Boyd McDonald has had several books
published of real-life sex-episode letters, with titles like *Sex, Meat,
Juice,* and the like.

"Piss-hole."

"Man-juice."

"Butt-fuck. They didn't teach you those words in Miss Pruitt's
Social Conversation classes."

"That's probably why you love them."

"Could be." Joey, irritatedly, takes his stirrer and folds it into a
knot, like a pretzel.

"Well, I find him too vulgar for my tastes."

"You would. You're such a priss. You probably never went to the
Mineshaft, did you?"

"Not that I recall," I say, hedging.

"It was the most interesting place in town to have a cocktail. All
of those leather grannies in their slings. The boys lined up, they didn't
care who. It was take a number, and next. With their opera gloves,
ready to plunge deeply into the matter at hand."

"I wouldn't sully myself with such crap."

"I wonder where they all are now? At the Dog Shed," says Joey,
referring to a decrepit leather-and-western bar in Chelsea, "the local
AIDS distribution center."

I blanch. Joey is just kidding, but even I have my limits. Bob
Broome is dying at Lenox Hill Hospital, and Joey is joking about
AIDS. "I think I'd better go now, Joey."

"Whatsamatter? I say something wrong?"

"No. I, uh, just think it's time to go home." I leave a five for the tab and go.

I run into Dr. Felix Braun on my way to the Monster. I'd met him a gym or two ago. He was standing with only a towel on around his waist, examining his tongue in the mirror at the sink area, surrounded by four or five blow-dryers in action. His chest hair intrigued me, a pattern of iron filings in a magnetic field. I stopped to chat casually. He didn't want to tell me at the gym what he did for a living, a profession that dare not speak its name in polite society. We went for frozen yogurt and papaya shakes across the street, at a health-food restaurant. Turns out fecal matter was his specialty. He runs a shit-lab in the Village and dispenses cocktails from hell in vast quantities.

Today, Felix has circles around his eyes, as if he hasn't slept for days. "What's wrong?" I ask.

"I've had a cold for more than a week."

"So? A week to ten days is normal."

"That's easy for you to say. I'm terrified it's AIDS."

"There's no sense in panicking."

"See this?" He indicates his throat. "I think my glands are swollen."

"I think that can be quite common with colds—temporary swelling."

"I don't think I had it a week ago, but who knows? Maybe. I think about getting sick all of the time. My friends are tired of hearing me complain about my health all of the time. I know I must sound like a broken record, but how do I know I'm not going to get sick? I can't get it out of my mind. I'd made an appointment to take the antibody test last month—I was this close to taking it—but I found out that even though they say it's completely confidential, the hospital keeps records, so I skipped out. I don't want to be denied insurance. I don't know. I might have it, and I might not."

"It's stupid to take the test. What difference would it make in your behavior?"

"The closest thing to unsafe sex I've had in the past three years was masturbating to a bodybuilding video on my VCR with someone else in the same room. We both wore rubbers. I still felt nervous."

"What do you want, shrink-wrap for humans? I bet you take your temperature so often you get high readings just from the friction of slipping it in and out of your lips."

"Let's not get graphic, B.J. Listen, I've done my will three times this past year."

"Do I get the condo in Florida?" The shit business is lucrative.

"Nope, but you do get free stool-tests for life should I kick off."

"Gee, thanks a lot. You'd hang up on me if I ever sneezed on the phone, wouldn't you?"

"So I'm paranoid; it doesn't mean they're *not* after me."

"Well, take care of yourself, Felix." I'm sure it's nothing that twenty years of intense psychotherapy can't cure.

"See you around, B.J."

I smile at the bouncer at the door of the Monster. Since the legal drinking age went up to twenty-one, more than a few bars check for ID at the door. A drag queen in a beehive plays show tunes on the piano. I hear a loud bass beat in the background. Downstairs, a disco ball twirls above a postage-stamp-sized dance-floor. Balloons and streamers hang over the main bar in the center of the room. The bar is packed on a Sunday night. I squeeze my way through the men standing against the wall and those sitting on bar stools.

In the corner I see Mr. Mackenzie, famed novelist and raconteur, in the midst of a rambling monologue directed at his screwdriver. Last month I read an interview with him in the *Times,* where he discussed his writer's block. Mr. Mackenzie hasn't come out with a new novel in years, and he used to produce one like clockwork every eighteen months. He catches my eye.

"Don't I know you? Of course, yes, the ill-fated visitor, the peripatetic guest. My wavering and indecisive failed concubine, won't you join me for a beverage, purely medicinal purposes, to blind, to numb, to deaden the pain? Seventy people. Do you have any idea? No, of course not, how could you? Most people don't even know seventy people, let alone know seventy who have or have had the plague. A. I. D. S.," he spells out, hissing. "Do you realize? Alive three years ago, now all of them gone or on their way out. Months went by, I'd be at three or four hospitals every day. I could tell you the visitor policies of every goddamned medical institution in this city. How could you know? How could you even guess what it's like?" His glass is empty. Anxiously, he signals the bartender for another. "It used to be fun to be gay. Remember those days? Of course not, you were too young. How can anyone comprehend?"

His voice catches; he sniffs, clutching his throat. "It's unfathomable. It's incomprehensible. It's beyond human comprehension." His hands tremble as he lifts his drink with one and knocks his cigarette into an ashtray with the other. Mr. Mackenzie spills part of his cocktail down his throat and places it back on its cork coaster. "I had a lover. He moved to Australia four years ago because he was afraid of it, as if it weren't going to cover the globe with its black cloud. After he left, I fell to pieces. I was sleeping fifteen, twenty hours a day. Deeply disturbed. That's what one deranged queen called me, as if he knew anything in his ivory tower." He rolls his eyes back, pauses, and takes another sip. "And then the phone calls began. This one was dying. Remember Tommy from the Ice Palace? Gone in a month. Heard from Fred lately? Went back to Iowa to die with his family. It's endless, I tell you, endless. I don't see any end to it. I can't tell you what it's doing to the community. Pretty soon there's going to be nothing left. Survival of the fittest. Shit. Survival of the celibate. And who could know that it would lead to this? Who could guess? No one." He gesticulates wildly with his stirrer. I think he's stone drunk, but he may be completely sober. "The last homosexual will die in the year 2030," he predicts. "The last heterosexual will die in the year 2065. Don't worry. We won't be around to say good-bye. But how could you be expected to understand? How could anyone understand?"

I'm scared of more than eggs.

Everything

This is everything I am afraid of: cholesterol, nitrites, AIDS, vagina dentata, forgetting my vitamins, salt, red dye No. 2, members of the legume family, large penises, small penises, AIDS, insomnia, asphyxiation, public and private humiliation, inadequate circulation, AIDS, crowds, stampedes, robbery, rape, murder, assault, battery, being hung up on on the telephone, AIDS, cancer, pneumonia, insanity, heroin, crack, Ecstasy, angel dust, free-basing, being buried alive, death by drowning, uncontrolled vomiting, AIDS, going to sleep and never waking up, being stabbed on the street, being shot on the subway, finishing the exhaustive lists I make up and having nothing left to do for the rest of my life, being touched by a bum on the street, leprosy, AIDS, calling up old tricks on the telephone and finding out they're dead, foreigners making jokes and laughing at me in their own language, being attacked by people of different socioeconomic and/or cultural backgrounds, being attacked by people of similar socioeconomic and/or cultural backgrounds, being touched by the friend with the voice like fingernails-on-blackboard who demands that I hug him at each meeting, becoming involved with an alcoholic, AIDS, and AIDS. There are more that I can't recall at present.

· 21 ·

September

*E*veryone has a friend who is dying.

Gordon calls me at work to tell me about Don, a playwright who lives in Brooklyn. Don is in the hospital with double pneumonia. "The doctors told him he'd be in the hospital for three weeks."

"Have you seen him?"

"Last Thursday. I get the impression that nobody else is visiting him. Don doesn't have that many friends."

"Is he taking anything?"

"He's in a double-blind experiment with a new drug."

"What's it called?"

"I think the name is placebo," says Gordon.

"Sucrose or dextrose?"

"Tic Tacs, I guess," says Gordon.

Joseph, the desperate former student who pursued Dennis relentlessly, is nursing Eduardo, his Argentinian lover. Eduardo fell behind in the rent and was evicted from his apartment a few months ago; he's staying at the apartment of the Circle Line tour-guide who was on the cover of *New York* magazine last spring in a story about the human side of AIDS. A few years ago, when Sheila and her husband, Alexander, came to New York for a weekend, we took the Circle Line around Manhattan, and he was our guide. Bright and vivacious, springing with excitement, he pointed out Ellis Island, the exclusive River House condominiums, where Henry Kissinger lived, and also Turtle Bay, where the guide's mother lived. Both he and Eduardo are dying. Dennis has visited Eduardo several times in his clerical capacity: to comfort him, give him courage, pray with him, listen to him.

Joey Romano knows a dancer named Paul whose face is spotted

with purple lesions. "I look at him and see the face of a dead man," says Joey bluntly.

"Don't write him off; don't give up on him," I tell Joey, cringing at his words. "Isn't there always hope?"

"Hope for what? Don't fool yourself, B.J. He's got 'Eighty-sixed' written all over his face. He's not going to make it through to winter." Joey is certain. "It's painful, but you have to face reality. The man is walking towards his grave."

Philip Moscowitz has a neighbor in Jersey City who is ill but doesn't want him to tell anyone about it. He doesn't want the pity of his friends; he doesn't want them to treat him differently than they do now. Philip drops over and makes him dinner a couple times a week: a barbecued chicken from the deli, a green health-salad, and rice pudding for dessert. "Some days I wish I could tell someone else who knows him. It's really hard, the burden of secrecy."

"I know. It's rough. Maybe he'll feel like telling his other friends later."

"I doubt it. He's withdrawing. He hardly sees anybody these days. Other than me and his brother, that's about all."

"Still sweating at night?" I ask.

"No, that was just a few nights in the dead of summer," replies Philip. "But my neck feels a little swollen sometimes."

"I'm sure it's nothing to worry about," I say.

"How's your friend Bob?" asks Philip.

"Still no change." I sigh.

"Do you think they're going to release him soon?"

"I don't know. I don't think he can manage by himself. He lives on the fourth floor of a walk-up building. Maybe if he hired a nurse full-time. But there doesn't seem to be much point in keeping him at Lenox Hill much longer."

"He's putting on weight there?"

"Not really. He's pretty stable."

"Well, catch you later."

"Yeah, back to the salt mines for me."

Every day we play round-robin at work on the telephone, telling each other about our friends' conditions. The news is never good.

At work I'm barricaded in my office like Hitler in the bunker, like Nixon with Kissinger, huddled in the Oval Office, praying on their knees. Outside, civilization is collapsing. The new mainframe operating system I have personally approved is going haywire; the computer is down half the time. Keyboarding and Operations are on the phone to me every hour with new complaints. Accounting screams for his monthly projections. My quizzical, quintessentially noninterfering boss is stationed in New Jersey. He sends me a telex in support, casually mentioning he will be off in Europe for the rest of the month. Should I need any assistance, well, he is confident I will weather any crisis on my own.

The phone rings. It's Gordon.
    "Hi, B.J. How are you doing?"
    "Oh, just fine."
    "I got this letter returned to me in the mail."
    "You forgot the zip code?"
    "Not quite. I had sent away for some porno."
    "I thought only us single guys bought those magazines."
    "Think again. Anyway, my letter came back marked 'Addressee Deceased.' I guess this guy was running mail order from his own house. It's kind of spooky." Gordon laughs his awkward laugh.
    "Yeah."
    "It's like I thought I was sending something to a business, and it turns out the guy who runs it is dead."
    "Did they mark it in red with the scarlet letter?"
    "*A* for 'Adulterer'?"
    "No, 'AIDS.' "
    "Oh, I get it. No." He clears his throat—a lot of phlegm today. "So Don is getting weaker. His mother moved into his apartment. She lives upstate. She visits him every day. At least I have company when I see him."
    "Bob is still the same. They're transferring him to St. Clare's Hospital."
    "How convenient," says Gordon, "that's right across the street from you."
    "Yeah, I guess that means I'm supposed to visit him every day now." Uptown I can visit him twice a week and not feel guilty about neglecting him.
    "When's he moving?"
    "As soon as they get an empty bed. Probably this Friday."

"I wish there was something I could do," says Gordon. "I feel useless, you know what I mean? I feel like a bulldozer is headed straight at me and all of my friends, and there's nothing I can do about it."

"I don't know. Join a religious or community-service group? Cultivate common interests? Speak to your clergy?"

"I think you're talking about how to get friends according to Ann Landers. Besides, I don't have a clergy."

"You can borrow mine."

"How's your friend Dennis?"

"OK. He's working at an AIDS hospice in the Village part-time."

"That's commendable."

"The lover of one of his former students died last week. He was there at the end."

"You know, I don't know if I could ever be a volunteer at GMHC as a buddy. I mean, I could handle answering the phones and giving out information—simple office work, data entry on their personal computers. But I don't think I could face the one-on-one relationship with a buddy dying of AIDS."

"I figure I've got my hands full as it is with Bob and all."

"Me, too, with Don."

"I mean, if you can't help your own friends . . ."

"Maybe it would be a little easier helping a stranger."

"I don't know."

"Well, I'd better let you go." Gordon clears his throat again. He eats constantly. I'm surprised I haven't heard him chomping on a carrot during our conversation.

"Snack time?"

"As a matter of fact, I'm going to have lunch with Joyce."

"But I thought the two of you usually have breakfast at ten together."

"She was late today. She came in at ten-thirty."

"Ex*cuuuuse* me."

"Why bother coming in on time when there isn't any work to do? This isn't going to last, you know. Pretty soon there are going to be cutbacks." The merger finally went through last month. A few people were laid off last week in another department. "The party can't last forever. We're just taking advantage of it while we can."

"Life at the country club." I sigh.

"Shall I pencil you in for squash at four this afternoon?" asks Gordon. "Dear, I'm not sure whether those of the Hebraic persuasion are allowed in the club."

"If they don't let me in, I'll take it to the Supreme Court," I mutter.

"Yeah, and our new Chief Justice, Rehnquist, will certainly hear your arguments."

"Welcome to America," says the hostess to me and Dennis.

"Does she think I'm just off the boat from Ireland or something?" asks Dennis.

"She says that to everyone. It's the name of the restaurant, silly."

"Oh, now I g-g-g-g-g-g-g-g-g-g-g-get it. Why-y-y-y-y-y-y didn't you tell me before?" Dennis picks up his napkin with a flourish and smooths it on his lap.

America is a trendy eatery on East Eighteenth the size of an airplane hangar with an endless menu that includes such American favorites as Pigs in a Blanket and Fluffernutter Sandwiches, along with a few exotic dishes with mushrooms flown in from Wyoming and sautéed toxic wastes from New Jersey. The reverse acoustic ceilings amplify the din to a decibel range appropriate for a wind tunnel. Straight singles in business suits are gathered at the gleaming-chrome elevated bar, sipping vodka stingers and exchanging stories about insider trading on Wall Street, wary about the next indictment. A larger-than-life-sized mural of the Statue of Liberty's head, atilt, covers one wall in soft pastels, drowning in what appears to be guacamole; facing it is an impressionistic razzle-dazzle wave of stars and stripes with a floating cow's skull à la Georgia O'Keeffe in a sky of washed-out blue.

"*This* is American home-cooking?" asks Dennis. "Ritz Crackers Mock Apple Pie? Space Food Sticks? Marshmallow Treats? The big question is, D-d-d-d-d-d-d-d-d-d-d-d-do they have D-d-d-d-d-d-d-d-d-dewar's on the r-r-r-r-r-r-r-r-r-r-r-r-r-r-r-r-r-rocks?"

We both order burgers. I tell Dennis that Bob Broome is moving across the street. I ask him how he is after Eduardo's death.

"It's rough. Joseph fell apart after Ed died last Thursday. I stayed over. It's just awful. I never got to know Ed that well. From what I hear, he was a real nice guy. He had been declining for the past year. He got nasty toward the end. It makes you nasty, dying. I think in his case it may have been something to do with the brain deteriorating. Sad, but your worst qualities are the ones that remain. Ed

270

was always complaining, those last few months. He kept telling Joseph to turn down the air conditioner; it was too cold, even though he was soaking in sweat. Or he'd tell him to switch the radio to another station when there was nothing on. He'd lose weight, lose all interest in eating, catch a cold, and they'd have to get him off to the hospital for some IV. Anyway, the last time, we were all there, crowded around his hospital bed last Thursday. His friend Andrew had flown in from San Francisco to see him. Ed was just hanging by a thread. And Morgan—he's into holistics and macrobiotics, he's pretty spiritual—Morgan had all of us come there at the same time. Ed had lost his vision. He weighed less than a hundred pounds; you could see he was just barely holding on. Well, Andrew walked into the hospital room, and Morgan started reading a beautiful passage, a spiritual passage about passing over to the next world. It was long and gentle and flowing. And at the end he said to Ed that it was OK to let go. And at that moment Ed sat up in the bed, looking straight ahead, a tear rolling down his cheek. And then he died."

Bob moves to St. Clare's on Friday. Thursday night, Dave Johnson and Jerry truck his possessions from Lenox Hill to my apartment. They were planning on storing his VCR, phone, and some flowers and stuffed animals in their West Village apartment when Dave remembers that I live right across the street. I don't particularly want to volunteer the space, but once nominated, I feel I can't decline. For an evening my apartment is redolent with the hospital smell, associations with Bob; the place is even more cluttered and disorganized than usual. The next day, laden with Bloomingdale big brown bags, we bring Bob's belongings to his room in two trips. The guard at the desk waves us through. This time we don't have to procure visitor cards. St. Clare's is relatively strict about adhering to visiting rules. Last fall I waited half an hour to visit a friend with pneumonia who lived down the block because two people were already in his room. The cards—eight by eleven, English on one side and Spanish on the other, laminated in plastic, frayed at the edges, and bent from use—contain visiting hours and room numbers on white adhesive-tape.

Bob is on the fourth floor. His room faces south. At the nurses' station a tall and slender West Indian woman sits, her long black hair in a braid. Behind her, on the wall, a blackboard tells Bob's room. I notice a smudged chalk entry, recently erased, after one of the room numbers.

St. Clare's is much less modern than Lenox Hill. A few years back the city closed down half of it, leaving only the emergency room open. The AIDS crisis revitalized the hospital. The green oxygen tank with chipped paint in Bob's room resembles an antiballistic missile, Dr. Strangelove's nuclear warhead on its cart.

"Great view, Bob," says Dave. "Look, right across the street I can see two men stripping," Dave kids.

"Hey, you can see the Empire State Building," I say, craning my neck from the corner.

Bob sits in bed. He looks wan. "I'm pretty wiped out," he says. "The move was exhausting." He stops, pausing for breath. He is very weak. "They had me on a stretcher in the hall for almost an hour. I thought they had forgotten me. The ride was bumpy. I think I'd like to be alone for a while."

"Sure thing," says Dave. "We'll be back tomorrow, won't we?" he says, looking at me.

"Sure," I say.

"OK, rest up. I'm sure you'll feel much better tomorrow. Take care." Jerry kisses Bob on his head. We troop into the bathroom to wash our hands with pHisoHex and leave.

"Remember how I told you that the doctors said Don would be in the hospital for three weeks?" asks Gordon.

"Sure."

"Well, they were right."

"He's out now?"

"His mother called me today. He died last night."

"I'm sorry."

"It's OK. I didn't think he would hang on much longer."

"How's his mother doing?"

"She seems to be taking it well. She seems to have prepared herself for it."

"So yesterday my friend Bob moved to St. Clare's. It's a long-term health-care facility for AIDS patients."

"Yeah, you told me he was moving. That's right across the street from you."

"I kind of wish it wasn't, you know?"

"Too close for comfort?"

"Something like that."

"Well, it won't last forever."

272

"I don't see the end."
"For Bob?"
"No, the plague."

Bob's parents come from Oregon for a visit. They're in their late seventies. His father is a retired Methodist minister. A few months back Bob told them that he was gay and suffering from AIDS. He complained to me how difficult it was dealing with his parents, and I sympathized from my own experience. His father was very strict and unyielding. Yet the moment they walk into the room Bob's face lights up. His parents' faces turn ashen when they first see him, then they smile through their tears. I forgot how bad he must look to them; I have seen the gradual decline. A gruff brother sits in a chair without talking much. Bob's mother has been writing him steadily. He receives a letter from her almost every day. They have been talking on the phone about once a week. His folks are in town for a few days. Dave and Jerry take them out to dinner. Before they leave, they tell me and David and Jerry how grateful they are to see Bob's room full of visitors. On different days they have met Marcy, Roxanne, and Ernie, who continue to come steadily. They leave on Monday. Dave leaves them alone in the room with Bob for half an hour, then drives them to the airport.

"I don't know what to say to Bob."
"Go with his moods," says my therapist. "Some days, if he doesn't feel like talking, you can just hold his hand. It's important that you don't leave anything left unsaid with him. Tell him how you feel."
"But I can barely express my feelings to myself."
"That's what we're here to work on."
"I wonder how much longer this is going to take. Some days I just wish he'd die and get it over with."
"It *is* difficult," says Neil.
"He always complains to me. It seems like he's usually much more cheerful to other people. I sometimes wish he hadn't chosen to confide in me. I don't want to hurt his feelings. He's right across the street, and I feel I have no excuse not to visit him every day, but I can't take seeing him there in the bed, wasting away, every day of the week. It's too much."
"You don't have to do anything. If Richard were sick, would you feel the same way?"

"I wouldn't mind visiting *him* every day." I have to put things into perspective. "But how do you talk about death to someone who's dying? Who has the energy to read Kübler-Ross with a friend in the hospital? I can make it through the pamphlets that GMHC puts out, but that's about all. Every day it seems to get a little worse."

Sensitivity Exercises for Death

1. Pretend the room is filled with helium. Glide across it effortlessly. You are a cloud passing overhead. You are drifting languorously, and you have no fear of falling. The air becomes fog and condenses. Now imagine the room is filled with water. Swim your way back to the other side of the room with slow, gentle, even strokes. Observe the reeds waving as you pass. Tropical fish ignore you. Your cheeks bulge with your last saved breath. Now exhale. Good. Don't be afraid. Breathing is no longer necessary. You are floating. Now imagine the room is filled with mud. Perhaps the water has thickened and darkened. The mud is viscous. Gradually make your way across the room. Watch out for rocks. The mud is warm and soothing. You hear muted music, the lower octaves from an organ. It gradually fades away. The mud hardens. Now it is solid. You are encased in concrete. Try to move. You can't.

2. Close your eyes.
   Now don't open them.
   Ever.

· 22 ·

October

*T*all buildings loom before me. I stand outside my apartment and look down Ninth Avenue. At Forty-second Street stand the twin apartment towers of Manhattan Plaza, grim reminders of two more miserable affairs. In the west tower resides Jefferson Peters, an ignoble lout who tortured me with his massive member and malign indifference for several months last autumn; in the east, Luigi Porcelli, who kept his focus on the TV as I did him, watching for his alias and phone number to flash on the screen of the gay cable-show personals, back in June of '82.

To the north, on Fifty-eighth, is Roosevelt Hospital, where John Lennon died in 1980. And across the street is St. Clare's, where Bob Broome is beginning to lose his mind.

"It's not so bad," I say, trying to sound casual. "Look at the view," I say for the thousandth time. "From my apartment, what do I have to look at but Wolf's Paint Store and the bus stop?"

"The Chrysler Building," says Bob.

"No, it's the Empire State Building."

"What time is it?" he asks, annoyed.

"Six-fifteen." I look at his radio alarm-clock nervously. I wonder how much longer I have to stay. I don't want to leave him alone.

"Oh," he says, lying back down on his pillow.

"Do you like this poster?" I have brought him a poster of the Eiffel Tower I bought in Paris a few years ago, a photo of the tower struck by two daggers of green lightning against a background of blue. I carefully hung the poster so Bob could see it from his bed without turning. Patrick had gotten silver streamers and decorated the pole at the side of the bed from which his IV was hanging.

"It's OK," says Bob. He went to Paris a year ago last spring for a few weeks. He had such a wonderful time that he had wanted to go back. Now all he wanted to do was go for a walk through Central Park and see the leaves change. "Did I tell you about what happened to my pen?" he asks, indignantly.

"I think I've heard this one before." I sigh.

Ignoring me, Bob looks straight ahead, right through the poster, and begins. "I had gotten this Parker pen when I left my job at Chemical, at a going-away party. I was very touched." Bob speaks slowly, laboriously, didactically. He wants to be sure that I understand the grave injustice. "It was my favorite pen. I asked Dave to bring it from the apartment so I could write letters and sign checks." Bob's handwriting has deteriorated. Last week Dave had to forge his signature on a rent check. He had Bob sign a blank piece of paper, and he didn't seem to notice. "Well, somebody took it. It's gone now." (Patrick and I had looked through Bob's drawer, stuffed with letters from his mother, wooden ice-cream sticks for half pints in paper cartons, bills, some holographic stickers I had gotten for Bob at Star Magic downtown, a *People* magazine, and other assorted junk Bob had accumulated the past few weeks. We couldn't find the pen anywhere. We checked the bureau, the closets, the bathroom; we asked the nurses. No one knew where the pen had disappeared.) Bob takes a breath. He moans. "And now I don't have my Parker pen." He starts to weep softly. "It was the only thing that was really my own here, and sombody took it."

I don't know what to say. I can't offer him any solace. It was just a pen. Jerry told him that he wasn't mad at the pen as much as he was mad that he had to stay in the hospital. Jerry calls Bob up every night at around nine, and they talk for an hour. Jerry and Dave usually visit around dinnertime. Jerry cries every night. Dave, who always sounds so flip to me on the phone, tells me it's getting to him, too. He cries—not just for Bob, but for everyone at the ward. "Did you see the junkie down the hall from Bob? He can't weigh more than eighty pounds. He's covered with KS lesions. It's horrible." His name is Sal. He always asks Dave to get him a Coke. Nobody visits Sal. You can practically see his heart beating through his shallow rib-cage. His fragile legs, bent at the knees, are pencil-thin. "And it's not just Sal. He's not the only one. That's what gets me. If it were only Bob, I could almost deal with it," Dave says to me.

"We'll get you another pen," I tell Bob.

"That's not the point!" shouts Bob. "It was the last thing I had, and now it's gone." He reaches for a tissue at the side of his bed, blows his nose, and lets his arm droop without releasing the tissue. "What time is it?" he asks.

"Six-thirty. Gee, I think I'd better go now. I'm meeting some friends for dinner."

"Nice to see you, B.J. I'll be seeing you tomorrow?" he asks.

"I guess so. I don't have any plans. Right after work, OK?"

"Thanks for coming."

I pat Bob on the head. I walk down the three flights of stairs, return the tattered visitor's card to the guard, and make my way home. I open a can of chicken soup and empty it into the pot.

"Donald's mother sent me a thank-you note," says Gordon. "She was grateful for the time I spent with Donald these past few months."

"That was nice of her."

"She also wanted me to tell her a little about Donald's life. She said she felt that she never really knew him."

"Do you want to start with the fabulous Mineshaft Cocktail Lounge and Restaurant?"

"Yeah. I can tell her I met Donald on Fire Island four years ago, but we didn't really connect then. We were taking different drugs at the time. When I was speeding, he was coming down."

"It must be nice to get real mail. You know who my most faithful correspondent is?" I ask Gordon.

"No, who?"

"Richard Dunne, the executive director of GMHC. It never fails. Every Sunday he sends me the same letter. It's always dated 'Last Sunday.' He tells me this heartbreaking story about visiting someone in the hospital with AIDS, and then he asks for my financial support. I wonder how many mailing lists I'm on."

"Do you know what I think? I think that when the city closed St. Mark's Baths, GMHC purchased their sign-up sheets."

"Very funny."

"How's Caroline, your pride and joy?"

"D-Day is approaching. According to the employee handbook, I can fire her next Friday. I've been waking up covered with sweat. I think it's night sweats, but then I remember it's just nerves over Caroline. I had another nightmare over her last night. I was the dean of a small liberal-arts college in Maine. Caroline and a troupe of radical feminists took over my office and kidnapped me. I had made some silly sexist remark, and Caroline convinced them I was dangerous. She was only out for personal revenge. They threw me into a burlap sack and were taking me to a submarine to torture me under the lake on campus while students lazily rowed above. Then I woke up."

"Well, they've finally started laying off people here," Gordon says.

"God, do you think you're next?"

"I'm practically the only one here who knows how to put together the PC's. Until I train a replacement, I'd say I'm fairly secure here. I'm hoping they'll offer me a package. To entice employees into leaving, they're giving settlements of up to twenty-six weeks' severance pay and a year's worth of Blue Cross/Blue Shield."

"Good luck."

"I went to see a headhunter last week."

"After work?"

"And ruin my evening workout? Are you kidding? I took a three-hour lunch. She was over on Forty-second Street. She said my prospects were quite good."

"Maybe if I switched jobs I wouldn't have to dump Caroline. I know it's going to be messy."

"You've given her every opportunity to shape up."

"I keep on wondering, Isn't it partly my fault? I mean, I'm a pretty weak boss. Of course, she has tried to walk over me. I haven't been firm enough. I don't want to just fire her because she drives me crazy like my mother. That wouldn't be fair. I don't want to fire her because I'm angry that Bob is dying. I want to judge her on her own merits, keep personal factors out of this. Trouble is, she drives me up a wall. How can I separate her performance from her personality? She's so fucking passive-aggressive. I'll tell her to do something, and she'll do it, but she'll take her own sweet time. I've been waiting almost a year for her to finish a project. I made the mistake of helping her out at the start, and now it's beneath her dignity to finish it."

"B.J., don't worry about it. She's a washout. You've been complaining about her for the past year and a half to me. Give her the boot."

"She's having a rough time now. I found out her husband is leaving her for another man. I mean—you know what I mean. Her husband, Liu Chou, only married her for the papers, about a year ago. Caroline didn't have an inkling. She thinks there's some sort of international homo conspiracy out to get her."

Gordon stage-gasps. "You mean she found out about the international homo conspiracy? I guess that means we'll have to rub her out before she gets to the press. Let's see, we could get a hairdresser to electrocute her on her next trim job. He could accidentally toss a plugged-in hair-dryer into the basin during her rinse. Or maybe we can contact the homo waiters' underground to off her the next time she eats out with a smidgen of arsenic in the bouillabaisse."

"Stop it."

"Look at it this way. If she loses her job and her husband at the same time, maybe she'll figure fate is telling her it's time to move. With any luck, she'll put some distance between you two."

"I *would* feel better if Caroline were back in Iowa. I'd even give her exclusive rights to the entire Midwest. She could keep it. I'd promise never to enter a single state, except perhaps en route on an interstate, and I'd limit myself to one rest-stop every two hundred miles, directly on the highway."

"Well, let me know how it goes. How's Bob doing?"

"Hanging on. He's beginning to lose his mind. It's scary. He keeps asking what time it is, and there's a clock right next to his bed. He got an infection from the IV in his right arm. They're running out of veins to stick him. Patrick tries to get him to do the leg exercises, but some days Bob is so irritable he can't finish. He's certainly taking his time," I say.

"The nerve," comments Gordon.

"I hate to say this, but I wish he'd get it over with."

"You mean die?"

"Yeah." It hurts to say it. "It's just—he can't do anything by himself anymore. I mean, he can't go for a walk. He can't eat without assistance. He can't concentrate to watch TV. He can't even control his bodily functions. I don't think he's capable of enjoying life anymore."

"How long has he been in the hospital?" asks Gordon.

"Ever since July."

"That is a long time."

"I know."

"You know what I think? I think that maybe he's just hanging on because he's too tired to make the jump."

"Into the next world? Come on, not you, too, Gordon?"

"J.k." Just kidding.

"I figured as much."

"You never were that close with him, were you?" he asks.

"Not really."

"Then why are you spending so much time there with him?"

"I don't know. I don't really have a choice. It's like I feel I *should* be there. I mean, how can I refuse him? Every time I see him, no matter how dim he gets, he always asks when I'm coming back to see him. I wouldn't want to be all alone in the hospital myself."

Why do I find it so difficult to separate Bob from myself?

On Friday at 4:45 I fire Caroline. It's as bad as I expected it would be. I talk about the problems we've been having over the past few years. She shrinks back in rabbit fear. She whines. Her face is white. I tell her things aren't getting better. She pleads. Tears run down her face. I am as diplomatic as possible. "I want you to think about this."

"What do you *mean*?" she whines. She cries without conscious effort; tears wash her face in a steady stream as she stares blankly in my direction.

"I mean it's time for you to think about getting another job." I hold a fixed frown on my face for fear of crumbling.

"Oh," she sobs. At this point Caroline lets go and joins her tears with tremors and shivers, racking sobs, hiccups, coughs. Gently, I close her door. I walk the long gray corridor to my office. I take my time packing my briefcase for the weekend. Cautiously, I take my leave. The light on her office is still on. The sobs have subsided.

Bob sits in bed, staring blankly at the wall. Patrick holds his hand, stroking it gently. I feel I'm intruding.

"No, sit down, B.J.," says Patrick. "Say hello to Bob."

"Hi, Bob. How's it going?"

He doesn't respond. His eyelids flicker as if during REM sleep.

"He's resting now," explains Patrick. "He's had a rough day." Patrick is visibly upset.

"So, how are *you* doing?" I ask Patrick.

"Oh, I guess OK. A little tired. My lover, George, flew to Chicago last Thursday. Now I've got the entire apartment to myself for a week. You'd think I'd go out dancing until dawn or be spending my nights at the Works, wouldn't you? But I've been feeling run-down for a while. I just go home after work or after visiting Bob and veg out in front of the TV. I'm so lazy, I'm not even reading mystery novels."

I feel exhausted from Caroline and Bob and AIDS. Limply, I try to enliven the conversation with some good-natured flirting. "You should have told me George was gone. I would have camped out in front of your apartment building in the hopes of rekindling our passionate affair. There's no need for you to sleep alone."

"What passionate affair?" Patrick giggles. "You must have been very subtle in wooing me, because, frankly, I don't remember this affair."

"How can you persist in ignoring me, your only true love? Can't you see I'm your destiny?"

"You mean there's no escaping you? That's not much better than George. I thought I was stuck with him. You mean now I'm trapped with *both* of you? I feel like a prisoner on a chain gang."

"Come on, it's not as bad as that, is it?"

Bob, who has been murmuring lightly for a few moments, turns to me and says, "B.J., you're too technology oriented." He moves back to staring straight ahead. I hear snatches of conversations going on in his head. ". . . move to New York . . . it will take six thousand . . . get a job . . . can stay with some friends in White Plains for a few months . . . making plans . . . fish wrap . . . not too sure . . . the seashore . . . out on the Sound . . . yes, easier said than done. . . ."

Patrick and I leave at eight. We have coffee and donuts at the diner at the corner of Fifty-fourth and Ninth. Patrick is shaking.

"I don't think I can take much more of this, B.J. You know, everyone says they didn't really know Bob that well. Like he was private and never really said that much about himself. Well, I only met him two years back, but we really got to know one another. We'd get together and talk for hours on end. Did you know that he wanted to be a doctor when he was a kid? He's been on top of things here, checking that the nurses give him the correct dosage of medication, asking the doctors all the right technical questions. Bob grew up on a farm in Montana. Did you know that he was majoring in agriculture until he was a junior at college? He had to drop out when his father got sick. He moved back home and stayed there for two years. Both of his brothers were married; they couldn't leave their families. When his father recovered—I think it was encephalitis—he decided that he should become a preacher. Bob left home then, went back to college, and finished with a degree in computer science. He moved to San Francisco, lived there for a couple years. He did some really incredible systems-work on minis in San Francisco. He wrote some programs that made a lot of money for his firm. I don't quite understand what they did myself; I don't have the background.

"But Bob and I would talk about our families together, growing up; it was sort of like in college, having an all-night bull session over a six-pack and a pizza. I'd tell him all about George and what we happened to be fighting about that week; he'd tell me about the latest in the series of cute blond all-American boys he had met at the gym or on the street. We'd just bullshit for hours. We got really close. And now, it's like he's not there anymore. I think we've lost him. It's scary. He's been sick so long; it *seems* like he's been sick so long. I don't even know him anymore. I don't want to be in the position of remembering this, what's left of Bob, instead of Bob. But that's not him in the bed anymore. It's like a shell of what Bob used to be. I'm so pissed. Why did this have to happen?"

"I don't know."

"Do you know anyone else with AIDS, B.J.?"

"A few passing acquaintances, but no one this close."

"Me neither. I was lucky, I guess. I hooked up with George seven years ago. We've had our moments. He moved to Chicago for two years, and we almost broke up then. But then, with AIDS, it didn't make sense. You don't change lovers midstream."

" 'How AIDS Saved My Marriage,' in this month's *Ladies' Home Journal.*"

"Cut it out, B.J. Sure, we had our rough moments. You expect the passion to die down in a relationship. George seems to get more and more rigid every year. It's funny. He's ten years older than me, and it didn't matter that much when I met him, but now the gulf seems larger. I feel like I'm approaching some prime. I want some excitement once in a while. I want to do wild and crazy things once in a while. And George would rather spend a quiet evening at home."

"Oh, Patrick, I'd marry you in a minute," I pledge, more serious than I'd care to admit.

He laughs it off. "I don't *want* to get married. You're lucky. You're single. You don't have to worry about farting in bed. You can sleep as late as you want. You can eat whenever you want. You don't have to fit your schedule to your lover's. If you want to go out and see a movie, you don't have to wait and make sure your lover wants to see the same thing or whatnot. You can be impulsive. B.J., I feel constrained."

"But safe."

"Yeah, I kind of feel safe. I'm not sure where I'd be without George. Where would I live? It's been so long since I've lived alone, I don't even know if I could manage it." He gives me a rueful smile. At times like these Patrick is at his most appealing, his big green eyes bright with whimsy.

"I guess the grass is always greener," I say. I long to wake up with someone like Patrick

"Hey, you could find a lover easy. You've got looks, brains, charm, appeal—"

"And easily the most neurotic personality in Manhattan."

"Well, you said it first." He laughs.

"How long do you think he's going to last?" I ask, seriously.

"I don't know." Patrick takes a deep breath and sighs. "It's so creepy, sitting there, holding his hand and listening to gibberish. I don't want to abandon him, but what difference does it make at this point?"

"I dread visiting Bob. You'd think it would get easier. That's the worst. Every time it gets a little worse. You'd think I'd get used to it."

"He's so helpless there."

"I wonder what I'd do if I were him."

"Me, too," says Patrick. It could just as easily be one of us in the hospital bed. "Well, I'd better be going now. George is supposed to call me tonight. I'd like to make him jealous and not be there to answer it one of these days just to see what he does, but not tonight."

"You're welcome to stay over with me," I quickly say, too eagerly.

"I'll take a rain check."

Monday I arrive at work, relieved that Miss Yamamoto has finally been dismissed. To my horror, she appears at ten. I shut my door and shiver with rage. Who does she think she is, Rasputin? Freddy from *Nightmare on Elm Street*? Caroline reminds me of the planaria we read about in high-school biology: Slice their heads in half with a scalpel, and they grow two in their place.

I play back the conversation from last Friday in my head and realize, in despair, that I didn't actually spell it out to her that she was fired. Shit.

She knocks curtly on the door and enters. "I have to talk to you," she says. "It's urgent."

"Caroline, I have a meeting in ten minutes."

"Could we meet during lunch then?"

I sigh. I'm planning on seeing Bob Broome at the hospital for lunch. "We'll meet this afternoon at two."

"It will only take a moment," she says.

"This afternoon. Two. *Capisce?*"

"OK," she says slowly. "Fine. Perfect."

After my meeting I grab a cab for the hospital. The nurse told me that Bob needed to gain weight. "Bring him food he likes from outside. We've got to get him to eat more. The hospital food isn't very interesting."

I get Bob some Afghanistan shish kebab from a tiny hole-in-the-wall restaurant on Ninth Avenue. I snatch up the visitor's card from the desk and jog up three flights. Bob sits, shivering, in his wheelchair in the hallway, staring. "It's so co-o-o-o-o-ld," he chatters to me. "Could you get me a blanket?" I go to his room and cover him with a bedspread, making sure not to disturb the catheter or the IV.

"I brought shish kebab. Do you like lamb?"

"It's OK." Bob struggles with the plastic silverware, trying to spear a piece, then he gives up. I cut up a piece into tiny bits and then feed him a little. Even last month I don't think I could have done this. The nurse told me that I could feed Bob one evening. I demurred. I didn't want to handle the utensils. In a way I am growing. Yet for each step I take, Bob recedes.

Bob tries to chew the lamb. It's difficult for him. The lamb is too spicy for him. I give him a spoonful of rice. He seems to like that. "I'm really not that hungry."

I check my watch. I'm more than halfway through my lunch hour. I spear, chew, and swallow rapidly, eating as fast as my father used to at home. "Listen, Bob, I've got to go now. I'll see you tomorrow evening, OK?"

"I guess so. Bye, B.J." I leave Bob as I found him, sitting in the hallway, staring at nothing.

I greet the nurse with the long black hair as I depart. Her name is Selena. She sees the aluminum container of shish kebab I left on the arm of Bob's wheelchair. Selena tells me her recipe for rice pilaf. I am half-listening. I look at the blackboard. There have been two erasures since my last visit. "You know, I prefer the gay AIDS patients to the IV drug abusers," she remarks. "They're a lot nicer. They're more interesting. Pretty soon the hospital will be filled," she says in an upbeat tone. Selena likes her job. I wonder if it is harder for the visitors, who know the patients, or for the hospital workers, who must endure an endless stream of dying people. I flee in despair through the rain-swept streets and return to the office.

At two I find that Caroline is out for blood. She digs her elbows into the trenches. She informs me that I cannot fire her without a hearing. She tells me she is in a bind because if she resigns, she won't be eligible for unemployment. At this point I will do anything to get her out of my hair. I check with Personnel and make an arrangement. She can quit and get unemployment; someone else will sign the papers. Upon hearing this, Miss Yamamoto leaves for the day.

On Thursday I find an urgent message on my desk. I call Miss Yamamoto at home. Caroline tells me that she is having problems with her divorce lawyer and that with not much cash on hand and no immediate prospects, she won't be able to pay him. She says that we must discuss the matter of severance pay. My blood is boiling as she asks for six weeks' severance. I tell her that I am sorry about her personal situation, but, frankly, I'm not responsible for it; furthermore, I believe that if she resigns, she will not be eligible for severance pay. "In that case, resigning might not be the most beneficial action for me," continues Caroline. Stonily, Caroline tells me that she has heard through the grapevine that another employee at Amalgamated received six weeks' severance pay. Sure, I mutter to myself, the second vice-president. Through thin lips I tell her I'll see what I can do.

I go to Personnel, blood pounding, hate in my every step, spittle at the corner of my mouth. I explain the situation. I tell Personnel that I'll be willing to go through with the bureaucratic sludge to fire her outright; it will be worth it to me to drive her into the mud. Personnel chews the cap of her Bic contemplatively. "Give her four weeks and tell her it's final," she says.

I relay the message to Caroline in as calm a tone as I can manage. During the conversation I mutilate several paper clips. Caroline gives me a noncommittal "That's very interesting" and then hangs up.

"Did you see the paper today?" asks Gordon.

"Give me a second. What page?"

"B-sixteen."

" 'Jerry Smith dies of AIDS.' "

"Former Washington Redskins football player."

"Well, he was honest about it. He admitted he had it. He came out to the press some time ago."

"Unlike certain fashion designers and movie stars who shall remain nameless."

"It isn't fair. There's no justice."

"I know." Gordon sighs. He clears his throat. "Aren't you sick of hearing about the Mets and the World Series?"

"It's mass hysteria. The city's gone crazy."

"It's like I go to work on the subway, and six people have Mets hats on. They're all talking about Mookie. Who would name her son Mookie?"

"I hear you." I drum my fingers on my table.

"How's your friend Bob at the hospital?"

"Still no change. He lies in bed all day, mumbling. His eyes roll back so you can just see the whites. He hasn't made any sense the past two weeks." I sniff audibly. I search through the morass of files on my desk for my Kleenexes and blow my nose.

"It's rough."

"You know, for a while all of my friends knew someone in the hospital with AIDS. Well, Bob's still there. He's the only one."

"Do you think AZT would have helped much?"

"I think he was too far gone. Who can say?"

"Yeah, I've heard there are severe side-effects. Anemia is usually so severe that many patients need regular blood-transfusions."

"Jesus, you know, you and I know so much maybe we should quit our jobs and go into joint practice."

"Well, it's too late now. Don't you get angry at all the red tape involved to get the drugs?" asks Gordon.

"The government's fucked. Look at the bimbo in the White House."

"That's Bonzo," corrects Gordon.

"I guess Bimbo is his wife."

"A lovely couple. Guess what?"

"What?"

"My mother sent me some mail-order cheese-food product from Wisconsin." Gordon's mother periodically attempts to communicate with Gordon by sending him painfully unsuitable gifts: polyester sweat-suits from J. C. Penney's in the wrong size, dried beef-jerky from Texas, and marmalade from New Zealand. He would drop off the clothing at the nearest Salvation Army. The bomb-shelter food he'd try to foist on unsuspecting friends.

"She means well," I offer.

"No, she's just guilty that she hasn't spoken to me in the past six months."

I guess we all have family problems.

Monday morning I have Miss Caroline Yamamoto's letter of resignation. I dash to the Xerox machine, make several copies, and start routing it to the appropriate people. By the afternoon she's changed her mind. She wants to resign effective two weeks later. She will be out of the office in two weeks from today; she will schedule her vacation to follow directly. In this manner she will get an extra month's medical coverage. She explains that she has cleared this through Benefits. I call them to verify this in her presence. I don't understand why I have to bend over backward. Benefits whispers into the phone, "Do it." I have no choice but to accede. I tell Caroline this is acceptable as long as she is off the premises in two weeks. She hands me a revised typewritten letter of resignation. Grudgingly, I return to the Xerox machine, make several copies, and start routing it to the appropriate personnel.

Tuesday she wants to retract. I tell her it's too late. She barges into Health Insurance with her tale of woe. Sobbing, she says she was totally unprepared for this, and she was in the midst of a legal battle. Health Insurance pats Caroline on the hand, clucks her tongue, and dispenses tissues. Through a stream of tears Caroline asks if Amalgamated can pay for her health insurance for the next six months. Health Insurance carefully removes her hand from Caroline's. "What?" Caroline tells her that a recent statute requires employers to allow their employees to remain on group health plan up to six months after termination. Health Insurance informs Caroline that this option is at the employee's expense. Caroline replies that she is certain she will be vindicated should she ever sue Amalgamated. Health Insurance says, "Just a moment," and calls Benefits, who calls Personnel. After a terse conference call Caroline is informed that Amalgamated has made an exception and will provide for her health plan for three months. Icily, Health Insurance says, "I trust that will be satisfactory." Caroline tells her she will think about it.

I go home, and there's a message from Richard in San Francisco. He's going to call me back tomorrow. The next day, his garrulous friend Stuart calls me. Richard is coming back to New York. Guess what? He's going to be staying with me. How nice for me. Bob Broome is in the hospital dying, Caroline is driving me crazy even as she leaves, and Richard is threatening to stay with me, indefinitely.

"He didn't speak to you yet?" asks Stuart.

"No, he just left a message last night." I look down and notice my left hand is trembling. "He can't stay with you, I suppose?"

"No, that would be out of the question. You know how he is with prescription drugs." Stuart, another manic-depressive, is on several. "I couldn't leave him alone in the house. Besides, the cats are pretty territorial here." Stuart has two mongrel cats, Gonzo and Faygeleh. His apartment always stinks of cat shit. "So give me a buzz when he tells you when he's coming," says Stuart. Stuart never loaned Richard money when he was in need. Stuart told Richard that lending money can ruin relationships.

"I don't know if I can handle him," I confess.

"Just be firm. Set limits."

"How long did he say he was staying?"

"Just until he gets his feet on the ground."

Just until the second coming of Christ is more like it. He turned me into a lunatic once; I have no doubt that in two weeks I will be a blathering idiot. Why does he want to come now? I was making progress in therapy. I had almost begun to identify myself as a distinct entity. If he comes, I'll start playing karma chameleon again and meld into his psyche. I will no longer be able to distinguish his angst from my own. Richard and me. Our relationship was as healthy and rewarding as Isabella Rossellini and Dennis Hopper's in *Blue Velvet*. Here I am, on the edge of a nervous breakdown. Can't Richard wait a bit? Like six more years? Richard has come back to haunt me, to plague me. And I can't tell him no. I'm terrified of Richard. I don't want to fall into his whirlwind of despair and get sucked under again.

Something else I've buried: Years ago Richard and I exchanged bodily fluids—you know, your typical high-risk sexual activities most conducive to spreading viruses. Fucking. Anal intercourse. *Taking it up the ass.* Didn't some part of me hate Richard for possibly infecting me?

"Do you think the reason I've stuck it out so long with Richard has been that I am subconsciously trying to cure my dead father of insanity?" I ask Neil Wollowitz.

"That's a possibility," he replies. "What do you think?" he inquires.

I think that if I wanted to play verbal rebound, I could have done just as well with a basketball backboard as with a therapist, and it would have been a lot cheaper.

Wednesday afternoon Caroline calls my dashing European boss. She needs to see him in a matter of the utmost urgency. He calls me from Jersey. "What's this about, Benjamin?" I explain the circumstances. He agrees it is time for a "parting of ways." He sighs. "I cleared a morning of appointments so I can see her tomorrow. I'll let you know what happens." I replace the receiver on the hook. Typically, I see my boss on the average of twice a month, usually for no more than fifteen minutes at a time, and Caroline managed to get an appointment for the very next day.

My boss gives me a report Thursday afternoon. Caroline asked if she could be transferred to another department. She mentioned some problems she was having with me, her boss, and thought it might be best to seek another supervisor. My boss offered her several leads for positions where he had acquired personal contacts. Throughout the meeting my boss remained cordial, diplomatic, and tactful. Caroline thanked him for his time. My boss tells me that he would prefer not to have another meeting with Caroline. He considers the matter dispensed with.

Gritting my teeth, I tell Caroline I will write her a letter of recommendation on the basis of her work, which has been more than adequate, leaving out mention of any interpersonal difficulties we encountered. Caroline asks if she may receive this letter by next Monday. Swallowing the bile in my throat, I tell her I will write it by then if I have time. I escort her to the door of my office. I shut the door after she leaves and spew a stream of invective in a torrent on a tan interoffice memo directed at Caroline on my IBM Selectric typewriter, then rip it into a thousand pieces and scatter them into the trash.

By the time Richard finally gets back to me, a week after he first called, I am ready for him. Stuart told me to set limits. "Two weeks," I say. "Two weeks, no money. And don't expect me to entertain you every night."

"Hey, wait a minute. I get this feeling that you really don't want me."

"Of course I want you; I just want to be clear from the start."

"Hey, I wasn't planning on staying forever. Just until I get my feet on the ground."

"It's a small apartment," I tell Richard.

"I know that. I stayed there with you, remember? After I got out of the hospital?"

"So when are you coming?" I say, keeping my voice neutral.

"Oh, sometime next week," waffles Richard. "I made the reservation." I see him riffling through his wallet, tossing scraps of paper to the ground on Castro Street. He's calling collect from a phone booth. I can hear horns in the background. Suddenly I hear a roar outside on the street. Pandemonium breaks out on his end of the line, too.

"What's the noise?" I ask.

"I think the Series is over."

"They're shouting here, too. I guess that means the Mets won."

"I suppose so. Well, I gotta go now. See you next week," says Richard.

"OK. Bye." We hang up. I size up the apartment. Can we survive two weeks together? Do I really want *another* albatross around my neck now? I can barely survive Bob's illness and Caroline's treachery. Do I really have to put up with Richard's insanity on top of everything? I feel my neck tighten. Reflexively, I check for swollen nodes. My forehead tenses. I can hear the blood pounding through my veins.

"I'm waiting for Bob to die. I hope it happens soon," I tell Neil Wollowitz. "I feel I have to keep visiting him, and there's nothing there. His eyes roll back and he just lies there, not making any sense."

"How do you feel?"

"I feel awful. I'm depressed. It shouldn't happen to anyone. It's draining, seeing him. I want to cry."

"Would you like to try an experiment?"

"I don't know."

"Let me tell you about it, and you can choose whether or not to try it."

"OK." I'll give it the old college-try, right? He's the therapist; he knows how to make it better, doesn't he?

"Lie down. Close your eyes. Relax."

I do as he says.

"Now think about Bob. You're in the room with Bob. He's lying in bed, propped up on the pillows. He's breathing slowly. His eyes are shut. He can hear you. Now, tell him what you want to say."

"I want to say I'm sorry that he's sick."

"Don't tell me what you'd say. Pretend you're talking directly to him."

I shake my head no.

"It doesn't matter. Say it however you want. Say whatever else you want to say to him."

I feel like an idiot and an asshole, but I ask Bob if he got fucked a lot, if he thinks that's how he got it. I want to ask him if he remembers what we did the night we spent together, but I feel very awkward in saying this. I feel guilty. He's dying, and I'm worrying about me. It's tough just thinking it. I apologize for asking him. He doesn't respond. I tell him that no one should have to suffer like this. I tell him I wish we could go for a walk through Central Park together. I tell him I'm sorry for all of the lost opportunities. Then I run out of things to say.

Neil notices I am finished. In a voice as cool as water he says, slowly, "Now, Bob is waving good-bye to you. He gets up from the bed and starts walking. Can you see him now? He leaves through the door. You can see his figure getting smaller and smaller as he walks off towards the horizon. His footsteps get softer and softer. Finally, his image shrinks to the size of a dot, and then he is gone."

I feel a profound sadness. A tear rolls down my cheek. I sniffle. I stiffen, open my eyes, and sit up. "You're trying to make me cry again, aren't you?" I accuse Neil. "I don't *need this*. Why are therapists so obsessed with making their patients cry?" Gordon told me that his therapist had spent the greater part of two years trying to get him to cry during a session.

"That's what you asked me to do, isn't it?" responds Neil.

"I don't know. You'd think I could trust you by now," I say by way of apology. "Fuck, this isn't working."

"I'm trying to give you the opportunity to express your emotions here. I'm trying to let you experiment with different techniques. There is nothing wrong with crying. It's a natural release."

"I know; you don't have to play Phil Donahue to me. It's just that—it's just that there's something private about crying. I don't know; I don't like to do it in front of anyone else."

"You don't like to do it when you're alone, either."

"Why should I?" I ask. "It makes me feel depressed. Isn't there some pleasure-pain principle that says that man avoids pain and seeks out pleasure?"

"B.J., you're in pain. Things are difficult for you now. It's hard for you to cope. Do you want to continue to go on the way you have been, or do you want to try to change?"

"Change is difficult."

"And you told me early on that you don't like doing difficult things."

"Yeah, it's like a double bind."

"Well, looking at the time, I think it's time to sum things up for today. I want you to think about what we've talked about today. Think about why it is difficult for you to cry. Perhaps you can remember earlier experiences of crying."

When I Cried

*I cried when I found the Ann Landers pamphlet "How to Make
Friends" buried in my mother's stack of papers on the kitchen table
in Rochester. My father had died a few years earlier. I was sad that
my mother felt so lonely that she had to resort to sending away for
a self-help pamphlet.*

*I cried when I was seventeen and I stood in the bookstore, and
everywhere I looked I saw books written by suicides: Virginia Woolf,
Sylvia Plath, Anne Sexton.*

*I cried in the checkout line of the A&P when I saw a cover story
on the* National Enquirer *on Rock Hudson's lover, Marc Christian,
and I realized that Bob Broome was going to die of AIDS.*

*I cried in the middle of a push-up at the Attitude Factory when I
felt a lump at the side of my neck and thought I had it myself.*

*I cried when I was four and my sister hit me on the head with a
lamp and made me eat dirt.*

*I cried when I was humiliated in gym in sixth grade, the sole
survivor of my team in a game of dodgeball, about to be gunned
down by five balls fast as bullets.*

*I cried when my father escaped from the loony bin when I was
ten. When we visited, we had to walk through two locked metal-
doors; there were two sets of keys. After several months they took
him off the locked ward and gave him grounds privileges. One day
he just walked to the bus station and took the first bus to Rochester.
He came home, woozy from medication. He knocked over a lamp.
His breath smelled of sulfur. He slurred, "I have a present for you,"
and he tried to give me a transistor radio. I shook my head no. I
wouldn't take it. I didn't want it. It was wrong. He was angry with
me. I still refused. He started shouting. And then the police came;
my mother had called the police to take him back. There were sirens*

and flashing lights. He struggled with the two policemen and suddenly became limp. Due to the medication, he had a bowel movement. "Ahhhh," he moaned. The police led him to their car. He was co-operative. "I don't want to go back there," he murmured, yet he walked passively as a lamb to the slaughter.

And now I am afraid of crying. I am afraid that once I start crying, I will be on a jag that won't end for days. I will never stop; I will cry and cry and cry. I have so much pain and frustration bottled up that if I ever let go, even for a moment, I'll fall to pieces.

· 23 ·

November

"*R*ichard, my crazy ex-boyfriend from San Francisco, never showed," I tell Gordon. "He was threatening to move in with me. He was supposed to arrive last Thursday. I skipped the gym and stayed home, waiting. You know how when you're waiting for someone, you can't really get anything accomplished? I was trying to read a *New Yorker* article, one of those endless six-hundred-page 'first of two parts' on Norwegian cheese, and I just couldn't concentrate. I'd put on an album and couldn't even listen to it. I didn't notice it was skipping at the end for a good fifteen minutes. It's like Caroline's out of my life, and now Richard has come back to take her place. And he didn't even call. I don't have his number, of course. He couldn't give me one; he's staying at a hotel, sharing a room with a woman, and he's not supposed to be there. If they find out, they'll hike up the rent."

"Why did you even offer to let him stay if he puts you in such a state?"

"I don't know. I feel I owe it to him. I was going to let him stay for two weeks and then boot him out on the streets. I'm sure he'd find somewhere else to stay. He always does. These alcoholics have amazing survival skills. You know, he asked me for money back in May—it wasn't much, just a fifty, because he was behind in the rent—but he needed it right away, and I said, 'Well, Richard, I can't really help you. If I send a check, it'll take three weeks to clear.' So he tells me that if I cable it, he'll get it the next day. And he tells me where I can cable it and what his account number is and what bank and what hours it is usually open. So I say, 'All right, just this once. But this is the last time, remember?' And it turns out it costs fifteen bucks to cable money. What a waste! It's like paying a thirty percent service charge. I don't know why I did it; I'm stupid, I guess."

Gordon coughs and clears his throat. "You said it, not me."

"You've got a cold?"

"Don't worry, B.J., you won't get the germs over the phone."

"Did I tell you last week during therapy Neil sneezed, and I tensed up like a cat—you know, the hair on the back of my arms stood on end. So he blows his nose and throws the tissue, ineffectually, missing the trash. You know, sometimes it annoys me that he's as much of a schmuck as I am. Why can't my therapist be better than 'last pick' in junior-high gym? So I told him that it really bothered me, that piece of Kleenex on the carpet. And he asks why it's bothering me, and I tell him I don't like germs. He asks me to think if there is any difference from having a Kleenex in the can and a Kleenex on the carpet. I stop and think and realize that, physically speaking, he has a point, but psychologically, it really drives me nuts. He says it's more AIDS anxiety."

Gordon clears his throat again. "Guess what?"

"What?"

"I told you about my friend Steven with ARC?"

"Yeah."

"He's taking an experimental drug now. The only way to get it in the U.S. is by being on a study. You know what?"

"No."

"He's using someone else's prescription. His doctor just gave it to him, told him not to ask any questions. He said that the guy who it was written for won't be needing it anymore."

"He's dead."

"I guess that's what he meant. Doesn't it really get you mad, how doctors have to lie just to dispense drugs? Doesn't it make you pissed? Why do they have all this red tape? Why don't they just release all the experimental drugs? The only way to get Ribavirin is to fly down to Mexico. It really gets me steamed up. People are dying, and the government is just wasting time. They don't give a damn. Two months ago they said that AZT would be generally distributed, and now it looks like it'll be another two months, and only for people who've had at least one bout of PCP, and it's going to cost almost a thousand dollars a month, and Medicaid might not pay for it. They're just bleeding people dry, bleeding them to death."

"It's fucked."

"You know, sometimes I'm glad that straight people are finally coming down with AIDS. You never saw much concern for a cure when AIDS was more or less confined to the 'high risk' groups. If AIDS had started out in Republican suburbanites in Grosse Pointe, I bet we'd have a lot more progress in research. I bet a lot more funds would have been spent."

"I hate to say it, but you're probably right." I pause. "Well, I hope the drug works for your friend."

"Me, too. How's Bob?"

"The same. He's been in a coma for about two weeks. You know what scares me? I've spent so much time with him these past few months that I'm afraid that this is how I'm going to remember him. I can't even recall what he used to look like; it's just a blur. I can't pinpoint it, the moment he changed from Bob into sick-Bob. But it looks like this is what will predominate. Now I guess I know why some people withdraw. They don't want us to remember them as dying. He's so thin, you can practically see the skull beneath the skin. It's like a death's-head."

Gordon clears his throat. "I think we'd better change the subject."

"OK with me."

He switches to falsetto. "Have you talked to our alkie receptionist lately?" Gordon sounds like one of those six-foot-five drag queens who walk down Fifth Avenue in the Easter Parade: extremely unconvincing.

"Yeah, I left a message for you yesterday. I guess she forgot to give it to you."

"When we were acquired by that multinational," he continues in a normal voice, "we got a new phone system. Well, that was two months ago, and Estelle still hasn't got the hang of it."

"Are you sure she's an alkie?"

"After every company party a few bottles of scotch disappear. She hides them in the desk drawer and takes nips during lunch."

"You're kidding."

"I'm not."

"Really?"

"S.b.t." He pauses and coughs. "Sad but true."

"You think you might get laid off?" I ask.

"Who knows? They're so disorganized here, it could take them months to even find out I'm on the payroll."

"Well, talk to you soon."

"Tomorrow," says Gordon.

The next day the phone rings at work.

"B.J., it's Joey."

"Oh, hi." I shuffle some papers.

"So what's new?"

I look at the clock and my date book. "I've got an interview scheduled for eleven-thirty. I'm trying to clean up my desk so Mr. Paige Skeffington will get the right impression."

"You're interviewing a *man* for Caroline's job? I bet you're going to test him on dick-tation, aren't you? Get that thing sliding in and out of his hot wet lips, you little devil."

"It's too early in the morning," I chide Joey. "I'm really not in the mood for trash right now."

"That's not what I called about," says Joey. "I have a tale for you. I told you my best friend, Tom, knows someone named Harvey who has AIDS. Well, Harvey had lent Tom around a hundred dollars a few months ago. Then Harvey got sick. He's in St. Vincent's. Tom went to visit one day. You know how some AIDS victims can get really cantankerous? Somehow this disease can bring out the worst in you, exaggerate your personal defects? Well, Harvey was always a feisty guy. He had this mean, petty streak. So he starts an argument with Tom, right there in the hospital room. He wants his hundred dollars back, now. Tom tries to calm him down. He doesn't have his checkbook with him. Who carries a hundred dollars around with him in New York? But the argument just escalates. The next thing you know, Harvey is telling Tom that he is barred from visiting him. A few days later, Harvey falls into a coma. Frankly, we all thought it was the end. We didn't expect Harvey to pull through. But he keeps hanging on for weeks. Then, just last week, he came out of it. It was a big shock. I thought he was dead. And do you know what the first thing he did was? The first thing he said—he couldn't even talk, he had to write it down—was to ask if Tom had paid him his money back. Can you believe it? The first thing out of a coma, and he asks if he got his hundred dollars back. Of course, Tom had sent him a check the night after the fight in the hospital. Isn't it funny? You expect someone to be noble when they're dying, to heal all the old wounds, to make peace with everyone, but it just isn't the case."

"Joey, how many people do you know who died?"

"Around ten, none very close."

"Five years from now, who will remember any of them?"

"We homos don't have any kids to remember us by," muses Joey, "and our lovers will all be gone soon after. Hey, maybe we should make a memorial like the Vietnam monument in Washington. We could have a wall with names on it—with glory holes, naturally."

"You know what I do, Joey? Every morning I try to recite the names of the people I know who have died. It's like a chant, a litany."

"That's spooky, B.J. Listen to my advice, my dear boy. Instead of this morbid remembrance, I want you to think about the *huge thing*. You know what I mean." With that, Joey cackles and hangs up. Sometimes I think Joey will never grow up.

I sit with Bob Broome at the hospital for my twice-weekly vigil. I'm there for maybe half an hour, reading magazines, talking to myself, waiting for Bob to die. I tell him my Caroline stories. "Rachel says I should feel sorry for Caroline. She's crazy. She'll be a crazy lady on the street one day, with her possessions in grocery bags and a shopping cart, and she'll be muttering that the C.I.A. has implanted listening devices in her brain so they can listen to her thoughts."

Bob says in a weak voice, "What's the weather outside?"

"Oh, it's been drizzling all evening; I'd say it's in the forties." I jerk awake, with the realization that Bob has woken from his coma. "Hey, Bob, good to have you back." I wonder if I should notify a nurse.

"I don't think I've been anywhere," he says irritatedly.

"You were in zombie-land for a couple weeks. You weren't making any sense."

"Oh, *really?*" he asks. He clearly doesn't believe me.

"Yeah, you haven't been doing that good since, I'd say, October 15, just sleeping a lot and murmuring in your sleep."

"And what day is today?"

"Let's see." I look around and see yesterday's *Post* on the windowsill. "Today is Wednesday, November 12."

"Oh," he says. "Hmmmmm." He tenses his brow. "I can't really remember much that well. Oh, well."

We chat for a few more minutes. Bob is hungry. I go to the nurses' station. The nurse gets a volunteer named Terry to come and help feed Bob. Terry has white hair in a long braid down his back. He is in his early fifties and pretty fey. Terry gives Bob a serving of canned peaches. Bob greedily slurps the juice from the spoon.

I go and call up Dave Johnson and Patrick. Patrick is euphoric. "Gee, that's great. It'll be wonderful to talk to Bob again. I'd thought we'd lost him completely. I really missed him."

Dave is more cautious. "This might be Indian summer for Bob, his last bloom of health. I don't want you to get your hopes up."

Patrick comes on Thursday and spends a few hours there. They talk, and then Bob rests, and then they talk some more. Patrick calls me up when he gets home. "You know, B.J., he's almost there, not quite."

"What do you mean?"

"Most of what he says makes sense. He's clear and lucid. But there isn't much continuity from one sentence to the next. We'll talk about the weather and then about his childhood in Montana, and then he'll ask me what time it is. Pretty soon we're talking about the weather again. I wonder why he's so interested in meteorology all of a sudden."

"It's a safe topic. It's not like religion or politics."

"Sure. Anyway, it's great to have him back. I felt like I was sitting with a vegetable."

For about a week Bob is close to his original self. He recognizes everyone. His friends who stopped visiting when he had been incoherent come back and visit, en masse, on the weekend. Everyone is animated and hopeful.

The wheelchair, in the corner of the room, sits unused. Bob takes no more jaunts down the hallway. Visiting Bob still takes a toll on me. He is so pale, so weak. His hair sticks up in sweaty tufts, remnants of a used carpet. Bob could be in his late sixties. The bones on his face are painfully prominent; you can see the pulsing in the veins.

Then he begins chattering again. His teeth chatter uncontrollably like a windup pair of false choppers from a novelty shop. He is cold, terribly cold. "They don't have the heat on, do they?"

Dave and I sit on the neighboring bed, our sweaters and jackets piled beside us. "It's fine, Bob," says Dave.

"I'm s-o-o-o-o c-o-o-o-o-ld." He clutches Sherlock, the stuffed dog from Dennis that I gave him for his birthday.

"Oh, he had a lovely day today," says Terry. "Bob went to the fair with his dog and his teddy bear, and they all had a wonderful time."

It hits me in the pit of the stomach. Bob is regressing to childhood. He's losing his mind again. At least he's not suffering.

"That's not Bob up there," says Jerry, crying. "That's someone else in his bed. That's a phantom. He's been gone for months now."

"There, there," says Dave, patting Jerry on his back. "It won't be much longer now."

I go up the next Tuesday. Bob is much worse. He's babbling. A bubble of spit forms at his lips, which move as if in silent prayer. It pops. Terry sits in the corner, knitting. "He's taken a turn," he says calmly, in a soft voice. The room has been stripped of valuables. Dave and Jerry have taken the VCR, the television, and the phone back to their apartment. They're afraid they will be stolen when Bob dies.

"Well, Bob, I'm going up for the annual pilgrimage, Thanksgiving with the folks. This might be good-bye, so take care." I don't know what to say. "I wish this didn't happen. I hope you're not in any pain." I'm speaking softly; I can barely hear myself. "Good-bye, Bob. I'm sorry." I leave him for probably the last time and go home to pack.

In the seat pocket in front of me is a paper bag in case I become nauseous in any of four different languages: "SAC POUR MAL DE L'AIR / SPUCKBEUTEL / BOLSA DE MARE / AIR SICKNESS BAG." People Express speeds me from Newark to Rochester in less than an hour. Sheila picks me up at the airport in a beat-up Dodge Dart, newspapers scattered on the floor, the back seat covered with clothes and towels, an oil can under the seat, a red brush and scraper for the windshield on the dashboard. "Alexander is coming later; he's watching a football game on cable," she says.

Four years ago they got married in a park in a civil ceremony with a woman judge who drove in from Elmira. The reception was held on picnic tables, with dancing nearby later on, with music from cassettes and a boom box. I brought a killer carrot-cake and a check; my mother swallowed her resentment and brought Grandma. Due to a scheduling calamity, a second cousin was getting married the same day at a synagogue. Aunt Maude hit Sheila's first and then went on to temple for Cousin Felicia's, leaving Mom and me alone with Grandma as the sole family representatives. Grandma, who was getting more and more dotty, wandered off into the woods during the ceremony. Sheila and Alexander went on a camping trip for their honeymoon. Afterward, Sheila complained to me that she had to do the whole wedding herself; Alexander didn't lift a finger. My mother told me she would have helped, but Sheila didn't ask her.

We don't go home directly. First we stop off at the Jewish Home for the Aged to pick up Grandma. My sister pulls into the driveway and says, "You go pick her up. She'll probably be in the dining room, waiting for dinner." I sign in at the desk and take the elevator to the second floor. On the walls of the elevator a big sheet of green construction-paper is tacked up, with this week's activities written in black marker. Grandma sits passively at a table in the dining room, which is otherwise unoccupied. Dinner isn't scheduled for another two hours.

"Hi, Grandma," I say, trying to give her casual clues as to my identity.

"Oh, hi, good to see you," she says.

"I'm here to bring you to my mom's for Thanksgiving dinner."

"I'm eating here," she protests. Her glasses are off, so the bags under her eyes seem even more pronounced.

"You don't want to go?"

"This is my home. I'm making dinner. Do you want to stay?"

"No, I flew in from New York City to have dinner with my mom, who's your daughter Selma. Remember Selma? She comes to visit every day?"

"Oh, I haven't seen Selma in years. My daughters, they don't come that often. It's too far. I see the other one a lot, though. What's her name?"

"Aunt Maude?"

"Yes, Maude, she's good. She comes to see me quite a bit. I think she was just here this morning. But Selma, I haven't seen her in weeks."

My mother was torn over placing Grandma in the home, but she really couldn't have her stay with her; Grandma was driving her crazy. Aunt Maude agreed it was the best thing. A few years earlier they had tried to place her in a supervised, private apartment-complex. Grandma was on a waiting list for eight months. When she finally got in, she refused to go. She said she'd be away from all of her friends at the Jewish Community Center. At that point she could walk with some difficulty, but she couldn't continue to live alone and was too weak to survive living at the complex. She needed medical supervision. Her heart was weak; she had to take several pills a day, and she would forget if she was left on her own. Grandma was in her mid-eighties. With great reluctance, my mother and Aunt Maude took her to the home. My mother visited six days a week, usually spending the entire afternoon with her or volunteering in the crafts activities.

"Come on, Grandma." I wheel up a wheelchair for her.

"Your name is?" she asks doubtfully.

"I'm your grandson Benjamin," I say clearly.

"*Oy, oy,* Benjamin, it's been a while, hasn't it?" She remembers that she likes me. Obediently, she pulls herself into the wheelchair. We ride down the halls to her room. I pick up her glasses, get her heavy red winter-coat, and then go and sign Grandma out for the afternoon at the nurses' desk. We take the elevator down. We leave the chair at the door, and I help her into her coat. We walk down the concrete walkway. Sheila is waiting at the circle, tapping her fingers on the steering wheel to the music on the radio. White smoke comes from the exhaust. Sheila has cleared a space in back for me to sit and tossed the papers on the front floor to the back. I usher Grandma through the door and buckle her in with the shoulder belt. "*Oy, oy,* who is this?" she inquires.

"I'm your granddaughter Sheila, remember?"

"Yes, of course, Sheila. You're a big girl now. Last time I saw you, you were this big." The last time she saw my sister was last Sunday. "Do you have a steady boyfriend?" she asks.

"You'll meet him at dinner at Mom's. His name is Alexander. You went to our wedding, remember?"

"Oh, I think you're mistaken. I don't get to shul that often anymore. You know, I don't walk as good as I used to. I'm sure I would have remembered a big wedding in temple."

Sheila guns the engine, and we're off.

At home Grandma wants to help Mom in the kitchen. "Let me show you how to make hamburgers. First, you put a little salt in the frying pan. Keep the heat steady."

"Mother, I'm making turkey. Hi, Benjamin. How was your trip?"

"OK." I kiss her on the cheek.

"Take Grandma into the living room and entertain her with stories about New York."

"OK."

"Sheila, your husband called. He wants you to call him back."

My mother speaks of him in pronouns, rarely calling him by his Christian name.

"OK, Mom." She dials. "Hello. What's up, Honeybun?" My mother winces. By some cruel trick of fate this is the same term of endearment that my father used to call her. "Shit. It won't start? Did you try to jump it? The cables are in the basement. Oh, the neighbors are away for the holidays, aren't they? Damn. Well, I guess I'll have to pick you up. In half an hour? I'll be there. Bye-bye, Hon." She hangs up. "The Duster's busted again. I've got to go pick up Alexander. I'm sorry, Mom. I was going to help you set the table."

"Well, what can you do?" says Mom dejectedly, in the classic Rosenthal shrug: palms upturned, elbows at sides, shoulders up, a frank look of resignation on the face.

I turn on MTV and sit in the corner chair next to the Picasso-clown reproduction. Grandma sits in a straight-backed chair from the dining room, thumbing through a color fashion-circular I've handed her. "Everyone looks so pretty," she comments. "This, I don't like," she says, referring to the David Lee Roth video on TV. "Too loud. They show too much, these days. What are they doing?" I turn the sound down. Now we're watching a Def Leppard video. "So you are living where?" she asks me.

"New York City," I reply.

"And you are in school?" she asks.

"No, I'm working. I've been working for several years."

"*Oy,* you look so young."

"Grandma, I'm going to be thirty next month."

"*Oy, oy, oy,*" she clucks. "I'd never believe it. The last time I saw you, you were this big."

My mother comes in with a piece of matzo in a napkin for Grandma. "She usually eats at around four. Give this to her so she isn't too hungry." I hand her the napkin. Obediently, my grandmother breaks off a small piece and puts it into her mouth. She has trouble chewing it.

"Ma, your teeth are in crooked. Here, let me help." My mother rearranges Grandma's plates, over her protests. "There, that's better."

"So who is coming to dinner? Should I bring some *latkes?*" asks Grandma.

"No, no, you don't have to bring anything, just yourself," says my mother impatiently. "Aunt Maude is coming. Her daughter, Bertha, is spending Thanksgiving with her in-laws." Bertha had eventually married her friend-who-is-a-boy-but-not-a-boyfriend, Sid. They are on Long Island for the holidays. "And Sheila, my daughter who brought you from the home, is coming with her husband, Alexander."

"Alexander. Did I meet him before?"

"Yes."

"I forget things, excuse me. A nice Jewish boy," she mutters to herself.

My mother frowns and curses under her breath. "Oh, and I think that Roger and Emily are going to drop by after dinner. Roger's your grandson; he was Reuben's son. Emily is his wife. They have four children. I can't remember their names. Let's see. There's Rosie, Theresa, Jeremy, and—oh, just ask Emily; I'm sure she'll introduce them."

Roger is a general practitioner. They live in New Hampshire. Roger wanted to have six children and Emily wanted two, so they averaged it out to four. Emily's another shiksa. She studied English literature in college. A homemaker, trapped in the hinterlands with nothing but educational television to keep her mind active, she's named the children after characters from *Masterpiece Theatre*.

"*Oy*, Reuben, is he coming, too?" Reuben was the apple of my grandmother's eye, her favorite (and only) son. He died of stomach cancer two years ago.

My mother pauses. "He won't be able to make it tonight." She and Aunt Maude had kept the news from Grandma for several months. They were afraid it would kill her. They didn't want her to go to the funeral. Eventually they told her, and she took the news hard. Today she seems to have forgotten.

"That's a shame," says my grandmother. "I would really like to see him. Do you think we can call him now at the last minute? No, I don't want to bother my Reuben. He must have already made plans. Oh, well, maybe next year."

"I think Grandma wants to lie down for a bit before dinner," my mother says. Grandma shows no signs of tiring to me, but I lead her to Sheila's old bedroom, and without questioning, she lies down for a nap. In a few moments she's softly snoring away. "If she doesn't get some rest now, she'll fall asleep during dinner," explains my mother. "Could you help me set up the table? The silverware should be in the cabinet drawer." I unwrap the plastic from the twice-a-year silverware and set six places at the dining-room table. This year we don't need the leaf.

Aunt Maude bustles in at five, laden with shopping bags. She's made her garden salad and a large pot of matzo-ball soup. Sheila and Alexander arrive at five-thirty. I wake up Grandma and show her the bathroom. "It's so confusing, so many halls and corridors. Tell me, in whose house am I this evening?" she asks me.

"Your daughter Selma's," I patiently explain. "It's Thanksgiving, and we're having you over for dinner."

"*Oy, oy, oy*, you shouldn't have to go to such trouble for me, an old lady."

"Mother, it's no trouble; everything is already made," breaks in my mother sharply from the kitchen. She and Aunt Maude are setting up the serving trays. My mother grumbles to Aunt Maude about Grandma's behavior. A few minutes later Mom shouts, "Everybody, come to the table. Dinner is served." Alexander is sitting in the living room, watching ESPN for some late scores. We take our places at the table, Grandma hobbling in last. Sheila pulls out a chair for her nearest the bathroom. I sit in the corner.

"So, Benjamin, what do you think about ContraGate?" asks Alexander.

"It's even better than Watergate—selling weapons for hostages in Iran and diverting the profits to the contras in Nicaragua. They're really going to nail Reagan on this."

Grandma says, "I came, it was light. The few hours ran away, and it got darker."

Aunt Maude interjects, "Reagan has so much public support I doubt this will harm him. Look at all the scandal and corruption that Mayor Koch in New York has withstood this past year. And that horse's ass is still mayor."

"The Teflon President," says Alexander.

"But look how fast it gets dark," says Grandma.

"We heard you the first time," my mother replies. "Who wants another kreplach for their soup? Maude, your matzo balls are the best," she compliments.

"Thank you," says Aunt Maude gruffly.

"It's delicious!" seconds Sheila.

"It really wasn't much trouble." Aunt Maude blushes.

"There's nothing like homemade matzo-balls," I chorus in.

"Really, there's no need to make such a fuss over it," says Aunt Maude.

Alexander has taken a tiny piece of the matzo ball and finished half of the chicken broth. "Alexander, come on, try it, you'll like it," encourages my mother.

"I'm saving room for your turkey," he says.

"It gets so early dark. I can't believe it," says Grandma.

"Mother, please!" says Mom.

"Hey, you don't have to yell at her," I say.

"I visit her six days a week in the home, you come home twice a year if we're lucky, and you tell me how to treat my own mother," says Mom. "It's not easy," she adds. "OK. Fine. I won't mention it again. But see whether or not it gets on your nerves after a while."

Mom picks up the soup bowls and takes them into the kitchen. She calls me in to help carve the turkey. This year she's made a cranberry mold, a recipe from Rochester's Hadassah cookbook.

"Cool Whip?" I ask.

She nods. "And Ocean Spray cranberry sauce."

I take out Aunt Maude's salad and a basket of rolls.

"Anyone want some margarine?" shouts my mother from the kitchen.

"I do," responds Sheila.

Grandma says, "To me it looks pretty dark."

I go back for the spread and a dish of sweet potatoes. "Use the bamboo thing," advises Mom, pointing to the trivet. A few moments later she joins us with the turkey, stuffing, and gravy. She sits down and then stands up, hand knocking her forehead. "Oh, my God, I almost forget the kishkes!" She rushes to the oven and turns off the heat. "Good, they're not burned." We pass the plates of food around. The table seems dwarfed by the mountains of food upon it.

"So much food, Selma, you shouldn't have bothered," says Grandma.

"It's Thanksgiving; we do this every year," says my mother evenly, giving me a sharp look. "Come on, Alexander, try the kishkes," admonishes my mother. Although she has fully accepted Alexander into the family, there is still a residue of resentment. Without realizing it, she is trying to convert Alexander subliminally by forcing him to eat ethnic.

"I think I tried it last year," says Alexander reluctantly. For some reason, the idea of stuffed intestines does not appeal to him.

"Give it another whirl," insists my mother.

"My honeybun is choosy," says Sheila. "He choosed me." She smiles, hugging her husband, puckering up the corners of her mouth into artificial dimples, a gesture that may have been endearing when she was eleven but reeks of affectation today.

Aunt Maude says, "Selma, your stuffing is out of this world."

Grandma takes a small bite of the turkey, chews it for a while, and then spits it out onto her plate. She stirs her sweet potatoes with her fork assiduously. I wonder if she has a plan. Suddenly, she drops her fork, giving up. "Ve are not used to dark weather, and as soon as it gets dark, I don't go out. *Oy, oy, oy.*"

My mother rolls her eyes. "Are you finished now, Mother? Would you like a little cranberry sauce?"

"I don't think so. Maybe some hot water." Mom whisks away her plate and starts the water for tea.

"How are Bertha and Sid?" asks Sheila. "I haven't seen them in months."

"They're pretty busy, working on the basement of their new house. They're converting it to a den." Aunt Maude was frankly relieved when Bertha finally got married. Personally, I think she could have done better. Familiarity breeds either contempt or marriage.

"Does everybody have enough food?" asks my mother from the kitchen.

"Plenty," shouts back Sheila.

"How do you think the Lakers will do this year?" Alexander asks me.

"I don't know. I don't really follow sports that much."

"Looks like the S.U. basketball team will do well this year. They've got a good chance to make it into the N.C.A.A. finals."

"Funny, when I came, it was so light, and before I looked around, it was pitch dark," says you-know-who.

Mom brings Grandma a cup of hot water. Grandma used to drink a lot of tea. Now she likes hot water with lemon and honey. Tiny and squat, she sits, shoulders hunched over, peering into her teacup. Grandma, so sweet and harmless, so cute, I have an urge to hug her.

"Should I wait a little for dessert?" asks my mother hesitantly, as if she never had people over for dinner. "Does anyone want coffee or tea now?"

"Later, Mom," I say.

"Selma, you've been up and down for the entire meal. Why don't you sit down for a while and let Sheila and me clear the table for you," offers Aunt Maude.

"Nonsense, you're my guest," says Mom, instantly springing up to clear the plates.

"Now, now, I insist," says Aunt Maude.

"You don't know where anything belongs," protests my mother.

"I'll just leave everything in the sink, OK? Sit and talk to your son. He just got in from New York."

"All right." She surrenders.

Sheila and Aunt Maude start stacking plates. A few minutes later, I hear a crash in the kitchen. My mother stiffens. "It's nothing," lies Aunt Maude.

"It's funny with me. I don't like it when it gets darker," says Grandma.

Alexander gives me a wan smile. I can see he wants to go back to the TV. I crack my neck. My mother sits quietly at the table, anxious about her good china. The doorbell rings, and Mom rushes to answer it. In bound my cousin Roger, his wife, Emily, and their four blue-eyed, blond cherubs.

"Hi, *Bubbe*," says Emily. "Want to say hello to your great-grand-children?"

"*Oy, oy, oy,* they're so cute," says Grandma animatedly, finally distracted from the effects of daylight saving time. "Here, tell me, what's your name?"

Rosie and Jeremy cling to Emily's print skirt. A five-year-old boy in overalls says shyly, "Jeremy."

"*Oy,* what a beautiful child," says Grandma appreciatively. "Come give *Bubbe* a hug." She opens her arms. They come, one by one, Rosie and Jeremy somewhat reluctantly, at their mother's urging.

"Would you like to have some tea or dessert?" asks my mother.

"No, we're stuffed. We just had dinner at Gussy's; you know she packs a mean plate. We just wanted to stop by and say hi. I've got a favor to ask. Can I drop off the kids for a few hours tomorrow afternoon?"

"Certainly!" affirms my mother. "It would be my pleasure!"

"We've got some shopping to do. I think we might kidnap Benjamin for the afternoon."

"That's fine with me," I say. I welcome any opportunity to get out of the house.

"Good to see you, Roger," says Alexander. "So tell me, what do you think about ContraGate?"

We chat for a while. My grandmother coos over how beautiful Roger and Emily's children are. My mother gives Grandma some hard candy to distribute among the great-grandchildren. Alexander turns on the TV, low. Sheila goes to the bathroom to wash her face. Aunt Maude talks about her ever-absent son, Herschel. Mom serves her famous cherry cheesecake and tea at the table. Roger is persuaded into taking a small piece. Then Emily announces that it's time to pack it up. The kids have to be in bed by nine-thirty. Grandma is very tired. Aunt Maude offers to take her home. Mom gives her a few pieces of cheesecake for Cousin Bertha.

After Aunt Maude is gone, Sheila tells us that she confessed to buying the matzo-ball soup at Zion's Delicatessen on the way over. "We were doing dishes, and she tells me that it's just our secret. Can you believe it? She tried making matzo balls, but she didn't have any eggs, so they just sunk like rocks in the soup."

"She never could cook," says my mother.

Alexander yawns conspicuously. "Honeybun, I think it's time to go home."

"You sure you don't want to stay a little longer?" asks my mother.

"Thanks for the wonderful dinner," says Alexander.

"Yeah, Mom, it was delish," says Sheila. "I'll see you later on in the weekend, Benjy."

"Well, all right. Good-bye." They leave, leaving me alone with my mother.

Roger and Emily come by the next day at around one. As usual, I try to sleep as long as possible during my visits. Consequently, I haven't shaved or showered when they arrive. Emily helps the children out of their winter jackets and deposits them in the living room. "Be nice to Aunt Selma," she says. I stumble into the kitchen, cleaning my glasses on my shirt, to get a glass of orange juice. I take a glass out of the cabinet, rinse it, and pour some juice from the pitcher in the fridge.

"You don't have to rinse it off. It's clean," says my mother, offended.

"Sorry, just habit." I'm used to running everything under water back in New York to get rid of cockroach shit. The glass had some dishwasher streaks anyway.

"Come on, Benjamin, let's get this show on the road," yells Emily. "Time's a-wastin'."

"OK, OK, I'll be there in a minute."

The three of us hop into their Saab station wagon, and Roger starts the engine.

"Where are we going?" I ask.

"It's a surprise," says Emily.

"You'll find out soon enough," counters Roger.

"Anywhere but the mall!"

"Worse than that." Emily grins.

"I don't want to know, then," I say, slumping back into my seat.

"So how's New York?" asks Roger.

"Just *fabulous*. I'm living right in the heart of Plague Central; people are dropping like flies left and right. You should come for a visit. Having a wonderful time. Wish you were here." Roger and Emily know I'm gay, so I don't have to keep my guard up and pretend I'm a heterosexual around them. Every once in a while I can even camp it up.

Emily turns around. "B.J., you'd better be careful. A friend died of AIDS last year from my hometown. It was terrible. We grew up together. I'm not going to go through that again."

"Well, I've locked the barn after the horses ran out," I say. "They don't know how long the incubation of this disease can be. It might be up to five years; it might be ten. I'm being safe now, but that doesn't give me any guarantees." I pause. "I've got a friend in the hospital right now. He's not doing well. I hope he's dead when I get back to New York."

"How can you say that, Benjamin?" asks Roger. "There's always hope. Maybe there will be a medical advance next week. A lot of people are out there working on a cure."

"Come on, Roger, you're a *doctor*. Don't act naive. Even if someone discovers a cure tomorrow, it will take at least two years before they test it and certify it. It's too late for Bob. He's been in the hospital for five months. He's lost control of his bodily functions. His mind is slipping. He's thirty-five years old, and he makes less sense than Grandma. When I left for Rochester, he slipped into a coma."

"Poor Bob," says Emily.

We sit in silence for a few minutes.

"Damn it, it isn't fair!" says Emily. We drive down Erie at thirty miles an hour. It snows steadily. The ploughs came through and salted the road early this morning, but we still drive slowly. For half a mile the only sound is the windshield wipers, rhythmically slicing through the wet snow.

"Here we are," says Roger gruffly. We pull into a large parking lot.

"You said we weren't going to a mall!" I protest.

"Stop your grousing. Six stores do not a mall make. Are you ready for Toys"Я"Us?"

"The day after Thanksgiving? Are you crazy?"

"We don't have stores like this in New Hampshire. It's now or never," says Emily.

Toys"Я"Us is huge, the size of a New York City block. Two aisles are dedicated to guns; half an aisle has Star Wars accessories. Emily and Roger, New Age hippies, steer away from the violent toys. They split up, agreeing to meet back at the cashiers in half an hour. I walk with Emily.

"Roger's generally good, but sometimes he slips. You got to keep him in line," Emily confides. "We're working hard at this nonsexist, egalitarian relationship, damn it. I've done my duty. I've worked overtime. When Roger married me, he might have wanted me to stay barefoot and pregnant, in the kitchen, for the foreseeable future, but he had another thing coming. I had him fixed right after Jeremy."

"Why not you?"

"Dummy, it's easier with a guy. The plumbing's more straightforward. Where's the Sesame Street aisle? I bet Rupert would love a Cookie Monster puppet."

"All these toys make me wish I were a kid again."

"Tell you what, Benjamin, you be very good and we'll adopt you. You can live with us in New Hampshire. All's you'll have to do is get the little savages dressed for school and out on the bus stop by eight-thirty. Me and you can play pinochle all day."

"Do I get my own room? Can I bring a special friend along?"

"Depends. Is he cute?"

"Yes and no. It'll probably be a different one every weekend."

"Deal's off. Now, Benjamin, you heard me earlier in the car, and I'm not going to repeat myself. Be careful! I don't want to lose anyone else."

"OK, OK. You've got nothing to worry about, all right?" Let her think what she wants.

We meet Roger at the cash register a few moments later. He has a pop-up book for Theresa and a space station for Jeremy. Emily and Roger jumble their purchases together on the conveyor belt. Roger pays by check.

We stuff the toys in the trunk so the kids won't see them and drive back to Mom's. The children are happily playing in the living room with my mother. She has a way with children.

"Thanks, Selma, you're a natural," says Emily. She stuffs her children into their coats and mittens. "Say thank you to Aunt Selma for a wonderful afternoon."

One by one they give Mom a kiss on the cheek. They leave in a rush. Emily shepherds them into the car. I hear "I want to sit up in front!" "You sat there last time!" "But that was just for a couple blocks!" I shut the door.

"Such well-behaved children," says my mother.

"Yeah, they're real nice."

"So where did you go?" she asks.

"Toys"Я"Us. Emily and Roger like to beat the rush."

"The biggest shopping day of the year."

"Yeah, I know."

"What did you talk about?"

"Oh, nothing special."

"I see." She waits for further information. None is forthcoming. I turn on the television. On TV the Red Cross has an ad encouraging people to give blood during the holiday shortage. "You used to give blood during college, didn't you?" she asks.

"Yep, but I'm not supposed to anymore."

"Why not?"

"Never mind." For the past four years gay men have been advised against giving blood and polluting the blood banks. Doesn't my mother know about this?

"Benjamin, you've been pretty sullen. What did you do, wake up on the wrong side of the bed this morning? There's no reason to take it out on your mother."

"Sorry," I say listlessly.

"Is there something wrong?"

"I told you over the phone a few weeks ago. I've got a friend in the hospital; he's dying from AIDS."

She blanches at the word *AIDS*. Her first reaction weeks ago was to tell me to stay away from people with "that disease." Now she tries to put things into perspective for me. "It's not easy for me, either. You know, three people died at the home this week. I go there every day to see my mother. She's not going to be around forever. I volunteer and help out in the crafts room; I go on trips with them; I help feed them at mealtime. We're all going to die. Your sister, Sheila, I'm lucky if she visits Grandma once every two months. I'm all alone in this big house. I hardly ever get out, except to see my mother. Dying is a fact of life. You don't know what it's like, to see your own mother sitting in the lunchroom all alone. If I don't look after her, who will? Last week she had a bowel movement in the shower. What's going to happen when I get old? You're off in New York; you've got your own life; you're not going to come home. Sheila's just struggling to survive. They barely make enough to make ends meet. I'm all alone. I thought it was going to be easier when I got older. You know, your father and I were going to go on a vacation to Italy the year he died. That was going to be the start of our sunset years. And one morning he wakes up, complains of heartburn, and passes away. I wonder, should I have called the ambulance sooner? It was too late. I'm all alone in this world."

I explode with anger I've been harboring for years. "It's always your pain that's real. Never mine. Nothing that happens to me ever matters. Listen, I'm sorry your life's all fucked up. I didn't tell you you have to spend your life looking after your senile mother, but that's what happens: People grow old, get senile, and die. But Bob is only thirty-five. And he's not the only one. The hospital wards are overflowing. A lot of people are dying, and it's horrible, and I'm not playing one-upsmanship with you; I'm not trying to compete. I didn't tell you about Bob to hear you tell me how much worse things are, how much more you suffer than me, how you're the greatest martyr that ever lived. Could I get a little sympathy for once? Every time I try to break through to you, to tell you something that matters to me—I've almost given up even attempting to communicate—you turn it back on me. You play your little guilt-trips on me. Listen, I can't take it any longer."

My mother, in tears, sobs. "Don't hate me! I'm your own mother. Why are you so mean? Why are you always picking on me? You misunderstood; I wasn't belittling you. You don't listen! I tried my best to raise you and Sheila well. I made some mistakes. Who knows how in advance? It wasn't that easy living with your father, you know—in and out of mental institutions half his life. But you try to remember the best. You forget the bad and try to remember the good.

Here I am, all alone in this world, and my own son hates me! It isn't fair. What did I do to deserve this?" She continues to cry. I offer her a tissue; she refuses it. "My own flesh and blood against me." She stumbles into the kitchen and sits down at the table in the dark.

"I'm sorry, Mom," I say, hesitatingly. "I didn't mean it. I'm just on edge a lot." I'm just on the verge of a nervous breakdown. I didn't mean to hurt her. She's so sad, a small woman in her late fifties, sitting at the kitchen table, crying in the dark. In front of her a handful of newspaper coupons is arrayed, ready to be sorted into separate envelopes. "You know me; I hold things in for too long, I never express myself, and then when they finally come out, everything comes out all wrong. I'm just so angry!"

"Did your *therapist* tell you that?" she spits out. "I could have told you years ago. There's no need to throw away money for common sense." My mother distrusts all therapists after what happened to my father. She stops sobbing, bitterness replacing grief.

Ultimately no permanent marks are left. A half an hour later I ask my mother if she wants to go to a movie. She says, "Fine, whatever you want to see."

"Do you want to see anything in particular?"

"No, you know I haven't seen anything out there. You make the decision. You go out a lot in New York. I never get to the theater. I'd like to see *Children of a Lesser God,* but you've already seen the play in New York. You pick." My mother last expressed a preference during the Crimean War: She wanted it to end; she wasn't taking sides. My mother, a compendium of every one of my flaws, magnified, sits at the table, endlessly deferring.

I take her to *Peggy Sue Got Married.* I drive the Pontiac serviceably. She asks whether I know the way, and I assure her I do, although I remember only the general route. My mother, the Greek chorus, the verbalization of my every fear and anxiety, winces at every turn, her head darting left and right in the back seat, scrunched down so she doesn't interfere with my rear vision. At the theater she opens her pocketbook, the contents a jumble of confusion, and searches for her change purse. I tell her it's my treat.

"But you paid for the plane fare from New York. It's the least I can do," she says.

"I insist." Why can't anything be simple at home, without a struggle of wills? The theater is falling apart. Seven rows are roped off, unsafe at any speed. We both enjoy the picture.

I return to New York, determined to forget the last few days with my family, the health crisis, the job I have to go back to on Monday, everything. I drop off my bag and rush down to the Spike. It's Sunday, five in the afternoon. The bars are filled with refugees from family weekends. The music is loud and insistent. Stacey Q sings about two hearts that beat as one. I'm drinking a Bud, leaning against the wall, watching a man in his late thirties standing near the pool table, a few feet away from the main bar in the next room. He catches my eye and looks down. He turns the other way.

A guy standing next to me in a leather jacket taps his foot to the rhythm of the music. He's drinking scotch on the rocks. His short salt-and-pepper hair is thinning at the top. He hides his blue eyes behind thick, wire-rimmed glasses. I glance at him casually, trying to take it all in. It's difficult to cruise someone standing next to you. You're not allowed much latitude of ambiguity. He wears a white T-shirt under his jacket. He has a firm, barreled chest. His stomach swells slightly. His Levi's fit tightly. He's not wearing a key-chain in his back pocket, which is a good sign. I decide he's fine: nothing to cause my heart to lurch or skip a beat, but good enough for tonight if he's interested. I always feel safer with men who wear glasses.

"Like the music?" I ask.

"Sure," he jumps in. "It's OK. I usually come here on Sunday afternoon for a drink or two to listen to the music, kick back, and relax."

"I needed to get out after visiting my family upstate for Thanksgiving. Did you have a nice holiday?"

"Yep. Went out to Jersey to see the folks. A lot of nieces and nephews. Oh, my name's Mario."

Probably Italian. I hope he's cut. "I'm B.J."

"Pleased to meet you." He grabs my hand and shakes it firmly, holding on a little longer than necessary. "So I ate too much, as usual." He pats his stomach. "Have to work it off at the gym next week, I guess."

"Where do you go?"

"Sheridan." He gives me the once-over and touches me on the shoulder. "You look pretty solid."

"I work out."

"Nice pecs," he compliments.

"Thanks. You, too," I say. "You planning on hanging out here much longer?" I ask. I hope I'm not going too fast. I haven't felt this horny in months.

"Depends."

"I was wondering if you'd be interested in something safe."

He gives me a grin. "Nothing but." He finishes his drink in a gulp. "How about now?" he says, rubbing my leg with his knee.

I swallow what's left of my beer. "OK," I blurt out.

We take a cab to my apartment. The unpacked suitcase sits in the closet. The rest of my apartment is relatively neat, owing to the fact that I straightened things out before I left for Rochester. I take two beers from the fridge that have been sitting there since August and give Mario one. I pull down the blinds and turn on the radio. Mario comes from behind and squeezes me in a bear hug, kissing the back of my neck. I rub his arms and turn to kiss him. His mouth is open. Mine remains shut. "Safe," I whisper when our mouths detach. Above the bed, like Martin Luther's ninety-five theses nailed to the door, is taped GMHC's safe-sex pamphlet "An Ounce of Prevention." Next to it is taped the list of regulations from the *Greenwich Village Gay News* which is usually found in the personals section, below ads that begin with "ATHLETIC MASC TOP," "THREESOMES," "CRAVE BIG DICK," and the like.

According to Freud, at least four people are present at every sexual act: you and your partner, and your mother and father. These days, when you sleep with someone, you sleep with every one of his partners for the last five years, which makes for quite an orgy in my book—considering that in all likelihood some of the past partners are now dead.

Erica Jong's zipless fuck has gone the way of the Edsel. There is no such thing as sex without angst anymore. The specter of death cannot be ignored, forgotten. Every action is accompanied with caution; every invention with doubt. I kneel at Mario's feet and slowly unlace his shoes. He massages my neck as I take off his shoes and socks. I put my hands under his T-shirt and make my way up the matted fur to his nipples, gently circling them. Then I reach around his waist, loosening his T-shirt. His arms rise like a child's as I pull the shirt over his head. In the back of my mind I note there is no swelling at his armpits, no visible off-color bruises. I rub his taut pecs with my palms and kiss him on the tip of his nose. He reaches for his beer, takes a slug, and then aggressively pulls my shirt off. We lie on the bed for a while, licking exposed flesh but avoiding mouths. I kick off my sneakers and roll down my socks with the other foot and push them off with my toes. I feel around Mario's pants at the crotch. He's hard. His nipples are thick and succulent. I circle them with my tongue, lapping gently, and then play with them lightly with my teeth. I feel for the buttons on his jeans. They pop open, one by one. I move off the bed and tug his pants. He arches his back as I pull them down below his hips. Mario is wearing Jockey shorts, with a tiny wet spot at the front. I pull his pants over his ankles and toss them on the couch. They fall to the floor. Expertly, he unsnaps and unzips my jeans, jerking them down to my knees. I roll over, and he pulls them off. We tussle in our underwear. The radio frequency unlocks and drifts into static. I get up to readjust the stereo. Mario finishes his beer. I return to bed. He hooks his fingers under the waistband of my Fruit of the Looms. My dick snakes out. I take off my underwear as he removes his. He looks better naked than I expected. I want to lick his cock, but I can't; I'm afraid to even touch it this soon because I might smear some precum accidentally on his nipples and suck them afterward. I feel confined, a million invisible strands of thread forming a skein of restriction. Mario lies on top of me, holds my arms by my head so my biceps are tensed, and slowly humps my stomach. His tongue snakes out lecherously and grazes his upper lip. He picks up speed, his fat dick slapping my stomach rhythmically. I strain my abdominals so the ridges appear. "Some grease?" I offer. He shakes his head no.

The phone rings. He raises his eyebrows questioningly on the fifth ring. "The machine's on; don't worry."

We hear my voice declare, "I can't come to the phone right now. If you want, leave a message at the tone." Then a beep.

Dave Johnson speaks tersely to the machine. His voice is hoarse. "B.J., it's Dave. I got a call from St. Clare's a few minutes ago. Bob Broome just died. His lungs had filled with fluid, and he drowned. I didn't want you to go there and visit him straight from Rochester and find out he was dead." He hangs up. I go limp. Mario stops. I wait for the tears to flow.

The Last Time I Saw Him

I think back to the last time I saw Bob Broome. All of the slots were filled on the blackboard at the nurses' station. He was strapped into an oxygen mask. His eyes were closed. I looked at his chest rise and fall, rise and fall. His breathing appeared labored.

And now he is gone.

I feel my cheeks. They are perfectly dry. The tears have yet to start.

· 24 ·

December

The service is held at a Unitarian church in the Village two weeks after Bob's death. All of his friends I met at the hospital come. Another thirty I never saw before also attend. A large floral arrangement decorates the podium, bathed in light. Dave and Jerry have hired someone to videotape the ceremony to send to Bob's parents; his mother had recently broken her hip and was too ill to travel. The service is really for them.

An actor Bob had been close to sings one of Bob's favorite Handel arias. Jerry reads the eulogy in a quavering voice. Then Dave comes up to say a few words. He talks about Bob's courage in the face of death. He talks about the time when Bob organized a surprise anniversary party for Jerry and himself. He recalls how stunned and then grateful he and Jerry were. Bob even made a German-chocolate cake. I didn't know that Bob knew how to bake. Then Dave calls on people sitting in the pews to give personal remembrances of Bob. No one volunteers. I look down at the sky-blue mimeographed program in my hands: "In memoriam: Bob Broome." A pair of dates bracketing a life. Jerry recites a brief anecdote about Bob's love of the ballet, how he never missed a performance of the New York City Ballet. I never knew Bob liked dance. Then Dave calls on me directly. I look up, stunned. I have nothing prepared. I stammer something about how I will miss Bob's dry wit and sarcasm. Roxanne stands in the audience. With tears in her eyes, she tells how even toward the end Bob was growing; he had told her of progress he was making in therapy. Marcy stands and says that throughout his illness Bob never complained, his spirits remained high. A few more people stand with recollections. Then a professional musician Bob knew plays a Bach fugue on the piano.

Dave and Jerry host a reception at their apartment. It's snowing heavily. I walk over with Patrick, sheltering him with my umbrella. "Jerry laid it on a bit thick in the eulogy, don't you think?" he says.

"What do you mean?"

"All that business about Bob making a tragic mistake. It kind of bothered me. I mean, he's dead and buried. It's hardly the time or place to dredge up his sexual activities."

"Yeah, I guess it was a little too much fire and brimstone. I figure he did it for the parents."

"Sure, blame the victim. That's the ticket. It's fucked. Goddamn it, AIDS is a disease. There's no connection between diseases and morality. I mean, like try to tell me that having hemophilia is immoral and getting blood transfusions is immoral and being inside a womb for nine months is immoral. There's no connection. And we have to sit through some Jerry Falwell shit speech at Bob Broome's memorial service? It's fucked," says Patrick. "The whole thing's fucked." He's very upset.

"I think he was just trying to warn those of us in the audience," I say gently.

"As if any of us doesn't know by now. Yeah, sure, he meant well." Patrick takes a deep breath and sighs. "I hope they have vodka. I feel like getting real drunk."

Bob Broome's brother has flown in from South Dakota. He sat in back at the ceremony. Now he sits uneasily in a bentwood chair, sipping a scotch. He's the only one present wearing a three-piece suit. A catered spread of crudités covers a table against the wall. To the left are cakes and Wedgwood china to serve them on. Another table serves as a bar. Patrick makes a triple Stoly, adds a curl of lime, and starts sipping. I try a little vodka on ice. I look around and realize that this is the last time I will see many of the people present. I stand next to Patrick, and we chat. I tell him to keep in touch.

The body has been cremated, in accordance with Bob's wishes. Jerry and Dave give Bob's brother a ceramic urn containing his remains. They hold on to Bob's apartment for another month, to dispose of his possessions. They haven't told the landlord Bob has died, only that he is in the hospital. Jerry and Dave keep the VCR. Patrick takes some clothing. I don't want anything.

A few weeks later I meet Patrick for drinks.

"You know, it's as if he went on vacation," says Patrick. "I mean, no one was actually there when he died. No one saw him pass on."

"I saw Bob last week."

"What?"

"In a crowd at Grand Central Station. He was hurrying for a train. I blinked, and he was gone. I mean, it wasn't Bob; it was just someone who looked like him. My therapist says it's quite common, seeing people who have died like that."

"That's strange."

"Nice shirt." Patrick is wearing a pink polo shirt.

"Thanks, it was Bob's."

"How could that be? He was six feet tall. You're closer to five-eight, aren't you?" I ask.

"I guess he bought it small."

"It fits you well."

"To a T."

"It's kind of creepy."

"Not to me. Whenever I wear this shirt I'll think of Bob."

"Not to change the subject, have you decided when you're leaving your lover and moving in with me?"

"Tomorrow," replies Patrick.

"What?"

"I'll need three drawers and one full closet. I hope you have room in the medicine cabinet for all of my Clinique-ware."

"Wait a minute."

"Oh, and I'm bringing the bird with me. George wouldn't make a good parent on his own."

"I think I'll have to reconsider."

"Chickenshit." Patrick laughs. We have a few drinks and then part.

Dave Johnson calls me and asks me what I'm doing with my time now that Bob has died and I don't go over to the hospital every other night. I don't know what to say.

Maybe the worst thing is that life goes on.

Going through my files at work, I find Bob's phone number on a slip of paper—one of his earlier hospital stays. I toss it. I neatly cross his name out of my address book and write "RIP" and the date to the right.

*   *   *   *

Richard is doing well in San Francisco. He lives with his most recent lover in the Haight. They are both practicing Buddhists. Richard grows bonsai trees in the garden in back. His T-cell count has stabilized, although it is well below normal.

Dennis and Chris are planning on going to Italy to celebrate their seventh anniversary. Dennis seems to be drinking more than he used to.

I turn thirty. Patrick thinks of Bob often. Every day I walk past the hospital where Bob died. Jerry does volunteer work there now. Dave calls me every so often to invite me over to brunch. I always decline.

I try to forget the Bob in the hospital and remember the Bob I knew before.

Epilogue

"So, they finally fired me," says Gordon.

"Where are you calling from?" I ask.

"Home. They couldn't have chosen more perfect timing, the week before Christmas." He coughs.

"That's awful."

"You know what's worse?"

"No."

"They didn't even fire me in person. They called me at home on Monday night to let me know they were letting me go." He coughs again.

"That's shitty. Hey, do you still have that cold?"

"Sort of," says Gordon. He pauses to catch his breath. "Well, I've got a card or two up my sleeve."

"What is it?"

"Maybe I'll tell you tonight. Are you going to the gym? You could drop over afterwards." Gordon lives a few blocks from my gym.

"Nope, I went last night. Come on, don't tease."

"Are you sitting down?"

"Yes."

"You're sure?" His voice sounds particularly nasal.

"Yes."

"I'm going to file an AIDS-discrimination suit."

"You're kidding."

"Nope."

"But you don't have AIDS."

"B.J., remember how I told you about my complexion? How my acne gets infected, and I get scared, and I go to my dermatologist just to make sure it's not KS?"

"Come on, Gordon, this isn't funny. Say 'J.k.' like you always do."

"Well," he continues, "last month he took a biopsy."

"Oh, my God."

"You know, it's sort of like coming out again. It takes a while until I feel comfortable letting someone know."

It's only KS, I think to myself. If it was PCP, he'd be a dead duck. KS, they've been known to last as long as five years. There could be a cure in five years. There *has* to be a cure!

"I'm not really ready for the whole world to find out, so I'd appreciate it if you could keep this under your hat for the time being," says Gordon.

"Sure. Whatever you say. Are you feeling all right now?"

"I'm nursing a cold. I haven't lost any weight or gotten any other symptoms, if that's what you mean. I feel perfectly fine. I saw someone from GMHC. This woman taught me how to use makeup that covers up the lesions on my face. I only have a few now, though I've got some on my leg, too." He coughs again. "Well, I've got an appointment with my attorney for this afternoon. I guess I'd better be going for now."

"OK." I'm practically choking. "I'm real sorry. Stay well," I say.

"Yeah, sure. Talk to you later."

"Good-bye." We hang up.

It begins as a gentle rain. Just a drop, for each illness, each death. And with each passing day it gets worse. Now a downpour. Now a torrent. And there is no likelihood of its ever ending.